Christine S. Drake

THE PRICE OF LOVE

A NOVEL

THOMAS NELSON PUBLISHERS
Nashville

Scripture quotations are from the KING JAMES VERSION.

Published in Nashville, Tennessee, by Thomas Nelson, Inc., Publishers, and distributed in Canada by Word Communications, Ltd., Richmond, British Columbia, and in the United Kingdom by Word (UK), Ltd., Milton Keynes, England.

Library of Congress Cataloging-in-Publication Data

Drake, Christine S.
The price of love / Christine S. Drake.
   p.   cm.
ISBN 0-8407-6732-3 (pb)
I. Title.
PS3554.R195P75   1993   93-1059
813'.54—dc20   CIP

Printed in the United States of America

3 4 5 6 7 — 98 97 96 95

For Karen Lee Rowley Mansfield

Psalms 126:5

1

"Dear Adam..."

Dear Adam! Jessy Flint paused in her writing to dip her pen into the ink bottle, knowing this little piece of stationery couldn't possibly hold all she wanted to say. The girl dabbed excess ink off her pen along the inside rim of the bottle so as not to blob any on this precious last sheet of Mother's stationery. *Mother!* Fighting back tears, Jessy continued her letter to Dear Adam. Dear, dear Adam. The dearest Adam in the whole world.

"In case my other letters never reached you, I'm writing again. You see, Father passed away when I was nine and after Thanksgiving, Mother—" Jessy paused before writing the word that had dealt such a crushing blow in her young life: "died."

It can't be true, but she knew it was, recalling her mother's final, fading whispers. How Jessy had strained to hear: "Resurrection and the life!" Those few words had spoken volumes to the girl leaning against the death bed. The faith that held on through death, beyond life, no matter what, had become Jessy's inheritance. Faithful mother and faithful daughter would see each other again in Paradise. God would wipe away their tears! Comforted by such hope, Jessy continued writing: "A friend of Mother's invited me to live with her until better arrangements could be made—"

How could Jessy express her urgent need tactfully, without sounding pushy? She peered out the window hoping the Lord's great sky would offer inspiration. What little she could see through the glass darkened by city soot looked grim. Turning from the clutter of smokestacks, Jessy plunged ahead bluntly, writing, "and I sure would like to meet you!"

Meet my brother! Seeing Adam Flint in person would be the most wonderful thing in the world. Her brother, her only living relative, had left home before she was born. Jessy pulled the worn, faded clipping from her mother's Bible. What possibilities it presented! But what did her brother look like? Jessy pouted, wishing the newspaper had printed his picture with the story. *I can't wait to see you!*

In her haste Jessy spattered ink on the letter. She finished writing in a rush, cramming her words around the ink blobs: "May I please visit you real soon? Yours very truly, Jessy Flint."

Satisfied with the message if not with the blobs, Jessy noticed she had omitted the date and quickly added February 16, 1900. After blotting and folding the letter and carefully placing it in the envelope she had addressed to the dear Mr. Adam Flint, Jessy ran to the post office.

On her way out the door, she grabbed her coat and hat, then pulled on her mittens as she flew down three steep flights of stairs. As Jessy rushed to the sidewalk, she patted her coat pocket, making sure the letter was safe. This precious letter was Jessy's one link to a new life in a new place a thousand miles from this dreary row of tenements.

Much to her distaste, the shortest route to the post office was straight past the shop where her father had once worked in wood, and his father before him. *Father.* The memory of him cut her like a knife. After he died, his carpentry shop was rented to a cobbler. The man inside had become so used to seeing the youngster standing on the sidewalk, struggling with her feelings, that he would pause to smile and wave at Jessy while mending soles.

Jessy waved gently and hurried on. Her pace slowed as she confronted half a dozen sets of railroad tracks. Just beyond them stood the post office, but the wailing of distant trains gave her pause. Seeing no train, she began crossing, picking her way over treacherous ridges of old ice and snow. She hurried when she heard the warning signals for an approaching train and felt relieved to have made her way across without having to wait for it to pass. Such a wait would delay her letter. Still, for just a moment, Jessy stood in wonder at the force, the speed, and the feel of the rushing train. Clanging bells, deafening whistle blasts, and spewing cinders overwhelmed all else. As Jessy closed her eyes and let the iron monster shake her bones in a strange and wonderful way, she realized letters weren't the only means of reaching her brother.

Tearing her eyes from the mailslot that had swallowed her letter, Jessy turned back toward the tenements. A sparrow, fluttering out from a thicket of weeds, twittered at her feet, then flew up and out of sight. Strangely moved, Jessy tried to see where it had gone.

Standing there, looking up, Jessy thought about God. "Trust Him in all things," Mother had said. And Jessy did trust with all her being.

"Dear God," she prayed, "Your eye is on the sparrow. And Your eye is on me. If it's Your will, please help me. Please bless my letter and please bless my brother. Please, in the name of your beloved son Jesus, please. Oh, and please bless the cobbler, too, and my neighbors, and . . ."

The only sound Jessy heard was the delicate call of the sparrow.

❦   ❦   ❦

A crow perched high in a pine tree swaying in the wintry wind of the vast American prairie. The bird had its eye on something far beneath its grasping claws. Behind a faded cottage near an empty Midwestern field, which in warm weather yielded up bushels of tasty corn crows love, lay a possible meal, and such a big, juicy one!

The crow, tempted by this feast but hampered by inborn caution, swooped down from the treetop through the unsullied air for a closer look. Perching on a lower branch, the bird cawed and cawed and cawed. No other crow answered. For a long while, the bird eyed the body on the ground. It remained motionless, sprawled on its back.

The crow descended little by little, calling with more variations, the sharp staccato proclaiming from deep within its broad black chest, "M-i-i-ine! This meal is mine! All m-i-i-ine!"

The noise roused the man a little. He reached out for the whiskey bottle lying a few feet from his hand. This sudden movement frightened the bird away.

The disappointed crow lit on the man's rustic mailbox. The bird, as if in revenge, sharpened its beak and dug its talons deep into the sign carved with considerable woodworking skill that proclaimed: *Adam Flint.*

❦   ❦   ❦

Jessy Flint leaned forward, wide-eyed and apprehensive, as the elderly farmer pulled off the road and across a creek frozen solid.

Ollie Gaad chuckled, "Here we are, Missie. Adam's place—your brother's bachelor paradise."

Paradise? Jessy, sore from her long train ride but anxious to see her brother's home for the first time, straightened on the hard wagon seat. While she hadn't been envisioning paradise on earth, she had expected something more than this little cottage, drab as ditchwater with its gray roof, gray porch, gray door, and gray shingling crusty as bark. A thin ribbon twisted from the chimney — gray smoke escaping a gray house, not so much a ribbon as the tail of a rat. She shrank down again, regretting the folly of heedlessly following her heart. Having journeyed a thousand miles, Jessy felt very much the stranger.

The buckboard had come to a rolling stop in a driveway alive with hens. They pecked around horse hooves and iron-rimmed wheels, their cackling accompanied by the grunting of hogs penned up in a nearby shed.

"Whooo!" Jessy cried, clutching her scarf in a driving wind that reeked of manure and left her breathless.

"Take hold a my arm, Missie," said the old gentleman as he eased her to the frozen ground. "What have I been sayin' 'bout that wind? Comes straight from the North Pole 'cross Canada with nuthin' in its path 'cept us! Easy, now, watch your step on that ice. Let's get down your bags."

"Yes, please. Let me help with those. I've got them, Mr. Gaad! Thank you!" Setting down her bags and taking his arm, Jessy shivered like the bare fruit trees lining the drive. "What's that strange noise?"

"Oh, that! Look there."

She followed the man's gaze to the barn, big as a cathedral. It was topped not with a cross but a rusty weather vane. The flying horse rattled crazily in the wind.

"You're hearin' March! Welcome to the Midwest, Missie!" Smiling broadly at her, he said, "Now let's find that brother of yours, whadya say?"

Now that this long-awaited moment had come, Jessy couldn't nod, much less speak. The conversation she'd had with Mr. Gaad during their wagon ride together had made her uneasy about meeting Adam Flint. A growing realization of her foolish risk was overtaking her. She stood frozen as the hard ground beneath her boots.

"Anybody home?" sang out Ollie Gaad as he walked toward the front door of the cottage. He whistled, knocked, and called out again but no one answered.

Behold, I stand at the door, and knock . . .

The verse of scripture comforted Jessy's heart, but the powerful odor of hog assaulted her nose. For so long she had looked forward to this moment with all her heart, but now, deep in her soul, she dreaded it. Losing her nerve, and without taking time to think through her predicament, she blurted out, "Mr. Gaad? Maybe my brother's off on a trip someplace. You said you haven't seen him in a while. Maybe I should turn back—"

"He's gotta be close by." Ollie jerked his thumb toward the roof of the little house. "Chimney's smokin'. Why, now, don't you look sad all of a sudden! Where's that sweet smile? You wanna meet him, doncha? "

Fighting doubts, Jessy nodded gently. "I want a home and family more than anything in this world."

"That's the spirit! Adam's probably in back out of earshot. Let's go find him!" When she didn't go along with him, he asked, "Are you comin'?"

Jessy shook her head. "May I wait here?"

"Sure, sure, Missie. That long trip musta wore you out." He moved away on his spindly legs with a speed that surprised her. As he rambled along the path away from her she heard him mumble: "Gossip sure ain't right. No matter what folks say I can't hardly believe Adam Flint coulda done murder."

There. He said it again. The farmer—a stranger who had befriended Jessy—had just repeated the very thing he had told her on the six-mile wagon ride from town: "Me and my wife don't believe gossip," he had said. "Adam Flint's no murderer." Jessy didn't believe it either. No, not Adam, not her brother Adam.

"No! Dear Lord, it can't be true!" she whispered. "My brother can't be a murderer!" Sinking into her scarf, she cried in anguish, "but what if he is? How long I've wondered what he was like and what I'd say to him the first time we met and what fun it would be getting to know each other, and now this! I prayed to be here, and now my prayer has been answered but if what Mr. Gaad says isn't true really *is* true, but—" With a start, Jessy rose up a bit from her wrap. "Oh, Lord, here I am in a panic and forgetting about You! I haven't even thanked You, dear Lord, for bringing me all the way here safe and sound! You've looked after me just like You promised. Mother always told me that whenever things looked impossible I was to look up to You."

For the first time, Jessy Flint really saw the vast Midwestern sky, really felt its awesome majesty. Here, under this glorious sky, under the same loving God of all, lived her brother Adam.

The crack of a rifle, then loud, merry shouts interrupted Jessy's contemplation.

"Great shot, Flint! Just great!" Still out of sight, Mr. Gaad sounded terribly excited. Soon he came into view, and he wasn't alone. He called out to Jessy. "Here he is, Adam Flint, in person!"

For the first time, Jessy beheld her brother. In another time, another place, Adam Flint might have been a mythical titan, a swashbuckler, a matinee idol. Though Jessy had never before seen him, he looked familiar. Something about him made her uneasy. He hardly noticed her.

"Killin' them and rats is full-time work," Adam said to Ollie as he stood his rifle against the porch steps. "Never shot a beaver before. Been tryin' to get this one all winter!"

Adam's voice — deep, rich, rolling, well modulated — suited his face and build. Jessy stood spellbound, silent, awestruck, listening to him speak. But the sudden aching wouldn't leave her. What was it, she wondered, this sinking feeling? Then she knew. *He looks like Father!*

"This bruiser dammed up the river out back and flooded my north field! Must weigh sixty pounds. Look at them teeth!" With one bloody hand Adam held up the unfortunate beaver. The powerful muscles of his arms and chest swelled beneath his coarse wool jacket. "Go on, Ollie, just feel that pelt!"

The old fellow's face glowed with admiration. "Beaver pelt that fine'll bring twenty dollars easy, not that it's all that much money to a high roller like you."

"Right you are!" Adam laughed as he put down his catch, grabbed a rag, and tried wiping the blood from his hands. They stayed red.

Her long trip, darkened by rumors and culminating with this first, disturbing look at her brother, left Jessy weak and confused. She felt as out of place as a sprite in an ogre's lair. What on earth had possessed her to come here? She eyed the road, wishing Ollie hadn't unloaded her bags.

"Well, guess I'll be goin' along. Mildred'll have dinner ready. Evenin', Adam, Missie." Ollie Gaad tipped his hat in Jessy's direction.

Adam looked up from his bloodstained hands. "Ain't you forgettin' somethin'?" Adam cocked his head toward Jessy. "Your granddaughter?"

Ollie laughed. "She ain't my granddaughter. She's Jessy!"

Adam looked like he had been stunned by an invisible sledgehammer. That Adam would suddenly appear so ashen, so astonished, puzzled Ollie Gaad. He stammered, "Y-you been expectin' your sister —" Ollie looked quickly from Adam to Jessy. "Oh, no, Missie, you didn't just show up uninvited?"

Despite the chilling wind, Jessy felt her face flush hot. "I'm afraid so, Mr. Gaad..."

Nothing broke the silence but the wind, the rattling weather vane, clucking hens, and grunting hogs. Jessy couldn't speak and Adam wouldn't. He glared at her with such intensity she squirmed inside her shabby coat. Hadn't he been taught it was impolite to stare? She clutched her arms tight to herself in defense. "Heavenly Father, what should I do?" she pleaded inwardly. "I've ruined everything. I never should have come! Now what?"

Ollie broke the silence with a cheery "Ain't you two gonna say hello?"

Of course! It was the least they could do. Jessy, thanking the elderly gentleman with her eyes, turned to her brother. "H-hello, Adam. I'm sorry for coming uninvited, but you never answered my letters. The postman said they were being delivered or they would have been returned to me, so I got the idea to take the train here to see you. I probably shouldn't have, but I just *had* to see you! I looked up Bethel Township on a map at the library. It took me five days to get here. It was supposed to take three but there was a wreck outside New York, maybe you heard? I've never been on a train before. It was terribly exciting..."

Gasping for breath, Jessy paused. She knew she shouldn't be babbling on like this, but she couldn't help it. Adam's mouth was hanging open, as if his jaw had gone slack. When he continued staring, she decided to press on. "I-I wouldn't have known how to find your house from the station, but Mr. Gaad introduced himself and offered me a ride on his way home. Wasn't that nice of him? He saved me quite a long walk. He said lots of other sisters visit you, but I thought I was your only sister ..." Jessy's voice trailed off. The implications of that last bit of news made her face flush red again.

Adam rolled his answer around the inside of his mouth like a juicy wad of tobacco before spitting it out. "How'd you ever know I was out here in the first place?" His green eyes, cold as the March wind, bore through her.

"M-mother saved a clipping from the newspaper about you winning a farm. I've still got it. W-want to see?"

Without waiting for his answer, Jessy pulled off her mittens, dropped to the ground, and began digging through her book bag. "I showed all the kids at school. None of them have famous brothers that made the news."

Pages flipped every which way in the wind. When Jessy paused to breathe warm air on her bare hands, she felt piercing green eyes on her and a dozen others as well. The roving band of elaborately marked hens had come to investigate. They eyed Jessy as well as one another with suspicion. The plumpest nestled on a book. Jessy shooed her away. With an indignant squawk, the bird departed, leaving behind one polka dotted feather. Still the stormy green eyes held on to Jessy like a vise.

"Here it is! There's not much left of it, though, with everyone passing it around." She smoothed the scrap of paper before trying to give it to him, but Adam had turned away from her. He was rubbing the back of his neck as if it ached.

He must be weary from a day of shooting at helpless animals, she assumed. Holding the clipping to her heart, she moved closer, speaking softly to his broad back. "I always wanted to know you, ever since I was little. All my classmates knew their brothers except me."

"You shoulda stayed put." His voice was soft and low and full of anger.

"I couldn't," she pleaded gently, still gazing up at the powerful form. "After Mother died, I couldn't keep my mind on school. I tried, but I couldn't stay there, living with neighbors."

Suddenly he turned on her. "You can't stay here either. Get back on the train and go home!"

"I don't have a home to go back to, Adam. With Mother gone, you're all I have. She prayed for you every day. Her last thoughts were of you. She talked about us being together, you and me. I tried explaining in my letters." Jessy looked into the distance, trying to make sense of this chilly reception. "Maybe you didn't get my letters after all."

His eyes sparked like kindling. "I settled out here so I'd be away from everyone and everythin'. Understand?"

Jessy nodded and shook her head all at once.

"Good," Adam barked. "Now get lost."

Jessy burst into tears.

"Ain't that just like a female!" Adam was livid, but the more he growled, the louder she sobbed.

"Now you done it!" Ollie came to the girl's defense. "Maybe I'm outa line here, Adam, and if I am I'm sorry, but what's the harm in her stayin' here with you? Look at her, a skinny child with the sweetest angel face. Such soulful eyes, too. Why, she's just like a motherless calf."

"I ain't no mother."

Of that there could be no doubt. Through her tears, Jessy began to giggle. The very suggestion was preposterous. Adam Flint looked like just about the toughest male who had ever swaggered the earth.

"Fine! A crier and a giggler all in one! It's more than a man can stand!"

Jessy clapped a hand over her grin. "I can be serious!"

"I need a kid sister like a bull needs—"

"Now, my boy, kids can be a real help on a farm. Mildred and me've raised nine of our own and two adopted. They don't stay young forever. They grow up fast and get married 'fore you know it."

"Married?" Adam peered down on the sprite.

"Well, maybe not for a few years yet, but like Mildred always—"

"She ain't my responsibility. Never was, never will be. Is it my fault my folks had a kid late in life?"

"Children are a gift from God."

"Ain't no gift I ever want."

So. Jessy Flint's long journey, sweet dreams, lofty hopes, and fervent expectations had come to nothing on a frozen prairie. For the last time, Jessy looked at the face so much like Father's. Adam truly was like Father, in ways too bitter to ponder. The hard truth of her brother's rejection would take a lifetime to put behind her. But for now, all she knew was that she must go. She turned and walked away, taking no notice of the thin brittle ice over ruts and hollows as it crackled and broke under her feet. As if in shock, she sank to her knees to gather up her books, but the sight of that little scrap of newsprint was too much for her to bear. Heaving sobs racked her small frame.

"Adam, be reasonable! Be neighborly!" pleaded the older man. "Ain't you got a heart?"

"Females use cryin' like a man uses these." Adam held up one meaty fist.

"I don't know about that, but I do know you can't hurt that sweet child. It ain't decent."

"It's all right, really, Mr. Gaad," Jessy stammered, tears streaming down her delicate upturned face. "I shouldn't have come. I think I can understand how my br— how Adam must feel." As she shuffled through her things, she added quietly, "God has seen me this far. He won't abandon me now."

Regaining his rosy outlook, Ollie Gaad flashed a bright smile to no one in particular. "Our God, He's somethin', ain't He? Just look at that sky! He sure does things up right, don't He, Adam?" Failing to draw a response didn't seem to matter to Ollie. "Your sister's had a lot on her, she tells me, losin' her daddy and momma both. A God-fearin' girl, too, nothin' like them so-called 'sisters' and 'cousins' you've had stayin' here."

"What I do on my own property's nobody's business, okay?" Adam began to pace. " 'Sides, no one but me's been here for a long time."

"You know what they say, Adam: It's not good for man to be alone."

"Says who?"

"Says the Bible."

Shrugging off Ollie's remark, Adam stopped short of an especially deep rut and sneezed mightily.

"God bless you!" two voices said as one. "Catching cold?"

Adam flushed at their concerned looks. "Nah! I'm healthy as a horse! But I-ah, a coupla weeks ago I musta stayed out too long and—" Adam scanned the tall pines where that pesky crow kept vigil, then turned back in the direction of the sobbing that had slowed to sniffling but, to his annoyance, had not fully stopped. "Maybe if *she* was a *he* it might be different. Her bein' here'd change everythin'."

"Would that be the end of the world?"

"It'd be the end of *my* world!"

"If you ask me, and you didn't but I'll tell ya anyway, 'cause I like ya and you're my friend, and I'd tell my own son the same if you was him: Your world could stand improvin'. And what about your duty to family?"

"You're right, Ollie. I didn't ask for your advice." With that, Adam turned to his sister. "You. Come over here."

Jessy stood and took a few hesitant steps, her eyes never leaving Adam's craggy face. He looked bemused. She felt her hair must be standing on end in this wind, twisting loose in all directions from under her hat. She tried smoothing it, and also her rumpled coat, not that her attempt made much difference, living in it continually as she had these last five days and nights. The coat was too small for her, anyway, and the sleeves too short. She put her arms across the stains and wrinkles.

"Closer!" Adam ordered her.

Jessy inched forward, forcing away memories of their father in an effort to see Adam for who he was. Her efforts were not in vain. There were differences, many of them. She was struck by Adam's rugged, God-given beauty enhanced by an active life spent outdoors. Thick brown ringlets fell across his forehead. He had dimpled cheeks, broad bow-shaped lips, perfect white teeth against ruddy skin flushed with the glow of life, and a generous cleft chin. Absently she touched the wisp of a dimple in her own, their shared inheritance from Father. There he was again. Adam Flint smelled of liquor, just as Father had. The memory made her glower coldly at her brother.

Scratching the back of his neck, he asked: "You play poker?"

"Of course not!" cried Jessy with disdain.

"Too bad. Ever work a crowd?"

"Have I ever what?"

"You heard me — panhandlin'." Adam reached out one big hand toward her while rubbing his thumb rapidly against his fingertips. "You know, goin' round beggin'. Askin' strangers for money. You'd be good at it, with them big brown eyes and those pitiful clothes. You probably got a whole trunkload of 'em someplace, huh? What an act! Not bad, not bad at all! Bet you're an old hand at takin' in suckers." Adam shot a glance to Ollie Gaad before turning back on Jessy. "Yes sir, a regular charity circus sideshow. Well, you don't fool me, sister." Adam turned abruptly and looked over his fields, deep in thought.

Jessy sidled over to Mr. Gaad, speaking softly so only he could hear her. "What's a char— What did he say about the circus?"

The old man shrugged. "I guess somethin' to do with his other line."

Still puzzled, Jessy pushed on with more important business. "You know, Mr. Gaad, I've been thinking. Maybe I shouldn't stay here after all."

"Now don't you let Adam's gruff ways trouble you. Nothin's ever come of them old rumors. We'll get this here straightened out."

"But maybe . . ."

"Your brother 'n me's been neighbors five or six years now. Adam's been over to our place many a time, and he never done harm to my girls. Between you 'n me, every one of 'em's sweet on him."

"Really?" Wide-eyed with astonishment, Jessy glanced around at the big, brooding figure.

While Ollie and Jessy huddled together, hens in search of a nibble paraded around Adam's boots. "Hey, stop that!" he yelled. "I'll feed you soon enough. That goes for you, too, Madame Fiji!" Ignoring him, the chickens retraced their steps. Madame, the most elaborately colored of them, paused to preen herself royally. "Females. Always wantin' somethin' from a man."

"Men need nourishment too, Adam."

Adam laughed shortly. "I guess you're right, Ollie. Everybody's after somethin'."

"Listen, this, ah, surprise ain't as bad as it seems," said Ollie. "Might even be a blessin' in disguise. Everyone knows you work like the devil was after you. Ain't you tired of doin' everythin' yourself around here? The girl can do lots of things to help you, like feedin' them chicks. On the way out here, she told me she likes to cook and bake." Gesturing at Adam's jacket, he added, "Bet she can sew your buttons back on so you won't be catchin' your death."

For the first time it was Adam's turn to appear open and hopeful, and Jessy's turn to stare with mouth agape, her jaw gone slack. Why did she ever talk so much about herself on the way here? She watched the elderly fellow pace nervously under the darkening sky, just itching to be on his way home.

Jessy hurriedly drew out her mother's change purse. Her one-way train trip in the lowest class coach had cost $17.56, a fortune to Jessy and nearly all her mother had managed to save from performing the most menial work. During the lean years after Father died, her mother had supported them by taking in laundry and sewing. Rather than pay the extra five dollars for a berth, Jessy had slept upright on a hard bench the whole way here. She had allowed herself $1.20 for food each day, the barest minimum. That train accident had caused unexpected delay and extra expenses. What was left? Six dollars and a few coins. "I don't have enough to go back, not that there's anything to go back to, but I can get a ticket to . . . someplace."

"Which reminds me—" Adam was on her in a flash, snatching the money out of her hands. "This all you got?" Adam looked genuinely puzzled.

"You give that back to me!" Jessy reached up, straining at him, but Adam was too big and strong for her. "It's all that's left of Mother's—"

"I bet." Roughly, Adam fended her off. His dimpled mouth curved into a nasty smile. "Thief."

"I've never stolen anything! Mother gave that money to me. It was all she had!"

"Liar. But, hey, I was a kid once myself." Pocketing the money, Adam patted his jacket. "I'll keep it safe for you right here."

"Please give it back so I can be on my way."

Like a weight lifter, Adam rolled his shoulders forward and back, flexing his muscles and breathing deeply in the cold. "No need to leave this minute." He scanned over the landscape. "It'll be dark soon. I decided you can stay the night so you and me can have a little talk. I'll ride you into town tomorrow."

Ollie Gaad exploded. "You can't mean that, Adam Flint! Turnin' out your own kin—the only kin you got left in this world! If that's the case, Jessy can live with us. Mildred'd love her. Come on, young lady, let's go."

"Oh, Mr. Gaad, I couldn't impose . . ."

"It's the least one Christian can do for another. You know what the Good Book says 'bout strangers and angels—"

"Angel?" Adam bristled. "That little faker?"

"I am not faking!" Now it was Jessy's turn to be livid. "How could you even think such a thing about me?"

"Don't give me that spiel."

Puzzled, Ollie asked Jessy, "What's he drivin' at anyway?"

Jessy looked bewildered. She had taken such care of Mother's savings, not wasting a penny of it. And what on earth was a *shpiel*?

Adam stepped between them. "Why don't you go home now, Ollie, before your dinner gets cold? You done your good deed for the day."

Ollie peered around Adam, to where Jessy was standing in his shadow. "And leave the girl here?"

"She'll be okay."

"Flint, you're up to somethin'! I don't like it!"

Adam crossed his big arms over his chest. "I thought we was friends."

"We are!"

"Look, Ollie, I ain't tryin' to run you off, but it's gettin' late and I got things to do." Adam jerked his thumb toward Jessy, "And she might as well help me."

"What about you, Missie? Would you like to come home with me or stay here with your brother? We got plenty a room."

"She's stayin'. We got family business to discuss. In private."

From Adam's shadow Jessy answered softly, "Yes, I suppose we should talk, seeing as I've come this far."

"Thanks for stoppin' by." Adam stuck out his hand to shake Ollie's.

Ollie shook, but warily. "If anythin' happens to that girl —"

"Nothin's gonna happen to her." Adam sounded genuinely peeved.

"All right, but I'll be back in the mornin' to make sure everythin's okay. And if you two need anythin', remember Mildred 'n me are right up the road. Evenin' to you both."

"Bye!" Adam said, sounding relieved. He walked quickly toward the sty where his pigs squealed for supper. "All right, I'm comin'!" Madame Fiji and her entourage strutted after him, clucking merrily at the prospect of a meal.

"Thank you, Mr. Gaad," Jessy said, running after Ollie. When she caught up with him she asked softly, "Pray for me. Please pray for both of us."

"You're the answer to a prayer, Missie." Ollie Gaad tipped his hat to her. "And if you need us, we're down the road a quarter mile — green house with the white trim. Don't forget."

"I won't. Thank you, Mr. Gaad."

"Now, remember, your brother's tough as nails, but he can stand lookin' after. He needs some of that real sweet love of yours."

"Do you really think so?"

"I know so."

"Mother said I should love others no matter how hard they are to love, because that's one sure way we can honor God and show we're His children."

"Your mother told you right." With a wave, Ollie Gaad rode off.

Jessy watched long after he was gone, growing aware of a new, intense isolation. She took comfort in the beauty of this place, the late afternoon sun blazing like molten copper over the land, casting the towering pines in bold relief. The vast panorama surrounded her in glory. The same wind that caressed her cheek drove a lone cloud across the sky. Emerging from behind it was a star, perfect for wishing. Filled with awe, she closed her eyes in reverence.

"Flood my land, will ya?"

Jessy turned to see Adam slitting apart the ill-fated beaver. With a sidelong glance he asked her, "Not afraid, are ya?"

She shook her head, her downcast lips a pale rosebud.

Pausing with the knife, his eyes caught and held her: "Won't do for you to live in this world afraid."

"I'm not afraid of anything."

Adam snorted in disbelief. "Still puttin' on an act! Yes sir, tonight you and me are gonna have a little talk." His big hands moved with practiced speed. He spread back the hide, ignoring the blood.

Jessy watched him walk to the pump, prime it, and rinse his hands.

"Wanna wash up?"

She drew close, put her finger in the flow, but quickly pulled away from the icy water. A laugh bubbled up from deep in his chest, the kind of laugh their mother would have considered dirty.

As he wiped his hands, he wagged his head at her and said softly, but with power, "Runt of the litter." Then he grabbed his rifle and headed up the porch steps into the house.

Once he was gone, Jessy scanned the sky for her lone wishing star but she was too late. Now another star sparkled near it.

❦ 2 ❦

Adam had gone into the dark, lifeless house. From the yard, Jessy watched the cottage brighten with lamplight. Soon he dashed back outside and past her, moving with the grace and stealth of an animal. Curious, she watched him heave open the cellar doors at the side of the house, then heard his light tread going down and coming back up the steps. When he emerged, his arms loaded with provisions, he passed by her again, snapping, "Plan on star-gazin' all night?"

"No, sir." Jessy followed him into the house with her things.

Inside was hardly warmer than out. Adam dumped the provisions on a counter: smoked sausage, a block of fresh butter, carrots, onions, potatoes, dull red apples. Jessy's stomach growled. Ill at ease, she clutched her arms in the cold. Adam arranged a fat log on top of the fire burning low in the hearth, then returned to the kitchen.

In the light of a lamp in the sitting room she glanced into the side rooms partially obscured by shadows. Without straying too far, she could see that one had a big bed and wooden chests, another was narrow, white-washed, and nearly empty, and the third was filled with sawdust, bits of boards, and woodworking projects in various stages of completion. *Just like Father*, she thought with a shiver — so much debris to be cleaned up.

In her smallest voice, Jessy said, "I can hardly believe I'm here."

"Me neither."

He rushed past her a few times, going about his business. The way he edged by made her regret having intruded into his life. Keeping her distance, she tiptoed about the bare wooden floor of the sitting room. It was a drab but peaceful blend of browns and grays with the stone hearth, knotty pine walls, bare windows, a simple wooden table and chairs, and a plain sideboard with a water pitcher, bowl of nuts, and an old crockery jar filled with pussy willows. Jessy liked pussy willows. She walked close enough to touch them but then noticed, standing near the sideboard in a

16

far corner, two long guns — a shotgun and the rifle. She drew back her hand.

From the kitchen, Adam watched her with shrewd hunter's eyes. "I don't suppose Pa taught you how to use a gun."

"He did. He always wished I was a boy."

Adam grinned at this. "You a good shot?"

"Father said I was, for a girl. He made me practice in the woods."

"Did he take you huntin'?"

"Yes sir, but I didn't like it. Mother didn't want me to go. She was afraid I'd get hurt."

Jessy moved toward Adam, but not too close. A washtub, basin, pots, and skillets dangled from hooks near the cast iron stove within easy reach of the cook, who was, at that moment, chomping on an apple. All the while he held her with the corner of his eye.

"See this box? In the mornin' I want you to fill it up with firewood. You can haul water too, from the pump outside. In this." He gestured toward a pail, but his attention was clearly on cooking.

Instead of buckets and firewood, Jessy regarded his fine head crowned with curls. His profile was distinguished by a blunt nose, square jaw, and prominent Adam's apple. She stared up at him in fascination, entranced by his commanding presence and tawny face. Adam was broad through the chest and shoulders, but slender at the waist. In all, he was well formed, manly, yet supple. She recalled her childhood Bible storybook with its splendid illustrations of another Adam, the first man. The sight of Adam Flint reminded her of a caption that seemed to suit her brother as much as it suited that first man: Humanity, the crown of creation made in the image of God, fell far from Him.

Adam rolled up the sleeves of his red flannel shirt, exposing the ribbed cuffs of long underwear. Even in the simple act of picking up an apple, his every motion exuded power. The crunching sounds he made proved more than she could bear. When had she last eaten? She tried thinking of something else.

"Catch!" Adam called out. He looked surprised when she caught the apple he tossed so suddenly. With grudging admiration he said, "Quick reflexes."

Grinning triumphantly, she asked, "Adam's apple?"

Jessy had made the big man laugh. "Too bad this ain't the Garden of Eden!" The crown of creation began peeling onions.

"Please let me help," Jessy said as she finished eating her apple.

"You can set the table and wash the dishes. Save that core for the hogs." Adam's hands were too busy to point. Instead, he gestured with one knee. "Under here."

Jessy sidled by him to drop her apple core into the pail. To his back she said, "That was delicious. Thank you. Where's the silverware?"

"In that drawer. Plates up there." He motioned with his head.

She found a mismatched assortment of forks, spoons, and knives, and a stack of plates, also of assorted styles and patterns. She selected the largest and plainest for him and the most delicate for herself, one adorned with pink flowers and gold edging. "Where are the napkins?"

"Why doncha take off your coat?"

She did so, but then held it tightly, as if the shadowy recesses of the house might be populated by coat-robbing bandits.

"Hang it up on one of them pegs and let's have a look at you."

As soon as she had hung her coat up she found her shoulders engulfed by his two big hands. Did he mean to squeeze the life out of her? she wondered, alarmed. She tried squirming loose but there was no escaping his grasp. She watched as he studied her, his inquisitive green eyes flickering with gold. With one hand he pulled the plain wool hat from her head and tossed it aside. For an uncomfortably long time Adam studied her in silence, taking in every detail. With a frown he squeezed her skimpy shoulders and bony arms, then turned her slowly around in a complete circle. At last he said, "Other than all that hair and them big brown eyes there ain't much to you." He let go of her all at once.

Jessy slowly regained her shape, like a wet sponge squeezed dry and suddenly dropped. Wondering at his strange behavior, she wanted to shout, "Kill many people with those guns?" But Adam was busy with the meal again, lifting lids and stirring the contents of pots with practiced hands.

She continued exploring. The washroom smelled good, like a well-groomed man, but the long, thick razor strap hanging near Adam's shaving mug made her cringe — another reminder of Father. She shut the door fast.

Wooden chairs, a stool, and a few large boxes stood facing the fireplace. Jessy found the sitting room stark without curtains, rugs, or pillows. The purple light of evening veiled bare windows. Except for the lamps and fire, the only brightness came from three lifesize, brilliantly colored circus posters hanging on one wall. Each depicted the human male in all his barbaric splendor.

In the center poster the he-man was wearing tights, facing the viewer squarely, his legs apart and arms up. He was standing in front of a circus tent. His muscles bulged from the weight of an enormous barbell topped by an elephant. Still higher, two showgirls faced each other, holding a sign proclaiming "See the Man of Iron, Only a Quarter!" Jessy noticed with delight a shapely purple mermaid, Madame Fiji herself, pointing up to the sign from her splash pool.

In another, the he-man, in fighting crouch, battled a trio of lions. His curls were tied around the crown of his head across his forehead, in the ancient style. The poster read, "Samson the Mighty and His Lions." In the third poster, a fighter readied to take on lesser beings. "Battle the Great Goliath—Coming Soon to Your Town! $50 prize to the man who can topple him!"

Although different artists had created and signed each picture, the strongmen resembled one another—dark, curling hair, beautifully proportioned physiques, powerful chests, tapered slender waists, long, lean, well-muscled legs. Clearly the artists had been inspired by the same strongman, mighty yet lithe. Odd, all the faces resembled Father's.

"What do you think of the Man of Iron—in person?" Adam asked.

"That's you in these posters?"

"You bet." He assumed the fighting stance of the Great Goliath, then, quick as a panther brought his head low and locked her wrists in his hands. "Can you wrestle?"

"Ow!" Jessy cried.

"Why, you're soft as mush!" Adam let her go. He flexed his upper arm. "Feel that. Go on."

Blushing, Jessy obliged, probing one rock-like bicep daintily with forefinger and thumb. "Gosh, you're bigger and stronger than Father!"

Adam backed away, his eyes suddenly bitter. At the stove he said, "When I was about your age, I ran away from home. At first I took any odd jobs just to eat, but before too long I was doin' a man's work, travelin' the country, poundin' tent stakes with a mallet big as you. Made a dollar a month, the months I got paid. One day, though, I became the star of the show."

Jessy drew near him. "Why did you run away?"

"I hated Pa. The more he beat me, the more I stood up to him." Adam rubbed the tip of his big blunt nose with the back of one hand. "I was tall as he was by the time I was fourteen, 'cept I hadn't filled out yet. I'll never forget the day I left home. He told me, 'Adam, you've grown too big to whip.' So instead he whacked me across the back with a plank. I got up swingin'."

Horrified, Jessy asked, "You hit Father?"

"You bet! I wasn't about to let him kill me!"

"He sure could be mean."

"Did he beat you?"

"S-sometimes." Jessy trembled, remembering. "M-Mother would beg him to stop. She told him fathers shouldn't provoke their children to wrath, like the Bible says, but he wouldn't listen. He was nothing like Mother."

"You sorta are."

"Do you really think so?" Jessy took this as an enormous compliment.

"Yeah." Adam prodded the potatoes baking in the oven and then gave her a quick little jab in the stomach. "Just like her. Soft 'round the edges and stuffed fulla religion."

"That's not nice to say."

"In my house I say what I want. Ma was drunk with religion."

"And Father was—" *just plain drunk.*

The wind sweeping across the prairie blasted the cottage until it creaked like loose flooring under a busy rocking chair. Jessy looked out to the purple void. She couldn't see the stars, but that didn't mean they weren't there. She assured herself: *God is here with us.*

"I get the feelin' you didn't like Pa any more than I did," Adam said.

"He always said I was a mistake. Mother said he talked that way because his business was slipping and I wasn't a son who could help him work."

"You were with her when she died?"

Jessy felt tears swimming up in her eyes and burning down the back of her throat. "The Lord took her fast. Pneumonia."

"Couldn't be helped."

No, it couldn't be helped, she thought, licking away tears. Her father's death could have been avoided, but not her mother's. Jessy looked straight into Adam's eyes. "How she cried for you at the end. She took my hand and kept crying your name, saying, 'Jessy, you know what you must do.' Before she died she pointed to her Bible on the nightstand. She told me all the answers I would ever need were in there, and then she held me as tight as she could." Their mother's hand was on Jessy still. A gust of wind rocked the house so hard the windows rattled. Jessy wiped away her tears and said: "All the way from the North Pole, that's what Mr. Gaad told me."

"Hmm?"

"This wind."

"Never thought about it that way, but he's right. Ever visit Unkajake's?"

"Yes! A long time ago. He lived out in the country, in a shack, with cherry trees and blackberry bushes. He let me have all the fruit I wanted. That's where Father taught me how to shoot, but I enjoyed listening to the song birds more. We didn't visit Uncle as often as I would have liked."

"I'd run there every time Pa'd get on me. Unka taught me to live on the land. How to farm, ride a horse, and tend animals. How to hunt and shoot and swim. How to fight. How to win. Pa'd beat me and off I'd go. Unka taught me card games, too, and . . . tricks."

Jessy neared the stove, enjoying the warmth. "What kind of tricks?"

"Oh, uh. . . " Adam blew the heat off a juicy bit of sausage.

Jessy watched and waited impatiently while Adam slurped the spoon clean. "What tricks?" she asked again.

"Huh? Oh, card tricks, craps. Time to eat. What'd you do with them plates?" Quickly he piled both high with food and sat at the table.

"Thank you," she said softly, taking a seat and bowing her head, awaiting Adam's expression of thanks.

Instead of a blessing, he snapped, "Eat before it gets cold."

"I'm sorry, I never did find the napkins."

"There ain't any." Adam dug into his food with two-handed gusto, fork in his left hand, knife in his right, never letting go of either utensil until he'd cleaned the plate. While he ate he rested both forearms against the edge of the table and bowed his head over his plate to achieve maximum leverage and speed with a minimum output of energy. He had downed two helpings of everything while Jessy was still nibbling daintily on her first. Between chews he asked, "Ain't you hungry?"

"Yes. Very."

"Doncha like the food?"

She answered truthfully, "It's wonderful. You're a good cook. What were you telling me about Uncle Jake?"

"He taught me a lot. Was he tough! Raised purebred bulls."

"It was a bull that killed him."

"No!" Adam looked truly crestfallen. "Unkajake?"

"Yes! Didn't you know?" Adam looked so lost, she said, "I shouldn't have told you." She stood to go to him but he gestured for her to resume her seat.

"Don't be sorry. That's life, 'specially farm life. Farmin's a gamble, more than any other business." From his seat at the head of the table, Adam gazed toward the fireplace, his face darkened by the pain of loss.

In the long silence, Jessy became aware of a clock ticking on the mantle, a mellow reminder of work waiting to be done. "Adam? Is it all right if I do the dishes?" When he failed to answer, she began clearing the table.

Her tender voice and little rustlings startled him. "The dishes can wait. Sit down and let's talk."

She sat, but with foreboding. This must be the 'little talk' Adam had mentioned to Ollie Gaad. She swallowed hard, not knowing what to expect.

"Now, I want the truth, straight and simple, with no tears and none of them hammy histrionics of yours. Where's the money?"

Jessy glanced at his jacket. "Still in your pocket, I think."

"I don't mean this chicken feed. I'm talkin' 'bout the estate."

"The what?"

His nostrils flared. "The money Ma and Pa left us. The proceeds from the sale."

"The sale of what?"

"The house on Oak Street, for one, and the furniture and Ma's silver and all. You musta ended up with a nice little nest egg."

"Oh! That!" Jessy smiled, relieved at last to understand what he was driving at. "The big blue house with the gables!" Jessy nodded happily, remembering. "With the swings in back and the picket fence and the rose trellis and the wishing well and the — "

"Yeah, yeah, yeah. What'd it sell for?"

Jessy's smile vanished. "I don't know."

"Musta been plenty. Who was the probate lawyer? I can wire him."

"I can't remember if there was a lawyer or not. I don't think so, but it was four years ago."

"You moved that long ago?" Now it was Adam's turn to be perplexed.

"Yes sir. The strangest thing happened after Father's funeral. Mother was still dressed all in black when these men came and told her they were owed money for Father's gambling debts. There were house payments due, too, and taxes, and on and on and if she didn't pay we would have to leave. She started selling things — first the silver, then her china, and then the furniture, piece by piece."

"Her dowry? She sold off what her folks'd left her?"

Jessy nodded sadly. "Mother cried to see her nicest things going one by one, and even then there still wasn't enough money to pay the bills." Jessy looked glum. "Well, one day some men from the bank came to put us out of the house and board up the doors! We ended up standing out on Oak Street with some pots and pans and clothes and books and the ironing board and some other stuff the junk man wouldn't buy. Mother prayed the neighbors wouldn't see. I never told her this but — " Jessy lowered her voice. "I saw some of them peeking at us from their parlors. It was awful."

Adam's powerhouse chest heaved with disgust. "It's hard to believe you were evicted, but, then again, knowin' Pa — "

"I wish it weren't true but it is."

Adam perked up. "What about Pa's shop? The tools — "

"His business went bad. He and Mother fought about money, and other things, too. They'd wake me up all the time, fighting in the night. It scared me listening to them."

"Pa wasn't exactly Mr. Charmschool. So you're sayin' Ma lost the house and you two moved to a dump, is that right?"

"Yes sir, and it really grieved her, but no one seemed to care about her feelings. When we first moved to the tenements, I thought Mother would never smile again but after awhile, things settled down. I missed the pretty roses and the swings, but I made new friends. The neighbors were nice, especially when Mother took sick and, well, they were real sweet to me after she—died. But they didn't have much and I didn't like having to take from them so that's why I left and came here and I'm sorry to have imposed but I didn't know what else to do, especially since Mother called for you so much when she was dying."

"Hmmp." Adam took the six dollars out of his jacket pocket and looked at it with a smirk on his face. "So. This is the estate."

Jessy had learned a new word: estate. It looked so small in his big hands. "What are you going to do with it?"

Adam roared with laughter. "That's a good one!"

Surprised and struggling to get the joke, Jessy laughed along with him.

"And here I've been, thinkin' you had it made, but bein' greedy decided to put on this big charity circus, comin' all the way here from New England just to sponge off me!"

"Ohhh! I see!" Now Jessy understood, or at least thought she did.

"And you made me mad, because here I am, the firstborn son, and I didn't care 'bout my rightful share of the estate, because I never wanted nothin' more to do with Pa and followin' in his footsteps, as he always put it to me, takin' over his business and all that hogwash. And I wouldn't have bothered lookin' into the matter till you showed up on my doorstep, lookin' like a lost soul beggin' for a handout."

For a moment, the two of them sat in silence digesting all of this. From his chair at the head of the table, Adam stared into the fireplace with an expression that defied description. The clock continued ticking, reminding Jessy of her duty.

"Should I do the dishes now?" When he didn't answer, she started clearing her end of the table. "That sure was a fine dinner, Adam. I can't remember when I had so much good food to eat. Thank you very much."

When she drew near him, he handed her the money. She reached out, but to his surprise, she didn't snatch it away. "No, thanks," she said sweetly, piling his plate and fork with hers in a neat stack, careful not to chip anything. "That money does belong to you, now that I think about it. In the Bible, it was the firstborn sons who inherited everything."

"Yeah," he said bitterly. "Everythin'." Adam stuffed the money into his pocket again and pushed away from the table. On his way to his chair by the fireplace he took a bottle and a shot glass from the sideboard.

"You're not going to get drunk, are you?" asked Jessy, her eyes wide with apprehension.

"Nah," said Adam, swirling the contents of the nearly empty bottle, "but I need a nightcap." He sat and stretched his long legs up on the stone ledge beside the fireplace, then yawned heartily.

A pile of papers on the same shelf as the bottle caught her eye. She walked closer for a better look. "My letters! So you did get them. Why didn't you answer?"

"Never was a writer. 'Cept for math and science and recess, I hated school. Hard sittin' in them little chairs all day while the great outdoors kept callin' to me. Soon as the teachers'd start talkin' 'bout grammar, I'd start lookin' out the window, or pickin' fights with my pals. Besides, I figured you musta been provided for and didn't need to come pester me."

Jessy smiled at the thought of Adam Flint, the biggest boy in his class, relegated to the back of the room so he didn't block the other children's view of the blackboard. Jessy herself was always seated up front, close to the teacher. She noted with quiet satisfaction how worn her letters looked, and stained but neatly folded. So Adam had read what she had written about Mother's death, one full page, and the quick reference to their father's death five years before. Jessy pictured Adam sitting just as he did now in front of the fireplace sipping his drink and reading her letters, thinking she had inherited a small fortune and wanted yet more. Hers weren't the only letters. "I see you get lots of mail."

"Used to get more."

"These smell as pretty as they look. Such dainty lettering." Jessy sniffed the envelope. "Mmmm. Perfume." The postmarks represented half the world.

"Put them away."

As Jessy did, she jangled two brass keys tied with red string. The tiny noise they made when she picked them up put Adam on the alert.

"Hey! Gimme those!" He held out his long arm in her direction.

Jessy handed them over and began washing dishes. From the kitchen she called out to him, "Do you get lonely sometimes?"

Adam answered by emptying the bottle into his glass. Gazing into the fire, he finally said, "He coached me in how to wrestle, till I could beat everyone around, even guys older than me."

"You mean Uncle?"

"He told me I could make some easy money wrestlin', usin' my strength. That's how I ended up goin' with the circus. At first all I did was put up tents and take 'em back down. I worked outside all day, rain or shine, always on the move. Split open more than my share of skulls. I been lucky. Made my pile without endin' up dead or maimed for life."

Jessy wiped all the counters and the table top, careful not to leave any spots. When she was finished, she went outside to toss away the dishwater, unprepared for a sight that filled her with wonder. The fruit trees, hardwoods, and pines were swaying in the wind, waving to the ink blue sky. Jessy came running back in, thrilled to her toes. "I've never seen so many stars! They fill up the trees like diamonds!"

"Can't see so many stars in the city, with all the lights."

"How lovely! No wonder you settled here." Stifling a little yawn, she asked, "Would you mind if I sit with you?"

"Have a seat." He booted a chair toward her.

Seated in front of the fire, Jessy began to feel the effects of a long and eventful day. The food had warmed her, but also made her sleepy. As she started to nod off, she heard Adam's rolling rich voice.

" 'Course I didn't become a star overnight. Had to pay my dues. Between matches I did other things—exhibitions, tests of strength, some boxin', carryin' pretty girls and lions around on my shoulders."

This roused her. "Lions?"

"Yeah. Good old Wilma. She was a newborn cub when I first joined up with the show. Cute little thing, at first. Big paws; quick and playful. I'd roll around in the sawdust with her, just for fun."

"You had her declawed, didn't you?"

"Nah. Wilma was smart. She wouldn't claw me. I had her trained. She loved to ride around on my bare shoulders. The manager decided we'd make a great act, so he signed me as Samson and his Lion. 'Course, wrestlin' was my best sport and how I still make a good livin'."

"You fight people for money?"

"Sure, why not? Men'll pay big money to see a match, even if it's rigged. They'll gamble everythin' they got if they think they can win. And when I wasn't fightin' I was learnin' every trick there was. Three card monty, shell games, fortune tellin', magic, snake oil. All that phony junk. Most days I'm glad I'm out of it, but there's times I miss the excitement."

"Why did you quit?"

Adam studied his glass. "Won this place in a crap game. Old goat who used to own it bet the back forty, then the front forty. He wanted to throw in his old lady, too, but I had to draw the line someplace. She was ugly enough to scare rats."

"Those poor people don't have a home now?"

"Poor people? Fools, more likely. Thought they could make some fast money off me. I showed 'em. 'Course, I figured I'd just sell it but I kinda liked the place once I saw it. Reminded me of bein' a kid at Unkajake's. Decided it was time to give up wanderin' all over with the fast 'n loose. Livin' here I could get plenty of fresh air and exercise, keep strong and fit, agree to a fight if and when I choose. Follow nobody's schedule but my own."

"Why didn't you ever come home to visit?"

He evaded her eyes by putting his glass on the crate beside his chair and picking up a sharp tool and a wooden block. "Meant to but one thing 'n another kept croppin' up. Road shows to do, always on the move. Practice every day. You don't get to be the Man of Iron lyin' around dreamin' 'bout it. You got to make it happen. Takes hard work every day. Pain. Sacrifice."

"Couldn't you have come home at Christmas?"

"Didn't care to see Pa. And, winters I'd go to New Orleans for ah—"

Jessy gazed into his face so long he began to stammer.

"Ah, for trainin'. Thought about home, sometimes, but just never got 'round to goin' back." Adam shaved thin strips of wood off the block. " 'Course, the folks coulda made the effort to see me perform but they never did."

"That reminds me! I brought you something." She emptied the contents of her bag on the floor—toothbrush, flannel nightgown, blouse, long wool stockings, books, Bible.

"Carried a rag heap a thousand miles?"

Jessy hid from him her ragged clothes and hurt feelings. "Here. For you. Father's and Mother's wedding bands."

He kept whittling. "You keep them. I don't ever want to get married."

"Me neither."

Adam cocked his brow. "No? I thought marriage was every girl's dream." Seeing that Jessy was adamant, he tucked the rings into his jacket pocket. His estate was growing.

Jessy kept digging in her bags. "And here's their wedding picture."

Adam took it from her. "What a pair." After looking at it long and hard, he propped it up on the mantle against the ticking clock.

Jessy continued unpacking. A pen went rolling off in one direction, her hairbrush in another. With a thud a small wad of papers hit the floor.

"What the — ?" Adam was out of his chair like a shot.

"Oh, those," she said as he grabbed her pretty papers. Much to her surprise he grabbed her as well. He lifted her off her feet and half out of her sweater.

"What're you doin' with my checks?"

"Mother gave them to me."

"Don't you lie to me. I'll slap you from here to Sunday!" He began shaking her like a rag doll. "Stole 'em, didn't you? Right out of the mailbox! No wonder the folks never bothered about me after I left home!"

"Mother gave them to me! I'd go to the library to find the cities on the map, and then I'd look up all the places you'd been!"

Ah, the pleasures those pretty papers represented to Jessy. Pinks and yellows and mint greens, no two alike, the delicately etched landmarks underlying the words and numbers, their mother's name — Esther Flint — designated as the payee and Adam's thick blunt signature on the bottom line of every one. Each pretty paper represented a different city — St. Louis, Chicago, Toronto, Philadelphia, New York, Paris, Vienna — the wonderful places her famous brother had visited. Jessy had improved her spelling, geography, and history working with those little slips of paper. But this was not a moment for peaceful reflection.

Adam shook her hard. "You got any more of these?"

"No. Please let go of me!"

He dropped her but not the papers. "Unbelievable. Absolutely incredible. To think I kissed this money goodbye ages ago." He fanned the pile like a card shark, rapidly and accurately counting aloud. "Six thousand eight hundred and fifty-seven dollars! Good as gold!" He slapped at the bundle with the back of his free hand. "My money's still in these banks right where I put it after workin' suckers. Money's been sittin' there molderin' all this while because them bankers were waitin' for Ma to cash these checks. When she didn't, they couldn't reach me because I was always on the move."

Jessy straightened out her sweater. "You don't mean to say they're valuable?"

"Bet your sweet life they are, as long as the banks are still in business. All I gotta do is get my banker in town to collect. Easy as that." Snapping his fingers, Adam sank into his chair. With a stunned expression, he turned back to her. "How'd you come by all these certified bank drafts? And you'd better not lie to me if you like livin'."

Jessy was still struggling with her crooked sweater and the twisted sleeves of her blouse. "I told you, Mother gave them to me."

"But why didn't she cash 'em in?"

"Knowing Father, he probably would have gambled the money as fast as it came, but he never knew about them. When mail was delivered, he was working or off somewhere. And, anyway, Mother told me they were no good."

"No good?"

No good like Adam, their mother had said, but Jessy couldn't repeat such a thing to him. Instead, she said, "Mother wanted to burn them but I begged her not to. I thought they were pretty. She said I could have them as long as Father never knew. She told me to tear them up and throw them away as soon as I looked up the places on the map, but I liked them too much to throw them away. She didn't know I kept them. She would've been mad at me knowing I disobeyed her. So I just carried them around with my school books."

"You said they couldn't make ends meet. That his business went sour."

"They couldn't. It did."

"So why didn't Ma cash these checks? You're not talkin' sense."

Jessy looked away from Adam, thinking her answer would be hurtful. Adam made a move toward her. "You answer me or else."

Jessy faced him squarely, uttering the unutterable in a rush. "Mother said she would d-die before taking money from you, and that's just what happened! Every time a check came, she called it Sin Money."

To her surprise, this revelation didn't anger him at all.

"Money's money. I earned it, mostly. Some I won. I sent some home, when I was fool enough to feel guilty 'bout runnin' off. I always wondered why they never came to see me perform. I still don't understand what it was she didn't like about my money, 'specially since she lost the house for lack of funds."

" 'Filthy lucre' she called it. 'Dishonest gain.' Mother said 'We'll starve and die by honest means rather than live and prosper on the income of a gigolo, even if that gigolo is my own firstborn child, my only son.' "

"Gigolo? My own mother called me that? I never took money from a woman in my life, even when I had the chance. You sure she said that?"

"Positive! She said, 'My son is engaged in vulgar entertainments, shamelessly displaying himself like a brazen idol before the low-minded masses.' I didn't understand what she meant. I'd run to the dictionary to—"

Adam exploded. "Vulgar? A brazen idol?"

"Mother forgave you though, at the end."

"That was big of her!" Adam fanned the bundle in Jessy's innocent, upturned face. "Well, I'll just relieve you of all this—what'd she say? 'filthy lucre'?"

"Yes sir." Having straightened her clothing, Jessy reached out to graze the pretty papers with one small hand. "I liked having what you sent to us. These helped me feel close to you. They've been so special to me, because they proved you were real, that I really had a brother, even though I never saw you till today. To tell you the truth, I'd rather know you for real than have a bunch of papers, even though they're awfully nice."

Jessy's long-winded recitations left Adam looking uncomfortable. At the moment, he was also speechless. First and foremost a man of action, he rolled up the bank drafts and crammed them into his jacket pocket which was now full to overflowing. He paced a bit, then raked back his hair from his temples with his two big hands, but his curls refused to lie flat away from his face.

Jessy asked brightly, "Are these papers like having more 'estate'?"

"You said it!" Adam's eyes blazed. "And to think a kid dumb as you come all the way out here, totin' these in a schoolbag."

"I'm not dumb."

"What you know about finance'd rattle around on a pinhead. These here are negotiable instruments."

"Really? What does that mean?"

Sighing, Adam raised his eyes to the rafters. "What morons, all of you, livin' like paupers, you lookin' half-starved, and me thinkin' how generous I been." Annoyed, he turned to her again. "And here you come with all this loot. Weren't you afraid someone'd grab you and steal these checks?"

"Why would anyone want to do that?"

His craggy face softened at the sight of her. "Plenty of crazies runnin' loose. Your mother would die all over again to know you'd taken a train by yourself carryin' around nearly seven thousand dollars. A naive kid like you comes all the way here to be with your infamous, brazen-idol, big, bad, vulgar, shameless brother. Weren't you scared spitless?"

"No, sir."

"I'll say one thing. Our folks didn't raise any cowards."

"No, they didn't." Jessy nodded happily. She decided right then that no matter what happened from this moment forward, she would always love her brother, but she was too shy to tell him so.

"So why didn't you cash 'em in?"

"Me? The checks weren't made out to me, and, besides, they're so old. Look at the dates on them." In truth, each check dated from Adam's glory days as a top performer. "Mother said they were no good. I don't know much about checks anyway, and I felt guilty not throwing them away like she told me to."

"I s'pose it's just as well you're such a dumb kid." Adam gestured to her belongings on the floor. "Got anythin' else I ought to know about? Buncha diamonds maybe?"

Shaking her head no, Jessy interrupted her yawning to giggle.

"You can stow your stuff in there." Adam showed her the narrow, chilly room with whitewashed walls, windows thick with frost, and bare shelves.

"Thank you, Adam." Jessy's breath steamed in the cold.

"There's pegs behind the door. 'Course there ain't no bed in there. I got a spare in the cellar but I don't feel like luggin' it up here tonight."

"Could I sleep by the fire, where it's warm? Is that okay with you?"

"Sure." Adam poked around in various rooms, tossing together a makeshift pallet for her piled high with horse blankets. He also extinguished the lamps.

When Jessy emerged from the washroom in her nightgown, she found him in near darkness, propped up in his chair, toasting his stockinged feet by the fire. He was sharpening the knife he had used on the beaver.

Once Jessy crawled under the blankets, she felt very much awake. The sound of knife against whetstone grated in her ears like a guillotine, not that Jessy had ever heard a guillotine, but she was sure it must sound exactly like the noise Adam was making. Regardless of her commitment to love always, she might as well face facts: The first time she saw her brother, his hands were bloody. Sure, he scrubbed his hands clean, but that didn't fool her one little bit. Adam had seemed friendly enough, even playful, but now she wondered if he was the one putting on an act. After all, Adam is the performer in this family, not me, she reminded herself.

In the eerie darkness, Jessy's mind began to race. Adam made his living putting on shows and hurting people for money. Now he had the cash, the checks, the gold rings, everything of value. There wasn't another house for — how far away did Mr. Gaad say he lived? And how fast could Jessy run in the dark down a strange road from a — a Philistine rifle-toting Goliath who towered over her like the one in the Bible who menaced a whole army and especially little David the shepherd boy? And Jessy didn't even have a slingshot, not that she'd know how to use one even if there was one handy which there wasn't and, besides, how could she find five smooth stones like David did, when here it was, the middle of the night? How long could a fourteen year-old eighty-eight-pound girl clad in a flannel nightshirt last in this cold weather and wind? Just like that ill-fated beaver, Jessy knew she had come to the wrong place. Involuntarily, she sat up, her eyes wide and hair standing on end.

Without taking his eyes off her, Adam slid the knife slowly across the stone. "Nightmare?"

"N-no. I'm n-not sleepy. All the excitement." Jessy's little heart thumped wildly under her flannel gown. Her mouth was so dry it was hard to talk. At last she stammered, "I'm th-thirsty. May I have a drink, please?"

Adam instictively reached for the bottle he'd left under his chair, then stopped. "Water's in the pitcher on the counter."

She crawled from the warm pallet into the chilly room, making sure not to turn her back on the knife-wielding ogre. Gulping cold water and shivering all over, she wondered if she should slide around him and rush back to bed, or grab her coat and run for the door. And where was her coat, anyway? Oh, yes, the pegs and coat-bandits. Fear was mashing Jessy's mind to mush.

Adam poked the fire with a heavy brass weapon with a pointed end. She stood behind him, watching his every move with her big bright eyes. The fire in front of him cast his shadow all the way up the wall, across the ceiling, and down the other side of the room. The shadow of the poker in his hand was at least as tall as the barn. Jessy's little mouth quivered.

"What's the matter with you, anyway?" He finally turned, annoyed. "You look like you seen a ghost!" He tossed the poker aside and sat down again, turning his attention to his whittling block. Under the pressure of his fingers against the sharp blade, wood shavings sprinkled to the floor.

There go my bones, thought Jessy, into itty-bitty, little . . .

"Go back to sleep. You're makin' me nervous!"

She was making him nervous!? What did Goliath-Samson Furry-Animal Killer Man of Iron have to be nervous about!?

In stunned silence Jessy watched him work, hands busy, turning the block this way and that, evaluating his progress. Flames leaped up in the fireplace, throwing monstrous quavering shadows of him on the walls. In this eerie light, Adam could have been a Canaanite baby-killing devil worshipper! And whatever was he making? Something to knock her out? A marker for her grave?

Feeling ridiculous and growing numb with cold, Jessy crawled under the covers, trying to shake away her foolish thoughts. Cold and stiff, she lay there like a corpse, but a corpse with a mind that churned like that weather vane outside in the wind. It was impossible to sleep. Twisting around on the pallet, she prayed: "Dear Lord, please protect me! If the worst happens, into Your hands I commend my spirit. In the name of Jesus Christ, Amen." She said it so fast she prayed the whole thing again, slowly, in case the Lord didn't understand her gibberish. She repeated herself several times.

Although sleep didn't come right away, praying calmed Jessy's heart. When a burning log dropped heavily into the ash, she opened her eyes a bit. Adam was dozing. Soft curls framed his rugged face. In sleep he didn't look like a devil-worshipping monster at all. He looked serene, boyish, like an ageless Greek hero poised for eternity. Yes, he was big and crude, but did that mean he'd murder her in her sleep? Yawning deeply, Jessy snuggled under the covers, enjoying the pleasant music of the fire playing a duet with the wind.

A city child, she had grown up in raucous noise that went on day and night — people brawling, cats in chorus, horse hooves on cobblestones, trains screaming in and out of town at every hour of the day and night. And now all she could hear was wind and fire. At last Jessy came to that chasm, sleep, which she had since her earliest childhood envisioned as God's loving arms. She slipped soft as an angel beneath His wings.

❧ 3 ❧

Jessy wakened to the striking of a match followed by banging around in the kitchen. From the racket, she knew a fire was being started in the stove. She was jolted by the thud of wood hitting the fireplace grate close to where she lay. Pushing deep beneath the covers, she struggled with eyes still closed to remember where she was, and why. Events of the previous night washed over her, the happiness and fear, the relief of clearing up misunderstandings.

"I awake, and I am still with Thee," she prayed with thanksgiving. Grateful for her life and such cozy comfort, she dozed off again, only to be roused by the sound of rock-hard coffee beans being crushed in a hand-cranked grinder. Soon the aroma of strong coffee wafted through the house. Adam's clattering continued as he moved about, slurping from his mug. Jessy, reluctant to venture into the chill air, began drifting into a dream of porters and railroad cars when her ears were pierced by the crowing of a rooster. She groaned and burrowed once more but was startled by a nudge against her foot.

"Mornin', Sleepin' Beauty."

Adam's boots soon faded from hearing as the front door opened and shut. Jessy struggled to recapture her dream, the magic of sleep, the stunning imagery of the American landscape unrolling before her through the windows of a moving train, but that annoying rooster repeated his vigorous wakeup call and roused a chorus of barking dogs. With all her will, Jessy held on to what by now had become a cozy pink velvet dream, but the insistent ringing of an ax forced her awake. She dressed to the thuds of wood being tossed about in the yard.

As Jessy folded the bedding and packed her few belongings, she looked around Adam's place at the fire blazing in the hearth, the circus posters, the fat pussy willows in their old crockery jar. She had been here less than a day and already Adam's place felt a little like home. Home! Straining not to think about what was not to be, still Jessy couldn't help but look longest and hardest of all at the empty chair at the head of the table.

Sighing, she consoled herself with the facts that her brother no longer considered her a faker and a cheat, and now had his rightful estate. Her long journey hadn't been wasted; it had a good purpose. Sad but resigned to her fate, Jessy set her bags by the door, said her prayers, and then stepped outside, lifting her long dark skirt as she went down the steps.

Adam, absorbed in the task of splitting firewood, didn't pause to chide her. " 'Bout time you was up. Too much sleep is no good for you. Makes you dull. Me, I never sleep more 'n four hours myself. Haul some of that seasoned wood into the house. Take a mix of hard 'n soft."

"Good morning. Oh, my! Did you cut all this wood?" Jessy paused to gape at the fortress of aging firewood Adam must have spent the winter cutting by hand. When she neared him, she said, "I've been thinking. There's a factory back East, a spinning mill. When they hire girls, they provide room and board. If you loan me my trainfare, I'll pay you back as soon as I can. I'm not asking for a handout, just a loan. I'll send you some money every payday. I could keep writing to you, that is, if you wouldn't mind hearing from me. You wouldn't have to answer my letters, not unless you wanted to. It'd be so good to hear from you!"

At that moment Jessy was entertained by a lively parade of hens strutting around her feet. Smiling, she turned from them to her brother. "And maybe if you felt like it you could write back and let me know how things were going with you and — and Madame Fiji ..."

Between blows with his ax, he snapped, "You don't like it here?"

"It's wonderful! But it's time for me to go and I've got to plan out what to do. I shouldn't impose on anyone — not back East or here. I really am sorry to have to ask you for money, but it would just be temporary, till I find work. I think the factory hires girls my age."

Jessy rubbed her hands together helplessly, wishing he would speak to her, but he had resumed working with concentration, control, and power. "I'm really glad we talked last night. I enjoyed hearing your stories, especially about Wilma, your baby lion." Jessy chewed on her lower lip, hesitant to continue but wanting to express her feelings, even though Adam wasn't listening. "It was real special to me, our visit, that is. We had lots to talk about, didn't we?" Jessy jumped out of the way more than once as Adam worked his ax. At last she wailed, "I'm freezing!" She blew hard through her mittens.

"Work'll warm you up. Pa teach you the difference between hard wood 'n soft?"

"No, sir."

Adam spit lustily. "Look." He startled her by making one sharp, clean downstroke that split a log into two perfect halves. With the ax he dug into one of them, lifting it to her nose. "Hard. See that grain? How tight and fine it is?" With one jerk of wood against boot, the wood fell free. He quickly and expertly dug the ax into another log, repeating the demonstration. "Pine. Soft. See? Not as soft as you. Get movin'."

When he forced the log to drop at her feet she picked it up gingerly, and carried it like a baby toward the porch.

"No, you dumbbell, I said take the seasoned wood into the house. What you got there stays out on the woodpile to age. It's green, like you." He threw himself into his work with such intensity he spoke no more.

It was fully morning by the time she had filled the wood box in the house, but still they labored on. Following the precise example Adam had set, she continued to pile newly cut wood beside the old.

"Owww!" Jessy winced and stiffened, then took off one mitten.

Adam put down his ax and was at her side at once. "Lemme see."

Jessy backed away from him, hiding her hand.

He grabbed her arm. "I said lemme see." Adam whistled at what he saw in her hand. "That's a beauty." Without letting go of her, he pulled out his pocket knife and opened it with a snap.

Jessy looked up to his impassive face with disbelief. She tugged against him in vain. "I'll be all right, really I will."

"Slivers don't come out by theirselves. Stand still."

"I don't think you ought to—"

"Don't tell me what to do." When she strained hard against him, he gave her a shake. "I said stand still."

Would he never be done squeezing and poking? Jessy wanted to scream. Tears ran down her cheeks.

"What a cry baby!"

As he prodded along the entry point of the sliver, she broke into a sweat. Then it was over.

"There! Look." Triumphant, Adam held up a two inch sliver for her to see. "Better wash your hand with plenty of soap."

Before she knew it he had pulled her to the pump and was priming it. "Me, I never notice slivers, my hands are so tough."

"This water is like ice!"

"You really are a baby!" He tossed a towel, stiff with frost, at her. "Go see if you can find us some eggs. There's a basket in the hen house." As he was about to resume his work, he paused and looked up. "Someone's comin'."

At first Jessy could hear nothing but soon a horse and wagon familiar to Jessy came to a halt in the yard. "Mr. Gaad! Good morning!"

"Hi there, Missie. I'd like you to meet my wife Mildred."

Jessy greeted Mrs. Gaad, taking an instant liking to the plump, pretty lady with her open, mild-looking face and hair streaked with gray.

"A goodly child, just like you said, Oll. We've come to take you home with us, Jessy Flint. You haven't been crying, have you, dear?"

Jessy rubbed the streaks across her face. "Yes, ma'am."

The Gaads stared at Adam in chill silence. He continued working, oblivious to their conversation.

Warding off the possibility of more rumors, Jessy said in a rush, "I've been helping Adam with the wood. He just took a great big sliver out of my hand." She held up her hand for them to see. "At first it hurt a lot but it feels better now. Adam made me clean it with soap right away."

The Gaads appeared to relax. "Are you ready to come home with us?"

"That's awfully kind of you both, really it is, but I don't want to be any trouble to anyone any more. There's factory work back East."

Adam sank his ax into a stump, rubbed his bare hands against his thighs, and dragged his hand across his chest with a seesaw scratching motion. Despite the morning cold, steam appeared to be rising off him, so damp and heated up he was from his labors. Sniffing the chill air, he approached the Gaads, nodding hello to them.

Jessy glanced up at her brother. "I've just been telling the Gaads that I can find work if I go back East."

Adam's temper flared. "And you might not! Trouble with you is, you don't think things through. S'pose you go all the way back there and find out they ain't hirin'? Or they don't hire girls as young as you?"

So Adam had been listening after all. Jessy stammered back, "I hadn't thought about that."

Adam nodded. "You hadn't thought about a lot of things. If they don't hire you, then you got no place to stay. And if they do hire you, you'll be stuck inside a machine shop twelve, maybe fourteen hours a day. Them machines can be dangerous. Tear hair and limbs off bigger, stronger folks 'n you."

"Oh, my . . . W-well, maybe I could work someplace else."

"Doin' what? You're fit to do nothin' 'cept wash dishes and maybe feed livestock. Maybe."

A growing hope sparked a smile in Jessy's eyes. "I can learn things."

Adam snorted, "Maybe."

Maybe! In the ensuing silence Jessy prayed a very fast prayer.

"If it's a job you want, there's plenty to do right here." Adam turned from Jessy to the Gaads. "Little Lady Luck here might be worth havin' 'round a while, as long as she don't make a pest of herself." To Jessy, Adam said, "I'll expect you to work hard, with no nonsense. Understand?"

"Yes, Adam." Dear Adam! Jessy nodded happily. "I'll work hard. And I promise I'll never be any bother to you whatsoever."

Adam didn't look the least convinced but the Gaads appeared satisfied. "In that case, think of our place as a second home. Our door's always open. And you're welcome to worship with us, Missie. Once a month the circuit preacher holds a meetin' at Standard Hall, 'bout four miles from here. Everyone's invited from all around."

Just as Jessy was about to accept their invitation, Adam prevailed. "You two don't ever give up, do ya?"

"Just bein' neighborly. Can't force folks to believe." Seeing that Adam had brought his arms over his chest in opposition to any further discussion of such an idea, Mr. Gaad changed the subject. Gesturing behind the seat, he said, "Got some milk and cream, if you want it. The wife baked these fresh this morning." He handed Jessy a basket covered over with a gingham napkin.

"And these are for you, Mr. Flint." Mrs. Gaad gave Adam two jars of jelly, blueberry and cherry.

Adam nodded to her and wiped his hands before taking them. "I'll finish makin' that hall stand for you in a coupla weeks. Need some hardware for it and the mirror, is all."

Mrs. Gaad looked pleased. "We're in no hurry. It will be a fine thing when it's finished, we know it. Call on us if you need us." With that, the elderly couple drove away.

"What wonderful neighbors!" Jessy peeked into the basket. "These smell delicious."

"You get them eggs yet?"

"No, sir."

"What're you waitin' for? Them biscuits to turn to stone?"

❧　❧　❧

Breakfast was much to Jessy's liking. Besides fresh biscuits, jam, and eggs, there was a hearty porridge with the richest cream and the sweetest syrup Jessy had ever tasted.

"Raised this hog myself," Adam said with a flourish as he dug into a plate full of bacon. He paused at the sight of her saying grace in silence. "Prayin' again?"

"I always thank the One who sent the food. Don't you?"

"I done the work. You can thank me. Whatcha got there?"

"Mother's Bible. She said I was to read it every day and pray the Holy Spirit opened my eyes to its meaning."

"Do that and you'll end up like Lucy Meredith."

"Who's she?"

With his knife Adam split open a biscuit. "Woman in town. Or, ah—was. There's, ah—all sortsa rumors goin' 'round. She believed all that religious stuff so hard she went crazy. Thought she could walk on water. Got drowned tryin', they think."

"Mother said the days we don't feed on God's Word are like going the worst sort of hungry—spiritually hungry. Once we die and go to heaven, we'll stand before the judgment throne and . . ."

"When you die you won't go nowhere. You won't know the difference. Death'll be the end of you."

"But the Bible says . . . "

"Forget what it says. There's nothin' after this life and anyone that thinks otherwise is a moron."

Jessy stared at him with unblinking liquid brown eyes. "But the Bible says there's resurrection and life eternal. The Lord himself shall descend from heaven with a shout and the dead in Christ shall rise first."

"There's no proof."

"I know that my Redeemer lives."

"Nobody can know that."

"But it's all written here, how Jesus died for our sins, and afterward, He visited with people, and ever since, the Holy Spirit comes to dwell among His believers."

"Hocus pocus! God's an idea dreamed up by cowards for kids and old women. I figure if God really did exist and if He's as all-powerful and all-knowin' as you folks seem to think, then He knows where I am and how to get in touch with me. But I ain't plannin' on seeing any burnin' bushes or corpses risin' up outa their graves." Adam jabbed another slice of ham and stuck it between the halves of a waiting biscuit.

"Jesus died to save us. Everyone, including you and me."

"Maybe you need savin', but I don't."

"Everyone needs savin'." Jessy winced. "I mean saving."

Adam's powerful chest swelled with pride. "I can take care of myself."

"We can't save ourselves. That's why God became a person, to show us how to live and to teach us how to pray, and to die for our sins so we won't have to, and then He sent His spirit so we'd know what to do and wouldn't feel alone or be afraid. Mother wanted me to be strong in the spirit. You, too."

"She dragged me to church when I was a kid. I gave up on it fast."

Goliath, indeed! Despite Adam's obvious powers and grand physical presence, his wonderful craggy face, his strength and fame, Jessy felt achingly sorry for him. Without faith in God he was doomed! Incomplete! A shell without substance. Lost in his sins. How could he be so blind to the truth?

"Can't believe in what I can't hear, see, or touch."

"And God and His promises are the only things I'm really sure of."

Adam sneered. "I seen how magicians trick a crowd, pull rabbits out of their sleeves, from fake bottoms in tables. Sheer illusion! But the crowds fall for it like it was real. Same with religion. Flummery!"

"God is real. And so are heaven and hell."

Pointing to his body, Adam said, "This is heaven; this is hell."

Jessy felt a great deep sob rising up in her. Excusing herself from the table, she went to the window where she could see the bare fields of winter. Some places were patched with snow. "Dear Lord, only You have the power to change this barren field to plenty, to bring forth bread from the earth, to give life, heal the blind, find the lost, raise the dead. Only You have the power to forgive our sins, to open my brother's eyes. Please take pity on him. Help him see Your truth. Please help me help him. In Christ. Amen."

Jessy struggled to collect her composure, finish her meal, and find her voice again. "Last night I didn't realize your farm was so big."

"Ain't much by some standards, but it's plenty for me. I been thinkin'." Adam went to the stove to refill his mug with coffee. "You're new to farmin' and there's few places more dangerous. I got four brood sows and a boar out back that weigh over 500 pounds apiece. They stay penned up. I'll show you how to handle 'em. This is the last of the cold weather. Soon the piglets will be born and in a few weeks, when the ground thaws, I'll start pickin' stone to get the fields clear for plowin'. Every year I plant a vegetable garden. A small part of the acreage goes to hay and oats for my horse and all the rest I put in corn to feed the hogs. Hogs is my business. I grow corn to feed 'em, and then, come fall, when the hogs are fat, I sell 'em but I always keep the meat off one for myself, same as what we're eatin' right now, and that sausage we had last night. I sell most of the herd for cash to buy supplies I can't make myself, like nails, salt, matches, and coffee. Sometimes I trade part of my corn or meat or extra hay for other things I need, like butter, cheese 'n cream."

"From the Gaads."

"Right. Dairy products galore to be had around here. Got a small ice house out back to keep 'em fresh."

Jessy wondered, "Wouldn't it be simpler to keep a cow?"

"Nope. Cows is dumb for one thing, 'n for another, they need to get milked mornin' and night." Adam raised his square chin with a sophisticated air. "And I don't like stickin' round here when I can be off someplace havin' a match."

"A wrestling match?"

"Right. Or playin' poker. There's few things in life I enjoy better. If I had cows I couldn't go nowhere for all the milkin' they'd need."

"I see." Jessy scraped the bottom of her bowl. "This is delicious, Adam, especially the syrup."

"It's from maple sap I tapped myself. Soon as this weather warms up it'll be time to tap them trees again." Adam worked a toothpick between his front teeth. "Soon we'll be gettin' into the busiest time of the year. I expect you to work hard. No time for nonsense."

"Yes sir." Jessy buttered a biscuit and slathered it over with cherry jelly. "Adam, there's something you need to know."

Adam stopped picking his teeth. "Don't tell me you're pregnant."

Jessy blushed furiously. "I should say not! I've never been with a man."

"Well, what is it, then? Don't just sit there with your mouth hangin'. You'll catch flies." Adam shook his head. "Never will understand women, not if I live to be forty."

"What I started to say was, ah, what I want you to know is that Mother loved you best." Jessy said this without a trace of jealousy. "She told me so. You were a beautiful child, she said. Everyone thought so. I was so plain and frail and small, she was always afraid for me. She prayed for us, for you in your wandering and me in my frailty. She called me her angel, sent from God to comfort her in her declining years, to fill the void after you left home. She said you were her prodigal son, her cross."

"That'd be her. Always talkin' like she had a screw loose."

"That isn't fair. Mother truly loved you. She blamed Father for driving you away from home and into a life of sin."

With a burst of energy, Adam scraped his chair away from the table. Now it was his turn to gaze out the window. "I settled here to get away from people—fans and lovesick females followin' me from town to town. Figured everyone'd leave me be. I wanted to get as far as possible from my past, but I can't ever seem to manage it."

"You can be forgiven and have a brand new life by trusting in God."

"Not me. I done things'd make your hair straight."

"God still loves you. If you want forgiveness you only need . . ."

Adam's eyes blazed. "You're just a kid. What do you know anyway? You been readin' all your life. I been livin'."

Jessy answered softly. "I came to be a blessing to you."

Adam wasn't listening. He was opening a new bottle of whiskey. He sat in his chair by the fire filling a glass. Jessy looked in the cabinet to see a row of unopened bottles. A shelf load of oblivion. So. This is what Mother was talking about that night she lay dying. How she ached for Adam's soul. *Now, so do I. I can't give him faith. But God . . .*

❧ 4 ❧

A month had passed. Despite Jessy's fervent prayers, Adam remained far from God, very much a man dependent on strenuous physical activity and strong drink. She noticed that his outlook hinged on factors that had nothing to do with her: the weather, private thoughts, and the amount of alcohol in his bloodstream. One additional factor had everything to do with her.

At this moment Adam came into the house, white with dust from the back forty, after a day picking stone. He tossed his battered felt hat on the usual peg with an expert hand. "Sittin' around readin' again?"

"I've only just sat down. I'm baking. Besides, I haven't had a chance to finish this and it's due back at the library Saturday." She showed him a thick history of American agriculture.

"Let's see how smart you really are. What was it I told you to get done first thing yesterday?"

"I just couldn't. B-but I fed and watered the stock. I washed clothes. I ironed and mended. I even wrote for the catalogs you wanted."

"What did I tell you to do first?" He grabbed her book from the table, and, with superb aim, pitched it across the room into the fireplace. The book went up in an orange blaze.

Jessy looked helplessly at the burning ruin. "Oh, no! Adam! That was a library book! How could you!"

"Easy."

"They'll charge a fine! A big one!"

"So what? I could buy that flea-speck Town Library if I felt like it." He grabbed her. "And I'll tell you somethin' else, sister. That book ain't all that's gonna go flyin'. You think you're better 'n me, doncha?"

Jessy did her best to avoid his blazing glare. "The hog house is disgusting."

"Like me, ain't that what you mean to say?"

"No, not at all." Still, she couldn't look at him.

44

He grabbed her and forced her around. "Look at me when I'm talkin' to you. Them pens need cleanin' every week and as long as you live on my land, it's your job."

"Let go! You're hurting me!"

He shoved her away. "Get started or I'll hurt you worse."

"Hog manure is the most disgusting ... it ought to be outlawed!"

"I'll rub your face in it if I like." When she failed to move, he raised his hand.

Jessy stepped backwards, her eyes on his upraised hand. "I've done all my chores, Adam, but working in that awful stench is—it's inhuman!"

"Clean it out or else. I got a lot of other things to do."

Jessy pleaded with her eyes but Adam only glared. "The cornbread's going to burn." She ran past him to the oven and pulled out a tray of muffins.

Adam watched with his hunter's eyes. "Now you're finished with that, you can get started with them pens. There's plenty'a daylight left."

Jessy smiled her prettiest smile. "Adam, please ... "

"Get the strap."

The blood drained from Jessy's face. "You wouldn't ... "

"You do things my way or else. Now get that strap." When she wouldn't budge he dragged her to the washroom and reached in for the strap himself.

Adam's razor strap, like everything else he owned, had been designed for years of hard use. She tried fending off the blows to no avail. With an iron grip on her, Adam herded her outside and down the steps toward the hated pens. The rank odor of hog manure soured the air even from this distance. "Adam! Please don't!" Screaming and crying, Jessy crumbled in the dust. "Stop it!"

"Givin' me orders, now, are you? I'll show you. You're not here to pick and choose what you feel like doin'. You hear me?"

Convulsing with sobs, Jessy managed to nod.

"I don't wanna lay eyes on you till you're done. You'll get nothin' to eat till you're finished. Stay in them pens all night if you have to but get the place cleaned out. Is that clear?" Over her crying he hollered, "Disobey me again, you'll get worse. I'll beat you up one side and down the other! Now shut up and get busy!"

She cried in pain, humilitation, and defeat, until there were no tears left inside of her. Once Adam was gone, Jessy sat up in the dust. She struggled to her feet and toward the pens.

The acrid fumes of the pens made her eyes burn. Fifty hogs, adults and newborns, generated a small mountain of waste. The shovel was heavy enough without their wretched manure. "No wonder the Prodigal Son came to his senses working in a pig sty," she said to the sows. After an hour of heavy labor, Jessy, dirty and tired, stepped outside for some fresh air.

She walked through the dusty fields to the fence that ran along the dirt road lined with trees. It pleased her to look up through their branches into the bluest sky she had ever seen. Not a cloud anywhere. She hadn't seen a cloud for weeks. Jessy slowly realized it hadn't rained once since her arrival, which explained why Adam had been so edgy. Without rain, he couldn't farm. All those pigs to feed and no way to plant food for them, or for people.

"Dear Lord, I've angered my brother. In truth, the thought has occurred to me that Adam is disgusting in some ways. Worse, he knows what I've been thinking. I could have cried when he said that. He's the brother You gave me to love, yet I've hurt him. Dear Lord, You know I love my brother. He's given me a home, a room of my own, and food to eat. He doesn't love me or You and I don't know that he ever will, but now he and all our neighbors need rain. Please, if it be Your will, Lord, remember us in our need. And most of all, dear Lord, my brother needs You. You must love him more than I do because You made him and breathed life into him. If You opened his eyes, I'd be forever grateful. Please help me be a light for him to see You. And please give me the strength to shovel that—awful stuff. Thank You. In Christ. Amen."

With a start, Jessy noticed people coming down the road, toward her. Three children, two boys and a girl, approached. The children spoke first.

"Hi. You must be that new girl, Jessy Flint."

"I'm not new. I'm fourteen."

"Ha! Listen to her! Been shoveling up after hogs, huh? Don't you just hate it?"

The smallest child spoke up loudly. "We hate it too, 'specially Luke."

Jessy nodded at this welcome surprise: company for her misery. "Who's Luke?"

"Me. I'm the oldest. I'll be thirteen next month."

"Where do you live?" Jessy asked the charming trio of young strangers.

"Two miles that way. You can visit whenever you like."

"Uh-uh-*uh*," moaned the girl.

"Whadya mean uh-uh-*uh*?"

"*You* know. . . " The little girl whispered something to Luke.

"That ain't true, Margie! No one's ever proved it."

Jessy interrupted. "Proved what?"

"Nuthin'."

The smaller boy piped up. "Adam Flint killed a lady."

Jessy flushed with shame. "Mr. Gaad said those rumors aren't true!"

Luke explained, "Lucy Meredith disappeared after Adam Flint moved in here, and so did his girlfriend from the circus."

Jessy's heart stopped. "What girl?"

"Why doncha ask him? The Sheriff looked and looked but he never found that circus lady Laurann, or Lucy Meredith either."

"Adam told me Mrs. Meredith drowned by accident."

Margie answered, "They dredged the lake but she wasn't there."

"Your brother chased us away from here!" complained the smaller boy. "He's a champion fighter but he won't teach us boys to wrestle. One day me and Luke and some other boys came to ask him to show us how to fight and he ran us off."

"Look, here he comes!" With that, the frightened children fled down the road rather than encounter Adam Flint.

Jessy panicked. She darted off at a diagonal, running with a strength she was unaware she had. Lungs bursting, she scrambled into the hog house. No sooner had she dropped the bar into the iron braces across the doors than Adam demanded she open up. Amazed by his speed and strength, she wondered what he was truly capable of doing, considering his temperament.

"Open up!" The heavy doors shook with his fury. "I wanna talk to you!"

The shovel Jessy hadn't wanted to touch an hour ago, she now grabbed and held for dear life.

"Jessy, lemme in!"

"Just try coming in here," she muttered quietly. "I'll — I'll what, Lord? Bash his brains out with this shovel? Some Christian I'm turning out to be." Jessy's mind raced. What to do? "Lord, I've offered my all — my life — to You, but do You want me to die today in a pigsty?"

"Jessy! Open up!"

"You c-can't come in. Yet. I-I'm not done sh-shoveling!"

"Who were you talkin' to?"

"K-kids. Neighbors."

"Who?"

"Luke and Madgie or Midgie. I never saw them before."

"Why'd you run?" When Jessy didn't answer, he rattled against the doors violently, shouting, "Answer me! What were they sayin'?"

As she swiped at her tears, she left a trail of manure across her cheek. "Lord, what should I do?"

One of God's commands and one of His promises calmed Jessy's heart: *Fear not. I am with you always.*

Jessy dropped the shovel, opened the door, and stepped outside, prepared for anything except what she found. Adam wasn't anywhere in sight. Mightily relieved, she prayed, "Lord, You really are merciful! I don't understand Your plan, but I'll keep trusting You all the same!"

🌻 🌻 🌻

Until darkness approached, Jessy cleaned pens while the massive sows suckled their young.

"You babies sure are sweet," she told them. When bigger sucklings crowded out the smallest, Jessy shouted, "Hey! Let him have some milk, too, you, you pigs! Poor runt of the litter, I know how you feel!"

By dusk, Jessy had nearly filled an old wagon with manure but still hadn't finished her work. Cautiously she stepped outside where all was calm. Knowing she couldn't go back to the house, she considered the hayloft as a resting place for the night.

With caution she ran through the yard and into the barn, past the rig Adam used for their weekly ride into Bethel. Jessy was halfway up the ladder to the loft when she wondered what was up there. Could one of Adam's victims be hidden in the hay?

Jessy dangled in mid-stride, wondering whether to continue up or run down and out in search of a new hiding place. There wasn't another hiding place except the cellar. *The cellar.* Jessy felt queasy. What was in all those boxes down there, and Adam's steamer trunks which he always kept locked with the only locks on this entire farm?

Jessy remembered finding those two brass keys of Adam's held together by a red string, and how possessive Adam was of them. How quick he had been to snatch them from her curious hands. She hadn't seen them again, but whenever she had gone down to the cellar to fetch anything, she had asked him what he kept in the trunks. Always he put her off with one-word answers, like "Stuff." Laurann's stuff? The trunks were of different sizes, but Jessy could easily have fit into the smaller one, had she been able to get it open. How big was Laurann? Jessy imagined Laurann, a contortionist, perhaps, or an acrobat, rolling herself into a ball, and being locked — stuffed! — in that trunk forever and ever. Adam's stuff!

Jessy imagined the whole drama in lurid detail, knowing that with his temper, Adam could do such a terrible thing. She swallowed but her throat was parched. Darkness was closing in faster than she could think.

Again came God's command, "Fear not."

Jessy finished her climb. She meandered through prickly fodder, covering the full length of the barn. Of one thing she was certain: Adam Flint's hayloft did indeed contain hay. She also found an old straw hat, a broken pitch fork, empty bottles, tangles of baling wire, a ragged neckerchief, rusty pruning shears, and a stray cat with four kittens.

"Oh, aren't you adorable!" Jessy whispered, picking up a kitten and cuddling it next to her neck. It mewed in her ear. "Oh, you are just darling! Let me see you." In the fading light Jessy could barely make out the little face. She held it close again. A rough tongue scraped across her cheek. "Oh, you sweet little thing. How'd you get up here anyway?"

"Jessy!" Adam was shouting for her from the yard.

Jessy let go of the kitten and grabbed the pitchfork. She stood still as a statue, her heart pounding. She heard an uproar in the henhouse. The flock sounded like it had gone mad.

"Jessy, for cripesake, where are you?"

Adam's powerful voice, slurred and drunken, rumbled through the encroaching darkness. Jessy dropped down when she heard the blast of a shotgun. Someone or something let out a terrific wail. The gun went off again. And again. Something scratched and scrambled around wildly in the yard, making panicky sounds that set Jessy's teeth on edge. Was he after her? From Jessy's hiding place, whatever Adam was shooting at sounded like an animal, too hefty to be a rat. Rats! There had to be rats in the loft! What was it that mamma cat lived on if not rats? Sweat trickled down Jessy's arms and legs. She crouched in total darkness now, too afraid to move.

"Dear Lord, please protect me this night." Startled by a crash she added, "And my brother, too. And all life!"

In the silence, Jessy crawled to the one opening in the loft that overlooked the yard. Adam had set a lantern on the ground. She saw him raise his gun and aim. He shot once, and then again. Wooden fencing shattered in all directions. Again he took aim, this time cursing. More wood splintered and glass shattered, too. Jessy hid her face in her hands and looked no more.

ชี ชี ชี

She wakened in pain, with aching joints and sore muscles. Welts throbbed across her back and shoulders, grim reminders of Adam's beating. Knowing her father would have done worse to her for disobeying him, Jessy felt ashamed of her behavior the previous day. Her hands hurt worst of all, so blistered they were from shoveling.

She crawled down from the loft and across the yard where she found a few fire logs knocked loose from the woodpile, an empty whiskey bottle and, lying in the dust, a dead dog with feathers in its snarling mouth, familiar polka dot feathers. Adam's guinea hen!

Jessy approached the dog slowly. She dropped to her knees for a closer look. "How beautiful you were. And Adam killed you. Shot you dead, didn't he, boy?" It was a dog like no other Jessy had ever seen, with generous thick red fur and long streaks of white.

On tiptoe she peeked into Adam's bedroom window. He was lying prone, fully clothed, still wearing his big boots. From the looks of him, she thought he would stay like that for hours.

Jessy chided her growling stomach but couldn't help thinking about Mrs. Gaad's hot biscuits. She thought of the open invitation, the nice folks just down the road, hoping Jessy might come and join their family.

Though tempted to leave Adam's place this minute, something he had said gave Jessy pause: She didn't take time to think things through. Her leaving would be a big move, and perhaps a bigger mistake, for even if the Gaads didn't say a word to anyone, the way news travels, the whole county would know Jessy had left and everyone would think bad of Adam Flint, worse than they already did. Jessy would never be able to face him again. It was bad enough to think he was a murderer. The way he acted, it was no wonder people talked. *But no matter what, I am my brother's keeper. Adam Flint is my only family living on this earth. If I don't love him, who will?*

Jessy glanced up at the sky. How strange it seemed, to be morning but so dark and gloomy. In the distance the brown earth and gray sky were divided along the horizon by a thin red line. Jessy made up her mind to stay, knowing that God had watched over her last night and would continue to do so.

Driven now by thirst and pain rather than fear, Jessy stopped at the pump for a long drink of water, and after a trip to the outhouse, began rummaging in the shed for work gloves to protect her blistered hands. She found shovels, brooms, hoes, rags, hay hooks, saws, rusty tobacco tins, fencing wire, a dusty ball of twine, rakes, even a perfect little bird's nest, but no gloves.

"What're you lookin' for?"

"Adam! You scared me!" Jessy dropped the nest. He smelled strongly of alcohol but appeared to be sober.

Still, to see Adam Flint, even unshaven and uncombed, to behold his stunning good looks at close range never ceased to amaze Jessy, she herself being so plain, so average, so ordinary. Between the two of them, brother and sister, there was no question who had been blessed with great looks. Green eyes illuminated with gold, thick dark curls, the rugged face and physique of Adam Flint were meant to be openly and lovingly admired, but sin, alcohol, and a nasty reputation marred the handsome image.

"I asked you a question."

"I-I'm . . . Good morning."

Adam nodded slowly, looking her up and down. In a sonorous whisper he asked, "What're you doin'?"

"Looking for work gloves. My hands—see? I'm about halfway done with that, ah, chore. Gloves would make it easier for me to finish."

"There ain't none. I never use 'em. Lemme see." Adam grabbed her hands, palms up, surveying all the blisters. "The hands of a reader. A dreamer."

"But they'll toughen up, don't you think? If I work hard like you? More I think about it, the gladder I am you gave me the job of cleaning out the hog house every week! It'll make me strong, like you. Besides, it's an important job, isn't it? You need that manure for the fields and the hogs need a clean place to bed down and tend their piglets. I've been meaning to tell you, those piglets are the cutest little things. I just love them." Jessy struggled to slow her nervous chatter. "About yesterday. I'm sorry I didn't do what you asked when you asked me to. Later, I thought about—everything—and how there hasn't been any rain and how upset you must be. I prayed for you. For rain. I'll do better to help you, I promise. Only I have to ask you something that's hard to say."

"Well?"

Jessy's little rosebud mouth trembled.

"Go ahead. Spit it out."

"Did you ever kill anyone?"

Adam punched his fist into the doorjamb. "Those kids!"

"Is it true?" When he looked away without answering, Jessy neared him. "Adam, you're my brother and I want you to know I'll stand by you no matter what. Even if the whole town and the whole world turn away from you, I never will. The first day we met you asked me to tell you the truth and I did. Now I want to know the truth from you, whatever it is, no matter how bad it may be. I promise I won't turn on you." She reached out and took his arm in her own two small, gentle, blistered hands. "Please tell me the truth."

Adam turned abruptly and looked her straight in the eyes. "I never killed no one. Never even laid eyes on that Meredith woman. She lived in town. There was rumors she drowned or somethin'. Who knows?" Adam shrugged his big shoulders helplessly. "As for Laurann..."

Laurann. The showgirl. "Wh-what about Laurann?"

Adam's eyes were moist. He looked scared, like a little boy. "She—she was beautiful. I might've married her, one day, if she stayed." His voice cracked. "One night we both'd been drinkin'. I don't remember what happened, but I woke up with scratches all over my face and chest and Laurann was gone." Adam gazed out across his fields. "We musta fought like wildcats, but I can't remember why. I looked everywhere for her. Ran ads in the trade and theater journals, but she never answered."

"I don't know what to say."

Adam turned to her full of frustrated rage. "You don't believe me, do ya? No one does! But no one has any proof I done anythin' against the law. And in America, a man's innocent 'til proven guilty."

"Yes, that's right. I learned that in school."

"Well, no one's ever found a shred of evidence to put the blame on me and they never will. One of the neighbors spotted Laurann walkin' toward town that night, but that's the last anyone saw of her."

Jessy braved the question eating away at her. "What's in the trunks?"

"Hmp? Stuff!" Adam looked back to the land again. "I shoulda never stayed on here."

"But you did stay. Why?"

"This is my place. No one and nothin's gonna run me off." He tipped his chin at her. "How come you stayed around here after yesterday?"

"Did you want me to go? I thought about leaving."

Adam wiped his mouth with the back of his hand, then touched her shoulder where he had laid the strap so hard. "You okay?"

She nodded. "I shouldn't have been reading when there was so much work to be done. I'm sorry. I won't act like the Queen of Sheba any more. But you really did scare me last night."

Adam looked blank. "Last night?"

"All that shooting, out in the yard, in the dark. Don't you remember?"

Adam looked genuinely bewildered. "No. I don't."

"You had your shotgun. I saw you. I heard you."

Adam, not knowing where to look, rubbed his palm against the back of his head. "Musta passed out. Happens when I drink too much. What happened?"

"You killed a dog, a red dog."

Adam's eyes filled with light. "That was no dog. It must be that fox that been's prowlin' round here."

"I saw him just now in the yard, right over there. The fox got into the hen house last night and you shot him."

"Yeah. Must be. A fox can do a lot of damage."

So can a drunk with a loaded gun, she thought. To Adam she said, "You had been drinking."

"Yeah. I slept solid like a rock."

"I hardly slept at all."

Thunder, booming directly over their heads, made them jump. Rain pelted them, and the dusty earth. Together they raced to the house. Jessy, shivering, went to the window near the stove where she could look up into the raging storm.

Adam stood close by, shaking himself dry. "'Bout time it rained. I was startin' to think all I'd raise this year was dust."

Jessy hardly heard him, she was so captivated by the storm. "I hurt so much I couldn't stay asleep, so I prayed for us, and for rain." She forced little droplets from her hair onto her hands. "And God answered," she said sweetly, holding out her hand. "For you and your crops."

Adam stood for a moment, speechless. The lightning gave Jessy's face an eerie radiance. He backed away from her.

❧ 5 ❧

The rains came and with them springtime with all its beauty and demands. While Adam plowed the fields, Jessy tended the big vegetable garden he had planted near the house. Adam's food supply was beginning to dwindle — what he had raised and stored in the cellar the previous year, the home-preserved foods Mrs. Gaad and her daughters had canned for him: vegetables, juices, rich broths. The bins filled high with potatoes, onions, cabbages and roots, plenty for the winter, were becoming empty. Now Adam, as well as his neighbors, must plant again.

Jessy delighted in helping him plant seeds in the garden and couldn't hide her enthusiasm about the harvest she knew would come: sweet corn, carrots, cabbage, potatoes, peas, onions, squash, beets, pumpkins, greens, pickling cucumbers, tomatoes, assorted beans, herbs, sunflowers — even popcorn. How excited she was one morning to discover the first young sprouts peeping out of the sun-warmed earth. Small eruptions in neat rows, they were her baby bean plants.

"Little Skinny" Adam had called her, noting her determination not to go hungry. Adam had spoken the truth. Jessy had suffered severe hardship in losing her parents. She looked forward to tending the garden with care.

There would be wild blueberries — and blackberries, too. They grew on bushes that fringed the back of Adam's farm toward the river. Along the drive Adam's fruit trees had already blossomed. Where only recently there were flowers, now there were tiny fruits — apples, cherries, plums, and pears — plenty for jams, jellies, pies, and punch. Come harvest, Mrs. Gaad would teach Jessy how to preserve food for the winter.

Now that Adam was busy planting field crops, every day he expected Jessy to prepare lunch and carry it out to him for a picnic. During this busy time of year Adam didn't like returning to the house at noon. Come summer he would welcome a shady retreat from the relentless sun, but not now. Today she found him turning the soil in his front forty acres, where his land met the road. She set down the basket, unfurled a blanket in the shade of a large elm, and sat down to watch him finish plowing a row.

Adam guided the horse with the same mastery he brought to every physically demanding task. The iron plow turned the earth in neat, straight furrows. He slipped free of the reins around his waist and unhitched the horse, removing the heavy leather harness. Before Adam let the animal feed, he looked over the roan carefully, including each hoof. Jessy could see how much her brother enjoyed working like this, out in the open, looking after the land and the animals. All the while, Adam talked to his horse in reassuring tones, his rich voice rumbling. He gave the animal a few friendly pats before joining Jessy under the shade tree.

Adam wiped the sweat from his hands, face, and throat on the moist towel Jessy had brought. He stretched out for a moment, and groaned in pain. "I'm a little sore today." Adam flexed his hands, arms, and shoulders as he spoke. "And I'm not the only one hurtin'. When you head back to the house, fetch me a jar of that salve in the shed. Looks like Milo's tryin' to raise a blister under his harness."

"Will he be all right?"

"Oh, sure. After the long winter doin' nothin 'cept haulin' logs now and then, he's gotten soft and tender."

"Like children wearing shoes the first day of school after a barefoot summer?"

"Somethin' like that." Adam dug into the basket. Besides enough water sweetened with honey to last him the afternoon, Jessy had packed cider and a large loaf of bread warm from the oven, beans baked with ham and molasses, sweet pickles, and potatoes roasted with onions and sprinkled with cheese.

"My version of the plowman's lunch. I read about it in a library book. Not that you approve of books."

"Cookbooks is okay."

Jessy noted with satisfaction how heartily he ate her cooking. She nibbled her own lunch as she looked about. "Look at all the robins! I've never seen so many in one place before. What do you suppose they're doing?"

"Catchin' worms." Adam popped a big chunk of bread into his mouth. "They think farmers turn the soil just for them."

They sat together quietly, enjoying the gentle breeze playing over the land. A few bees murmured above their heads. Jessy felt a little sleepy listening to their hypnotic song.

Once Adam had finished his lunch he stretched out on his back. With his head resting on his folded arms he gazed up through the tree branches into the cloudless sky. "Rain tonight."

"How can you tell?"

"I can taste it. I can feel it. I can even hear it."

Jessy peered up through the tree where Adam was looking. Strain as she might, she couldn't taste, feel, or hear anything like the next rainstorm. "But how can you tell?"

Adam had dozed off. The demands of this season had taken their toll on him. Jessy looked at his long frame, a mountainous range of rugged blue denim, complete with cliffs, gaps, ravines, and palisades. He seemed an outcropping of the earth, as much a part of this place as the tree under which they rested. No wonder the talk of the town hadn't been able to budge him from his land.

Far off she noticed a small cloud rising up in the road. "Someone's coming, Adam. On horseback. Straight this way. It's a man dressed in black!"

Adam struggled up to see. "Minister," he said and sank back down again.

Jessy stood up to shake her skirt free of crumbs. "He'll be here any second, Adam."

"They're like crows! Big, black birds pokin' their beaks 'round here. Christ!"

Jessy winced. "He's calling you, too, Adam."

"Who is?"

"Jesus, our Lord. He's calling you, too."

Adam gave her a murderous look before covering his face with his hat.

She smiled sweetly at the preacher. "Hello!"

"Good afternoon! I'm Reverend Edwards. You must be Jessy Flint. I'm sorry not to have come by sooner to greet you, but I cover the whole tri-county region. We've had more than the usual number of funerals, weddings, and baptisms. But welcome to Bethel Township! We're glad you're here!"

Jessy blushed shyly. "Thank you. I'm sorry I haven't attended services, but —"

"I'm not sorry!" came Adam's voice from under his hat. "Her mean old brother won't stand for such nonsense."

Jessy blushed. "My brother isn't as mean as he pretends."

"Don't bet I ain't."

"Hello, Mr. Flint." The minister reached out his hand to shake Adam's but Adam remained supine, his face still covered by his hat. The minister withdrew his hand, but said pleasantly, "Just came by to let you know that we'd be delighted if Jessy worshipped with us. And, as I've said before, Mr. Flint, the church is always open to you, too."

Adam murmured something vulgar.

Apologizing, Jessy asked, "'Why doth the heathen rage?'"

Adam muttered, "There's times I'd like to throw her to the lions."

"No one can say my brother is lukewarm."

Adam tore off his hat. "And just what's that supposed to mean?"

The minister explained. "The Lord would prefer us to be cold or hot rather than indifferent."

Adam stood up and brushed himself off. "If Jessy 'n you'n the Gaads wanna believe in nonsense, go ahead, but leave me be."

The minister pulled a Bible from his saddlebag. "This isn't nonsense."

"Get off my property."

The minister retorted with the speed and fury of a Gatling gun, the pitch and volume of his words spewing and sputtering like boiling lava. "Now, see here, Adam Flint, you'd better listen to me if you know what's good for you and especially for your eternal soul, which I might say is in the most dreaded state of perdition! You are headed *straight* for the bottomless pit, and *fire* will rain down from God out of heaven and devour them that have displeased Him, and they will be thrown into the lake of fire and brimstone where the beast and the false prophet are and shall be tormented day and night for ever and ever. And whosoever is not found written in the Book of Life will be cast into the lake of fire. Remember, my fallen friend, that the wages of sin is death. Even now you are dead in your trespasses, yea, *dead* though you appear alive."

While the minister paused to wipe the corners of his mouth and mop his forehead, Jessy stood in rapt attention, glad there was more to come.

"But, sir, there *is* a remedy made possible by the death and resurrection of our personal saviour, the Lord Jesus Christ. Hear me, Adam Flint, hear the Word of the Lord, for even though your sins are like scarlet and though your particular sins have been many and varied and horrible, nevertheless, Jesus Christ guarantees your redemption if you will but turn from your wickedness, repent of your sins, and accept Him as your personal saviour. The choice is yours, whether to continue on the road to fiery hell, or be washed clean as new-fallen snow by the sacred Blood of the Lamb. This is the day of salvation. What is your answer?"

For Jessy nothing was as important as this challenge to her brother. Certain the very angels awaited his answer, she waited breathlessly to hear what Adam would say.

Adam, who had been chewing on a piece of straw the whole time, took it out of his mouth and said very softly, "Jessy, go get that horse salve."

"Now? Can't that wait?"

"You heard me. Go on. Do as you're told."

In shame, Jessy stared at the ground. She rubbed her work-worn hands against her faded skirt.

Adam threw the piece of straw at her in a fury. "You move when I tell you!"

Shaking with foreboding, she went on her way. Just for a moment, her soft brown eyes mourned in silence to the minister.

Jessy searched the shed for the salve behind odd contraptions and parts of contraptions on the shelves, the uses for which she hadn't the slightest idea—cast iron gadgets with small wheels, greasy gears, pulleys, handles, and cranks. The place was so dusty she had a sneezing fit. Just then, the minister, red faced, tore by on his horse.

Jessy raced back to find Adam resting comfortably under the tree. "What did you say to the minister?"

"Among other things, I told him where to go."

"Wherever it was, he sure seemed in a hurry to get there."

Adam roared with laughter. "Like a bat!"

Jessy's brow furrowed in consternation. "You said something bad to him, didn't you? I can tell by the way you're laughing. Sometimes you're, you're horrid!"

"Keep talkin' that way and you won't be able to talk at all." Adam propped himself up on one elbow. "Faith is for weaklins. By the time I was your age I was doin' a man's work and leadin' a man's life, in all its particulars."

"Sin is nothing to brag about. If you truly want to be forgiven, no matter what you've done, all your sins could be wiped clean, if you repent, if you step out in faith and trust God, rather than rely on your own —"

"When I want a sermon I'll ask for it."

"You need one!"

"Want another go-round with that strap?"

"No, sir, never again."

"What you got last time was nothin', believe me."

"I believe you."

"Glad we understand one another. Get that salve?"

"Is this it?"

"Yeah. Come over here 'n lemme teach you somethin'. "

Jessy followed him dutifully and watched him rub salve over Milo's tender flank, meanwhile being taught the anatomy and care of a plow horse.

"See?"

"Yes, sir."

"Good. What's for supper?"

"Supper? I hadn't thought that far ahead . . . ham?"

"I'm tired of pork. Tonight we'll have chicken."

Jessy trembled. The hams had been salted and cured last winter, but the chickens still strutted the yard hunting for cracked corn.

"You kill one like I showed you."

"Me?" The last time they had dined on chicken, Adam had forced her to watch as he had wrung the poor thing's neck and drained its blood. She had helped pluck feathers and gut the carcass. Adam had stressed how acceptable and proper an end it was for any farm animal raised for food.

In the rare beauty of this springtime afternoon Jessy couldn't imagine herself doing the deed. Except for the adorable, newly hatched chicks that Adam allowed to remain unmolested for a time, Jessy wasn't exactly fond of chickens. In her egg gathering they had made her life miserable with their painful pecking, but fashioning one into tonight's supper was another matter entirely.

"Don't look at me like that." Adam glanced over at her as he adjusted Milo's harness. "Has to be done. Otherwise we'd be overrun with the fool things. I told you not to get sentimental over them chicks. They've led a soft life, softer 'n me, that's for sure. I don't fatten 'em for the fun of it."

"Yes, sir," Jessy said forlornly, gathering up the picnic basket and blanket.

"You better get used to the idea. Before you know it, them piglets you think are so cute'll be hogs ready for slaughter, even that runt you've taken such a fancy to. Just do as I say and stop lookin' at me like that!"

Jessy watched him go off, talking to Milo in his soothing sort of way and turning another perfect furrow. On Adam's farm she had begun to witness the continual cycle of life and death. As a child of the city she could remain blind to the obvious but not here—eating meat required butchering. She was acting the hypocrite and she knew it, for despite the grizzly preliminaries, she had relished the chicken dinner Adam had cooked for her—fresh, tender morsels topped with the best dumplings she had ever tasted, better, even, than Mother's. With a deep sigh Jessy approached the barnyard. She passed the brood hens with unseeing eyes and deaf ears. Postponing the inevitable, she went into the house and set about her afternoon's work.

As she did, she thought about the minister, how hard he came down on her brother, without winning him for the Lord. *Adam's heart is dry and barren, just like this land before the rains.* She knew it would take a miracle to open his eyes.

Jessy swept around his chair near the fire. Every night, long after she had gone to sleep, he whittled. Each morning she would find shavings and sawdust on the floor. For all his skill and speed as a carpenter, Adam worked slowly at whittling. He paused after every little motion, studying the wood in his hands, looking at it from all directions. She wondered what he had been making of the block he had started on the night she first arrived. It still appeared solid except for a distinct taper at one end.

Her mother used to say there are two kinds of people in the world, the quick and the dead. The quick are in the Lord, she would tell Jessy, with spirits alive to God. The dead were—well, like Adam. Just as the minister had said, "Though he appears alive he is dead in his sins." He was dead like the block of wood, and not good for anything but burning. Jessy swept up and tossed the shavings into the fireplace. She stared into the flames, mesmerized.

"Fire, you are a terrible and wonderful thing," she said. "At the end of the world the angels will come forth and separate the wicked from the just, casting them that offend into the furnace of fire. Will my brother be cast into the fire? Will he die just as he has lived, in his fallen state?" The fire burned so brightly it hurt Jessy's tender face.

"Dear God, You wouldn't throw my brother into the fire, would You?"

But what would it take to unlock Adam's heart? Jessy remembered the two brass keys tied with string she had found, the ones Adam had taken from her and hidden. As she swept the floor she wondered about his battered steamer trunks in the root cellar beneath her feet. Jessy had never seen anything like them. They were covered with colorful stickers from all over the world. Adam's name was painted in elaborate gold script embellished with stars. Around all four sides of each trunk, circus animals paced wildly behind golden bars. Leopards, lions, and tigers bared their fangs. What was Adam hiding?

She heard a sound. Someone was coming up the drive. Not Reverend Edwards again! After the way Adam treated him, Jessy felt she would never be able to worship with the community of Bethel, not ever.

❧ 6 ❧

From the sitting room, Jessy observed the stranger through the screen door. An ancient fellow with watery blue eyes and a beard reaching his waist was standing in the yard peering through the door at her. "Afternoon, little lady. Come see what I've got for you today. Are you alone?"

Jessy's reluctance faded when she spotted Adam coming toward the house. His long strides covered a great deal of territory in short order. Jessy was reassured to know that Adam kept such a keen watch even from a distance, blessed as he was with the vision of a hawk.

"Hi. Adam Flint's the name." Adam reached out to shake hands.

"MacPherson, peddler-at-large. Good to see you."

"Heard you got the typhoid some time back. You over it?"

"Yes, got through it, thanks be to God. Many souls don't."

"I have a couple of things to trade, if you're interested."

"Sure, sure. Let's have a look. You're the carpentry fella."

Adam nodded at the peddler and then, on his way into the house, turned to his sister. "You haven't taken care of that chicken like I told you."

"No, sir, not yet."

Adam glanced toward the washroom, where he kept his razor strap.

His glance was not wasted on Jessy. Knowing it would be either a chicken or her hide, she quickly, quietly assured her brother, "I'll do it, I promise!"

"Good. Why doncha see if MacPherson's got anythin' we can use."

Jessy needed no second invitation to step outside and look at all the merchandise the peddler had hauled from one farm to the next in his horse-drawn wagon—everything from pans to hats. While they browsed, the peddler shared news of several counties, a service everyone along his route greatly appreciated after a long winter in isolation.

"Yep, the typhoid hit Stone Grove and Three Oaks pretty hard again."

"Bethel Township, too," said Adam.

"This time, forty-seven died, including a family of nine, all but the baby, can you beat that? Funerals sure kept the preachers busy. And weddings! Suzanna Webb's to that Senator's son from the State Capitol was to be the wedding of the century. Young fella had everything— money, looks, law practice, career in Washington if he wanted. Planned on Paris for the honeymoon, but two days before the ceremony, she turns the young man down cold. No one knows why. Upset her family, 'specially her father, George, the lawyer."

Adam nodded. "He wouldn't see anyone, clients included, for weeks."

"And the Kimballs aren't happy with their son, Leo, quitting college. Came home because he missed farming. Can you imagine that? Great baseball pitcher. I suppose you know that Amos Winslow passed on. He owned the bait and tackle place over at the lake. The folks that used to live here in your house're in Kentucky with their son and his wife and three children but the Missus is ailing. Her eyes went, you know. And, oh, Sam Ackworth's back from working his way through Texas to Mexico. New school's going up—"

Adam and Jessy listened while looking at pocket watches, brooms, strainers, and cuff links. With her encouragement, Adam selected a small but attractive set of silverplated spoons, forks, and knives. He showed her a record book. "You can keep accounts for me. How much seed we plant. How many bushels we harvest. The birth and sale of animals. Prices we pay for goods and services. The weather. Everything."

"I'd like that," agreed Jessy, "but we'll need pens, ink, and blotters. And I do need some sewing supplies... What an adorable bonnet!" It contrasted dramatically with Jessy's work-worn clothing. She didn't dare touch it, for it looked expensive. To her surprise, Adam told her to try it on.

"Looks good on you. What else you got, Peddler-at-Large?"

"These books are two for a nickel."

"Oh, Adam, may I?"

"I s'pose."

While Jessy selected several books, the men negotiated terms. Adam traded two wall racks he had made during the winter. They were handsome things of maple with tiny milkglass knobs and doors on miniature hinges. "Mighty fine, Mr. Flint. You are a craftsman indeed."

"Cash only for this."

"Oooh, that's a beauty. One of the finest decoys I've seen."

"Adam, did you make this? It's wonderful!" Jessy admired the lifelike duck carved in wood and delicately painted. "Are you making another one out of that block you whittle on every night?"

"Yeah. I like ducks. That's a male blue-winged teal. Circus friend taught me how to carve 'em between shows."

"Before I go, a special bonus for the young Miss. Hand painted in Japan." With a flourish, the peddler flicked open a fan so Jessy could see both sides. "Blossoms and a stylized river. And on the reverse, a Bird of Paradise." He fanned his beard with a flourish.

Jessy pored over all of its detail before taking it from him, still open, with the greatest care she could manage. The fan filled her hands with color. She turned up to Adam with an angelic expression, wisps of hair framing her face like a fragile halo. "Isn't it lovely, Adam?"

Adam couldn't hide a most bemused expression. He rubbed his chin with one big hand.

Jessy ran her forefinger lightly over the edge of one delicate pleat. "Isn't it wonderful? Look."

Adam wiped his palms on his trousers before taking it from her. In his big hands the fan resembled an exotic butterfly.

"Just think," said Jessy, "this came from halfway round the world."

"Some time I'll tell you what I remember of the Orient."

"That's right, you went there. I saw a sticker on one of your trunks."

"Fan that fine'd cost you fifty cents in the mail order catalogs. Well, folks, been my pleasure. I'll be on my way." The peddler climbed aboard his wagon and flicked the reins of his horses.

"Thank you, Mr. MacPherson, especially for the fan. It's lovely!"

The peddler smiled at Jessy. "Fair child, you have an eye for beauty. May your life be filled with it and nothing but! Good day, now."

Adam walked off, but not toward his fields. Meanwhile, Jessy put away their new possessions, then took up that unfinished block of wood Adam had been working on, knowing that someday it would be a beautiful bird. "And Dear Lord, now I think I see what You might be doing. This wood is like Adam, in a way. He's being fashioned in Your hands, and I'm one of the tools You're using to mold him into what you want him to be. How glorious!"

Screeching distracted her — a disturbance in the hen house that could only mean one thing. Jessy ran outside. Adam met her in the yard. He handed her a dead chicken. "You do the rest, like I showed you."

Jessy nodded, taking the poor feathered creature from him. Still warm! But she had been spared the dreadful deed. She probably wouldn't be so fortunate the next time Adam wanted chicken for dinner but for now Adam had taken pity on her, maybe because of what the peddler had said. "Thank you, Adam. I'm grateful to you."

"And one other thing. You look pretty ragged to me. You'll need some decent clothes to go with that new bonnet. You can pick out what you need from that catalog we got in the mail the other day."

"Really? Thank you, Adam!"

"Oh, and I'll be needin' more manure. Once you get them pens cleaned up, I'll show you how to spread it."

"All right."

"When you see the harvest you'll thank your brother. You'll come to love manure."

Jessy couldn't hide her smile. God was with them, she could feel His presence here in this place, at this time. "Yes, Adam."

"What's so funny? Quit lookin' at me like that! Sometimes I think you're crazy as Ma."

"Yes, Adam."

❦   ❦   ❦

In a half hour Adam was back in the yard again, shouting for her. All around, trees were shaking in the wind. Adam was straining to hold Milo by his bridle. The nervous horse kept rising on his hind legs.

"What's the matter?"

"Look at the sky to the southwest." Adam pointed at the horizon.

"What could it mean, a green sky? And in the middle of the day."

"Didn't I tell you it would rain?"

"Yes, you did."

"This looks bad — could be a tornado. Hail stones. Ruined crops. Death and destruction for people and livestock. Then again, maybe nothin'. But whenever you see a sky like this, run for cover. No, not in the house."

"Where then?"

"To the cellar. Go on. Run!"

"But what about you?"

The wind was picking up so much speed Adam had to shout to be heard. "Gotta get Milo under cover. You go on now. Hurry."

The moment Jessy stepped outside she could see how wrong everything looked. A sickness had come over the land. The sky in the far distance appeared to be churning. How fast everything was changing. The beautiful blue sky of noon was now strange, eerie, greenish-gray, phosphorescent. Jessy reached the double doors just as the rains came mingled with ice pellets. They bounced against everything in their path with a terrible racket. Jessy hurried down into the cellar.

She skirted by Adam's gaudy steamer trunks painted with circus animals. Before she could once again consider what they might contain, thunder shook the earth all around her. Jessy strained on tiptoe to see through tiny windows at ground level. Hail stones pelted the new grass. Adam came along just as another crack of thunder shook her. The force broke a tree in two. The crash was tremendous.

"Adam!!" Jessy wailed in the near darkness. She shivered in the damp. What if . . .? Adam living—and dying—without God. . . The consequences terrified her far more than the storm. The storm raged on but Adam didn't join her in the cellar.

At last in he came, drenched to the skin, half covered in mud and gasping for breath. Rainwater dripped from each curl. Adam rubbed mud off his mouth with the back of his hand.

"Are you all right?"

Adam's lips curled into a derisive grin. "Aw, don't tell me you're concerned."

"Of course I am. What happened?"

"I got knocked down when that tree fell."

"Your arm's bleeding," Jessy said softly. "Here, let me." She daubed his elbow with her handkerchief. "This cut's full of dirt! We'd better get it cleaned up as soon as we can."

Adam wouldn't stand still. He left little puddles as he paced. "I'll be okay, but the garden won't. Hail's murder on crops. If this weather keeps up, it'll wipe out everythin'."

"We'll have to start all over again?"

"Maybe. It's happened before."

"But all that work . . ."

"That's life on a farm. A gamble. No guarantees."

Suddenly the sun broke through the little windows. The storm had passed as quickly as it had come. Already the sun was melting the hail but the new grass and young garden crops that had emerged only days before had been battered down. Jessy's heart sank. All the young crops gone in an instant. Life was so fragile, and the world so dangerous.

Jessy followed Adam toward the hoghouse. Their path was blocked by the ruined oak. "Perfectly healthy tree pulled up by the roots in one stroke. Ruined! Useless now for anythin' but firewood. Take days to cut this monster up and get it out of the way. Look at that."

Jessy was looking, wide-eyed and terrified, at the size of the tree that had been struck down in a flash. Upright, it had not appeared nearly so big as it did now. Trunk and branches barred the way from the hoghouse to the cottage, just where Adam had been running a few moments before.

She looked up at her brother's powerful, vibrant form, so like that tree, thinking, he had nearly been cut down in his prime. All life, even one as vibrant as her brother's, is fragile, precious. "You could have been killed."

"But I wasn't."

"But if you had . . . "

Adam pursed his mocking lips, "Aw, gee, you're worried about me."

Jessy answered earnestly. "You might have been killed."

"Just luck I wasn't. I take it you don't believe in luck."

"I believe that God has spared you for a purpose."

"To spend three days cuttin' this tree into firewood?"

"Adam, be serious."

"You're too serious. For a kid, you think too much. Oh, now don't pout. Your face'll get stuck that way." Adam poked at her upper arm. "How's that muscle comin'? You can give me a hand with the two-man saw. That'd sure be a help." Adam moved away, down the drive, looking for other damage. "Fruit'll be okay." The little trees had stood up well in the passing storm. "Course, the weeds look healthy as ever. Ain't that always the way. What are you all moon-eyed over?"

Jessy girded herself up. "Do you ever think about dying and meeting your Maker?"

"No, I don't. Got more important things to worry about, like reseedin' that garden 'n gettin' that tree outa the way 'n tryin' to get the plowin' done after the whole field's been turned into a mudslide..."

Believing that if he didn't wake up to the truth, his own fate would be like firewood, she called out: "Adam?"

"What?! I got work to do."

Jessy began to whimper.

"Cryin' about me, too? Well, whadya know about that?" Adam grinned so broadly his dimples appeared. "Anyone'd hear you, they'd think you was the one nearly got killed instead of me."

Jessy sniffled.

"Well, I'll be! You really are worried about me. No one's ever worried about me. Scared I'll leave ya all alone? No such luck."

"I'm worried you'll die in your sins, without coming to know the Lord."

Adam gave a short laugh. "If there is a God, then it's His business to know me, not the other way 'round. Lemme show you somethin'. Over here. Look at the weather vane. Come on. Snap outa that cryin' jag and listen to me."

So practical, Adam was, so down to earth. Jessy looked up at the sky where he was pointing, only half-listening to him explain about tornados. Yes, the weather vane pointing, in that direction over there, southwest, he said. The sky is so big and we're so small, she thought, more concerned with the vastness of God's universe and the urgency of the Gospel than Adam's rusty old weather vane. For now the sky appeared benevolent, the wind calm. But how quickly things could change.

❦ 7 ❦

"Adam Flint's a man makes a father thankful he don't have daughters."

Jessy overheard them enjoying a noisy game of checkers on the other side of the counter, behind the high pile of dry goods at the general store. How dare the men of Bethel talk about her brother like this. Did they know she was there? Did they care? Now they were laughing. The longer she listened, the angrier she got.

"Regular hell-raiser, that Flint!"

"Coulda charmed the serpent outa Eden."

"Or the horns off the devil!"

"He got ways to make the women risk all, and lose. Your move, Ben."

"Remember the day Flint first showed up at the train station, dressed to kill, with a pair of the fanciest ladies ever seen around here?"

"Set this town on its ear, he did."

"You shoulda seen them girls, all satin and rouge and feathers! What a sight the three of them made."

"Once he set up house, the girls came and went in a steady stream. Terrific, all of 'em. King me! Redheads, blondes, brunettes. Showgirls."

"With plenty to show!"

Every trip to town was the same. Adam and Jessy would ride in each week and suffer gossip in the shops, on the streets, at the pharmacy. Even while he waited for her to check out library books, there were always a few people whose eyebrows would raise in her direction as she browsed through the shelves.

Adam would go about his business as he always did, posture perfect, a head taller than everyone else. Old gossip was mingled with new. No issue was ever dead and buried, including the fate of Lucy Meredith and her house, standing idle, a constant reminder of her inexplicable disappearance. Now the checker game continued along this track.

70

"Real shame Lucy's place is going downhill. Used to be the prettiest place in the county. That lawyer fella, George Webb, says the estate'll be tied up in probate for years if he can't find an heir. Shame."

"Wouldn't want it myself. The place is cursed!"

"Double jump!"

"Triple! I win!"

"Which you want this round, red or black?"

"Red. I always play the red."

Now as the men babbled all at once, Jessy checked her shopping list. The first item was napkins. She found some that were suitable and inexpensive, and also dishcloths to replace Adam's which were worn through. Jessy frowned at her list. The next item, tea, was shelved on the other side of the counter.

The gossip being bandied over the checkerboard stopped abruptly as Jessy Flint rounded the corner. She looked at the men's faces, one by one, more in sadness than in anger. Not a hand moved a playing piece while she stood there. She wondered why grown men would chatter like geese. Were they trying to warn her about her evil brother?

"Ready to go?" Adam had come up behind her quietly, nodding hello to the men who were slow to resume their game of checkers. "What's goin' on?"

"Oh, nothing." Jessy smiled brightly at Adam despite her sorrow.

Slowly a new game began, and a new conversation that did not focus on Adam Flint.

Adam pulled her aside and spoke softly. "Banker says those old checks of mine are bein' paid up slow but sure. Not all but most. Got back nearly two hundred dollars this mornin'."

"Does that mean we can afford napkins? These are the best buy, I think."

"Sure."

"I'll hurry."

"No need to. I still gotta get supplies. Meet me up front when you're done."

Adam walked down the aisle toward the front of the store past two young women shopping for country chintz. Jessy noticed both of them turn in his direction, eyelashes fluttering, watching his every move until he was no longer in view. Both raised up on tiptoe and strained their heads after him. That too was always the way. No one, man or woman, felt neutral about Adam Flint.

Jessy finished shopping in a rush, glad to go outside to help Adam load their rig with bundles — flour, sugar, salt licks for the livestock, a new harness for Milo, lamp oil, matches. Among the people watching them, Jessy noticed a few elbowing each other. She busied herself with the work at hand.

Someone ran toward them, a beefy young man with his hat in his hand. "Adam Flint? Are you Adam Flint?"

"Yeah?"

"I'm Jim Frazier." He shook Adam's hand. "Folks 'round here tell me you're the one to beat."

Adam smiled. "At what?"

"Arm wrestling. They say you're the best. I'm passing through town and thought maybe we could have a go at it, you and me, in there." The fellow indicated the store the Flints had just left.

Adam sized up the man. "No, thanks, I'm . . . "

"Afraid?"

Adam smiled coolly. "Yeah. Afraid I'll hurt you."

Frazier flashed green in the air. "Thirty dollars to the winner."

Adam called out, "Jessy, watch our stuff. I'll be right back."

As if on cue, men came running from all directions, headed after the opponents and into the store. The sidewalk flooded with spectators. Jessy squeezed through the crowd to the store windows but flower boxes and gingham curtains blocked her view. She wriggled to the crack between the double doors, hoping to get a glimpse of her brother and Jim Frazier locking arms in combat, but all she could see was the back of a man's jacket. The noise inside was horrendous, with much scraping of chairs and coarse shouting.

"What's going on in there?"

Jessy turned to a strapping fellow. "My brother —" Jessy peered through a crack. "Someone challenged Adam to a fight."

"Adam Flint?" The newcomer pressed close to her. His cheek lightly grazed her own. "Wish I had some money on this one."

A shout went up from the crowd, then a roar of laughing conversation.

In a few moments, excited spectators burst through the doors, pushing Jessy and the newcomer aside. Adam soon appeared, pocketing his winnings. Men poured out after him, surrounding him, clapping him on the back. "Your fastest time ever! Beautiful!"

Someone shouted, "Get the Doc! Frazier's arm's hurtin' real bad."

While some people went back inside to gape at the unfortunate loser, Jessy continued standing with the newcomer. Adam approached the two of them, hollering, "So this how you behave the minute my back is turned!" He grabbed Jessy away and gave her a resounding slap in the face.

The crowd was stunned.

From the painful stinging, Jessy was sure her cheek would be red for days. With her hand over her face she whispered, "Everyone's looking."

"Let 'em! What's the idea, anyway?" Adam yelled. "Didn't I tell you to watch our stuff? What were you doin' with him?"

"Nothing. We were just being friendly," Jessy answered quietly.

"That's your problem, Jessy. You're too friendly." Adam eyed the young man with extreme displeasure.

Jessy moaned, "But we were just talking."

Adam spit mightily. "Talkin', my foot. I catch you with a guy again — any guy — I'll fix both of you. You're too young to be talkin' with boys, understand? You're not gonna end up like ... "

At that moment a woman in the crowd caught Adam's attention. He returned her warm, admiring gaze. From a distance their lips caressed.

The young man took advantage of the interlude. "See here, Adam Flint, you're nothing but a bully, hitting a young lady."

Adam lifted the fellow up by his shirt. "You're right. I should've started with you, Tom Lester." With a heave Adam tossed the fellow into the street. He would have done worse if Jessy hadn't interfered.

With both hands and all her force Jessy could hardly manage to hold on to her brother. "Let's go home before you get arrested."

He shoved her away and stormed into the street where Tom Lester lay in a daze. Adam kneeled over him and lifted him partly by the lapels. "Stay away from my sister." Then he dropped the fellow back into the dirt. Adam stood up, wiping his palms against each another. "Find my hat," he ordered Jessy. "I'm goin' for a beer."

Jessy looked around for his best felt hat. She dusted it off before handing it to him. "Here it is."

With practiced hands, Adam set his hat at a rakish angle that best suited his curls and commanding profile.

"And what am I supposed to do while you drink beer?"

"What I tell you to. Watch our stuff." He lifted her up easily onto the carriage seat. "Stay right here and don't move. Hear me?"

"The whole town can hear you."

Some onlookers laughed. Adam's face darkened with hot blood and cold defiance. He scanned the crowd from one side to the other and front to back, as if daring to take on the whole lot of them. When no one budged, Adam turned to his sister. In a voice meant only for her he said, "This is one time you better start prayin'. I'll be back in five minutes."

Jessy bowed her head, hoping her red face couldn't be seen. She studied her hands, red and raw from ceaseless work. She could feel the presence of the crowd around her. The Flints had provided yet more grist for the gossip mill. The onlookers spoke openly, as if Jessy were deaf.

"Well, now, that's a switch, Adam Flint concerned over a girl's honor."

"Boot's on the other foot. It's okay for him to take up after half the women in the territory, but if someone so much as talks to his sister —"

"You see him sizing up Melinda?"

"Yeah. She was doin' some sizin' up herself. Did you see her?"

Jessy twisted her handkerchief into tortured shapes. Eventually people moved on, except for one young woman dressed in delicate pink and half hidden under a pale yellow parasol.

"Jessy? Jessy Flint?"

With great reluctance Jessy looked down to see a dazzling beauty with silky golden curls and blue eyes.

"Is he always like that? Your brother, I mean?"

"Writing a book on the subject?" Jessy asked. Some of Adam's sarcasm was beginning to rub off on her.

The girl laughed nervously, exposing her pretty teeth. "Oh, please excuse my forwardness. We haven't even been introduced." She extended one dainty white-gloved hand to Jessy. "I'm Suzanna Webb. I live here in town. Your brother is quite, ah, well, we've never seen anyone like him. They say he might have murdered someone! Maybe two!"

"It isn't true," Jessy said, despite her suspicions. "There's no proof he did any such thing."

"Forgive me. I'm going about this wrong. What I meant was, he has quite a reputation and I for one would like to know the facts. The truth."

"Why?"

"Because . . . I shouldn't have troubled you. I'm sorry."

"If you must know, I hate the way people talk behind my brother's back. It's cruel. No matter what they say he's amazing. And you can tell all the gossips in this township I said so." A familiar form advancing toward them caught Jessy's eye. "Uh-oh. Here he comes."

Jessy watched Adam approach, the unmistakable build, the astonishing good looks, the smooth powerful stride. In a moment he had covered two city blocks and had crossed the street. Soon he was sitting beside Jessy with his capable hands on the reins. Jessy turned to the girl with the parasol but she had left.

They hadn't gone a block when Adam blurted out, "Did Tom Lester touch you?"

"He was trying to see the fight so he put his cheek next to mine."

Adam brought the horse to a halt. He squeezed the reins, his jaw bunching angrily. "Why, that no-account . . . Jessy, you're at a dangerous age, and pure. Believe me, this world is full of wolves all prowlin' around for somethin' good to attack and devour."

"Like that red fox after your hens?"

"Exactly. Purity is a fleetin' thing. Once it's gone, and it can go in a moment, it's gone forever and you can never get it back."

Jessy nodded quietly, but her mind was racing. Wasn't Adam a fine one to talk about virtue and purity? As they rode on, she said, "But that Mr. Lester just bumped into me. I can't believe he meant any harm."

"I shoulda broke his neck. Next time I see him, I will."

"The way you carry on, no wonder people talk."

"I was defendin' you."

Nursing her injured cheek, she said, "You hurt me."

"All right, so I'm quick tempered. High-spirited, too. Them crimes?"

"You could get into awful trouble by —"

Her words were drowned out by the roar of an approaching train. The air was filled with bells and clangs and whistles and the shouts of men conducting business along the railroad line running parallel to the road.

Adam and Jessy were at the outskirts of Bethel near the cemetery, the place where the bustle of the town dissolved into the solace of the countryside. Jessy had calmed down enough to enjoy the beauty of this day, the bounteous fields opening into splendid vistas on either side of the road. Meadowlarks flitted on fences. A cool breeze soothed her burning cheek.

The horse stopped when a cat scrambled across the road in front of their carriage. Adam turned to look in the direction it had taken. Jessy followed his gaze to a desolate two-story house of faded elegance amid overgrown hedges beneath ancient trees. Nature crowded in from all sides. Coal soot blasting from a thousand passing trains had settled over the house like a shroud. Although Jessy had passed this way before, she had never asked what this house once was, not until now. "What is it, Adam? How strange it seems."

"That's Lucy Meredith's place."

Jessy felt a chill. Indeed the place did seem cursed, as those townsmen seemed to think. She drank in the sight, the faded porch with its empty wicker chairs, a dozen planters but not one flower, the tatters of an American flag waving to a parade long past. Adam flicked the reins but Jessy turned, staring. "Look, Adam! A light's on inside."

"Where?"

Jessy pointed. As soon as she did the light was gone.

Adam pressed the horse forward. "Ain't been a light on in Lucy Meredith's house in a long, long time."

"But I saw it."

"Musta been the sun shinin' off a window."

"You must be right." Feeling foolish, she sank down in her seat. A long while passed before she told him about the girl with the parasol.

"Who was she? What'd she want?"

"She said she wanted to know the truth about, ah, you know."

"Idle curiosity. Whole town's got nuthin' better to do than butt into other people's business. She good-lookin'?"

"Adam, really .... As a matter of fact, she was gorgeous."

His green eyes glinted brightly. "Well? Who was she anyway?"

"Suzanna Webb."

His chiseled face warmed with sudden pleasure. "Yeah?"

"I shouldn't have told you."

Adam grew serious. "You tell me everythin'."

"I already have."

"You like that Tom Lester?"

"I don't even know him."

"I do. He better keep his distance. You're a good girl and I want you to stay that way. It's what your mother'd want."

The town was far behind them now. As the horse clopped along, Adam surveyed the countryside with keen interest. "Corn looks good. If the weather holds we'll do all right this year. And today I made some money."

"You won the fight."

"Sure did. Wish they was all that easy."

"You hurt that man."

"He asked for it. I tried to warn him, the idiot. You heard."

Jessy nodded silently, wondering why there was so much human misery in the world. At her father's burial, when she asked her mother that question, came the reply, "Because man is bent on his own will instead of God's."

Jessy reached down for a book at her side. "Want me to read to you?"

"Not from the Bible."

"How can you be so prejudiced about something you've never read? It's the best book in the whole world!"

"Watch yourself."

With a sigh she put down the Bible and picked up the library book she had checked out that morning. "This is a history of the American Civil War."

"Now you're talkin.' Lots of fightin'. Best ever. It's my favorite war," he said with a devilish grin. "I been to some of the battlefields."

"Really? Tell me about it."

And so Adam did, the rest of the way home.

Listening to his stories, Jessy realized she did indeed learn much from reading, but Adam, for better or worse, learned from living.

❧ 8 ❧

Jessy was in the kitchen one afternoon in late June when she heard a knock at the front door. She finished squeezing a lemon before seeing who was there. She faced a pair of wiggling feet in wildly striped stockings. Jessy giggled in surprise.

The body quickly turned upright, light as air in the turn. "Excuse me, Miss! Little joke of mine. I thought Adam Flint would answer the door. He still lives here, doesn't he? Mailbox sign says so."

"Yes, of course he does." Jessy smiled at the man, a robust redhead who seemed to grin with his entire body. "You must be one of his circus friends! I'm his sister Jessy, his *real* sister."

"What a nice surprise! And how do you do? I'm Beau Bally, but you can call me Bo."

"Oh, yes, of course! You're a performer, like my brother!"

"Well, I'm not the star he is. I'm too much the clown."

"Thank you for the lemons! They arrived this morning. Adam loves them! I just finished making lemonade. Why don't you have a seat out here on the porch while I get it. There's a nice breeze today. Adam should be here soon. He's greasing the pulleys up to the hayloft."

As Jessy turned back to the kitchen she noticed Bo's valise, sleeping bag, and banjo case on the steps. "Did you come by train?"

"That's right. Rode in from Chicago. Had the lemons shipped up here to you from Florida. I live down there when I'm not on the road."

Soon Jessy was back with a pitcher of icy fresh lemonade and a large plate of buttery shortbread sprinkled generously with confectioner's sugar.

"Why, thank you. Just the thing for a summer day." Bo covered his knee with a napkin and dug in. "You make these? They're good! So you're Adam's *real* sister. He's had plenty of them other kind. Girls were always wild about him, lucky devil."

Jessy smiled shyly. "Do you travel all over the country?"

"Yes, but I spend most winters down South. If I ever gave up the circuit I'd have to settle down somewhere and I suppose it would be Florida, but I don't know if I could sit still in one place for very long. Course, all this travel gets tiresome." Bo sipped his lemonade while scanning the grounds from the porch. "This place hasn't changed much since last time I was here. Looks like it's time to cut hay."

"Yes, how did you know?"

"I grew up on a farm. My father's got a big spread in Iowa. My whole family's in the farming business, everyone except Old Bo. How's Adam? Has he been working hard?"

"Yes, always. My brother has energy enough for four people. How long have you known him?"

"Since we were boys, both of us looking for work. I stop by here whenever the circus is within shouting distance. Just finished a string of one-night stands in the Midwest and a three-nighter in Chicago. I'll catch up with the crew in Windsor or maybe Montreal. I'm part owner now so I have some privileges."

Jessy refilled Bo's empty glass.

"Thank you. You perform? Don't think I've caught your act."

"Me? Mother never approved of even one performer in this family."

"Adam isn't teaching you an act?" Bo looked genuinely concerned.

"Oh, he's always wanting me to become stronger. He thinks the human body is everything. I think the spirit is what's most important."

"My daddy always said, 'Fear of the Lord is the beginning of wisdom.'"

"How I wish Adam would see that truth! We go round and round and never come to any sort of agreement."

"Adam Flint's a hard man." Bo might have said more but he couldn't stay serious for long. He smiled at her. "You'd make a good clown. The sad-but-funny kind."

"I've never even seen a circus, but I've read about them." Jessy spooned a chip of ice from her glass into her mouth. "Adam makes me lift a lot, to build up my arms and shoulders. I can't lift myself up by my arms, not yet, but I keep trying."

"That's the way, slow but sure. I doubt many people outside the circus or farming can lift their own weight."

"Adam thinks chin-ups are fun but to me they're torture."

Jessy thought of her brother's physical prowess, his abilities to lift and pull and climb. He was built for action, the more strenuous the better. Not satisfied with the exertions of farming, he worked out with a full set of weights. He had even rigged up a chin bar and other gadgets in the barn so that he could scramble up a rope or walk a wire when he felt like practicing. He spent hours working out stunts such as swinging himself end over end while holding onto a rope with one hand. It was this last stunt that revealed something he hadn't liked. Adam's hands had begun to shake.

Jessy noticed how much this troubled him. To steady himself, Adam would have another drink, which only made the shaking worse. She felt powerless to help. As she sipped her lemonade, she wondered if she should confide in her brother's best friend, but decided not to appear disloyal. Instead she said, "I wish I were coordinated like Adam. He says I'm just at that awkward age. Please have some more shortbread. I baked two whole trays full this morning."

"Thanks. Don't mind if I do. You know, I don't feel so bad about Adam being way out here, now that he's got family with him, someone who cares about him and can look out for him. Well, speak of the devil!"

"Bo! When did you bounce in?" Adam looked genuinely pleased. He rubbed his greasy hands on a clean napkin before shaking Bo's hand.

Jessy poured Adam's lemonade while he dropped into a chair on the porch and propped his long legs up on the railing. "You'll be stayin' a while?"

"If you'll have me. And have I got a match for you!"

"Not Mad Mountain Malone again. That guy nearly killed me!"

Bo roared with laughter. "I thought the both of you would land in a hospital. This fight will be something else entirely. Gus 'The Gunboat' Gastonby. Here are some pictures of him."

"Don't believe I've had the pleasure, or displeasure. Looks nasty." Adam studied the pictures while draining two glasses of lemonade. "Never saw him fight."

"I have, and believe me, Adam, if there's a man in this country who could beat him, you're it. You're the toughest competitor I know. You pick the place and the time, he says. Four thousand dollars to the winner. Three-second fall. Have you been training?"

Adam waved his arm over the landscape. "This here's the gym."

"How about if you and me train every morning for the next month. I'll help you farm the rest of the day. Your sister ever see you fight?"

"Yeah, but the match was what you call spontaneous." Thinking back to his feud with Tom Lester, Adam tipped his chair onto its two back legs and rested his feet on the railing, smiling.

"Brawling again? Will you ever learn? People should pay to see you fight. Jessy, if the Man of Iron wrestles The Gunboat you must see it from the best seat in the house, front row center. Have you some money saved?"

"No, sir, I don't have any money."

"Too bad. You could make a tidy sum betting on your brother."

"Gambling?" Jessy went numb.

Adam was thinking out loud. "Four thousand ..."

"Fifteen percent for me, same as always, from the gross receipts."

"And the loser?"

"Five hundred plus expenses."

Jessy hardly heard the rest. Her brother was going to do something dangerous, for money, and folks would gamble on the outcome. Something bad might happen to Adam, and him so far from God.

While she prepared dinner, Bo tuned up his banjo. As the men sat outside, talking the night away, Bo strummed tune after tune, melodies that made Jessy think of happy times in faraway places. Before she fell asleep she prayed for the men, even for the one called Gunboat.

In the days that followed, Jessy would peek into the barn to see Adam and Bo struggling, two athletes locked in combat. Although Bo's physical appearance was not as imposing as Adam's, he was in excellent condition. Those first few days, in fact, Bo clearly had the upper hand. At one point Adam collapsed in the hay, groaning, "I think I died. What have you been doin' since I last saw you, Bo, wrestlin' grizzlies?"

"Nope. Gators! I keep telling you to visit me in Florida some winter." Bo carried on a conversation while walking around on his hands. "I own twenty percent interest in Cowboy Joe's Birdland. It's a gold mine."

Adam caught Jessy's eye. "Seems harmless, don't he? Wrestlin' alligators, for pity's sake."

"It's simple," said Bo, righting himself. "A trick. You hold their jaws shut and keep clear of their tails. A snap compared to wrestling you and grizzlies, and the tourists love it." Now Bo was balancing himself on Adam's prostrate chest, seesawing on a board across the top of a ball.

"You'll squash my brother," said Jessy indignantly.

"Never mind, Jessy. Just fix me up an ice pack." Adam groaned heavily. "Better make it two."

And so that first week went. Jessy wished to avoid the barn altogether with its grunts and groans and terrific thuds but the two men usually called on her, needing one thing or other. Never sure of what she'd find, she had learned to knock and shout her arrival before entering the barn.

"You're bleeding!" Jessy watched Adam squeeze his nose to stem the flow. "Here!" Jessy's hankie barely fit around her brother's big blunt nose.

"Wish I had a nickel for every nosebleed I ever got wrestlin'. Hey, Bo, toss me a towel!"

"Now you're in for it!" Bo shouted as he attacked Adam from behind.

"Don't get any funny ideas," Adam roared, resuming the struggle with a passion that surprised Jessy, with the fire Bo had meant to kindle.

Within a week it was Bo who was doing the groaning and begging for ice packs. Watching Adam in action, Jessy felt she was seeing him with new eyes. She became aware of something their parents must have missed, a trait Father had tried to beat out of Adam and failed—his inborn need to compete. He had natural drives and a need to strive, to use his body in the most intense physical way. He was tenacious, determined. He loved winning. Jessy saw that Adam not only reveled in the struggle but somehow needed to struggle. It was the struggle, she noticed, that made him strong. Perhaps Adam needed to struggle with God, within his soul, before he could see His light. She wondered if her brother, like Jacob, was wrestling with an angel.

🙋 🙋 🙋

"Your brother's a real champion, greatest I've ever seen, and I've seen the best," Bo confided one night as they finished eating dinner.

"That's kind of you to say, Bo!" Jessy was filling the kettle. "Would you like some tea?"

"Yes, please."

"Adam?"

"You know I never touch the stuff. Tonight I'll have my usual."

Until now, Adam had avoided alcohol. Bo's presence had been a steadying influence on him.

Bo, quick to notice and share Jessy's concern, said: "I'll never forget your brother's first fight. Remember Wham Willard the Wonderman?"

Adam laughed. "How could I forget?"

"Jessy, your brother was no more than sixteen at the time, but strong as an ox. Wham Willard was the star of the show, until Adam came along. We traveled together, up and down the East Coast. Adam and I put up staging for the fights. Being roustabouts, we could watch the performers. Every night we saw Wham in action. He would offer a twenty-dollar goldpiece to any man in the audience who could wrestle his shoulders to the mat to the count of three. We saw Wham fight many times, but he never got beat. I wouldn't go near the guy but your brother figured out how to take Wham down and keep him there."

Adam obviously relished this grand moment in his past. "When I finally challenged him he laughed at me. Got the crowd laughin' at me too. Asked me how old I was. While he laughed, I thought of all the things I could do with the prize money. In those days, twenty bucks sounded like a fortune to me. While he was playin' up to the crowd, I rushed him and knocked the wind outa him, like that." Adam snapped his fingers. "As soon as he went down I was on him, puttin' on all the pressure I could muster. Then somethin' I didn't expect happened. I never figured on the roar of the crowd even though I had heard them shout for Wham in every town he played. For the first time, the crowd was cheerin' for *me*. The more they shouted, the stronger I felt. And I won the prize! Winnin' made me want more. Before long I took over Wham's act. Star of the show. The Man of Iron."

Bo stopped playing with his spoon. "Never could figure out why you left when you were still on top."

"Don't you know?" Adam pulled out a bottle from the sideboard. "Because I was gettin' to be Wham's age when he went down. On the road ten months out of twelve every year, fightin' six nights out of seven every week, always on the move, a man gets tired and sore. I had some close calls. Too close. I wasn't about to let some up-and-comer knock the wind outa *me*, robbin' *me* of applause. I figured I'd leave a champion, not a loser."

"But you'll take on Gunboat."

"It's a sport now, not my bread 'n' butter, now that I got this place."

Glancing at the bottle, Bo said to Adam, "Do you know that when Wham couldn't fight anymore he couldn't find anything better to do than drink? Got the shakes. Died on Skid Row."

"Yeah?"

"That's why it bothers me to know you started drinking. I've seen too many good men ruined. You know how people in our business feel about alcohol. For your own good, I want you to cut out the booze."

"Drop it, Bo."

"Make me."

The two men jumped to their feet with fists clenched. The tablecloth twisted so violently the china snapped to the edge of the table. They who had been staging mock fights really meant to fight this issue in earnest.

"Oh, please, don't!" The men ignored Jessy and glared at each other. Jessy knew that if she came between these two men, she would get her skull broken, at the least. Dear Lord, what to do?

Fear not, came His reply, *for I am with thee. I have redeemed thee. When thou walkest through the fire, thou shalt not be burned.*

Then a sound broke through the oppressive silence diverting everyone's attention. The tea kettle sputtered, splashing hot water out of its spout and onto the stove. Jessy raced away from the table in search of potholders. Inwardly Jessy thanked God for fire and water and the power of prayer. "I picked blackberries for dessert," she said cheerfully while she made tea. "I was going to bake a pie but I know you are both in training and don't want sweets — or anything else — to spoil your hard work."

Though neither man moved, their fists relaxed. Adam flexed his big shoulders before grabbing a fork hanging at the edge of the table. As he tossed it slowly between his right hand and his left, he studied Bo's face.

Jessy came between them to rescue plates perilously near the edge of the table. She turned her warm brown eyes on Bo. "More than anything I was hoping to hear some music tonight, if you would be so kind."

"Wouldn't dream of disappointing you. Any cream for those berries?"

"Yes, of course. What about you, Adam? Care for some blackberries?"

Adam sank down into his chair. "A few. But no cream." He slammed his washboard stomach proudly. "Don't want to put on any flab."

The crisis had passed. Adam left the bottle alone. The subject of drinking didn't come up again during Bo's visit, but Jessy wondered how long Adam's abstinence would last.

❦ 9 ❦

True to his word, Bo Bally arranged the fight between Gunboat Gastonby and the Man of Iron. It would be held in August, at Azleton, a three hour train ride from Bethel. As in past years, record crowds were expected at this, one of America's largest, most popular roadshows.

Much to Jessy's and Adam's sorrow, though, once Bo arranged the advance publicity, he had to leave them. A boy on a bicycle delivered a batch of telegrams to their door, all but one about the fight. Among them was a serious but sketchy appeal. "Oh, no! An emergency in Florida," he explained to Adam. "I'm sorry but I've got to go. Your fight's all set, though, see?" He handed Adam the telegrams about the upcoming fight with Gunboat. "Wish I knew what was going on in Florida. This message hardly says much at all. Look." He showed this, too, to Adam.

While Bo packed, he made Jessy promise to answer his letters, seeing that Adam never did. Jessy was sorry Bo left, and uneasy about Adam's fate.

Still, she couldn't contain her curiosity when Adam went to the cellar to go through his steamer trunks. Now, at long last, she would see what he had been hiding. Following as close as his shadow, she expected him to chase her back upstairs but he didn't. She watched him take the two brass keys from his pocket, still tied together with the red string, and open both trunks. She coughed uncontrollably at the odor of a dozen stale cigars he had locked away.

"Oops, forgot these were in here." Adam savored a Havana Supreme. "Aw, too bad. Definitely past its prime. Here's one of the posters from my last fight. Bo had these printed up for me."

Jessy read the colorful hype. "This was last year?"

"Uh-huh, and with the same show that's comin' back to Azleton. Made some friends last year. Maybe I'll get to see some of them this trip."

Adam pawed through golden boots, satin arm bands, ragged sweat shirts, old circus weeklies and playbills, calendars, faded train schedules, sequined garters, playing cards, ticket stubs, capes, dice, valentines, and letters bundled together with pink ribbon. "Here!" he said, tossing a picture in her direction. "Me and Little Wilma. She was just a cub then."

"A baby lion! How adorable!" Jessy admired the sepia photo of the fetching feline perched saucily on the broad, bare shoulders of Samson Flint. "Gosh, Adam, your hair was so long!"

"Samson had long hair, too, till Delilah gave him a haircut. Fleeced by a woman, the fool. Won't happen to me, you bet your sweet life on that." Adam pushed the delicately tinted bundle of love letters deep into the trunk, out of Jessy's reach. He was careful not to squash extra copies of the posters displayed upstairs in the house. They were rolled inside a packing tube. For his fight Adam selected the golden boots, white tights, and a leotard shimmering with golden spangles.

Jessy was flabbergasted. "Mr. Gunboat looked plain in Bo's photos."

"This is too much, is that what you're sayin'? Guess you're right." Adam settled for black tights and a dark singlet, black high-topped boots that looked expensive, and a leather tie for his curls. "This is all I'll need. Let's go. Oh, wait. I better trash these cigars."

While he was otherwise occupied, Jessy exclaimed, "What're *these*?" lifting out the flimsiest, sheerest undies she had ever seen, nothing like the plain thick white all-encompassing cotton armor she wore, and her mother and grandmother before her. Jessy spotted some long black garters, too, held together by a silky band.

"Hey, small fry! What're you doin' with those?"

Puzzled, Jessy asked, "Were these Laurann's? Did she wear such . . ."

Adam flushed redder than she'd imagined possible. "Yeah. They were hers. She left 'em here. I saved 'em for her, thinkin' she'd come back someday. Gimme that!"

"Is this why you keep the trunks locked? Does the Sheriff know?"

"Sure he knows. He went through everythin' I own. Had a good laugh at me 'n Laurann's expense, too, the dirty—" Adam muttered blasphemies. "Don't look so shocked. I seen flimsier stuff 'n that."

"Really?" Jessy picked up a spangled bauble, the use of which she couldn't fathom. "But what good can such flimsy things do?"

Adam flustered, "Plenty!"

"But they can't be very warm. Are they comfortable?"

"How should I know?!? You're too young to—hey, put those back!"

Jessy would have liked nothing better than to spend the rest of the day reading Adam's fan mail, but he locked both trunks and pocketed the keys again. Still, she rested easier after that, knowing that although their contents would be considered downright shocking to polite society, the trunks contained nothing the Sheriff thought relevant to a murder investigation.

❦ ❦ ❦

When the Flints arrived in Azleton, the road show was in full swing—rides and games, bands blaring, acrobats tumbling, and posters announcing the big fight between the Man of Iron and The Gunboat tacked to every post, wall, and storefront.

A welcome committee of sorts met their train—Adam's old friends and admirers, mainly showgirls, full-bodied, long-legged, and smiling. With the exception of her own bath time, Jessy had never seen so much exposed flesh in her life, nor so much brilliant color. Their costumes were as flimsy and bangled as anything in Adam's trunks. Jessy followed the swirling mass of red, lime green, and pink netting toward Adam's dressing tent.

Women vied to carry luggage and look after Adam who was dressed in his finest suit—cream silk—with a luxurious tie and polished Italian boots. The women wasted no time latching on to his arms and bouncing round in front of and behind him as they made their way to the dressing tents. "Our long-lost gentleman farmer!" the girls teased. "Back to resume his career."

"No, no," said Adam, grinning. "Much as I'm delighted to see you girls, this is strictly a business trip. One fight and goodbye."

"Goodbye! You only just got here, Adam Flint! And with a girl friend."

"*Sister*. Mind yourselves around her."

"You're so adorable when you make jokes!"

"Hey, easy, honey! Save it for after the fight." Adam pushed away one particularly affectionate blonde dressed as a golden peacock.

An auburn beauty announced, "In your honor, I've asked for the day off. The first one I've had in three weeks."

Another girl squeezed between them. "Me, too. This way, love."

Exhibits spread in paths arranged like the spokes of a wheel. Jessy, taken with a passing menagerie including baby elephants, didn't dare lose sight of Adam and his entourage amid the long rows of tents. She was impressed to see that his was the largest of all.

Upon entering, Jessy beheld, open-mouthed, the spacious, luxurious quarters — red velvet sofas, thick oriental carpets, gilt-framed mirrors, white dressing tables, racks full of costumes, and ornately enameled folding screens which allowed several entertainers to change clothes between shows.

Apparently Adam had seen it all before. While showgirls and roustabouts arranged his luggage, he busied himself before a full-length mirror. With dimples showing and without taking his eyes from his reflection, he loosened his tie and said to Ruby, the auburn beauty, "Long, hot ride."

"Let me help you." She touched the top button of his vest.

"Not in front of my sister! Besides, I need to relax before the fight."

"I understand, sweetheart. Later?"

"Maybe." Adam gave her a look that said, *Absolutely*. "Right now I wanna get freshened up. I'll take some ice water if you got it."

"Right here, darling. Everything you could ever want, ready for you."

While she bathed his face, two other women pulled off his shoes. Another handed him a tall glass of water.

Removing his tie and sinking back into a stack of satin pillows on the sofa, he asked, "So what've you been up to, Ruby?"

"The show toured South America, elephants included. Avalanches, mud slides, earthquakes every day, a civil war, and general mayhem. But without you, darling, it was dull. How I've missed you."

"You hardly know me."

"Maybe that's why I missed you."

He threw a pillow at her. That's when he noticed Jessy, dressed like a school girl, still standing at the entryway. "If it's all right with you, Adam, I'd like to see the elephants."

"Good idea." He tossed his wallet to her. "Take some money. Fight won't start till tonight. Go on all the rides. Get some lunch. Tell the barkers you're my sister. They'll treat you special. Be sure to see the nickelodeon."

Jessy took a little money but looked hesitant when she returned the wallet. "I don't know where to begin."

"Say, Ruby, howsabout showin' my little sister around? You know, look after her. That'll give me a chance to rest up."

Ruby looked hurt beyond words. Her beautiful face turned brittle, as did her voice. "Spend my one day off with a kid?"

"Oh, don't worry about me, Adam. I can find my way around without troubling this lady."

"This *lady* owes me a favor. Doncha, Ruby?" Adam nudged the woman from behind with his bare foot. "Remember? Go on, the two of you, and let a man get his rest."

In silent fury, Ruby, dressed only in a thin magenta chemise and fishnet stockings, disappeared behind a screen. When she emerged a few moments later, she looked positively chaste in a plain shirtwaist dress. "Let's go, kid," she said through clenched teeth.

"Gosh, this really is nice of you to take time for me, Ruby. Is it all right if I call you Ruby?"

"Sure, kid, sure. Let's start with the flea circus."

At the mere mention of fleas, Jessy began to itch.

ಀ   ಀ   ಀ

"I don't know which I liked better," said Jessy as she finished her second hotdog, "the games, the rides, or the fleas. I guess the fleas, especially the one that twirled the tiny beach ball! I could have watched all day!" Jessy smiled happily at Ruby. The two had found a table under the trees where Jessy admired her new toy tiger.

"Never saw a girl win one of those." Ruby was referring to the sight, just an hour ago, of Jessy swinging a sledgehammer onto a contraption that rocketed a ball to the top of a seven-foot pole where it struck a gong. The deed stunned everyone, Ruby and Jessy included.

"The game was rigged so you'd win, seeing you're related to Adam Flint."

"Oh. And I thought I did it all on my own." Jessy was crestfallen. "I ought to give back the prize."

"It was meant for you to have. Enjoy it."

"If you think it's all right, then I will! It's the first prize I've ever won and I do like it! Thank you, Ruby, for spending your day off with me. I know you didn't want to."

"Believe it or not, I'm enjoying myself. Afternoons, I help the magicians and tumblers and at night I sing. I seldom get a chance to see a sideshow unless I'm working it." Ruby studied Jessy over her soda. "It's been fun for me to see a kid look at life with new eyes. You're a good kid. I noticed you said silent grace before you ate."

"Did that bother you?"

"No! You made me think of my dad. I haven't thought about his saying grace for a long time. Seems so long ago when I left home. I haven't been back in nine years."

"Are your parents still living?"

"Oh, yes," said Ruby happily. "And I have four brothers and two sisters."

"How wonderful! Do you all get along?"

"Used to."

"They must miss you a lot."

"I don't fit in with them anymore, but a sweet kid like you wouldn't understand. I was like you once. I began my singing career in a choir!"

"You must have a wonderful life," Jessy said. "Your work must be fun!"

"Fun?" Ruby said with disgust. "This is a hard way to live, harder than you could imagine."

"I thought living on a farm with my brother would be easy but it's constant hard work. I think it might be fun to join the circus."

"I've never told anyone, but I'm sick of my life."

"There isn't joy away from God," Jessy said with feeling. "If we have the whole world but we don't have God, then we have nothing. If we have nothing but God, we don't need anything else."

"Take my advice, honey. Stay sweet like you are. What I'd give to be that girl in the choir again, with a new chance in life. I'd do things differently, but it's too late. I'm past my prime and don't have a future."

"We all can have a glorious future!" Jessy stopped herself from saying more. She heeded Adam's advice by thinking things through. "My brother says I'm a terrible prig. He gets mad when I explain my beliefs. I won't say another word unless you want me to." Jessy sipped her root beer.

"In this business, I've heard everything." Ruby looked hard. "What could you say I don't already know?"

"For one, I believe anyone can begin again. It's never too late, if that's what you really want."

"Impossible!"

Jessy picked up her stuffed tiger. "I thought I won this prize on my own strength, but someone saw to it that I won. You say I should keep it and enjoy it. Well, it's the same with faith in Christ. By dying in our place, He won the prize of salvation for us. The question is, will we turn away from our sins and accept His gifts? We didn't earn them, but He wants us to have them. And we can't have a wonderful future without Him. Salvation's something we can't earn on our own, no matter how hard we try. We have to depend on God."

"If it could only be that simple. I turned away from God years ago."

"God hasn't turned away from you."

For a moment, joy transformed the hard lines of Ruby's face into glowing beauty. "You're right. My parents would agree with you." Her radiance faded as soon as it had appeared. "But forgiveness is for people like you, not me."

"We've all sinned, and we can all be forgiven."

"Your way is too hard!"

Jessy cried, "Living without God is what's hard! I know you think I'm just a kid, but life would have been impossible for me without faith. God is always with me, no matter how confused or upset I am, no matter what goes wrong, or what stupid thing I might do. He'll be with you, too, Ruby."

"I really should pray, but this isn't the time or the place."

"I'll pray for you, Ruby, if you want."

"Shows you what kind of life I've been living! My name isn't even Ruby! The manager made me change it when I joined the show! I'm Mary Smith!"

Jessy watched the new woman weep and pray in silence. When she lifted her head, she said, "This morning when I woke up, I knew today would be wonderful. I thought it was because I'd see Adam Flint, but being born again is beyond anything I had expected! Do you think I'll always be close to God? I'm weak, you don't know how weak, Jessy. If I sin, I'll be doubly lost."

"God won't fail you," Jessy assured her. "Once you're His, you're His!"

"All things are possible with Him, that's what my folks believe. I'm so happy! I want them to know!" Ruby—now Mary—stood. "Let's go to the telegraph office. I'll send a wire home. They'll never believe this!"

"Oh," smiled Jessy, "I think they might."

❦   ❦   ❦

After sending the telegram, Mary and Jessy came upon amateur wrestling matches in progress on the fairgrounds. One of the wrestlers, dressed in blue, was crawling to the outside of the ring. His opponent, wearing green, grabbed him from behind with both arms and locked his fingers tightly to gain control. Blue strained and struggled but couldn't break the hold. His shoulder muscles, bared in the sleeveless singlet he was wearing, flushed pink. The flush spread across his chest and back. One quick move and Blue was brought low. Green pressed his opponent's shoulders to the mat. A referee dropped down and slapped his hand once, twice, three times. The match was over. Both wrestlers got to their feet. The referee held up Green's arm for all to see. Blue shook his head like a wounded bull. Slowly he stood and shook the victor's hand. As the two walked away, another pair of wrestlers prepared to enter the ring.

"Never could understand these fool things," Mary admitted quietly.

With a grin, Jessy said, "Adam explained to me: 'This sorta wrestlin' in one form or other goes back to ancient times. The winner is the one who can take the other fella down 'n hold his shoulders to the mat to the counta three.' Adam said that in the first few seconds of a match, he can usually tell which wrestler will win. 'Nine times outa ten, the fella who gets the first takedown will win the match.'" Jessy delighted in imitating Adam. She pursed her lips the way he did, forcing her dimples to show. "'Cuz he gets a mental boost from gettin' the upper hand quick, and that boost'll carry him through to victory.'"

Mary laughed. "You sound just like him! Look! Here come two more wrestlers! Let's test Adam's theory."

Two men, one in black, the other in white, approached each other on the innermost part of the mat. A moment later, Black grabbed his opponent by the knee and took him down to the mat. A few more moves and Black had won.

"Adam was right!" Jessy screamed amid the roar of the crowd.

"Wish I had bet a few bucks on *that* fight." Mary clapped her hand over her mouth. "Uh-oh." She looked to heaven, her face filled with awe, fear, and hope. "Jessy, can I tell you a secret?" Motioning for Jessy to withdraw from the crowd, Mary whispered, "I love your brother. I've loved him from the first time I ever laid eyes on him, last summer. I want to marry him."

Jessy sighed deeply. "Now that you're a Christian, you need a Christian husband. I'm sorry to say Adam is not the kind of man you need."

"How could Adam be lost with you to guide him? When you were speaking to me I could feel the Spirit moving my soul for the first time ever."

"Sometimes I think Adam hates me worse than anyone, just for sharing the truth with him. I try not to take it personally, because he's spiritually blind. I pray every day God will open his eyes so he can be whole. It hurts me a lot that Adam's so lost, but he just doesn't understand how much he's missing." Jessy shrugged helplessly, wondering if she would ever see the victory. "I want the best for Adam, but he's got to want it for himself."

Jessy and Mary returned to the tent where they had left Adam earlier in the day, but he was gone. Mary suggested that Jessy rest while she went on her way. Gratefully Jessy lay down on the sofa. The sun was still high over the tent, warming the earth, but Jessy needed rest after the long train ride and the exhilarating events of this day.

As she made herself comfortable, she prayed: "Thank you, Jesus, for what You did for Mary. And thank You for letting me take part in Your glorious plan for us. And thank You for such a wonderful day!"

While Jessy rested she was aware of show people moving in and around the tent but the day's excitement left her yearning for sleep. She buried her head under one of the satin pillows.

When she stirred, the sun had shifted down to the lowest corner of the tent. In the dim light, Jessy could hear Adam warming up for the fight.

"Almost time to go," he called to her.

When she finally fully wakened, it was getting dark. Adam was nearly dressed for his match. She watched him pull his jacket over his shoulders to keep his muscles warm. As Jessy sat up, she felt a piece of paper slip off the sofa down to her feet. It was a note from Mary. After smoothing her hair and putting on her beribboned hat and pretty blue jacket, she rushed out after Adam.

"Have fun today?" he asked.

"Oh, yes, Adam! It was one of the most wonderful days possible."

"Where's Ruby?"

"I don't know, but she left me a note. I'll read it to you if you like." Jessy scrambled to keep up with him and keep her hat from flying away. " 'Dearest Jessy, Just received a wire from home—short but sweet. My folks asked me to come back right away. They've been praying for me all this time and can't wait to see me! The prodigal daughter is going home! Jessy, you will always and forever be my very special friend. I'll never forget you and what you've done for me today. God bless you, always, and goodbye. Love, Mary. P.S. Please tell Adam I'll pray for him.' "

"Who's Mary?"

"Mary is Ruby's real name. Gee, I'll miss her."

"Thought we had a date after the match. Well, there's plenty more rubies round here. She was too clingin' for my taste anyway. Can't imagine the Ruby I know prayin' for nobody. You musta had somethin' to do with that. Only you could turn a bawdy show like this into a missionary's old home week."

"I won a prize! I rang the bell with the sledgehammer."

"Musta been rigged."

"That's what Mary said, but I could swing the hammer."

"Yeah?" He whistled appreciatively. "Willya look at this crowd!"

"They're all waiting for you, aren't they?"

"And The Gunboat. Gonna root for your brother?"

"Of course! Loud as I can!" Softly she added, "May God be with you."

"Here, hold my jacket. Watch the suede." Adam's singlet was cut to reveal his exquisite physique, the broad powerful chest and shoulders that had made him famous. A path through to the mat opened miraculously before him. He moved forward, with Jessy tagging behind. She trembled at the sight of his opponent. "Oh, dear, don't tell me *that's* The Gunboat..."

The last thing she remembered hearing was Adam's whisper: "Oh, well, I can only die once."

❦ 10 ❦

Adam raised his arms in appreciation of the roaring crowd. Photographers and reporters pushed in from all sides, and behind them, men shouted encouragement or discouragement as they felt so inclined. It was a rough crowd, rougher than Jessy had ever seen. Her heart beat wildly amid the cheers of a thousand men.

The two wrestlers, standing toe to toe in the center of the mat, were of roughly equal height and weight, but there the similarity between them ended. Adam's weight and muscle were beautifully balanced across his shoulders, down his torso, and through his legs. His upper body was shaped like a V, the broadness of his chest perfectly balanced over his slender waist and hips, whereas Gunboat resembled an upright cannon topped off with a bald head that seemed all of a piece. Unlike Adam's arms, sculpted and swelling in great curves and shadow as a result of years of training, Gunboat's were thin and knotted. While Adam's smooth shaven face, form, and agility were classic, to Jessy The Gunboat looked ferocious, dressed in red like a demon, with a goatee, and half cross-eyed besides. All Gunboat lacked was a pitchfork and a tail. Jessy broke out in a sweat, concerned for her brother's safety.

Someone was trying to make a speech, but the audience was so uproarious no one heard. The opponents sized each other up, shook hands, and began pacing in quick circles. Adam was first to reach down with both hands and slap Gunboat's knees, trying for a grab.

"Like breaking down a table," Adam had once told Jessy, but the wrestling moves he had used with such success against Bo had no effect on Gunboat. Still the men kept upright, moving. Now Adam was the one being grabbed. He went halfway down, slipping on one knee.

Remembering Adam's theory, Jessy screamed, "Oh, no, Adam, don't let that bully take you down first!"

Adam must have heard, or at least felt the same way, for he struggled up to his feet, pushing hard with his great back and shoulders to escape

95

and reverse Gunboat's murderous hold on him from behind. Both men strained to the utmost.

Now Adam was in control. He had managed to take Gunboat halfway down, and held on fiercely to the man's knotty, straining arms. Adam worked with his legs as well, trying to twist one of them, then the other, around Gunboat's to topple him over. Gunboat stiffened. Adam shoved mightily, fighting against the arching bridge Gunboat had become. Jessy noticed Gunboat turning pink. His bald head, neck, and shoulders flushed with strain. By comparison, Adam looked cool, comfortable, his green eyes clear and unclouded, but his face was tense with concentration.

Gunboat surprised Adam with a sudden lurching of his hips. Adam countered with a surprise of his own. He dropped down, swung himself under Gunboat's crotch, and knocked the man over on his back so quickly Gunboat shook his head with uncertainty.

Adam seized this opportunity to hurl himself on top of Gunboat, pressing him down on his abdomen, using both arms to go for the pin, but Gunboat strained to keep one shoulder off the mat, denying Adam's victory. The two struggled together as one, reversing one another's holds, escaping and holding, escaping and holding. Neither seemed to have an advantage.

The crowd that had so eagerly hollered advice early in the match was now reduced to silence, stumped in a deadlock along with the wrestlers. The referee demanded a pause in the action. Both men got to their feet, shrugged their shoulders, then reached forward, locking arms in combat once again. This time Adam tried a cradle, a move he had practiced repeatedly on Bo and had carefully explained to Jessy. He grabbed Gunboat, who was on all fours like a dog, by one arm and one leg and tossed him down to one side but Gunboat snapped himself away to a half standing position.

Adam lost his temper now. Jessy could see a storm brewing in those green eyes. She knew there was no stopping him when he looked that way. With one furious burst of energy Adam stunned the crowd and Gunboat by raising the red devil up across his mighty shoulders and then tossing Gunboat down to the mat. Adam again threw himself on Gunboat, who appeared dazed and limp from the fall. With all the strength Adam possessed he pushed against his opponent's shoulders, pressing them down to the mat, but Gunboat struggled viciously for a release.

"Dear Lord, please help my brother. He looks like his heart might burst!" Burying her face in her hat, Jessy cringed at the scrambling sounds on the mat, the shouting and screaming all around her, the grunts and groans of the two men locked in combat.

And now it was over. One, two, three!! shouted the referee.

The crowd roared its approval. Jessy peeked and saw the referee waving her brother's arm high in victory. Adam reached down to help Gunboat to his feet. The two men shook hands again to the cheers of the crowd.

Jessy rushed forward to congratulate Adam but a mob of reporters, photographers, and girls surged ahead of her, moving away with Adam high aloft on their shoulders. Jessy caught up with Adam at the winner's table, where he was being paid his cash prize.

"Oh, Adam, I never dreamed a fight could be so exciting! I was so scared for you! You're so fast, so strong . . ."

His green eyes dazzled with shrewdness. "Not bad for an old man?"

"No, sir. But still, I was so scared for you . . ."

Adam laughed and hugged her close. His rock hard body was soaked with sweat. He drew her aside. "Take this."

"Your winnings?"

"Half of it. Put it inside your jacket. Crooks won't think a kid'd be carryin' so much loot. As soon as I get cleaned up and change my clothes, I'll wire Bo his share and then head to the poker game I got lined up."

"Gambling? What would Mother . . ."

"No sermons. I'll see you later."

"Can't I stay with you?"

"Not on your life."

"So what am I supposed to do while you play poker?"

"There's plenty to do around here—a kid's dream! See you later."

"When?" The fairgrounds were already lit by gaslight, brighter than anything she had ever seen before, a bewildering maze spreading in all directions. "Where?"

"Where else? The Paradise Club!" With that he was gone, swallowed up by well-wishers and girls.

After Adam disappeared from sight, Jessy roamed in the garish night for something to do, amid thronging masses of spectators. There were many entertainments she had not yet seen: An enormous musical pipe organ drawn from town to town across America to this spot by a forty-horse hitch, and curiosities Jessy found fascinating, bizarre, or both. There were bearded ladies, snake charmers, somersaulting midgets, two-headed calves, belly dancers, clownish acrobats, exotic tigers, and more.

As the evening wore on, she met with Adam from time to time. It wasn't hard to find the Paradise Club, a building that occupied an entire city block just beyond the fairgrounds. The tinkly sounds of more than one honky-tonk piano filled the air. On her first visit, while finishing her second triple-scoop ice cream cone, Jessy thoughtfully regarded the bouncers outside and the big brass sign, Paradise Club, floating on puffy white clouds. There were smaller signs, too, banning loafing and loitering.

Through the night, Jessy, always on the outside looking in, wondered why the same women, fancily dressed, appeared often, but going in and out of the club on the arms of so many different men. From time to time, Adam stepped outside for air, with more than one girl in tow.

"Got a great little poker game goin'. Hang on to this for me," he would say, handing Jessy money. Sometimes he took money from her.

The roadshow continued unabated until long into the night. Jessy didn't miss a thing. All this activity had given her an enormous appetite for treats. She had just paid for her third cotton candy when a man stepped out from the shadows, his bare arms covered in tattoos. Jessy thought he was one of the entertainers until he put a knife against her throat.

"Gimme that rolla money or I'll cut ya!"

Like a fool, Jessy struggled with the thief, but he slammed her down and grabbed the money. Sick and dizzy, she gradually became aware of a crowd forming around her. It was some time before she felt strong enough to stand. Wondering how she would ever explain such a thing to Adam, she rushed to the Paradise Club, but he had left. They found each other soon enough, in court.

11

Jessy squinted into the early morning light streaming from a window above and behind the judge's head. The night before, she had tried in vain to talk to Adam, but the police had kept her away. Now, from the entryway of the courtroom, she inched forward through a mob of officials and onlookers. When she reached Adam's side, she whispered, "Adam! I have to tell you something!"

"Ssssh." Adam wouldn't even look at her. He looked like he had spent the night in gin joints and a drunk tank, which he had. He focused on three points: the judge, the crowd near the bench, and his own handcuffed wrists.

"Mr. Flint, Mr. Adam Flint, you are charged with public drunkenness, disturbing the peace, assault and battery, indecent exposure, fornication. It appears you had rather a full night in our fair city of Azleton." Demanding order, the judge glared at some noisy spectators.

The large crowd was growing larger. Police had worked through the night until the jail and this court were filled to capacity.

"Mr. Flint, please tell the Court how you managed to accomplish all of these misdeeds in only one evening?"

"I can't say, exactly. I musta blacked out at some point. The last thing I recall was headin' to Hazy's Tavern with them girls over there."

Adam pointed with both bound hands to a throng of girls accompanied by uniformed guards. The girls moved and shifted together, alternately giggling, groaning, whispering, and hiding their faces with their hands.

Down went the gavel. The judge turned sharply to his left. "Order in this Court. If you women persist in causing a distraction, I shall charge you with contempt. Mr. Flint, please continue."

"Well, Your Honor, the truth is the more I drank the better them girls looked. Me 'n Maxine 'n Molly 'n Charlene went out back after a while, and we was havin' a really fine time when I felt this hand on my shoulder and I said, 'You so 'n so, can't you see we're busy?' And next thing I knew, I was being hauled to my feet, which made me mad enough to take a swing at whoever it was interruptin' us, but Your Honor, you'd done the same if you'd been caught in my position."

When the crowd laughed, the judge banged the gavel down again. "Mr. Flint, despite the fact that you are a showman, you will confine your fighting to the professional circuit and your lovemaking to private places. One night to serve. That has already been served. And a three hundred dollar fine."

Adam nudged Jessy. "You heard the man. Pay up."

"Can't you pay it?"

"I only got twelve dollars on me. Hurry up, I wanna get outa here."

Jessy whispered too. "I've been trying to tell you since last night—the money you gave me to hold got stolen."

Adam exploded. "Your Honor, we been robbed! Fine city this is! Over the course of last evenin' I gave my little sister here a total of $3,973 to hold for me and she just told me it got stolen!"

The judge called for order and looked at Jessy, "Suppose you tell this Court what happened, Miss... Miss?"

"I'm Jessy Flint, Your Honor. Sir."

"And what is your age and relationship to the defendant?"

"I'm fourteen, sir. I'm Adam's sister."

"Please tell us what happened, in your own words."

"Well, sir, real late last night, or maybe early this morning, I was eating cotton candy, when a man grabbed me and said, 'Gimme that money or I'll slit your throat,' or something like that, I'm not sure. I tried to fight him off and he pushed me down. He must have seen me take a hundred dollar bill from the roll of money I had with me. I was keeping it here in my jacket." Jessy turned her empty pocket inside out so the court could see. "Anyway, he took the money and ran. People must've seen because some of them helped me and some others ran after him, but I'm not exactly sure because in all the confusion I hit my head and everything went fuzzy and next thing I knew a lady was helping me up, and the man who stole the money was gone, but I found the police station and told them what happened, and they said the thief had been arrested, but they wouldn't give the money to me because it had to be held for evidence, all three thousand seven hundred..."

"Three thousand *nine* hundred and seventy-three dollars," Adam corrected in a crisp voice.

"How very interesting," mused the judge. "And won't you please tell us how you happened to have such a vast sum of money in the first place?"

"Let me answer that."

"Mr. Flint, you will not interrupt. Go ahead, Miss."

Jessy heard Adam groan as she plunged ahead. "It wasn't my money at all, sir, it was Adam's winnings for fighting and gambling, two of the things he loves doing a lot of. After he beat the Gunboat, Adam went off to gamble. I went to the Paradise Club like he told me to do, but the big men in charge at the door wouldn't let me inside on account of my age, so I asked them if they would kindly let my brother know I was waiting outside for him, and after that, for practically the rest of the evening, Adam would come out every so often to hand me money he was winning at poker and shooting craps and such."

The crowd whooped with laughter until the gavel brought order in the court.

"I found out later that when Adam finally finished in there, he told the men at the door to tell me the next time I came back from the roadshow that all the gambling had made him thirsty and it was time to start drinking 'for real' and I was to wait at his dressing tent for him, only in the meantime, I got robbed, and when I was at the police station trying to get back the money, that's when it was I saw the officers bringing Adam in, but when I tried to talk to him and tell him what had happened to his money they said he was sleeping off a drunk and couldn't be roused and truth is, he did appear to have passed out cold. Sir." At last Jessy had run out of story and breath.

The judge, too, was speechless, but not for long. He asked the Constable to approach the bench.

At that moment, a prisoner was brought in, his arms covered in tattoos.

"There's the robber, Your Honor!" screamed Jessy.

The Constable addressed the Judge: "Your Honor, this knife and all this money were found on the defendant at the time of his arrest. After he robbed the girl, he was chased down by some men in the crowd who disarmed him."

The judge glowered from the bench as he addressed the robber. "Stealing from a child! Despicable! This isn't the first time you've been up before me, is it, Bartholomew? The last time you were here I promised to throw the book at you if you caused any more trouble."

"Yes, sir, I do remember you said exactly that and believe me, had I known that kid was any kin of Adam Flint's I wouldn't a gone within ten miles a her for double the haul — I mean, money, Your Honor, Sir!"

"So how do you plead, Mr. Bartholomew?"

"Guilty. And I'll be glad to go to jail, sir, only just don't let that Flint near me."

"Mr. Flint, your reputation precedes you. Let the money and the weapon be recorded as exhibits and the money duly returned to Miss Jessy Flint."

Jessy quickly counted out three hundred dollars to pay Adam's fine. The guards returned his belongings to him and unlocked his handcuffs. Adam ran his fingers through his tangled curls before setting his hat over them at the usual rakish angle.

"Mr. Flint, you are to leave this county today, you are not to come up before me again for causing a disturbance, and you are to examine your conscience as to the proper example to set for your sister, a minor."

Adam took more interest in adjusting his vest and brushing the back of his hand over the generous lapels of his suede jacket than listening to the lecture. "Am I free to go?" he asked curtly.

"As far as I am concerned, Mr. Flint, you are *too* free. You are a man living without controls, without restraints. And, off the record I would add that unless you mend your ways you are courting disaster. Next case!"

"Be seein' you," Adam said with a smile to the crowd of disheveled, disorderly girls being herded toward the bench. To Jessy he muttered, "That Maxine definitely looks better in the pitch dark."

"Is that a nice thing to say? Speaking of things said, what did the judge mean when he . . ."

"I'll do the talkin', Little Miss Law and Order." Once they were outside he really began fuming. "For a girl your size, you sure got a big mouth! I thought you'd never shut up in there!"

"But the judge asked what happened and I told him the truth," Jessy said with a hurt look. "Besides, while you were having your idea of a good time I nearly got stabbed to death and had my new clothes ruined."

Adam surveyed her this way and that, noting her wilted ribbons, mud, and grime. "You'll live. Now hand over the money."

Adam flipped through the roll with his usual flair for all matters financial, hangovers notwithstanding. "What the...? Two hundred six bucks missin'!" He spun back toward the courthouse.

"No need to go back in there. I can explain."

"Don't tell me you spent all that money on cotton candy."

"No, sir."

"Well?"

"I, ah, last night while I was waiting for you outside the Paradise Club, this lady came up to me..."

"What lady?"

"I don't know her name, but she was sobbing her heart out because her husband had lost his whole paycheck gambling and they needed the money desperately for food and on top of everything else their baby had been sick and they had doctor bills and the lady herself was ailing and..."

"And you got suckered out of two hundred and six dollars of *my* money?" With one hand Adam grabbed Jessy by her scraggly ribbons and with the other he fingered his Italian leather belt. "Just wait till we get home."

"But the lady said..."

Adam pushed her away, saying, "If you ain't the naivest kid on this green earth."

Jessy's eyelashes fluttered. "What do you mean by that?"

Adam spit on the sidewalk. "She was no lady and nobody's wife and she got no bills and no sick kid. She got no nuthin' 'cept my hard earned money and a talent for makin' up sob stories to fleece suckers like you. She pulled one of the oldest tricks in the book and you fell for it. You got suckered outa *my* money."

"I don't understand it. She sounded so sincere, Adam. She really did!" Jessy answered with wide-eyed innocence. "Besides, it's more blessed to give than to receive and if we do good unto the least of these we do good unto Christ and anyway you won that money gambling and gambling's a sin."

"Where'd you ever get that idea?"

"They cast lots for His garments."

"Who?"

"The soldiers. At Golgotha. At the foot of the cr..."

"Yoo-hoo! How glad I am to see you again!" A poorly but neatly dressed woman standing in front of the county assessor's office across the street was waving in their direction. She hurried across, pushing a baby carriage. She smiled radiantly to Jessy and took Adam's hand for a brief moment. "Is this your brother, Jessy? Oh, thank God for both of you, that you had mercy on me and mine." She waved a handful of receipts. "I've already been to the bank and have just settled part of our debt to the doctor. From now on, my husband's boss will pay our bills out of Burney's paycheck *before* he has a chance to gamble it away. And see how the baby loves the toy tiger you gave her, Jessy! I'll always remember your kindness in our time of need. God bless you both."

Jessy looked up to Adam who had the oddest expression on his face, one of reluctant benevolence. "This is the lady you said suckered..."

He elbowed Jessy hard. "Ssssh!"

"What did you say, dear?" the woman asked Jessy.

"Nothing, ma'am. It's good to see you again and know everything's going to be all right. We're so happy we could help. Aren't we, Adam?"

"Yeah, yeah, our pleasure," he said while tipping his hat and admiring the woman's porcelain skin.

The woman, appearing visibly shaken by Adam's ruinous good looks, stammered her farewell.

While the woman went on her way, Jessy said, "I'm sorry I made you mad."

"Huh? Ah, forget it. But next time you feel generous, give away *your* money, not mine." He scanned both sides of the street with his sharp eyes. "I could eat a horse. You hungry?"

"I feel sick." In truth, Jessy looked and felt queasy.

"Too much cotton candy and funnel cakes, I'd say. Decent breakfast is what you need. There's a restaurant 'round the corner." Adam began walking toward it in a hurry. "Last time I was in town they served me a nice fresh rainbow trout, melon, and scrambled eggs. Sure go down good this mornin' with a Bloody Mary."

"A bloody what? Which reminds me, what did the judge mean by 'fornication'?"

"Don't you ever let me hear you say that word again! It's indecent!"

"That's what I was afraid it meant."

Meanwhile Adam was buying the morning paper from a newsboy. The two-inch headline proclaimed FLINT TORPEDOES GUNBOAT and, in smaller type, word of Adam's arrest. Flicking the paper with the backs of his broad fingers, Adam asked her, "Look at that free publicity. Proud of your brother?"

"No," she answered, noticing that a crowd was forming around them.

Adam basked in their admiration as he signed autographs.

Pride goeth before a fall, thought Jessy.

❧ 12 ❧

That unforgettable autumn Saturday began with an unruly hog, all 300 pounds of him, breaking through two fences to avoid the restraining noose Adam had tried to loop around its snout. While Jessy distracted the animal with a taste of maple syrup daubed on the end of a stick, Adam dropped a burlap bag over him. Together they hauled the animal onto the wagon. Soon five more hogs were on board, each tied in its own cocoon.

Jessy felt heartsick for the poor hogs who had been raised and fattened for a one-way train ride to Chicago's meat processing plants. The rest of their sty mates, except the one Adam would butcher for his own larder, would be shipped to market over the next few weeks in the same fashion as these unfortunates. When slaughtering time was over, Adam would be left with his trusty boar and breed sows to provide him with new litters the following spring. Life and death, life and death, so went the cycle on Adam's farm.

How fast the time had passed since, shortly after Jessy's arrival, she had witnessed the birth of piglets—sweet, helpless, nursing babes. Keeping their pens clean had kept her filthy during spring, summer, and fall. They would greet her with contented grunts whenever she arrived with buckets of corn, home-cooked leftovers from the dinner table, tender treats from the vegetable garden, and surplus milk and cream Adam bought from dairy farm neighbors. Piglets, even the runt she had once held on her lap, had fattened to three times her weight and were now headed for doom.

Naturally, she felt protective, and even angry. "Won't they smother in those bags?"

"Nah. I do this every fall. Gotta get 'em to market somehow. It's a long ride and I don't want 'em hurtin' each other or me. This is the best way. They'll rest easy all the way to the railroad yard."

"They were such cute babies."

"They got ugly mighty fast. I told you from the start not to get attached, not to name 'em or hold 'em."

"Still . . ." She bowed her head. A fast, nearly wordless prayer more like a groan, fleeted through her mind. She felt a little silly praying for hogs, but they were, after all, God's creatures headed for slaughter, so like us all.

"Ready to go?"

"Not quite. I'll be right back!" Preparing for the long ride herself, Jessy ran to the outhouse.

There, while seated on the rustic throne, she reached for an old mail order catalog. Adam, as his rural neighbors, didn't squander money on store-bought luxuries like toilet paper, not when other kinds of paper arrived free by mail. Much of the catalog had already been used, but Jessy, being an avid reader of anything and everything, perused the dog-eared fragments with interest. Soon Jessy's attention fell to drugs.

There, amid the promised cures for rheumatism, blood builders, nerve tonics, brain pills, lung restorers, and Dr. Rose's Obesity Powder, was an illustration of a man guzzling straight from an upturned bottle. The man didn't resemble Adam, but the bottle was about right. Jessy shifted around on the wooden seat without taking her eyes from the ad:

> A cure for any liquor habit — guaranteed!
> Sample — 50 cents.
> 12 boxes — $5.
> Full treatment — $9.

A permanent cure! Jessy read the ad more than once, always taking pause at the cost. She didn't have fifty cents, much less nine dollars. Would Adam give her the money? Not if she told him what she wanted to buy with it and he was sure to ask. She couldn't very well lie. How to get the cure and yet keep it a secret? How to make Adam *want* to stop drinking? *That* was the question. She jumped when she heard him coming up the walk. He rapped on the door a couple of times.

"You fall in?"

"No, sir."

"Well, hurry up. Think I like waitin' around with a buncha pigs?"

Giggling, she said, "No, sir." Quickly she ripped the ad out of the catalog.

"You laughin' at me? What's goin' on in there? Don't tell me you're readin' again." Now he sounded like he was really steaming.

"I'll be right out." When she heard Adam walk down the path, she glanced over the ad once more. A cure in a bottle. It sounded too good to be true. Jessy knew that what Adam needed was a cure from the hand of God, but just the same she tucked the ad into her skirt pocket.

❦   ❦   ❦

The Flints waited their turn at the railroad station jammed with other hog farmers and their families. Once Adam's hogs had been weighed in, he was paid for their total poundage. As hundreds of squealing hogs were being loaded into waiting boxcars, Jessy covered her ears and looked away, glad to be riding toward the town center to do their usual errands at the bank, library, post office, and general store.

While Adam selected coffee, salt, hardware, and other things they needed, Jessy bypassed jars of candy and barrels of rice, meal and nuts, suspenders, longjohns, axle grease, lime, chamber pots, shoelaces, moustache combs, hammerheads, washboards, mason jars, and lamp chimneys. Jessy needed new skirts. The ones she had worn all summer were beyond hope, their ankle-length hems frayed by chewing hogs. She examined bolts of wool and corduroy, but prices were high. When she looked for Adam to discuss the matter, she heard the shop owner call out to her, "Your brother said for you to meet him outside Mo's. Me, I never touch strong drink so soon after breakfast. Surprised they let him in Mo's any more, after the brawl that time two years ago. Flint didn't start it but he sure did finish it."

Jessy left the store in a rush, walking the two blocks briskly, anger welling up within her. She found Adam's horse Milo waiting patiently in front of the tavern, only his ears flicking casually. When the town clock struck the quarter hour, then the half, and Adam failed to emerge, Jessy boarded the rig and began reading a library book. Jessy read five full chapters, but Adam still didn't emerge. She fed Milo some of the oats Adam kept in the bin under the seat, but there was nothing for her to eat. She fished deep in her pockets for a coin or two to buy a snack but as usual, they were empty, except for the ad promising addicts a cure.

The warm morning faded into a damp and chilly afternoon. Now she could no longer concentrate on her reading. She could only think of Adam who would be terribly drunk by now, long past the friendly stage and approaching his belligerent worst, when his speech slurred and his hands grew into fists, when he committed wrongs his mind would all too conveniently forget.

As the day grew old, the noise filtering from the tavern grew louder, men's voices mingling together and breaking loose in bursts. It would be warm in there, cozy with fires all about and liquid heat being poured from bottles and kegs down the lusty throats of men who talked and laughed while keeping women and hungry children waiting in the cold.

Jessy's bones ached. She set her books aside and stepped down to the street on shaking legs, cramped and cranky from sitting so long on a hard wooden bench on a chilly autumn day. She reached the tavern door but paused at the sign: Not for ladies.

Nor gentlemen, she thought grimly. Like an avenging angel, Jessy pushed through the tavern doors. Odors wafting out from within brought past and present together in sickening collision. *Father!* Memories of searching on Saturday nights, opening doors like this, looking for Father rushed into her mind. What had started as a rare occurrence became a weekly event, then daily, until her searching came to an end.

Through the smoky haze she could see the rough outlines of counters and tables littered with old bottles, dirty glasses, and the ashes and stubs of stale cigars. The combined stench made her choke. Where was her brother's face amid so many?

The bar keep snapped, "Can't you read? No ladies allowed. Goes for kids, too."

"I'm looking for my brother Adam."

"Hey, Adam! Adam Flint! Your sister's here lookin' for you!"

Conversations stopped. Heads turned. Jessy hoped the floor beneath her would open and swallow her.

"He's right here, darlin'," someone called.

She could see Adam, far back, trying to focus on her. He looked terribly drunk, worse than she had ever seen. She ran to him and whispered, "We ought to leave now for home. It'll be dark soon."

With his free hand he patted her arm clumsily. With his other he raised up his glass. Before she could take it from him, he stood up, drained it dry, and keeled over. Horrified and helpless, Jessy felt the floor shudder as he crashed down. For a moment, all activity within the tavern stopped. It was a long way down for the big man.

Jessy dropped down in the gloom. "Adam? Are you hurt? Say something!"

A few customers came close.

"Well, I don't believe it, the Man of Iron finally had one too many."

"Looks like you're here for the night, little lady."

"Can we carry him outside to the rig?" Jessy asked.

Two men tried but failed. It took four men to drag Adam outside. Drunk themselves, yet accustomed to the hard work of farming, they hoisted and squeezed Adam onto his wagon less like a fellow human and more like a side of beef. They pushed from behind, shoving the long frame head first against the tins and boxes purchased earlier that day, atop the six empty burlap bags still reeking of hog. Adam growled in pain.

Jessy winced. "Is he bleeding?"

"Nah. He'll sleep it off. Can you get home okay?"

"Certainly," Jessy answered with a confidence she didn't feel in the least. She took the reins. "Milo knows the way home as well as I do."

"Champion drinker if ever there was. Never saw a fella put it away quite like him."

You didn't know our father, she thought bitterly, snapping at the reins in the fast approaching twilight.

On the way home, Adam demanded she stop so often she considered leaving him by the roadside. It was dark now and they still had a mile and a half to go. The pines had turned black in the fading light. When he asked her to stop yet again so that he could relieve himself she ignored him.

From behind her came Adam's "Whoa, boy, Whoa!" His familiar, commanding voice brought Milo to a dead stop despite the fact that Jessy held the reins. Adam stumbled to the ground, cursing her, the world, and the Lord God Almighty.

While Adam stumbled to the bushes, Jessy yearned for home and a cozy fire, doing her best to ignore the crude noises he was making, his slurred threats and cursing. She covered her face in her hands, fighting away the truth she had avoided so long: *Adam is just like Father.* All the unhappiness of her parents flooded her heart and mind. The damp night air cut through Jessy. What could be taking so long?

"Adam?" When he didn't answer she scrambled down from her seat and groped along in the darkness. "Adam? Where are you?"

"Lemme alone, for godssake ..."

"It's for His sake I can't leave you alone," she said as she moved toward the direction of his moaning. "I was too young to help Father but maybe it's not to late to—" With heartfelt tenderness she reached out to him, saying gently, "Adam, let me help you." She groped for his arm. Her hand grazed the suede of his jacket.

Without warning he snapped around violently, swinging and hitting her in the face. She wailed in pain.

"Shuddup!" With both hands he caught Jessy around her throat.

He held on so tight she couldn't breathe, much less scream. Jessy fought for her life, scratching the hands that clutched her throat in a death grip. On that dark country road, Jessy could only wonder, *Where is God?*

❧ 13 ❧

A violent wave of nausea forced Adam down. He released his hold on Jessy. She fell to the ground, gasping for breath. Despite her pain, she ran for her life, down the road into the night. She stumbled forward, throat aching. From the throbbing pain, she knew her eye was turning black. No time to give in! Running nearly two miles down a dark country road proved to be one of the most difficult things Jessy had ever attempted. The landscape, familiar by day, seemed strange, shadowy, bizarre by the light of a crescent moon. Fallen leaves crunched underfoot. Night creatures rustled in the undergrowth. Horses neighed and pawed the meadows on both sides of the road. The thought of Adam catching up with her, finishing her off, and leaving her in the bushes for dead spurred her on with an endurance she never knew she had. With every step Jessy thought of Laurann rotting in the bushes where Adam must have left her. Now Jessy was convinced he was a monster, capable of anything.

She passed warmly lit houses of neighbors, decent families at home where the Flints would be if they had any sense. Forcing herself to plan ahead, Jessy thought things through, just as Adam would have advised. Before young David faced Goliath, he picked up five smooth stones. Jessy resolved not to face her raving brother barehanded. She would show this modern Philistine the error of his ways. Justice would be done.

When she heard the familiar babbling of the creek, she knew she had come home. Hurrying, knowing Adam could catch up with her any minute, and trembling with pain, she climbed the four porch steps and pushed through the unlocked door into the house. In total darkness she ran one hand along the wall until she came to the match holder. A few wooden matches spilled out onto the floor but she managed to grasp one and strike it. Quickly, she put her plan into action, lighting all the lamps she could find. She set them about the house, the porch, and the yard. Saturday night would soon be Sunday morning, the day of the Lord. She must be ready.

Jessy hauled Adam's entire supply of liquor bottles outside. She emptied the sideboard and dragged the crate from under his bed, the one he had just received direct from the Kentucky distillery. She searched his every hiding place, making sure she'd removed his entire supply. With a cool head and steady hand she emptied every quart, pint, and gallon on the ground. She discarded enough alcohol to keep Adam and his household in turmoil for months. There would be nothing alcoholic in the house for Adam and nowhere to buy any for soon it would be Sunday, the day God commanded be kept holy.

Only now did she seek relief from her pain: cold water from the pump for her face and throat and a few crackers for her empty stomach. Before she took a seat by the small fire, she loaded Adam's double-barreled shotgun and kept it close at hand. Then she extinguished all the lamps but one. Even as she rested, she kept her hands on the gun.

In the darkness she heard the rig approaching slowly up the drive, halting and moving, halting again. Adam had come home. He sounded terribly, terribly drunk. Jessy renewed her grip on the gun. She sat still as a rock, listening to him muttering orders to Milo. Adam's voice sounded strange, unnatural, more like a beast than a man. Something flashed and sparked deep inside her memory, an old fire she thought she had extinguished long ago. Where had she heard that fearful groaning before?

Now the spark burst into flame deep within her. She could no longer deny the truth: her father's viciousness prevented her, for a time, from believing that God is a loving father. Laban Flint was hateful to his own family—his wife, son, and daughter. Knowing their father had driven Adam away with his cruelty, that afterward he had regretted Jessy's own birth, she strained to banish the vivid images frolicking like demons inside her brain. Jessy realized that although she had put her father out of her mind, she had never truly forgiven him.

Quietly, breathlessly, she approached the window. She hid far back in the shadows, listening, holding the gun. Adam must have been feeling his way down from the rig. She heard the doors of the barn being opened, then Milo being led inside. After a long while she heard light footsteps in the yard, Adam moving on the ground across the drive. He was very close to her now. Only the porch and the wall she leaned against stood between them. She waited for him to climb four little steps and open the door that was never locked. Holding her breath, waiting in darkness, she wondered why he didn't come inside. She could feel her bones creaking within her from the strain of standing still so long, holding such a heavy gun. With every heartbeat the delicate, swollen tissue around her eye and throat throbbed painful reminders of Adam's brutality. Silently she sank to the floor, murmuring wordless passionate prayers up to God, the Heavenly Father of all, but never did she let go of the gun.

❦ 14 ❦

The early morning sun brought light but not warmth. Jessy wakened where she had waited for Adam to enter the house, but he never came through the door. Where was he on this strange Sunday? Across the township — the country — the world — the Living Body of Christ would be at worship, searching for the peace that passes all understanding. While the family of God sought His Word, Jessy Flint sought her brother. Outside she went, still holding the gun. Not far from the house, she found Adam Flint lying in the dirt.

Dust thou art, and unto dust shalt thou return.

Until this moment, Adam's appearance had never failed to impress her. Until now, Adam Flint had appeared more wondrous than the sky and stars above, for Adam, unlike inanimate things, had been created in the image of God Himself. Always, Jessy had been able to see the good in Adam. Until today. Adam Flint was, after all, a man of the flesh, gone far from God, with a man's ways and a man's needs, living for himself, by himself, and for all his toughness, plagued by the crippling weaknesses of man.

She approached with caution, coming within a few feet of him, this idol of millions, lying in the dirt. *Fallen from heaven, O Lucifer, son of the morning, cut down to the ground.* The void inside Adam that could only be filled by God was being drowned instead by alcohol — *just like Father.* History had repeated itself; lightning had struck the same family twice. Jessy tried to shake away the distant past but failed.

Adam looked dreadful, the wreck of a man on the brink of extinction. His lower jaw was swollen and purple, his hair and clothes encrusted with vomit. The body God had formed and infused with life and breath lay still as death. Was Adam dead? Had he gone to judgment, leaving her without a family but sparing her this morning's dreaded confrontation? Had time run out for Adam? Had he died without the blessings only Christ can offer the willing heart? Had he gone to eternity without salvation?

Jessy looked for signs of the life that is so precious, so fleeting. With an odd mixture of relief, pity, and dread she noticed the fingers of his right hand quivering in the dirt. Adam had the shakes from consuming so much liquor. *Thou art filled with shame for glory.*

She looked upward for solace, but this morning's strange gray sky loomed over her, devoid of beauty. The damp wind made her shiver. The faintest drops of moisture falling from above touched her cheeks and mingled with her tears.

"Dear Lord, You who raised Lazarus from the dead, You Who can do anything, will You raise my brother from his spiritual death? This pathetic creature is dead in spirit, dead to Your truth. He will surely come to ruin if he goes on like this much longer."

She gazed upward, waiting, hoping for an answer, but nothing happened, only the continued falling of a cold mist which grew more intense with each passing moment. She turned up her collar against the chill, then stepped across the yard and crouched under a tree where she could observe Adam but be hidden from him should he waken. Dead leaves swirled around her. The light rain turned to ice crystals that scraped her face and bare hands. She longed for shelter but knew she was safer out in the open where she could observe Adam. She reasoned that he wouldn't be able to remain supine much longer, the way the weather was worsening.

By now she knew the enemy well. There had been many mornings-after in which to observe him. How well she knew the pattern. Once Adam came to, he would crave a drink, a quick shot to steady his nerves, but his shaking would worsen and he would take another drink, continuing until he was insensible, violent, out of control, strong as a bull and capable of anything, including murder. But this morning would be different. She clutched the gun butt close to her chest.

He roused from his stupor. Shielding his face from the icy mist, he covered his eyes with one hand while the other probed his swollen jaw. He struggled to sit up, then looked around in a daze. He hardly noticed his wretched appearance. He didn't bother to glance at his jacket or vest. He didn't seem to care that the beautiful suede of which he had once been so proud had been ruined by his own filth. At the moment he had more urgent business. He rubbed his mouth and ran his tongue over his parched lips. Slowly he got to his feet and staggered toward the house.

He climbed the porch steps on unsteady legs. Soon he shook the house with his rage. Even though Jessy had expected as much, still she cringed to hear him thrashing about, ransacking drawers and cupboards, slamming doors from one end of the place to the other, his boots thundering across the bare wooden floors. He was calling her name with that bestial voice he had acquired in the night, no doubt due to the injuries he sustained in his fall at the tavern and when he was shoved like a slab of meat onto his own rig.

"But you won't remember that," she murmured. "You won't remember anything, not even trying to strangle me on the road last night. How many have you killed? You'd kill me right now if you could get your hands on me."

Coolly she got on one knee to steady herself with the heavy gun. Her father had taught her well. Adam would come running outside again any minute now. *Be sober, be vigilant; because your adversary the devil, as a roaring lion, walketh about, seeking whom he may devour.*

With clenched fists, Adam burst through the front door and down the steps. Scanning the yard with his wild hunter's eyes, he yelled, "Jessy, wherever you are, you're dead! You hear me?"

He stormed to the side of the house and hollered at the cellar doors, "You down there?" It was then he saw what she had done. He kicked the empty bottles in a fury. "Every stinkin' one! I'll tear your head off! Where are you?"

"Here I am," she said in a loud clear voice, "but I would have been dead on the road if you had finished strangling me last night."

Adam was about to charge at her, his fists clenched, but the sight of the gun changed his whole demeanor in an instant from raving child to crafty, wary adult. The hunter had become the hunted.

With his eyes fixed on the barrel, he relaxed his fists and opened his hands to show they were empty. He displayed them to her in an eloquent, mute gesture of helplessness, but they were shaking so much he forced them to his sides. He tried that smile of his that had always charmed, but this morning his lips and dimples failed him, encrusted as they were with old blood and vomit. He reached up to rub his mouth.

"Don't move! Keep your hands down."

"All right. Don't get excited." His swollen jaw trembled. "Let's be reasonable."

"You can't be reasonable, not when liquor's concerned. You nearly killed me last night and you'd finish me off right now if I didn't have this gun."

His green eyes flickered over her, coming to rest on her battered face. With one hand she pulled her collar open to reveal the bruises his fingers had made around her throat. "Look at what you did to me."

He shook his head lamely. "I don't remember."

"How convenient for you." She renewed her two-handed hold on the gun. "I remember every detail."

"All right, so I lost my head. I'm sorry! But you can't shoot a man in cold blood. Kill me and you'll spend the rest of your life in prison!"

"Everyone around here knows your reputation. They'd take one look at me and know I acted in self-defense. How many people have you killed?"

"I told you before, not one."

"Then two? Or maybe more?" Jessy cocked the trigger. "How many?"

"Put that gun down before..."

"Don't you dare come any closer or I'll shoot."

"You can't fool me. A nice little Christian wouldn't aim a loaded gun at her own brother."

Jessy aimed up and pulled the trigger. When broken branches and acorns dropped down over his head, he ducked. "You made your point!" he shouted. "Let's let bygones be bygones. I hurt you and I'm sorry. But right now, more than anythin' I need a drink! Look at my hands." He was close to tears, shaking worse than ever.

Jessy stiffened her backbone. "There's not a drop of liquor left in the house, and today being Sunday, the bars are closed. What you need instead of a drink is a nice long walk to jail. I'm going to walk you there at gunpoint, every step. Last night you would have strangled me if you hadn't been so sick from drink. My guess is you've tried the same thing before, at least twice. It's time justice was done."

"No, I swear." Adam, usually oblivious to pain, cradled his jaw with one hand. In truth he sounded as if he were in agony, but he faced Jessy squarely. Looking her straight in the eyes, he pleaded, "I never saw Lucy Meredith in my life. From what I hear, after her husband died she was always goin' off somewhere on the train, visitin' all around the country. There's no tellin' where she ended up but," he jerked his thumb at his chest, "it's for sure I never saw the woman in my life. And as for Laurann, I told you before, she left here one night and I never saw her again."

"I don't believe you. How can I? You can't even remember what you did last night and look at me. I'd be dead right now . . ."

"Put that gun down and let's go inside and talk."

"No." She steadied her aim on him. "I want the truth."

"I already told you." He held out a shaking hand. "I need a drink and I need it bad."

"What you need is to stop drinking forever. It's killing you. Can't you see what's happening? You're disgusting. Just look at yourself. You won't listen to anyone — not to the judge, to Bo, to me. What will it take before you see reason? If you had killed me last night you'd be in jail today waiting for your own execution!"

Adam's head hung down, motionless. "Do I stink as bad as I think I do?"

"Yes."

"Mind if I take this off?" He took off his jacket and let it drop.

Jessy watched him shiver from the cold and shake from drink. Adam was truly the most pathetic human being she had ever seen, save one. "When you drink you become just like Father."

Like an angry bull, Adam reared up his head and lunged for her despite the gun in her hands. "Don't you ever tell me that again!"

The sudden feeling, the anger and raw hurting in his voice, surprised her. Knowing she had struck a nerve, she pressed on. "You look like Father. When you drink, you smell like him and you talk like him and you get violent, just like him. I saw him push Mother down the stairs once when he was drunk. I was only four years old but I saw him do it. Mother wouldn't tell anyone. She wouldn't let me go for help. For a month she stayed inside, healing. She let him get away with violence but he kept on hurting her and me."

Although Adam cringed under her condemnation, Jessy knew that after last night she must not allow herself to feel sorry for him. This was her best chance — and her last — to make him see the error of his ways. "I can't understand why you drink something that makes you sick and dependent and so mean you hurt people who love you. You're no different from Father."

"I'm not like him." Adam was indignant now. "Never was, never will be. You're lyin'. Pa was a lot of things, but he wasn't a drunkard."

"Then he must have taken up the habit after you left home. Drink ruined him and his business and . . . and it *killed* him."

"What?" Adam looked at her in disbelief.

"Yes. It's true. I hate remembering what happened to him. It hurts . . . too . . . much." Jessy's voice dissolved into nothingness. There in the chilling mist of that vast Midwestern prairie, Jessy, age fourteen, had become nine years old again and it was summer. "All night I've been thinking about the last time I ever saw Father. Mother told me to forget what I had seen that day but I can't. I'll never forget what happened to him as long as I live.

"He had been missing a whole day and night. Mother and I went looking for him. We walked the hot city streets for hours, going from one bar to the next, asking if anyone had seen him. Mother's feet started to hurt so much we couldn't go on. She was ready to drop in the heat. We went home and waited but Father didn't come back. The next morning a policeman came for us. He took us to a street we didn't know, to an alley behind some shops. A crowd of people watched us. Mother didn't want me walking back there with her but I did. I let go of her hand and ran ahead. She called for me to come back but I wouldn't."

Jessy could still hear her mother's hard breathing and see the policeman holding the woman's arm to steady her. Jessy's body, a mourning vessel, was so deeply filled with sorrow that tears rose up, burning like acid in her eyes and throat. She looked at nothing. She was hardly aware of Adam or the silence hanging over them. She spoke slowly from her trance. Each of her words seemed weighted down. The images she dragged out from within her were not merely etched; they were engraved, emblazoned, indelibly printed for all time.

"The pavement was slippery, yet it hadn't rained. The shopkeepers threw garbage back there in the alley. Some of the trash cans had toppled over. It was so slippery, I fell down in the mire. I scraped my knees but I didn't notice, not until . . . after. Mother and the policeman came up behind me. I saw another man standing at the far end of the alley, looking down. There was Father, lying on his back, staring up. I thought he was playing a game so I looked up too but there was nothing to see except tenements, with laundry hanging out to dry. People stared at us from their windows and porches."

"When I got closer to Father I noticed a puddle of blood around his head. Till the day I die, I won't forget how he looked, but mostly I remember the flies. The policeman kept shooing the flies away but they kept going back to Father's face. Some landed on me. They crawled all over me — on my shoes and up my legs." With shoulders trembling, Jessy shooed away green-black flies from her face even now. "Mother called his name until the walls echoed all around us. 'Laban! Laban!' she screamed. She kept asking why. No one would tell her the answer. Strangers came and stared but they couldn't tell us why."

Jessy was silent a long while. When she brushed away a fly near her face, she slowly realized it was only the icy mist falling from the leaden gray sky. She felt too tired to keep holding the gun and too weak to try stopping Adam from taking it from her. When she let out a small sob, he put his hand on her shoulder.

"I never knew," was all he said.

The tears began to roll down her cheeks in earnest. "It isn't the kind of story anyone wants to tell or hear, but the same thing will happen to you if you don't stop drinking, and you're all the family I have left in this world. How do you think it makes me feel to see you destroying yourself?"

Adam set down the gun and pulled her close. "My little sister. Everythin's goin' to be all right. I promise." He looked into her eyes with a new tenderness. "I'll never drink again. I promise you I never will. I know I'm poisonin' myself slow but sure. I gotta stop. I just never knew how, or when, but I can't go on like this. You know what the first thing was I thought of this mornin'? Lyin' in the dirt feelin' like my jaw was broken, and all I could think about was gettin' another drink. It never stops — one drink leads to another, but I never have any peace. When I get drunk, there's a blank, a dead space, but that ain't peace. For too long I been outa control and I don't like it. I wouldn't blame you if you killed me. Hey, now who's shakin'?" He studied her injured face. "I musta been crazy. Can you forgive me?"

Jessy nodded with enthusiasm. "Of course."

"That's my girl. Let's get inside." Still holding her, he led her toward the house.

"Adam, if you quit drinking, I promise I'll never tell anyone what happened last night on the road, not as long as I live."

"It's a deal — best one anyone ever offered me."

Jessy studied her bruised face and throat in the mirror. "It's good that the Gaads have gone upstate to visit friends. They'll never know this happened." She turned from the mirror. "And Adam, I want you to know I never wanted to hurt you with that gun. I just didn't want you to kill me. Are you mad at me?"

"Mad? Course not!" Adam gave her a reassuring hug. "You got courage. You stood up to Adam Flint. There's not many people on the face of this earth'd dare do that. I'm proud of you."

Jessy knew her brother must have been in terrible pain — physical, mental, and spiritual. He had sunk as low as a man could but perhaps now he could start to climb back up.

While he washed up and made coffee, Jessy put a few logs on the fire, but the stamina that had carried her this far had vanished like smoke. The fury of Saturday night and the confrontation of Sunday morning had caught up with her at last. As she warmed herself, she dug her hands into the pockets of her skirt. She felt a piece of paper in one of them.

"Water's hot. Want some tea?"

"Yes, please. Let me help you."

As she went to his side, she pulled the paper from her pocket. *Beat the Liquor Habit*... If Adam kept his promises, then Jessy had felled Goliath without a stone, without a bullet, without money, and without drugs. Rather she had triumphed with the help of the unseen God. She was convinced God had prevented disaster on the road last night and then again this morning. Jessy took comfort knowing their father's death, as tragic and unnecessary as it was, hadn't been entirely in vain.

Overwhelmed by God's mercy, she went back to the fireplace and leaned against the mantle. There, she looked from her parents' wedding portrait to Adam's steadily ticking clock. On that Sunday morning more than ever before in her young life, Jessy was mindful of her past, present, and future, all of which were in the hands of God. She buried her head in her arms. "Heavenly Father, thank You for this miracle, for Your peace, Your love. Thank You for Adam, my brother. Please give him the strength and the grace to keep the promises he made today. And thank You for being loving and true, not like our earthly father who failed us both. There is no use praying for the dead, but please help me forgive my father. I can't without Your help."

As a new peace calmed her heart, the peace only God could give, she sipped her tea, thinking God's promises are true: *But they that wait upon the Lord shall renew their strength; they shall mount up with wings as eagles; they shall run, and not be weary; and they shall walk, and not faint.*

Adam interrupted her contemplation. "Ice'll ease the swellin' of that shiner." Before he went to the ice house, he looked at her face closely, turning her head into the light. "Boy, am I sorry."

She smiled shyly. "Oh, I'll be all right."

Still, Adam was furious with himself. "If I ever so much as *look* at liquor again you say to me, 'Shiner.' Hear me?"

"Yes sir," Jessy said with a little grin. "Shiner." She sipped on her tea. "Today is a great day. A new beginning."

Inwardly, she knew her joy would not be complete until Adam followed Christ and claimed His promises in faith. Although Jessy longed with all her heart for Adam's conversion, she couldn't imagine it coming to pass without a miracle. But this morning, she believed in miracles more than ever.

❦ 15 ❦

"From Bo," Adam said, showing Jessy the letter he had just pulled out of his mailbox. "Fool got *married* over Christmas. They planned on comin' here for a visit but she's expectin' already. Man gets married, everythin' changes." Adam sounded miserable.

"So *this* was his big emergency in Florida!" Jessy took the letter and read the joyous message from the happy couple. Snow was falling, big sloppy wet flakes. She had to protect the ink from running off the pages. "We'll send our congratulations at once."

"Hmp!" Adam was thumbing through the rest of his mail and glancing at the latest seed catalog. While snow fell over him, he became fully absorbed in pictures of luscious tomatoes, and sunflowers heavy with seed, their faces turned toward a blazing sun.

Jessy smiled, seeing a connection between the two pieces of mail. Spring would surely follow this long winter and with it would come a great harvest. Bo married, and soon to be a father! Today had been hard on Adam. News of all sorts, not only Bo's letter, had bombarded his defenses.

They had just come back from town where Adam had been forced to listen to the barber, Shakes, talk nonstop about the weather, hog futures, and embezzlement at the county level. Jessy had read a magazine until the barber's monologue penetrated her concentration. She watched Adam sink into the lather of a professional shave, his face swathed in hot towels, steam rising from them in torrents, his blunt nose looming above white fluff. Just as he seemed to doze, his sharp green eyes snapped open. Shakes had struck a nerve.

"Should of seen the spread they gave June and Jim. Too bad you missed the weddin'."

Adam looked disgusted. "I'll never stick *my* neck in a noose."

Shakes, grinning openly, maneuvered his gleaming razor along the sculpted curves of Adam's throat. "D'you know Chip Wilson's gettin' married? Oh, and Tom Lester proposed to Amy Price."

"Amy Price? That school marm?" No matter how much Adam may have disliked Tom, he disliked marriage more. "Poor Tom."

"Now, marriage ain't so bad, once a body gets used to it."

"Like castor oil?"

"You'll see, one of these days. Why, you'll fall for some little beauty somewheres and it'll all happen so fast you won't know what hit you."

"Not me. I'm no fool."

Once Adam was properly shaved and anointed, the barber cranked up the chair to begin the haircut. Thick brown curls fell in profusion along the rim of the chair and over the barber's shoes.

"You got the hair of Samson himself! Didja hear Jim Farnsworth died?"

Adam's eyebrows shot up. "What of?"

"Tree he was cuttin' down fell on him. Crushed him to death. Didn't find him till yesterday. Livin' alone like that. Should of gone to stay with his son and daughter-in-law in Eider, but he was too stubborn."

This news hit home. Yesterday Adam and Jessy had been cutting down trees, pines and a half-rotted monster hardwood that didn't fall quite as Adam intended. He and Jessy had barely escaped disaster. Adam was always teaching her things, giving her practical advice about the work they did together — the best way to handle an ax, how to notch a tree so it would fall away from you, but he had warned her, "No matter how careful you are, trees can twist as they go down. You never know how they'll land."

Shakes wasn't finished. "Hear about Luke Cratchworth? Lost his footin' patchin' the roof. Fell thirty feet onto a hay rake; they say he'll never walk again, if he lives." The barber snipped his scissors in the air for emphasis. "That family's had it hard. Fall before last his brother Bill got shot deer huntin'. This summer his cousin Duane Tubbs got killed by lightnin'. Sittin' in a boat, fishin', mindin' his own business. Never knew what hit him."

"I heard. No guarantees in life," muttered Adam. "None whatever."

Despite Adam's casual tone, as soon as he paid Shakes, he made an unscheduled trip down Main Street through the falling snow. Jessy had run to keep up with him. When he made a sudden turn and started banging on a door, Jessy noticed the sign: George Webb, Attorney-at-Law.

The lawyer didn't open immediately. Instead he looked through the glass at Adam. "What do *you* want?"

"Business." Adam entered like royalty, Jessy lagging behind, dutifully scraping her boots before stepping inside. Adam opened his jacket and removed his wide felt hat. He flicked snow off in all directions.

The attorney eyed him up and down with annoyance. The contrast between the two men couldn't have been more pronounced. How odd, Jessy thought, to see a man dressed in better-than-Sunday best on no special day at all. The lawyer's glasses were framed, not in iron like most of the people living in and around Bethel, but real gold like his wedding band. His gray hair was thinning to baldness. He puffed on his pipe, but it must have gone out, for Jessy could see no smoke. The man's solid, stately bearing held her in marvelous fascination.

His office was no less striking. The walls were lined with mahogany bookcases crammed with leather-bound volumes, their enigmatic titles embossed in gold: torts, contracts, Blackstone, probate. Certificates, family portraits, and hunting scenes adorned the papered walls and oriental rugs the polished hardwood floors. Bottle green curtains hung across the lower half of the broad bay windows, allowing light from above but protecting the attorney's visitors and work from the eyes of casual passersby. An old fire snapped and sparkled, its glow framed and reflected in rich maroon tiles and a polished cherry mantle. The pleasant odors of hickory and wood oil clashed with Adam's perpetual scent of earth and hog.

Without being asked, Adam took a seat. He folded one long, well muscled leg over the other into a broad figure four and, resting his elbows on the arms of the leather chair, set the tips of his fingers together. Over the resulting steeple, Adam fixed his green eyes on the lawyer. "Ever since Duane Tubbs got killed, I been thinkin' to have me a will."

"Well, I'll be! Adam Flint has finally realized he is mortal."

Adam eyed the man coldly. "You don't like me and I don't like you but you're the only lawyer in town and I don't see why I should have to ride to Zinnithia just for a will." To Jessy he snapped, "Sit down. This will take awhile."

Jessy sat, still wrapped for the storm raging beyond the glass. The attorney, sighing deeply, knocked the ash from his pipe and set it down amid a litter of papers, seals, stamps, and open books. "Come on, Mrs. Cat, let me have my note pad." A cloud of angora flopped out of the way, but not without casting a sultry glance toward Webb.

Someone was knocking on the door. Before Webb could answer, a young woman entered in a swirling gust of snow. Jessy recognized her at once. She was the gorgeous girl with the dazzling smile and azure eyes who had spoken to her once from beneath a parasol. Today she wore a blue velvet cape sprinkled with snowflakes. The generous hood that framed her face was lined with white fur. She began talking at once. "Daddy, you'll never guess what!"

Adam, looking as if he had been shot, managed to stand and nod to Suzanna Webb.

"Please sit down, Mr. Flint. I'm so sorry to interrupt. I didn't realize you were in the midst of a consultation. My news can wait, Daddy."

"Are you sure?"

"Of course. It's nothing, really, Daddy..."

George Webb smiled. "I'll be home about six."

"All right, Daddy." Though Suzanna spoke to her father her last glance was for Adam. Her expression appeared warm enough to melt snow.

Looking uncomfortable, Adam resumed his seat, squirming around, folding and refolding his legs. Licking his lips, he resteepled his fingers. His green eyes bore down on the lawyer. "As I started to say, if somethin' happened to me, my sister wouldn't have no family left."

The lawyer nodded. "Do you have a guardian in mind?"

"The Gaads've said they'd take her in."

"And I suppose you'd want your sister to be sole heir of your estate."

Adam smiled slyly. "Or what's left of it after all the bills are paid."

Mr. Webb asked a few more questions and then tossed his pen down. "All right, Mr. Flint, I'll draw up the papers in the next few days. You can stop by to sign them whenever you're back in town."

On their way home through the falling snow, Adam hardly spoke a word, except to tell Jessy, "Just don't get the idea you own the place... I ain't dead yet."

"No, sir," Jessy said, feeling uneasy at the thought. Lightning, falling off a roof—life was fraught with peril. She wanted to ask about the obvious and apparently deep-seated animosity between the attorney and her brother, but she kept that to herself, knowing that Adam had probably offended everybody in Bethel Township at one time or another.

ȭ ȭ ȭ

Two weeks later, Adam signed his will, with the town's dentist and a young law clerk serving as witnesses. George Webb told Adam, "In the event you marry, this will would of course be invalidated."

Adam's face grew strangely wistful, the rugged lines of it softening. Swallowing hard, he nodded to show that he had heard the attorney. As he stuffed his copy of the will inside his thick wool jacket, he asked, "How much I owe you?"

"Twelve dollars."

Jessy watched Adam pay the man in cash, pulling rumpled bills out of his pocket. On their way out the door Adam caught sight of Suzanna coming toward her father's office, her cape whipping up violently around her in a blustery wind. Adam did everything he could to avoid running into her. The girl held her ground in the gale, looking at the Flints as they rode off.

Once they were well on their way home, Jessy asked, "Isn't Suzanna Webb the one the peddler was telling us about last spring? Didn't she call off her wedding to that Senator's son?"

"Yeah."

"She was the one who asked me about you that time." While Jessy picked her next words, she kept her eyes on Adam's jaw. "I think she likes you."

Just as Jessy had thought, Adam's jaw tightened visibly. "When I first moved here, I wanted her more than I ever wanted anythin' or anyone in my life. Her father said he'd shoot me if I ever got within fifty yards of her." Adam appeared furious with himself. "It was after I showed up at her place one night drunk as a skunk. No wonder the old man took offense. I made a complete fool of myself. She was a minor then, too. I really did it, screamin' outside her window at two in the mornin'."

"But you don't act like that anymore, not since you quit drinking."

"Try tellin' old man Webb that."

"You still like her, don't you? And she likes you."

Adam avoided her eyes but he couldn't hide the dimple in his cheek. So it was true. Suzanna Webb had turned down every suitor because she was in love with Adam Flint. "You know what Mother used to say."

"What, 'Don't act like a jerk?'"

"No!" Jessy laughed. "'If two people were meant for one another, God would shake the world to get them together.'"

"He ain't goin' through all that bother for me."

"Probably not," Jessy said wryly. "But He might for Suzanna Webb."

❧   ❧   ❧

It was March when Adam decided to replace the wooden doors, jambs, lintel, and some of the stairs that led down into the cellar. It was Jessy's lot to hand him tools. Adam had been making so much noise wrenching out old nails and ripping apart rotting wood, neither heard the visitor approach, a man on horseback dressed in black.

Without pausing in his work, Adam said, "Lemme guess. Another new minister?"

"Yes, sir. Avery's the name, from the Church of Bethel." In vain the man extended his right hand to Adam. "Came to invite you to a barn raising."

Adam paused to spit. "Who for?"

"The Eberharts. Lost nearly everything in a fire a couple of weeks ago—barn, house, livestock. Neighbors have put up a new house, but they can't put up the barn without a community meet. If the weather holds these next few days, we plan to make a weekend of it. Work right through, hold Sunday prayer service out there instead of at church. Ox roast on Saturday. Twenty-six families have agreed to help."

Adam said nothing. Jessy could see his tongue working around inside his mouth. When she could no longer stand the silence, she blurted out, "I'll help, if my brother says it's all right for me to go."

"That would be splendid, Miss Flint. We'd be grateful for your presence. And here's something for you." The minister reached into a saddlebag and handed her a book. "I ordered enough for all the young people in our community."

The Shepherd Calls His Flock. Jessy set down the hammer she had been holding to examine the beautiful little volume. "It looks wonderful."

"Give it back, Jessy."

"It's free, Mr. Flint."

Adam eyed the reverend sharply. "One thing I've learned, nothin's free in this life, 'specially gifts from preachers. Give it back, Jessy."

With great reluctance, she did what Adam told her. "Thanks all the same," she said softly, her face burning with shame.

"If the Eberharts need a carpenter, fine. But otherwise you're wastin' your time."

"I appreciate your feelings, Mr. Flint. And I am glad to know you'll help a family in need. God will bless you for it." The minister mounted his horse quickly and easily. He was halfway down the drive when he called out, "See you both Saturday if the weather holds."

Adam wasn't listening. He rummaged around looking for something. "What are *you* lookin' at, sister? Find me that nail claw."

"How could you be so . . ."

"I said, find me that nail claw. You deaf?"

Jessy searched a pile of tools and rotted lumber. "Is this it?"

Adam snapped it out of her hands without a word.

She watched him working with his back to her, his muscles straining, tearing wood apart and breaking it down with his hands at a furious pace, tossing old lumber in her direction, demanding this, that, and the other tool. Jessy winced at the uproar he was making. She stood frozen, studying him from the landing. His knuckles were scraped and bleeding, the palms and fingers scratched and torn. He slowed every now and then to wipe his hands on his faded brown cord trousers. He finally paused to look at her. "You gonna stand there all day like a dummy?"

"Maybe."

"Maybe you'd like a whippin' too."

"What'd I do?"

"Nothin'. That's just the trouble. Either make yourself useful out here or get in the house and scrub floors. Only quit starin' at me like I was some kind of freak on parade."

"I'm sorry. Do you want the medicine kit?"

"What for?"

"Your hands."

With a snort he turned away. "Think I'm a baby like you?"

"Adam."

He turned back full of anger. "What is it now? I'm gonna waste the bloody weekend givin' free labor. What more do you want?"

"Courtesy."

Adam showed her a tightly clenched fist. "How's this?"

"You're impossible."

"You only just figured that out?"

"You know what your trouble is?"

"As a matter of fact I do—a whinin' kid that better mind her own business unless she wants her hide tanned. You got dinner ready?"

"When have I had time? I've been out here helping you all day."

"Then get inside before I throw somethin' at you."

Jessy ran inside, not waiting for him to make good his threat. As she worked in the kitchen she heard Adam's wrenching and pounding about in the cellar beneath her, as if it were some private hell where he was being driven by demons. Why, she wondered, perhaps because of a guilty conscience? Adam Flint had sinned mightily against God and humanity. Guilt was robbing him of peace. After all the scenes he had made over the years, how could he face the community? Adam had stopped drinking, but he couldn't erase his past. He blustered and stormed, putting up a front, keeping people away from him.

When it grew too dark to work outside, Adam flung open the front door with a force that startled her. As he breezed through the house to the washroom, flinging off his jacket and shirt, he demanded hot water. She inched toward the basin with the kettle, then backed off to watch him add cool water from the pitcher. She stood at a distance, as he bent over to wash his hands and face, droplets falling into the basin from the big blunt nose and curling locks.

"What're you starin' at?" Adam threw the soap down with such force it spun around the dish and sailed off into space. "Supper ready?"

"Yes sir."

"Well, put it on the table!"

Jessy didn't move. He seemed surprised to see her still standing by the doorway watching him dry his face. "What's come over you today?"

"People would love you, if you would let them. That minister . . ."

"That minister wouldn't come near me if he knew all I'd done."

"I don't think that's true at all. He's a Christian. Christians forgive. God forgives. And what God forgives, God *forgets*."

Jessy studied his face, his eyes, hoping the bitterness would be replaced with peace. But the hardness about him remained. Jessy spoke more to the heavy kettle in her hands than to him. "Dinner's ready for you if you're ready for it."

"I'm ready. I thought I made that plain."

Jessy prepared the table, making sure the linens were immaculate, setting out everything he could possibly ask for in a valiant effort to please. When he sat at his place she put an old but well-polished ladle and brimming tureen before him. She was so preoccupied with ensuring that everything was in place she had to be told to sit down. She kept her head bowed while he filled her plate and set it at her place. Then he filled his own. While waiting for him to begin eating, she said grace inwardly, her eyes shut tight. Before she finished, Adam began talking.

"First thing tomorrow you'll start haulin' away them rotted timbers."

"Yes sir."

"Stack 'em by the woodpile."

"Yes sir."

"When's the last time you swept out the fireplace?"

"Saturday."

"Needs doin' again."

"Yes sir."

"When did you shovel out the hog house?"

"Tuesday. I think Sheba's . . . " Jessy blushed violently.

Adam smiled. "Yeah, she is. Sheba's a good mother. Dependable every spring. You're gettin' to know somethin' about hogs."

Jessy nodded, pleased with herself. She was getting rather powerful too, in a young-womanly way. "I've grown four inches over the last year."

"You eat good, better 'n you used to."

"It's easy to work up an appetite around here," she said with a smile. Relieved his mood had lifted, she said, "I'm sorry if I upset you today. I didn't mean to. I hope you're not still mad."

Adam shrugged his big shoulders. "I wasn't mad at you."

Jessy took him to mean that he was mad at himself. She felt this was so, even if the Man of Iron would probably prefer to die rather than admit such a thing. "Know what tomorrow is?"

Adam paused in his chewing. "Groundhog Day?"

"That was a month ago! Guess again."

"Thursday." Adam's face radiated a perfect blend of humor and sarcasm.

"Tomorrow I will have been here a whole year!"

"Seems longer." His bemused expression hadn't changed. "Toss me them rolls."

Jessy handed him the basket. "Who are the Eberharts?"

"Don't know 'em but I seen 'em around. Gimme the butter."

"What do they look like?"

"A buncha kids, six or seven of em, half grown, all redheads."

"Oh, I think I know who you mean." Jessy felt sorry for them. "Is it all right if I bake some extra bread for them?" When Adam continued eating without answering, she asked, "Have you ever raised a barn before?"

"Coupla times."

"How's it done?"

"You'll see." He stared at the cupboard, the one that once served as his liquor cabinet. He knew she was looking at him. "I know, I know. Shiner!"

It had been six months since Adam had taken a drink. He clenched one battered hand into a fist and cupped it inside the other. Jessy had the uneasy feeling that before the weekend was over, she'd see more raised than a barn.

These last six months had not been easy for Adam, as he struggled to overcome his desire for drink. Evenings were hardest. That night he went so far as to go to the empty cabinet. He stood there, looking from it to her. Jessy, standing in the kitchen, didn't face her brother empty-hearted, empty-headed, or empty-handed.

"This afternoon I found this tin of cocoa powder on the top shelf of the cupboard. There's a recipe for hot chocolate on the label. Maybe after I do the dishes we could have some? And maybe popcorn, too?"

Adam went to the stove and took the tin from her. "Forgot I had this."

"After Mother lost the house she never had money for chocolate. Is it all right if we use it?"

"Sure, sure." He took the milk and sugar she had set out and began mixing and stirring everything together in a pan.

"I remember a long time ago having hot chocolate after a day of ice skating and building snowmen! What a wonderful day that was!" As she washed the dishes, she asked, "What was the most perfect day you ever spent, the one you'd do all over again if you could?" When he had no answer she asked, "Well, if you could spend a perfect day, what would you do?"

"How do you come up with these questions anyway?"

"Oh, I don't know. I just like to have something to look forward to. To hope for." As Jessy set out two mugs, she said, "Mmmm, that smells delicious!" She rattled around looking for the canister of dried corn kernels they had grown in their own garden.

Adam filled the mugs and took them near the hearth. While he built up the fire, Jessy got out the corn popper, a lidded metal box poked through with holes and fitted with a long handle. In it she put a small batch of kernels.

"Careful, or you'll burn it like last time," Adam chided gently, taking the popper from her and shaking it deftly over the blaze. Soon the kernels were exploding nicely.

"Thank you, Adam," she said as she took off her apron and sat beside him. "So what would you do on your perfect day?"

Adam emptied the fluffy popcorn into the bowl Jessy had set out and began munching. "Oh, I guess a perfect day'd be one spent with the woman I love, a woman who loves me and would be true to me. Maybe we'd go on a long drive and sightsee and have a picnic—fried chicken— and we'd make each other laugh a lot. Someone I could be true to. An impossible dream!"

"No, it isn't!" Jessy sipped her cocoa, savoring its richness. "I'll hope and pray your best dreams come true."

Looking as if he hardly believed her fanciful notion, still he enjoyed the snacks and the fire. Soon he began whittling, saying, "I'd better get started makin' my share of pegs for that barn. Can't use nails. They'd rust."

"I never thought of that." She said, watching his hands at work, "You know, if I ever needed a new barn, you'd be the first person I'd ask for help. You must be the best carpenter in the whole county!"

"I doubt that!"

"I don't!" Jessy glanced at the duck decoy he had made over the last few months, looking so real on the mantle. "Why, you're an artist in wood! That bird is so real it might quack! I think the Eberharts will be fortunate to have your help."

Adam formed one peg after another, rapidly tossing them into the crate by his chair. "When I was in the circus, I tried carving a hobbyhorse for the merry-go-round. Did I ever tell you that story?"

"No," said Jessy, fascinated. "What did it look like?"

As Adam launched into one of his fond memories, Jessy inwardly noted that he appeared to have forgotten entirely about the empty liquor cabinet. Listening to him with rapt attention, she happily finished off the bowl of popcorn. With a grateful heart, she knew her brother was gradually changing for the better.

❧ 16 ❧

Adam and Jessy arrived at the Eberharts' just after eight in the morning. There must have been forty men with their families there already—small children playing, older ones turning sides of beef on roasting spits, women of all ages tending open fires, preparing vats of gravy and vegetables for the noon meal. After a long winter of isolation, Jessy thrilled to see so many people gathered together in one place.

Adam hauled his tools, tackle, ropes, and a sack of wooden pegs off his rig and walked across the fire-blackened earth to join the men who were already laboring on the foundation of the new barn. They were laying wooden girts across a vast bedding of stone and mortar sixty feet wide and ninety-six feet long. Jessy heard Adam whistle at the imposing dimensions of the barn to be.

"Doors'll be twenty-two feet high," the Master Carpenter explained, "for loading in hay. And a gambrel roof. For extra stability, every beam will be doubly supported from below."

Jessy admired the blueprints, a maze of triangles formed by uprights, verticles, and bracing. The stark beauty of the design impressed her. Adam, tracing lines on the plan with a forefinger, explained how the gridwork they would raise would support the loft and roof. "We'll put these bents together on the ground first, eight of 'em, and then raise 'em into place with ropes and pikes. Sheer manpower! See that?" Adam pointed to the open air above the foundation. "By sundown that space will be filled with barn. You watch. See that lumber?"

Jessy looked at the massive piles of wood. They meant nothing to her heaped on the ground, hundreds of solid oak timbers, each one numbered for ready assembly, had already been cut to be dovetailed into one another without a need for nails. For other parts of the structure, Adam and the other men had brought along the wooden pegs they had made to use instead of nails which would rust and disintegrate. A thousand wooden pegs lay heaped on the ground.

"See that lumber?" Adam tapped again at the architectural diagram. "Every piece has a place in this plan." With that he left her to join the other men in the day's work.

Once the timbers had been laid across the barn floor, the teamwork of raising bents began. As the first bent went up, the only comparable experience in Jessy's mind was Bible illustrations she had seen of Roman soldiers hoisting up the cross of Jesus from the ground with ropes and setting the base into a waiting hole with what she imagined was a deadly thud.

In raising the barn, a dozen men rode on the bents while twenty more strained with ropes to haul up the framework, riders and all. Against the bent stood more men armed with pikes, spiky poles twenty feet long. When the Master Carpenter gave the order, every man worked in unison. As the riders were raised, they lowered the pikes one at a time against the bent. Once the bent was upright, other men on the ground steadied it with ropes and poles, setting each upright squarely into the mortises of floor timbers. The second bent was raised and connected to the first by means of girts, braces, and pegs. The sound of mallets was deafening.

The whole morning was taken up with raising and fastening bents. Jessy watched in awe as men pieced together the seemingly meaningless piles of wood into a perfectly sound structure fit for man and beast.

Adam moved nimbly up and across the spidery framework, often twenty or thirty feet above the ground and then even higher once the horizontal plate was erected across the bents. This plate would bear the heels of the roof rafters which were being cut and neatly stacked on the ground.

"Your brother sure has changed since you came along."

With both hands full of clean towels, Jessy turned from the spectacle to regard the two young women she had often seen in Bethel. "Do you think so?"

One girl answered, "He doesn't drink anymore. Doesn't swear. Doesn't fight."

The other sighed, "And he's better looking than ever, too."

"Don't tell him we said anything, promise?"

Before she could respond, Jessy caught sight of Suzanna Webb in the distance, fluttering a big table cloth over a picnic table which women soon covered with pies and cakes. The women moved on to the next table, spreading out another cloth and setting out more food.

Reverend Avery approached, looking flushed and weary from the morning's work. When Jessy saw him she felt tongue-tied and embarrassed, but to her surprise, Adam joined the minister where all the men were washing for the meal. Jessy overheard the men talking as she set out towels for them.

"You are a fine carpenter," Avery said to Adam. "It's always a pleasure to see an expert at work."

"Say, about the other day, don't take what I said personally," Adam said. "It's just that as far as religion goes, I got my fill a long time ago."

Before the minister could respond, one of the men asked if he would say the blessing. For the first and last time all day there was a moment of silence followed by the minister's words of grace over the vast meal and congregation. The minister gave thanks for all who had helped a needy family, for the good weather, for the bountiful food.

Out in the yard temporary tables had been set up where the men could eat the lavish meal, their only payment for a hard day's labor. From where they sat, they could see the barn, a testimony to careful planning and teamwork, a monument to man's ability and reason.

One of the men near the minister said, "Look at what we're building, so beautiful and useful, and all from what looked to be a disorganized pile of lumber."

The minister smiled and nodded. "Yes, the plan of a Master Carpenter. And there's a Master Builder at work in our world, too. Life has a plan, a purpose. And we are all a part of God's plan. Think I'll try a sermon on that theme, Roger, thank you."

The day's work continued until the great wooden skeleton stood in the landscape. The following day, the roof would be shingled and the exterior painted bright red. Toward twilight, Jessy caught up with Adam as he was gathering his tools.

"Adam, do you suppose we can stay?"

He looked reluctant but also bone-weary. "Might as well. I'm too tired to make the trip home tonight and back here again tomorrow mornin'."

One of the organizers overheard him. "Plenty of room at Thompson's place, just across the road. It's okay to leave your rig here with the others. The Eberhart boys will see to your horse. Thompsons got a fine new barn themselves — can hold thirty-five people easy, and the band."

"Band?" Adam questioned sourly.

"Saturday night party for everyone."

"Music? Really?" Jessy tingled with delight.

"I'm gettin' some sleep."

"Elkhart Boys'll make enough noise to wake the dead."

"They won't disturb me," Adam said as they started with a small crowd in the direction of the Thompson place.

On the way, Jessy nudged Adam. Suzanna Webb ran up the road to embrace a newcomer. Adam's sharp green eyes burned at the sight of her hugging a man.

"Who's that?" Jessy wondered.

Adam squared his shoulders and clenched his teeth in anger.

"Hey, Jeff!" someone shouted. The man with Suzanna responded with a wave of his hand.

Two of the girls who had befriended Jessy during the day closed up behind the Flints as they walked toward the Thompsons'. "Who's that Jeff fellow over there?" Jessy asked them in a hush.

"Jeffrey Webb, Suzanna's brother. Teaches seminary in Pine Bluff. He must have come home especially to help the Eberharts."

Jessy smiled happily. So Suzanna hadn't been hugging her boyfriend after all. She quietly passed on the information to Adam who nodded coolly. Still, Jessy noticed how he appeared to relax at this news.

Soon thirty or more people were packed into the Thompson barn, listening to music, eating fried chicken, and all talking and laughing at once. At nightfall the dancing began. While the band took a break, Jessy caught sight of her brother. Far from the exhausted wreck he had appeared to be before supper, he stood amid a lively group that included Suzanna Webb. Every now and then Jessy could hear a rare and joyous sound, Adam's distinctive, rich rumbling laughter rising above the music and general merriment. Later still she noticed couples drifting away between sets, leaving the barn for fresh air. Jessy thought she saw Adam Flint disappearing in the moonlight with Suzanna.

For weeks afterward, Adam wasn't quite the same. Jessy noticed that he ate only two helpings of dinner instead of his usual three or four. "Spring fever?" she ventured. Adam wouldn't answer.

Stranger still, Adam Flint, a resolute hog farmer, began visiting dairy farms and invested a small fortune in sound young heifers which he expected Jessy to tend. The young females, prize Ayrshires, had pretty faces and fine red and white coats. Jessy suspected Adam was up to something.

"Who's going to milk these cows?" she asked him.

"Who do you think? With you around to do the work dawn to dark, I can get into the dairy business."

"What about the hogs?"

"You can take care of them too. What else you got to do?" Meanwhile, Adam, who had been such a recluse, and who until now had seldom ventured off without her, took advantage of any pretense to go off alone to grange meetings, horse shows, auctions, political rallies and the like, always dressed in casual but beautifully tailored clothes. He constantly demanded that Jessy iron his best shirts, silk ties, and vests. The miracle was that he always returned sober.

Right after supper on a beautiful June evening she watched him preen himself before the mirror.

"Going somewhere again?"

"Uh-huh. Poetry reading at the Gables."

"*Poetry*? You?" Jessy laughed. "Adam Flint's got a girl!"

"I should be back by ten. And no, I don't have a girl. At least not officially. Don't wanna get myself shot by some enraged father, you know."

"Oh, Adam, not Suzanna Webb?"

"Ssssh. You brush my hat?"

Jessy handed him his new felt. "Honestly, Adam."

"What? I haven't done a thing wrong."

"Lately."

"Lately," he nodded, setting the cream-colored hat over his shining curls. His green eyes sparkled merrily.

Jessy was worried. Adam could all too easily get himself shot. For so long she had prayed that something good would happen to Adam. She hoped God's hand was on Adam now, guiding his path.

That night, Adam returned, not at ten but at midnight. He rapped on Jessy's door, rousing her from sleep to announce, "I'm gettin' married. Elopin' next week, when George Webb leaves town on business."

Half awake, Jessy groaned, "You're marrying Suzanna Webb?"

"That's right. She never wanted anyone else for her husband but me!" said Adam proudly. "Turned down a dozen suitors, waitin' for me to sober up."

Jessy thought of the pampered darling. "Suzanna Webb living *here*?"

"She loves me and I love her."

"What about her father?"

"We'll be married before he knows anythin' about it. Course, I'd rather marry her with his blessin', but she says he'll never go for it."

"Mr. Webb doesn't know?"

"Nope. Neither does her mother. Got the license already, see?" Adam showed it to her. It had been issued in the next county. "Got a preacher lined up to do the honors, all nice and legal."

"I hope you know what you're doing."

"Sure I do. And my will's all in order in case Webb goes on a rampage."

In the lamplight, Jessy shivered for his mortal soul.

"A man can die but once," he said, smiling happily.

But after that, the judgment. Jessy was worried.

❧   ❧   ❧

Wearing her new dress, Jessy stood before Adam. He had insisted she order it from the mail-order house in Chicago. It was shimmering pink taffeta trimmed generously with Belgian lace. Her new high-topped boots were made from the finest kid with small French heels. What a joyous time she'd had when Adam let her select whatever she wanted from the wish book. He had shunned her frugality, insisting that she order the prettiest dress of all. He explained that because he wasn't buying liquor he could well afford the best for her. Gratefully she had accepted.

Adam looked her over with such care she proclaimed, "Honestly, you'd think you were taking me to an auction like one of your feeder pigs instead of to your wedding!"

Adam laughed. "Now how come I never thought of that? I could get rid of you and make some money while I'm at it."

"I do believe you would do it if you could."

"I will if you don't hurry up."

"I'm ready. What about you?"

"How do I look?"

"Splendid, but I think you should have a flower in your lapel."

"Good idea. Go pick me one, but hurry up." As she ran off he hollered, "And no dandelions, hear me?"

"Would I do such a thing?"

"No tellin'. Pick some roses for Suzanna."

She was back in a few minutes with a handful of fresh flowers, and a pink rosebud for his lapel.

"Now where's them dried lima beans?"

"Lima beans? In a jar under the counter. Why?" She watched him drop a few beans into his pocket. When he didn't reply, she asked, "Can I read something to you while we ride?"

"Sure. No, not the Bible." He grabbed a book on their way out the door—*Horse Ailments and Their Cure.*

As they stood in the doorway, they looked at the spotless little cottage bathed in the warm light of late afternoon. A summer breeze played through the house. "Just think," said Jessy, full of excitement. "Soon we'll be three."

"Don't remind me. I might change my mind." With that, Adam lifted her up into the carriage without any apparent effort, taking care to put her down gently on the seat without rumpling her finery. He nodded in approval as he watched her putting on her new wide-brimmed straw hat trimmed with silk flowers and satin brocaded ribbons.

Once they were moving down the road, he said, "You ought to get cleaned up more often. Make an effort to look your best."

It was true. Jessy worked and studied so hard she took little interest in her appearance, consciously avoiding any outward displays.

"You're not bad-lookin'. But you tend to be careless. I don't like it."

"But it isn't easy to look attractive slopping hogs."

"I mean when we go off somewheres. You ought to take pride in yourself."

"Yes, Adam, I'll try to do better."

"But not too much pride."

"Yes, of course, Adam."

"On second thought . . . you'd better not bother."

"But you just said . . . "

"Forget what I just said. Never mind how you look. I don't want boys comin' 'round after you."

"How can you give me these morality lectures when you yourself . . ."

". . . don't have any morals?"

"Strange how your morality isn't fixed in God."

"Enough about me. Read about those sick horses."

"But *you're* the one who's sick."

"Nonsense. I'm in great shape. Never felt better in my life." He stuck out a hand for her to see. "Look. Steady as a rock. No more shakes."

"I'm talking about your spiritual health. Your soul."

"The condition of my soul, assumin' there is such a thing, which I doubt, is none of your affair."

"Is too."

"Is not."

"Is too."

Adam reined in the horse under a glorious stand of oaks. Light streamed down through them in broad golden rays. "Either get off the subject or get off this rig right now. Walk home from here and cut wood the rest of the day for all I care." When she didn't budge he said, "Well?"

Jessy frowned.

"I won't be nagged to death by a half-grown girl."

"Yes, sir."

"Now don't go frownin'. Makes you look awful. And sit up straight or you'll wrinkle your new dress."

"Yes, sir."

"You're gettin' out of hand. Worse than a litter of pigs."

"Thank you, Adam."

"You're welcome," he snapped.

They were on their way again but now his expression seemed more appropriate for a funeral than a wedding. This was his day and she had spoiled it. Jessy determined to be merry for his sake and his bride's. She sat up straight, thumbing through the book, trying to work up enthusiasm for the subject. "Chapter One: Horse Colic." Soon she was interjecting her reading with her own silly comments. Adam joined in with remarkably realistic sound effects. They giggled like mad. Luckily no one else was on the road that day or they might have thought Adam and Jessy were suffering from sunstroke, dressed in their best as they were, and neighing like horses.

🌿 17 🌿

They arrived in Bethel at suppertime. "Deserted, just like I figured," said Adam, pulling off the main road onto a broad, tree-lined street. He passed some of the finest homes in town before bringing Milo to a halt.

"Come on," he whispered, helping Jessy to the ground, "and be quiet."

On tiptoe, her crisp taffeta skirts rustling noisily, she followed him around to the back of a huge Victorian house. With perfect aim he flicked one dried bean after another at an upstairs window. He stopped when he heard someone coming. From the shadows, Suzanna appeared, a vision in lavender. Jessy was struck, even in the fading light, by her beauty. The June air carried her delicate fragrance. "How romantic," whispered Jessy.

"Wow," Adam murmured as he took Suzanna in his arms. "I've missed you . . ."

"Darling," she whispered.

They kissed with such feeling Jessy backed into the bushes. Between their kisses, the couple managed a few murmurs in plain English.

"My things are on the back porch." Suzanna tried taking hold of his hand but he showered hers with kisses. At last she nudged him toward her luggage. "Watch out for Mother's gardening tools. They're all over the place."

"Anybody home?"

"No one except Aunt Mil and she's nearly deaf. Daddy and Mother will be at the capitol until tomorrow. They don't suspect a thing. I put them on the train myself, first thing this morning. And Matt's at his Every Wednesday meeting. With Mother and Daddy gone, he'll probably stay out later than usual." Suzanna paused, startled. "What was that noise? Oh, Jessy, it's you. My, but you look *lovely*. You ought to dress up more often. What fine features you have."

Adam nudged Suzanna toward the back porch. He exploded when he saw the huge pile of luggage. "Why don't you take the piano while you're at it!"

"I'd love to! Would it fit? Oh, but you're joking, aren't you?"

"What's this?"

"A carpet sweeper."

"I don't own any carpets."

"As I was packing, I wondered if I had everything I needed."

Adam grinned as he held her. "I got everythin' you'll ever need."

"Oh, yes, you're all I could ever want," she answered, melting in his arms. "I knew that the first moment I ever saw you, right here in this yard. Do you remember, Darling?"

"Vaguely," murmured Adam, while caressing her bare throat with moist, tender kisses. "I was really loaded that night."

The bride-to-be tightened her grip on the sobered man of her dreams. Somewhere a dog began barking, then another.

"Hey, you two, shouldn't we be going?" Jessy called out.

With great reluctance, the couple heeded her and packed up the rig. There was room for so few of Suzanna's things. Soon they were on their way to the home of the minister of the Greater Harvest Assembly of God in Pine Bluff. Even from outside, the place appeared to be rocking.

"Some friends to wish us well," explained Suzanna.

"From the noise, half the state must be here to see The Man of Iron go down for the count."

A happy throng, the young elite of Bethel, greeted the couple. Jessy was astonished at the array of hors d'oeuvres arranged around a castle of a cake trimmed in white rosettes.

Adam greeted the crowd with the confidence of a born showman. "Well, it's finally goin' to happen. Adam Flint is about to meet his doom."

Everyone laughed except the bride. The hurt in her fabulous face demolished Adam's strongest defenses. His bachelor smile dissolved into contrition. In a moment they had made up and drawn close, ready to forsake all others. During the service, Jessy paid rapt attention, finding the exchange of vows rich with meaning. *What God has joined together, let no man put asunder.*

"Oh, dear heavenly Father, how wonderful!" she prayed, "Please bless this happy couple with much joy." For so long she had prayed something good would happen to Adam, and now he was madly in love. Once he placed a little band of gold on Suzanna's waiting finger, the deed was done. The two were one. Adam kissed his bride with such intensity everyone burst into cheers.

❦   ❦   ❦

Jessy didn't sleep well that night. She'd had too much cake and too much excitement. After the celebration and long ride home, the newly-weds had devoted a great deal of time to getting settled in. The bride, dainty as a ballerina, had kept her athletic groom busy arranging and rearranging her belongings until he insisted they both retire.

Jessy dozed fitfully in the room next to theirs, hearing their low talk, the courteous but nervous excuse-mes, soprano and bass, the movements of two pair of feet, Adam's barefoot and light as a cat, Suzanna's pattering in high buttoned shoes. Disturbing Jessy's slumbers, hairpins dropped like a handful of tacks bouncing in all directions across the polished wooden floor. The low bass continued, punctuated by the timid but enchanting full soprano. Jessy couldn't make out the words but the whole seemed right to her. Outside, bugs and bullfrogs provided a rousing summer chorus.

Inside, the struggling and sighing continued, pierced by breathless, gasping womanly cries. Jessy sat up in bed, her heart pounding. Something must have gone wrong, she thought. Harsh memories of parents in the throes of bitterest despair came to her mind. For a moment all was still, tense, as if a clock had been overwound and its driving energy had suddenly come to a halt. But then she heard the rich, sonorous voice of her brother provoking merry feminine laughter. Once again, the marital clock began ticking in perfect harmony.

Jessy got out of bed and went to her window, wondering if ever before tonight there had been such a rich blue heaven vaulted by stars and crowned with this pearl of a moon. She could easily make out the broad form of the barn and, against the darkest blue heaven, the fragile silhou-ettes of fruit trees, their limbs adorned with twinkling stars. All the heavens moved in subtle harmonic progression, everything perfectly ordered, balanced, shimmering, beautiful. To the Maker she whispered, "Thank You, Your Majesty."

In the heart of night, fireflies illuminated the landscape. Jessy mar-veled at these living stars that, driven by the unseen Hand of God, filled the night with such beauty. As bullfrogs and bugs reached their peak

performances, Jessy heard the newlyweds tiptoe about the kitchen. A soft
breeze played through the house, purest air clarified by hundreds of acres
of growing corn and sweet grasses. When a thousand crickets stopped
chirping in unison, Adam and Suzanna laughed together. Soon bugs and
frogs began again as if with one great voice. Amid their music, loving
whispers of the newlyweds began again. Jessy jammed her pillow over
her head and fell asleep at last.

❦   ❦   ❦

Up at five, alone, Jessy began a fire in the wood stove and made coffee.
She did all her usual morning chores, feeding and milking Adam's herds,
tending the garden, and gathering eggs. Three hours later she wondered
why the newlyweds hadn't yet emerged. Adam had never in his life slept
this late, even after one of his bygone drinking binges. After making
herself breakfast, Jessy sat at the table sipping tea and nibbling fresh
strawberries while browsing through Suzanna's scrapbooks. For years
Suzanna had clipped stories about Adam from the newspapers that
tracked his career as a fighter, his feats of strength, his scrapes with the
law. Suzanna had preserved the good with the bad.

Jessy paused when she heard bare feet moving. Adam tiptoed from
the bedroom in nothing but his pants, tousled and unshaven at the
disgracefully late hour of nine A.M. Suzanna sighed and shifted in the
great oaken bed behind him. "My bride has refused to have any more to
do with me until I shave," he explained cheerfully as he stepped into the
washroom. "Do I smell coffee?"

Jessy tiptoed to him with his big mug filled to the brim. "Is everything
all right?"

"Right as rain." Adam's eyes sparkled merrily. He had never appeared
so young, so alive. Sharpening his razor on the long thick strap and then
lathering his face, he asked, "Do the chores?"

"Yes, sir."

"Milkin'?"

"Course."

"Drive the cows out all right and clean up after them?"

"Yes, Adam."

"Churn butter?"

"Not yet."

Adam frowned at the table where her books lay. "Why not?"

"I plan to, once I finish breakfast."

"Get the bread started?"

"Uh-huh."

"Feed the chickens?"

"Yes, sir."

"Forget their supplement?"

"No, sir. Got the eggs washed and put up, too. Nell's on the nest again and so is Zoots."

"Good. How're the hogs?"

"Fine. But we need to spray the potatoes for bugs again."

"I was plannin' on doin' that tomorrow. Today I'm havin' a honeymoon." He finished shaving, gulped his coffee, and disappeared into the bridal chamber.

Grudgingly, Jessy set to churning cream into butter, a boring job made tolerable only by reading as she worked. Standing on the porch, with the open Bible before her, she was pondering what it meant to put on the whole armor of God when she noticed George Webb and the sheriff, who was armed, coming up the drive.

"All right, Miss, where's your brother?"

"What do you mean to do?" Without looking behind her, she could sense Adam coming close on bare feet. "Don't, Adam, they have a gun!"

"Then come inside and stay low."

"No!" She felt Adam drawing close, pressing his bare arms above her head, against the door jambs.

Webb looked disgusted. "Hiding behind a girl."

With one knee Adam nudged Jessy. "Thought I told you to get inside." Still Jessy didn't move.

"Where's my daughter?"

Adam savored the words. "In my bed. Asleep."

"You rotten ..."

Jessy saw the sheriff make a sudden move. Terrified, she turned to look at Adam. He grabbed her by the shoulders. "Get inside!"

"No!" She twisted away to face the men. Adam restrained her by the shoulders.

"You're too late, Webb," Adam called. "Not a thing you can do. We're already married, legally, by a minister. Suzanna's of age. She came with me of her own free will. Got the marriage license right here if you care to see it, and I got a slew of witnesses." Adam squeezed Jessy's shoulders. "Here's one."

At this, the sheriff put down his gun, and Jessy sighed with relief.

Adam rubbed his long thigh muscles before speaking out. "Look, Webb, my past isn't exactly . . . but I love your daughter and she loves me. I would've asked for your blessin' and married her out in the open, but she said you'd never consent. I promise to treat her right, make her happy. You can see her now or any time you want. I'll go get her for you if you like."

"I'm right here, Darling." Suzanna, her hair flowing and wearing a silk robe, came to her husband's side and put an arm around his bare torso. "Hello, Daddy. It's true, everything Adam told you. You know I've always loved him. When Adam proposed to me, I was the one who insisted we elope."

A young goat wandered through the yard. "Uh-oh, Daniel's loose again," muttered Jessy.

Webb looked on, disgusted. "Suzanna, come home with me where you belong."

She curled closer to Adam. "This is where I belong."

"When I think of the suitors you've had: rich, powerful, connected."

"Daddy, we've been over this before. It's no use." With a radiant, loving face Suzanna looked up at Adam. "Here's the man I love."

"So this is how it ends," said her father, crushed. "I gave you everything you ever wanted. Hopeless. I wash my hands of you."

As the men left, Adam said to his bride, "Too bad. I kinda like your old man." Suzanna sobbed against his chest. "Hey, change your mind?" he asked her in his gentle rumbling way. "Homesick?"

"My home is with you — always, wherever you are. I just feel sorry to have hurt Daddy without wanting to. I love him very much."

Adam rocked her in his arms. "Of course you do. And he loves you. In time he'll come around, when he sees how happy we are together."

"You don't know him like I do."

"My little Sue-Sue." Adam nibbled playfully at her open lips.

She blushed and let out a squeal. "What will the neighbors think?"

"No one within screamin' distance," he said, the devil in his voice. His lips brushed downward past the delicate softness of her throat. Suzanna moved backward, to the bedroom with Adam close behind her.

Jessy ran in the opposite direction, flying down the porch steps and calling, "Mr. Webb! Mr. Webb! Wait! Please!" Once she had caught up with him, she said in a rush, "I know you hate my brother, but he's become a different man since he stopped drinking. He really loves your daughter, and she loves him. They have their own sort of language. I don't understand it, but I can tell he's happy for the first time since I've known him. For a long time I've prayed that God would bless my brother. Adam needs a loving wife. He really does."

Webb seemed to soften, listening to her. "I heard he quit drinking but I didn't believe it. He's been such a troublemaker around here ever since he first showed up." George Webb sighed. "He's lucky he's got a sister who cares what happens to him."

"And a wife."

"But you don't understand. My daughter could have had *anyone*."

"So could my brother."

"You got me there, young lady! But they're wrong for each other."

"Love conquers all! That's what I believe."

As Webb started to board the rig, Jessy called out, "Would you like some strawberries to take home with you? I picked them this morning."

"No, thanks. I'd better be on my way, but I'll rest better knowing you'll be out here with my girl."

"You can come visit whenever you like, you and Mrs. Webb. We're family now, aren't we?"

"Can't say I could ever enter Adam Flint's house, but thanks for asking. Do me a favor? Tell Suzanna her mother and I will send the rest of her things, what she left behind on the porch. And the piano, too, if you have room for it. She always loved it so, and her music."

"Oh, she'd like that very much, Mr. Webb. Goodbye." As the rig disappeared, Jessy dug her bare toes into the dust. To the south the sky looked green and churning. Trouble for sure.

❧ 18 ❧

Jessy gave in to the rooster's crowing. As she sat up in bed, she thought, truly, *In the sweat of thy face shalt thou eat bread, till thou return unto the ground; for out of it was thou taken: for dust thou art, and unto dust shalt thou return.* For his disobedience, Adam was banished from Paradise, to till the ground from whence he was taken. So too Adam Flint, and Jessy.

She put on her long, faded denim skirt, cotton blouse, stockings, and boots. After she brushed her luxurious, waist-length hair — the color of the richest, darkest earth tinged red — she bound it neatly away from her face.

"You're a practical girl, Jessy Flint," she told herself in the mirror. "Practical, plain, hard-working. Your faith is practical too." She glanced upward, adding, "Thank you, Lord, for this day, for Your bounty, for the gift of life, for the fruits of our labors."

She hurriedly joined Adam and Suzanna at breakfast. It was high summer, her second with Adam, and there was much work to be done. Always a hard worker, now Adam seemed doubly driven to provide for his new bride, working himself — and his sister — harder than ever. While Suzanna took charge of the house, Jessy worked side-by-side with Adam. If she disliked the eighteen-hour days he planned for them, Jessy kept her complaints to herself. Long ago he had made it clear that, if she were to live under his roof, she must earn her daily bread.

There was hardly time for reading now or for anything but work. Jessy's education advanced by doing, as she learned the meaning of survival. In addition to caring for the hogs, every morning she helped Adam milk his dairy herd, twelve cows in all. Once the milking was done, they drove the cows out to pasture. After cleaning stalls, Adam and Jessy carried the morning's milk to the cellar to cool. A heavy load it was, too, but she grew accustomed to carrying it by following Adam's practical advice. She had learned to separate milk from cream with a hand crank and to churn the cream into butter. Adam seemed perfectly content to teach her how to do some dreadfully dull, muscle-building chore, and then leave her to slave away while he expanded his farming business or put in crops. He used a varied rotation, each crop enriching the soil for the next. Small grains were planted one year, the second, wheat and oats, the third, hay (either clover or alfalfa), followed the next year by field corn, his most profitable crop by far, and food for his livestock. Whichever crop, Adam planted seed in a perfect grid by means of a horse-drawn planter.

Once the corn sprouted, the battle against weeds raged unabated through August. This work fell to Jessy. She learned to hitch a horse to a cultivator, to walk up and down the rows of corn, burying weeds first in one direction and then crosswise, taking care never to disturb even one stalk of growing corn. The horse stepped as carefully as Jessy did. In the process of killing weeds, Jessy covered ten acres a day. She estimated she walked twenty miles in this lonely fashion, covering eighty acres of corn four times in the growing season. Once the leafy green stalks reached above her head, they shadowed the weeds so they couldn't grow. They withered and died without her intervention.

Just before the corn ripened in late summer, Adam hauled out a steel-toothed hay rake. A spidery machine fitted with a driver's seat, it was operated by gears and levers and drawn by horses. Adam mowed the tall hay and, with Jessy's help, raked it by hand onto a wagon fitted with an oversized platform. Together they cut and loaded a ton of sweet hay from each acre. Every bale had to be tied and hoisted by pulleys and horsepower to the loft of the barn. Filling the cathedral-size barn full of hay at the height of summer was hot dusty work.

Suzanna was appalled to see her new husband and sister-in-law dripping with sweat, parched and burned from the sun, working by day and even by the light of the moon because nature demanded that certain tasks be done right then, not tomorrow or when they were less tired.

At twilight, after two weeks of haying, both roasted by the sun, brother and sister were in the yard shaking the first few layers of hay dust off themselves. From the house came a melodic, "Adam, Darling, come and see!"

Creating a small cloud of dust as he went, Adam ascended the porch steps, passing two freshly baked pies cooling near the window.

Holding up new curtains, Suzanna said happily, "Look! I've spent nearly the entire afternoon working on them."

Adam scratched and frowned. "I hate ruffles," he muttered, then returned outside.

Suzanna burst into tears.

Jessy ran inside to comfort her. "I like ruffles a lot, not that my opinion counts for anything at all around here."

"You're absolutely right," came Adam's growl from outside.

Jessy stammered, "What are you doing out there?"

"I own the place, remember? Come out here." Adam's voice was low and menacing.

Jessy slowly walked toward him, her face red. "You heard what I said just now?" she asked in a hush.

"I hear everythin'. Prime this pump for me." While Adam pulled off his shirt and rinsed dust off of himself, he continued chiding her. "Any more loose talk from you and you won't be able to talk at all. Now go inside and make yourself useful."

Shame-faced, Jessy climbed back up the steps to ask her teary sister-in-law what she could do to "make herself useful," this after putting in a day of field work that would have exhausted a team of oxen.

From outside, Adam's rich voice penetrated the vale of tears: "Suzanna Webb Flint! That's enough!"

His terse order might have effected the desired result if Jessy were concerned, but it had the opposite effect on his wife. When Suzanna continued crying, he yelled and cursed for quiet.

"How could I have ever wanted to marry Adam Flint?" Crying all the harder at her cruel fate, Suzanna wailed, "He's a beast. An absolute beast!"

"I'm a *what*?" came the booming response from outside.

Jessy echoed in clear, ringing tones, "Suzanna's says you're a beast, Adam, an absolute beast!" Jessy was pleased with herself for getting Suzanna's inflection exactly right.

Suzanna, horrified at hearing her epithet repeated with such accuracy, dashed into the bedroom, slamming the door and leaving a trail of ruffles behind her. Adam rushed inside, flung open the bedroom door, and shouted, "Don't get me wrong, sweetheart! I like ruffles—on you!"

"You stay away from me, Adam Flint!"

"Sweetheart—"

"Don't you 'sweetheart' me—you, you, ooooh!" With all her might, Suzanna threw her hairbrush at him.

Adam ducked in plenty of time but the hairbrush made a savage dent in the door frame. To Suzanna's further distress, he found this display rather amusing. "Missed! Wanna try again? I dare you!" As she retreated from him, he walked closer, taunting her. "Come on! What're you, scared?"

Suzanna had backed all the way into a corner, her eyes bright with fear.

Just as he reached out to her, Adam stopped cold at the sound of laughter. He wheeled around to see Jessy standing in the fractured doorway snickering at him. On the wall behind her, billowing like a colorful frame, were the circus posters proclaiming Adam's legendary powers. Mr. Man of Iron exploded like shrapnel. "Laugh will you?"

Under his withering look Jessy backed off, stammering, "I'm sorry, Adam, I only—"

He took a few steps toward her but his feet got tangled up in the trail of ruffles.

Jessy giggled all the more.

"Get outa my sight! Go for a walk!"

Jessy stood tall against him. "I've been walking all day!"

"Walkin's healthy! I done plenty in my time. Get out and don't come back till I call you!"

"And just how long will that be?"

"All night maybe! Can't a man even fight in peace?!"

Jessy, wisely deciding not to debate such a remark, fled to the creek for a refreshing swim. When she returned, she was surprised to find the house in apple-pie order. Although Suzanna's hair was in disarray and her blouse untucked and half unbuttoned, she looked at least as radiant as she had at her wedding. Adam looked refreshed, relaxed, and distinctly cheery as he rummaged about, all the while listening to her tell about the eggs she had gathered that day. He beamed with pride, saying, "That's wonderful, sweetheart, just wonderful! Is this the new catalog? Good! Did we get any other mail today?"

While all this gentle domestic chatter went on, Jessy looked around with serious misgivings, stealing a wayward glance at their room. Other than the rumpled bedspread, all seemed normal.

Raising his sights over the catalog, Adam called out, "Looking for somethin', Jessy?"

"Damage."

Adam and Suzanna laughed, dropped what they were doing, and embraced.

Jessy coughed politely. "When's dinner? I'm hungry!"

At this reminder, Suzanna broke loose from Adam's hold to remove two golden loaves from the oven. She slathered the crusts with fresh butter and stirred a big pot on the stove. "The stew isn't ready yet."

Jessy was torn between hunger and weariness. "Do I have time to take a nap?"

"A little one," answered Suzanna. "I'll call you when it's time to eat."

As Jessy rested in the sitting room, she overheard Suzanna whisper to Adam, "Do you think she's all right?"

"I wore her out today. Now it's your turn."

Jessy heard giggling and a great rustling of clothing as the pair headed for the bedroom. "You shameless woman!" Adam called out. "How could I have ever lived without you, Suzanna Flint?"

In that zone between wakefulness and sleeping, Jessy recalled thanking God that, despite occasional fireworks, the new couple was getting along just fine.

Much to Jessy's relief, a hard rain fell that night and all the next day, curtailing outside work. Still, there were always tasks waiting to be done summer or winter during wet weather: shelling corn, repairing harnesses, cleaning stalls, making coops, mending screens, sharpening tools, building troughs and sheds, oiling hinges. Since Adam had invested all his savings in livestock, he couldn't afford to discard anything until it could no longer be repaired.

Once the rains stopped, Jessy and Adam began another arduous field task, harvesting potatoes. He turned up the long rows of vines with a horse-drawn rake. The spidery machine dug into the mud, turning it up and over without damaging the potatoes which were then picked out by hand and tossed into crates that each held sixty pounds.

Afterward, Adam handed crates up to Jessy, one after another, while she stood on a platform wagon, noting how strong she was becoming. In her mudstained clothes, Jessy asked him why it always rained just before the potato harvest. Only hogs, dogs, and little boys liked wallowing in so much mud. For this, Adam had no answer.

During meal time, Suzanna would remark at how humbling it was for her to share food with the two of them, knowing how hard they worked to make sure the family didn't go hungry. She would take one of Adam's great hands, gnarled from continual toil, and kiss it sweetly, making Adam grin like a boy.

Always Jessy silently thanked God for Suzanna and for the way she lifted Adam's life with love.

❦ 19 ❦

Everything had been readied for this week in May—tiny sweaters, soft new bonnets, little coverlets, wee booties, the cradle Adam had made. Suzanna's friends had come to visit, bearing gifts, asking her to return to Bethel to give birth, but she insisted on bearing Adam's child at home. If she missed seeing her family, she never said so.

The Flint house, once bare and barren, had been transformed by Suzanna's magic touch. Over the months since her elopement, she had brought countless new comforts to the stark little house. Bare floors were warmed by her thick, hand-braided rugs. Every bare window was now graced by curtains. Adam's hard wooden chairs were softened with colorful, plump cushions. The country kitchen glowed with finery; the table brimmed with wonderful cooking. Suzanna's music filled the air.

But Suzanna had no religion. That fact drove Jessy to prayer as much as Adam's lack of faith. Suzanna regarded church as "the place you went on Sundays to please your parents." She knew all the hymns by heart, sang them, played them on the piano, but the Word of God meant little to Suzanna. Jessy had hoped their marriage, blessed by a minister, would spark a dawning faith in Adam's heart, but it had not. Still, he had never been happier. Suzanna was all Adam wanted in a woman. These days, the Man of Iron and his bride thought of little else but when their child would be born, happily reminding each other what the midwife had told them: "Green apples fall when they're ripe."

"Seems more like a pumpkin than an apple. Look at him kick!" the couple gleefully noted together.

Praise the Source and Giver of life! Jessy marveled at the blessed union from which emerged this babe, so much like a seed planted and sustained in darkness. This unborn child, this treasure hidden in darkness, waited for the light of day. *We wait, too,* thought Jessy whose joy felt boundless.

It had been a soggy spring. Between drenching storms, Adam and Jessy had prepared the soil, spread manure, put in the crops. Jessy spent a good part of March in the cellar, cutting root potatoes into pieces for spring planting, while Adam built a silo. He had invested everything in his herds and fast horses for show and breeding. By May Suzanna, in her ninth month of pregnancy, had fashioned wardrobe enough to carry the child to its third year.

During a sultry twilight she began to ail. She asked Adam for ice. He made his way through a rainstorm to the ice house and back. Without hat or coat and already soaked to the skin, he returned to find Suzanna and Jessy terribly excited. She said it was time for him to fetch the midwife. Adam left at once on his fastest horse to seek out Mrs. Garner, who lived three miles away.

Despite the rain he made good time. He dismounted his horse and ascended the woman's porch steps all in one motion, and banged on her door with all his might, until he nearly broke it down. After much fumbling with the latch, the midwife's husband opened the door, complaining, "Hold your horses, Adam Flint! First babies don't come as quick as all this!"

Hiding his temper, Adam wanted to shout, "You old-timers are all alike!" Instead he only asked if Mrs. Garner could come right away.

"Sure, soon as she gets back," came the reply.

"Where is she?"

Mr. Garner pulled on his pipe, emitting a long stream of smoke before answering. The old fellow's slowness forced Adam into a panic. "Gone to Milbank. Mrs. Turner's having her third."

"But my wife! It's our *first* and she's got to have help."

"You first-time fathers are all alike," the old man said calmly.

Meanwhile, Jessy heated water, got the scissors ready, and did everything just as the midwife had instructed on her last visit. Impatiently, Jessy went to the window, wishing Adam would return. Evening chores remained to be done. The cows would be balky to drive in and slow to milk with all the rain, but cows and unborn babes were not to be rushed.

Suzanna reassured her from bed. "Go on, honey, I'll be all right. I'll sing out if I need you."

"But with all this rain I know I won't be able to hear you."

"Go on, this will take time. I'll be fine Jessy, really I will."

It was nearly midnight when Adam returned with Mrs. Garner. A waterfall cascaded off him onto the floor as he ran to the bedroom.

The midwife took command. "Mr. Flint, we're in for a long night. Why don't you change and have some supper?"

"You're more concerned with me than my wife?"

"I've seen many such cases—young fathers like yourself catching their death of cold."

Cautiously, Adam approached the bed and took gentle hold of Suzanna's little hands. He kissed her lightly. "My sweetness. Sorry I took so long. It's been a big night for babies to be born!"

From her bed, Suzanna, drenched with the sweat of her pain, smiled bravely. She touched his wet curls. "Mrs. Garner's right, you know. Please change into dry clothes. For me."

Once he was out of hearing, the midwife declared, "Never thought that boy'd get married, much less become a devoted family man. You must be just the wife for him."

Suzanna smiled and tried to answer but couldn't. Her pain was now overwhelming.

By dawn a milky fog covered the land. Adam, exhausted and unshaven, had gone from the house to begin the day's work. "It's my fault," he said to Jessy. "I killed her. She should've never married me. Her father was right."

"You love each other as much as any two people can."

There were tears in his eyes. "She'll never live to deliver my baby. It's too big for her." Adam disappeared into the fog.

"No!" Jessy cried after him. "It can't be true!" She returned to the bedroom, asking for the hundredth time what she could do to help.

"Jessy . . . " Suzanna tried squeezing Jessy's hand but was so weak, Jessy could barely feel it.

Jessy was scared. Throughout the long night, Suzanna had remained patient in this extreme test of womanhood, but now her blue eyes were lifeless. There was no fight left in her. To hide her sorrow, Jessy went to the window. Facing the ghostly morning, she let the tears slip down her cheeks. There would be no new baby, no joyous wife. The shadow of death would fall over Adam. Having loved and lost Suzanna, neither he nor Jessy would ever be the same. Death would swallow up mother and child. "Father, oh Heavenly Father, children come from You and go back to You. All I ask is that this baby be born, if it's Your will. But please stay with us whatever Your will may be, whatever comes…"

"My dear God!"

Jessy turned, startled. She had never heard her sister-in-law calling upon the Lord.

"Jessy, come here!" demanded the midwife. "Look! The baby's head—it's bald. Do you see? Quick, hand me those towels. Hurry!"

When Jessy looked again, the baby's profile was in plain sight. "How beautiful," she said, watching the midwife wiping the eyelids and a perfect little mouth. Tears rolled down Jessy's cheeks as she watched the slippery shoulders and hands, plump and dimpled, then the whole body twisting forward, trailing a blue rope of umbilical cord.

In triumph, the midwife cried, "Thank the Lord, weeping may endure for a night, but joy cometh in the morning!"

"Yes," responded Jessy, her heart bursting with happiness. "Our sorrow will be turned to joy, and our joy no one will take from us." Carefully but merrily she hugged Suzanna before running into the fog.

She found Adam only after calling a dozen times. He was still castigating himself for the loss of his own fair bride. "There you are! I looked everywhere for you," she gasped. "He's here! Stephen's here!"

"Stephen? A boy? But Suzanna? What about…"

"She's going to be all right. She'll need a month of bed rest, but she's fine. Stephen looks just like you! He even has a dimpled chin! The midwife thinks he's the biggest baby she ever delivered. He's got the hiccups!"

"Hiccups? My son? Really?" Adam said this as if it were the most remarkable event in the history of western civilization.

Laughing and crying together, they ran home. For the first time Jessy could keep pace with Adam's powerful strides. From the yard they could hear healthy baby cries.

"Listen, Adam! Your son has your temperament!" With practiced skill, she dodged Adam's playful swing in her direction.

Later the neighbors came, and old friends of Suzanna's to bill and coo over Stephen Flint, the most perfect child ever born, the most beautiful, the smartest, the hungriest, the dearest, the baldest, the most lovable, the loudest. Father and Mother would simply nod in agreement, for indeed Stephen was, like all newborns everywhere, the greatest.

❧ 20 ❧

"**M**ug-gy!" said Adam, sweating profusely after his morning round of work. He poured himself coffee and sat down for breakfast. "You sure you don't mind if I go over to Sweet Elm today?"

"Of course not, Darling. You've been planning on going to that auction for weeks." Together Adam and Suzanna took a final look at the list of equipment that would be sold that day. Adam handed the flier to Jessy, asking, "What do you think?"

While Jessy studied the list he turned to his wife. "And you'll stay off your feet as much as possible?" Adam made it sound more like an order than a question.

Suzanna nodded, a warm smile lifting her features. Horatio's tail thumped heartily beneath the table. Adam peered down to see Stephen's puppy, and also noticed Suzanna's ankles. "Go back to bed. You know what the midwife said."

"I only just got up! Honestly, Adam, you sound like a mother hen."

"Second baby's supposed to be easier but you look all in."

"It's just the heat."

"It should rain today and cool things off." Adam pushed himself away from the table. "I got a long ride. Better get goin'. Jessy! See to things while I'm gone."

"All right. Suzanna and I have an agreement—if I take Stephen blueberry picking, she'll bake the pies."

At the mention of his name, Stephen, wearing only a diaper, toddled forth to grapple with one of his father's trunklike legs. Looking up, he tugged at heavy denim with chubby fists. "No, son, you stay home with Mum and Aunt Jessy." Still Stephen refused to let go. With bare little feet he mounted the toe of one great boot. Adam picked him up on his way out the door. The women followed, with Horatio bringing up the rear.

161

Before Adam climbed aboard his rig, he handed his son over to Suzanna. "Blueberry pie, you say?"

"And a roast."

"Mmmm." He leaned over to give her a kiss, mmming again. "Want anything from Sweet Elm?"

"More jelly jars. At least two dozen."

"Bye, Dad-dee!"

"Bye, son. Be a good boy."

The trio watched Adam drive away, the team moving slowly in the heat. "At that rate they'll never make it," Jessy said. "It's a two-hour ride in cool weather."

"It's not even eight o'clock and I bet it's eighty-five already. Let's take a look at the thermometer."

As if not wanting to hear the exact reading, the dog retreated to his cool nook under the porch.

"Eighty-six in the shade! It'll be a hundred by noon," predicted Suzanna.

When the women returned to the house, Suzanna dropped into a chair at the table, overlooking the wake of breakfast dishes. Jessy began cleaning up, with Stephen following after her.

"Hope Adam can get that corn sheller." Jessy had accompanied Adam to more than one sale of the Tri-State Auctioneers. "It's hotter in here than it is outside." When she realized Suzanna hadn't said a word she turned to see her sitting in uncharacteristic stolidness, resting her head on an upraised hand. "Why don't you go back to bed? I'll mind Stephen."

"Oh, I'll be all right. Haven't slept well these last two nights, hardly at all. I've been having strange dreams. Big black elephants charging . . . "

"So go back to bed."

"No, there's too much to do." Suzanna began wiping dishes. "I need to put up some of that squash this morning."

With heads tipped together the two stared out the window at the garden. Jessy said, "By next week we'll have enough vegetables to fill up this room."

And so they spent the morning washing, slicing, and peeling vegetables. The hot kitchen grew hotter with all the boiling and canning. By lunchtime every counter was filled with a colorful array of jars—green beans, yellow squash, red peppers, tomatoes, sweet pickles. Suzanna began marinating the roast for dinner. The exquisite aromas roused Jessy's appetite but Suzanna left her lunch half eaten. She got up and stood by the back door in search of a breeze.

Jessy ate a big lunch topped off with leftover walnut layer cake. "Best you ever made, Suzanna!" she said, scraping the plate of the last moist crumb.

"I'm glad you liked it. I didn't get to taste it."

Jessy stopped dead. "I'm sorry. I would have saved you some."

Suzanna laughed. "It's all right. I'm not hungry." She sat down heavily. "Sure hope it rains. It would certainly cool things off."

"Adam's never been wrong. When he predicts rain, it rains. Wouldn't a nap make you feel better?"

"I suppose so." Suzanna studied her swollen ankles. "They've never been so big, have they? I sure hope this baby's early. I don't know that I can take another two months of feeling this way. I'm sure Adam is tired of me."

"Impossible! He absolutely adores you and you know it."

While Jessy carried the newly canned foods to the cellar, Suzanna finished the dishes, set the roast in the oven, and fed Stephen, fresh and frisky from his nap.

Jessy took hold of one chubby little fist. "Want to pick blueberries?"

Stephen squealed with glee as Jessy lifted him up and kissed him profusely. "We'll get you all dressed up. Where's your shirt?"

Without bothering to take off her apron, Suzanna limped into the bedroom. Jessy called after her. "Need anything before I go?"

"No, honey, I'll be fine. Thanks for minding Stephen." Suzanna closed the drapes in the bedroom before sitting on top of the covers.

The last thing Jessy heard as she went out the door was the sound of shoes dropping to the floor and the gentle creaking of the bed as Suzanna settled down for a nap.

🐛　🐛　🐛

"Not too many or you'll get sick. Look at you! What a mess!" Jessy shook her head. Stephen's hands and mouth were purple with berry juice.

While Jessy picked blueberries, the dog explored the bushes. At one point he barked so insistently Jessy stopped to investigate. "Oh, it's only a garden snake! He won't hurt anyone." Without further noise the dog cowered off but Jessy took care where she stepped. "Stephen, stay close to me. Come on."

As she took his hand, she noticed the southwestern horizon turning a sickly green. Above, the clouds were densely black and churning. Jessy remembered Adam's warnings. Without hesitation she picked up his son and raced toward the house. The wind grew fierce. Thunder cracked overhead. The vast open fields seemed like yawning traps with nowhere to hide. Jessy's mind raced ahead of her feet. Was there enough time to reach the house? Would a ditch be safer? Lightning crackled through the southwestern sky. The eerie green and black mass drew closer. Jessy decided she could reach the cellar in time.

Heart pounding, she set Stephen down while she grappled with the bulkhead doors leading beneath the house. Why had Adam built them so heavy? And where was Suzanna? Why wasn't she down here already? How could anyone sleep through such a storm?

"Be brave, sweet potato," she murmured to Stephen who nodded, imitating her calm demeanor. "Good. That's my boy." Jessy took one precious moment to survey the cellar. Where was the safest spot to leave a toddler? The carrot bin. When Stephen tried to climb out she closed the lid over him. His cries convicted her of high treason. "It's a game, sweetheart. Aunty will be right back! Don't cry!" High winds drowned out his cries.

Up the stairs of the cellar she went two at a time, and up the porch steps calling for Suzanna. In the near darkness that now consumed all, she saw that Suzanna was still lying in bed.

"Suzanna, wake up! We've got to get under the house!"

"All right," came the sleepy reply. Suzanna didn't budge.

"Wake up! We can't stay here! Adam said we should always take cover in weather like this." Jessy saw that Suzanna's ankles looked worse than ever. "Suzanna. Suzanna! Listen to me!" Jessy made Suzanna sit up. "You've got to get out of here!"

The woman who had not slept for two nights now groaned from the deepest recesses of sleep, fighting to be left alone. Coming to herself, with half-open eyes, Suzanna asked, "Where's Stephen?"

"Downstairs, and that's where we're going."

"It's just a little wind, for heaven's sake. I've seen storms like this all my life. Nothing much ever . . ."

The drapes, hurled upward by the wind, were being beaten against the ceiling. In the sitting room, a picture fell from the wall, frame and glass crashing and scattering over the floor.

"You'd better put on your shoes." Without waiting for Suzanna to respond, Jessy was doing it for her, in her haste mixing right and left but jamming the shoes on regardless.

"I'll never make it, Jessy, I'll only slow you down. You go. I'll get under the bed."

"No!" Jessy roared above the din of wind and thunder. "I can't leave you here! Adam would never allow it!"

"Go ahead, I tell you! I can't walk."

"Then I'll carry you."

Suzanna was now fully awake and very angry. "You're crazy!"

"You're crazy to stay here. There's no time to argue!" With one smooth motion Jessy took hold of Suzanna's arms and rolled her off the bed and across her own shoulders. Jessy powered into a standing position. "Even with child, you're not much heavier than a crate of potatoes," Jessy declared. Years of demanding physical labor were paying off in a way no one could have envisioned.

Jessy negotiated the bedroom doorway with ease but once she neared the porch the wind nearly knocked them over. Flying debris filled the air but Jessy didn't stop, even when sand grated against them and the wind threatened to tear off their clothes. Still not a drop of rain had fallen. It took all of Jessy's strength now to descend the porch steps, and make her way around the side of the house to the cellar. She rolled Suzanna off her shoulders and helped her down the steps.

"Under the table would be best." Jessy referred to the heavy oak table covered with cooling jars of vegetables and the morning's milk and cream.

It was so dark inside the cellar Jessy had to feel her way past Adam's steamer trunks and up the stairs to close the double doors of the bulkhead. If he were here, she knew he would take time to examine the thunderous mystery approaching them. She braved a look. Were it not for the vivid network of lightning, Jessy would have been able to see little, so dark was the afternoon sky. It seemed as if a rearing black elephant were galloping over, or a roaring demon with a thousand angry mouths all droning as one. Here was Suzanna's dream! The heavens Jessy so loved had turned sickly and glowing beyond this spiraling black funnel that seemed to suck up everything in its path. When a host of objects flew past — a clothesline, part of a hay baler, newspapers, even boulders and trunks of trees — Jessy shut the doors and latched them tight, appreciating Adam's abilities as a carpenter now more than ever. She crawled past the bin, alive with a two-year old, to hide under the table with Suzanna.

"How clever of you. Stephen's protected on all sides."

"Wish we could fit in there too!"

"My ears hurt!" wailed Stephen from among the carrots.

"Mine, too," said Suzanna.

From high above them, through the small grilled windows ringing the earthen cellar they could hear hailstones beating the land. Strange, thought Jessy, the sound of trains had never reached Adam's farm before. They were more than five miles from the railroad line and yet the roar of engines was deafening, as if locomotives were rolling over their heads. She held on to Suzanna, praying amid the raging noise. As the world caved in over their heads, Jessy wondered, *Is this like falling into the hands of the living God?*

Floorboards, brickwork, and loose plaster rained down into the cellar, followed by hailstones as big and hard as marbles. How long this lasted Jessy couldn't tell, but when the noise of storm and hail had ceased, the earth was deadly quiet, disrupted only by Stephen's wailing. When the dust cleared, the pale light of day flooded the cellar. Suzanna and Jessy stirred from beneath the table. The cellar was filled with rubble. They moved with caution, to the sound of tinkling glass. Mixed with hail, rain, and construction debris, freshly preserved squash, beans, and tomatoes oozed underfoot. Odors of spilt milk and dill pervaded the air.

"Ow!" Suzanna nicked her hand on glass in an effort to reach her son.

"Watch out! Those rafters are loose up there."

"Wish we had helmets."

"And gloves."

"And shovels. Good thing you thought of my shoes."

Together they forced their way toward the bin, pushing aside cinder blocks and planks to open the hatch. Stephen was sobbing and dirty but unharmed. Suzanna snatched him up with a glad cry.

When they climbed free of their refuge, they found they were refugees still. The landscape had been changed in a twinkling. Where lovingly pruned fruit trees and century-old oaks had once graced Adam's yard, nothing could be seen. The house was gone, not simply blown down but blown away. Even his sturdy bulkhead doors that had so well protected his family were gone. The angry demons with a thousand voices had swept all away, leaving behind only the wreckage of the cellar. The women were stunned. No more than half an hour had passed since Jessy had stopped picking berries. She helped Suzanna into a seated position on the uppermost cellar step.

"If I had stayed in the house . . . oh, Jessy, you saved my life! You saved Stephen and me!" Suzanna cradled her abdomen. "You saved all three of us! But how did you carry me here? How did you ever manage it?"

Quaking helplessly, Jessy said, "I couldn't lift so much as a candle now." The miraculous strength that Jessy had displayed had left her. She scanned the now benign sky. "God gives us strength and grace as we need it, to face what comes in this world."

"It was a miracle, Jessy. Plain and simple."

Jessy didn't respond. She was taking stock of their situation. They faced a staggering crisis and she was the only one present with the physical ability to deal with it. "The barn's all right, except for the roof, but the corn crib's gone, and everything in it. Boy, is Adam going to be mad."

"Adam! Do you suppose he's all right? Isn't Sweet Elm toward the southwest?"

Until that moment, Jessy hadn't considered the direction of Sweet Elm but she realized Suzanna was correct. With feigned bravado Jessy answered, "Adam is too big and tough to be swept away by a mere tornado. I'll find a place for us to settle in. Looks like it's going to rain before too long." Wherever the vast midwestern sky wasn't gray or green it appeared black.

Jessy entered the barn with caution but backed out again when she saw the damage. Heavy timbers dangled overhead. She knew repairs would be needed before the next rain or the tons of hay and grain stored there—feed that represented a summer's toil and the coming year's income—would be ruined. There wasn't an animal in sight. Every cow, calf, and horse had been set out to graze that morning.

From a rise she could see that most of the fencing had been uprooted and blown away. The hen houses were gone. Except for a few disgruntled chickens, she could see none of Adam's livestock. When she came across their rooster half dead and twitching in pain, she killed him as quickly and painlessly as she could manage. "Goodbye, old faithful. Never thought it would end this way for you." She thought of Sweet Elm, where the big auction tents would be set up. How many more lives would come to an end this day?

The only building in tact was the hog house. Three of Adam's prize sows were huddled in a far corner. She gladdened at the sight of them. "Hey, girls, am I happy to see you." They grunted in reply, coming closer when they realized she was scooping feed corn from a bin. She went to them, stroking their backs as they ate. She talked to them in reassuring tones, as Adam might if he were there. *Adam.* She tried not to think of him. "You girls thirsty?"

When she went to the well behind their pens, she found it had been sucked dry by the tornado. She could hear a slow trickle as it filled from an underground spring. Fortunately the pump was still intact and working.

Distant thunder sounded to the south. "No, not again," she wailed. Though it was only mid-afternoon, the sky appeared dark as night. The flesh of her hands looked blue in the weird light. Rain began to fall in solid sheets like waves. She hurried back to Suzanna and Stephen. The three made their way to the hog house, becoming drenched in the rain. Why had no one come to their rescue, or were their neighbors in a worse fix themselves?

"I'll go to the Gaads for help. Adam always said if . . ." Adam again. Jessy stopped, not wanting to upset Suzanna.

Suzanna took tight hold of Jessy's hand. "No. The weather's too bad for you to go off in the open. There could be another tornado."

"All right. I'll wait for the weather to clear." Before they ducked inside, Jessy noticed a piece of straw imbedded through the solid oak lintel of the doorway. "Look. It won't come loose. It went straight through."

"That wood must be four inches thick."

"Oak is so hard and this straw is so thin."

"I've never seen such a thing."

"The wind drove straw through solid oak." Jessy touched it in awe. "Like the Word of God," Jessy said in a hush. "It goes where it will, driven by the Spirit into the human heart."

The skies poured over them now but they lay in dry, fresh straw. "How good it is to be inside, even in the hog house. I used to hate it in here, when I first came to live with Adam. He made me get to like it. Good thing I just cleaned it out yesterday!"

Stephen cried alternately for food and for his daddy. Suzanna nursed him a long while. Once she had rocked him to sleep in her arms she said, "Jessy? I know it was a miracle from God that saved us through you. How could I ever have doubted in Him? I'll never doubt Him again."

"Amen," said Jessy, in something of a haze.

"I've lived so long without prayer, turning my back on God. I went to church every week as a child, to please my parents. I was there in body but my mind, my soul, were elsewhere. All that time wasted! But no more. I'm His!" Suzanna turned to see her son asleep without a care.

"That's how God means for us to be, like children, trusting and faithful, resting in Him no matter what happens." Jessy relaxed despite the raging storm blasting all around them.

As the storm raged, they prayed, especially for Adam and all their neighbors, and then they rested, as helpless and trusting as children.

❦ 21 ❦

Jessy wakened slowly, painfully, when sunlight streamed through the windows above her head. Her hair and clothes were still damp from the previous day, and her throat sore. She struggled to gather strength to face this day. The first sight she saw that morning was a lovely one—Suzanna and Stephen asleep. Disturbing the image was the growling of Jessy's stomach. She hurried from them to find something to eat. Although she hoped by now to see that Adam had returned, and that their neighbors were safe, Jessy saw no one.

The fact that the house was gone struck her fully now, and threatened to overwhelm her. The night rains had collected in the cellar. She waded in to find a shelf of unbroken jars along one wall—applesauce and beans from the last harvest. She set a few jars beside Suzanna, then went outside again, feeling mortally alone. The well had filled again. Birds greeted the day with song. She wished she too could sing, even in this. Another sound reached her, mooing. Though the cow didn't belong to Adam's herd, Jessy could see from her udder that she had gone through the night without being milked. "Poor girl, I'll try finding a pail." She brought the fresh milk to Suzanna.

"Good morning, love." Suzanna smiled with an inner warmth that defied storms and swollen ankles and the painful doubts of yesterday. "I've given my life over to the Lord, Jessy. My brother will be so pleased. Jeff has prayed for me for years, did I ever tell you?"

Jessy remembered seeing Jeff, home from seminary, to help the Eberharts when they had lost all in a fire. "He must love you very much."

"I never realized how much till last night, as I lay here thinking about, things."

"It's hard for Christians to see the ones they love most live without faith. That's how I feel about . . ." Adam again. Regardless of her own feelings, Jessy must not mention his name and risk upsetting her sister-

170

in-law. "Look, Suzanna, I'm going to the Gaads for help. You'll be safe here. The sky looks clear. I'll be back as soon as I can."

Making her way on foot, Jessy found and mounted one of Adam's horses. As she rode bareback she noticed that most of Adam's pasturelands had been unaffected by the weather except for a broad skipping path of naked earth where the tornado had touched down, lifted, and touched again as it moved away from their farm. While clover and alfalfa looked richly green in some places, oddly shaven in others, Adam's corn crop had been beaten down by hail. Months of labor under a merciless sun were gone in a day. Jessy estimated Adam's loss as nearly total, which pained her all the more as she passed on to neighboring farms unaffected by the weather. Mr. Gaads' corn looked fine. Envy struck her heart as she rode past broad fields where corn stood six feet tall. Such was the fickleness of nature. One farm was ruined while another stood in perfect order. It was only when she reached the Gaads' barn and house that she paused.

"Oh, Lord, forgive me," she whispered as she slipped off the horse. The five-bedroom farmhouse had been reduced to rubble. Roof tiles, two-by-fours, and broken furniture were piled in heaps. Half the barn had been sliced off and carried away. What remained standing resembled a stage long after the final curtain. The second story loft dangled precariously. Most of the hay stored within had tumbled to the ground in disarray.

Jessy took a few hesitant steps, calling out for the Gaads. In answer she heard nothing but the rusty slurring whistle of a meadowlark. Each sprightly trill sent shivers through her spine. She neared the ruins. Inside walls stood partially upright, their flowery wallpaper exposed to the world like a doll's house. Jessy tried climbing the wreckage but hastened away when her footing threatened to collapse. Surely no one was in there. Surely the Gaads must have seen the storm coming. They knew the danger signs as well as anyone. Perhaps they were at the auction, or at a neighbor's. Before she had gone a hundred yards, though, she encountered neighbors coming her way.

"Jessy Flint. You and yours all right?"

"All but Adam."

"He hurt?"

"I don't know. He went to the auction yesterday."

"Storm hit your place?"

"Yes, sir. Took the house away, and everything in it. Suzanna's back there with Stephen. I came to get help, to the Gaads, only..."

"Did you talk with them?"

"No, sir. Maybe they went to a neighbor's?"

The men looked at each other before one spoke. "You go on home now. We'll see what we can do here and then come by your place as soon as we can."

Home. The only home she had known since the death of her parents was gone. The Gaads were to help if ever she were in need, that's the way Adam had planned for such an eventuality. Where was her refuge now? Come what may, God would be Jessy's home, as He always had been and always would be.

On the way back, her horse shied repeatedly at all the fallen trees and dead animals. One unfortunate calf from a neighboring herd had been impaled by a spike driven by the wind like a spear. She found Horatio, Stephen's pet, drowned and half buried in the mud. She dismounted at the sight, kneeling beside him. "Poor pup, your barking warned me. You're the real hero. You saved us all."

Jessy knew that all living things must die. Yet amid death and decay, life in all its variety of forms went on with an insistence that transcended her grief. Stray pigs destined to become the pork chops and bacon of America were having a glorious time in Adam's ruined corn and vegetables. Now that the fence had been blown down, more than a dozen, none of their own, were hogging down in the garden. Chester Whites and Belted Hampshires as round and rotund as barrels uprooted Jessy's tender plants. As she muttered, "Glad someone's having a good time today," she noticed something that made her forget everthing else — a muddied wagon and familiar team stood in the drive. She glanced at the new corn sheller with a Tri-State inventory tag. They had no corn crop but they had a corn sheller. What did it matter?

"Adam!" With a delighted cry she dismounted the horse and ran, crying, "Thank God you're home!"

He poked his head out of the hog house. "There you are! I leave you in charge for one day and you let the house blow away!"

"You look like you spent the night in a ditch."

"How'd you guess?"

She laughed for the first time in two days. "You did? Really?"

Adam's clothes were plastered to his body by mud. "Nearly got blown away tryin' to get home." He held the back of his head with one hand. "Got hit with somethin'. Knocked me out cold. I didn't come to until this mornin'. I got back here as fast as I could, but the roads are filled with fallen trees. Suzanna told me what you did, how you saved her life..."

"But the Gaads—I have a terrible feeling that..." With a sob Jessy realized that mourning is the price of love.

While he held and comforted her, he marveled at the view around them. "How could the barn have stood up through a tornado and the house just vanish into thin air? Beats anything I've ever seen." He looked at her and declared, "You're a mess. Let's get cleaned up. Is the pump still workin'?"

Once he began rinsing mud off himself, he began bleeding from numerous small cuts. The knot at the back of his head was the size of a plum.

"You sure you're all right?"

"Well, I don't exactly feel like rope dancin' but I can't think about my aches and pains at a time like this. We got work to do, fences to mend. Got to see about that barn roof before the hay starts moulderin'. You'll help me pull a tarp up there for now. And we have to get to Bethel before dark. Suzanna's in no condition to be out here at a time like this."

While Jessy helped him hunt for tools and haul his trunks from the cellar to the barn, he found one of his most productive hens, a white graced with brilliant red comb and wattles. She had lost most of her feathers to the tornado, but her eyes appeared sharp and clear. Jessy heard him whisper, "You'll grow them back, won't you, girl?"

"Sure she will. She's just had an unscheduled molting."

Adam set her down carefully and seemed to brighten watching her nibble at the cracked corn Jessy had brought out from the hog house. At the prospect of being fed, a few more hens sallied forth from hiding.

"Adam, I feel terrible about your place."

"Couldn't be helped."

"It was such a nice little house," she sobbed.

"We're not alone in this, that's for sure. There's been damage all over. Two counties, maybe three, were hit, that's what I heard comin' back."

She took small comfort in this. Even if they found all of their livestock, there was hardly any corn to feed themselves or their animals through the coming year. Adam's farming losses were nearly total: a dozen cows dead or missing, along with four calves and an aging boar; twenty-seven feeder hogs nearly ready for market; half his chickens drowned or plucked alive by the winds. Of his eight short yearlings being raised for beef, only two were found. One had to be destroyed due to an injured leg. In going to the auction, Adam had taken and thus had spared his best team but all of his other horses were lost except for the one Jessy had found. As Jessy had discovered, high winds and hail had decimated most of the corn crop. Garden vegetables close to harvesting had been pelted into rotting garbage.

Together Adam and Jessy worked in frustrated silence. Their full year's work of planting, breeding, and cultivating was ruined in one day. Orchards that had taken forty years of nurture were no more. Adam's savings, too, were gone, tied up in all that had been swept away by the storm.

They could search for years and never find what became of their belongings—their clothes, including Jessy's best shimmering pink dress, Suzanna's scrapbooks and handmade rugs and delicate needlepoint, the baby's clothes, Adam's furniture, the savory roast Suzanna had put in the oven, the oven itself, the kitchen and everything in it, the gleaming copper and matching china Suzanna had so prized. Most of all Jessy mourned the loss of her mother's Bible. But, still, they were alive, and Suzanna had turned to the Lord. Perhaps the storm, in driving all apart, would draw all together in some way still unclear to Jessy.

"We'll get a loan," she overheard Suzanna say to Adam.

"I've never borrowed in my life. Now I'll end up a failure like my father."

"Plenty of people borrow money. My father has. It's no shame. We'll pay it back. We should thank the Lord—"

"For what? Look at us, sittin' in a pig sty! I promised to take care of all your needs, give you a decent home—"

"My parents will help us."

"Sure."

"My love. My good proud love. That bump on your head hurts me just looking at it. Come sit by me and rest."

"I got work to do."

"I need you more than anything right now."

During the ensuing calm, Jessy slipped away unnoticed.

In late afternoon they boarded the wagon, Adam and Suzanna up front, Jessy in back with Stephen asleep by her side. The ride to town took them south, in the reverse direction of the tornado's path. Mangled trees along the way told the story. Few farms had escaped damage. Some homes were gone without a trace, but for rubble and the rectangle of a cellar. Homes on either side of the road had been ripped apart as if by a single blow. Houses toppled onto barns, barns leaned over sheds, trees flattened roofs. Sometimes for a space of a few hundred yards, no damage would be apparent. Again and again the tornado must have hovered along the ground, sweeping everything in its path, only to rise up and drop again in its furious path northward.

"Worst disaster I've ever seen," said Adam.

"God has blessed us, Darling. We should be grateful."

"Blessed? I'm ruined. I put all my money into that place. If there is a God, how come He struck down believers' places same as mine?"

"You can't expect life to be perfect for believers. This world is full of tribulation."

"But why did this happen?"

"We can't expect to see the whole of God's plan, but there are blessings in all things."

"For now we see through a glass darkly," added Jessy from behind them.

As they got closer to Bethel, the damage seemed even more readily apparent due to the dense massing of buildings. Suzanna whispered, "Darling, do you suppose Mother and Daddy's home was..."

Until now, Jessy tried not to think of the effects of a tornado on Bethel. The closer they drew to the Webb home the less they spoke. Only Adam looked ahead, come what may. One by one, they passed the buildings that had been hit: the bank, the post office, the dentist's office, the barber shop, the blacksmith forge, the grain elevators, even the railroad lines were twisted by the unearthly force. The roof and steeple had been blown off the church. Ironically, the Lucy Meredith house, deserted for years, stood untouched. It must have been undergoing restoration, for a scaffolding obscured the facade.

"Don't that beat all," said Adam, admiring the graceful two-story. "Nice new paint job, too."

They made their way through town, where he pulled off the main road and onto a side street toward the Webb home. Suzanna reached for her husband's hand.

"Whatever it is," he assured her, "we'll face it together."

"I've been so stubborn. I should have tried to make peace with them long ago. I really should have tried."

"Easy now. Can't have you bearin' our child right here in the street, now can we?" Adam cradled her just a moment. "Look."

In the fading light of day Suzanna's childhood home was alive with the glow of lamps. "Thank God."

"Come on, easy on those ankles," he said, as she stepped down to the curb. Carefully, he helped Suzanna into his waiting arms. "After I leave you and Stephen here, Jessy 'n me'll find some place to put up for the night."

"Nonsense. We're a family. We'll stay together."

Fighting back his emotions, he carried her up the steps. The aroma of home cooking filled the air, and the voices of a dozen women. From the sound of activity within, the Webb house must have been turned into an emergency center. Adam paused on the veranda, not daring to knock on the door. It had been three years since Suzanna left this house. In all that time, she hadn't seen or spoken to her parents. Letting go of her was the hardest thing Adam had ever done. He set Suzanna down lightly on her swollen feet, and as calmly as he could, he said, "Goodbye, sweetheart."

"No!" Suzanna clutched at him with all her might. "Darling, I need you."

"And I need you but . . ." Arguing, they backed into the shadows.

"You have not because you ask not," Jessy said, but they weren't listening. Weary of trying to keep Stephen from squirming in her arms, she decided to take action. "Come on, we're brave, aren't we, Stephen? The worst they can do is refuse to let us in." Jessy knocked on the door.

An elderly woman opened it. "Come right in, you poor darlings! What a beautiful child! You're just in time for supper! You young mothers seem to have suffered the most in all this, you poor girls. Clean diapers in the washroom to your left. After supper, your boy can bed down in the guest room with the other children."

"You don't understand, you see . . . "

More women gathered around them. "Why, it's Jessy Flint. I didn't know you were a mother. When did you get married? Or did you?"

"I didn't. I'm not. I mean—this is Suzanna's—" Jessy stood there stammering, dressed in her filthy rags in the stylish Victorian hall with a plush carpet at her feet and a crystal chandelier glowing over her head like a halo. "Umm. I shouldn't be here at all. I'll be on my way—"

"You'll do no such thing. What's a family spat at a time like this? We'll look after you like we have all the others, isn't that so, Mrs. Webb?"

All eyes turned to a small girlish woman with graying hair and a flushed but pleasant face. "Did you say this little boy is Suzanna's?"

"Yes, ma'am. Your grandson, Stephen." As she turned so Mrs. Webb could see him, Jessy prayed he would behave himself long enough to charm his grandmother into submission.

"Oh, what a love, what a perfect angel!" While her friends beamed at the sight, Mrs. Webb touched the loose, golden ringlets of her grandson for the first time. "He has Suzanna's eyes, but these curls, this darling little dimpled chin, well, just look at him. May I hold him?" Mrs. Webb took her grandson from Jessy's arms. "Oh, aren't you a darling boy. Your grandfather had forbidden me to—" Fear gave Mrs. Webb pause. "Since yesterday I've been afraid to ask where Suzanna is—"

"Outside arguing with Adam. She won't come in without him, but he won't come in. Won't you please invite them in, ma'am, out of sheer Christian charity if nothing else? Suzanna's due again soon and she's in a bad way." Jessy chewed on her lower lip. What a big mouth she had some times. What should have been said with the utmost delicacy had sounded so blunt.

Mrs. Webb flew toward the porch, then stopped at the sight of a group of men coming up the stairs from the street. Jessy winced to hear the distinctive lawyerly voice of George Webb, Esquire.

❦ 22 ❦

"**D**on't worry, I was just leavin'," Adam snapped for all to hear. He burst through the open door to be confronted by the women standing in the hall. Glowering like a bear, he towered over the ladies. "Jessy, come on, we're goin'. Where's my son?"

"He's right here and I don't ever want to let him go," said Mrs. Webb, nestling Stephen's little face close to her own.

Suzanna stood between her mother and her husband, no one knowing what to say. When George Webb came in, Adam headed out. Jessy ran to follow.

"Darling, please don't go." Suzanna was in tears.

"What else can I do?" he whispered helplessly. "You stay here, you and Stephen. I need to get away and think." He ran his hands through his hair in exasperation, wincing when his fingers grazed the knot at the back of his head.

A crash in the kitchen drew everyone away from the hall except George Webb and the Flints. "For the time being, my errant daughter and her child can stay, but I won't have Adam Flint under my roof. I don't care what sort of ill wind blew him here."

Without saying a word, Adam left. Jessy looked at Webb in bitter disappointment.

"You can stay, Miss. I have no quarrel with you."

"If you reject my brother, then you reject me, too," Jessy told George Webb. Then she trailed down the steps after Adam.

Suzanna, limping badly, tottered to catch up with them. "I'll try to work on Daddy," she whispered. "You look after Adam, won't you?"

"Of course." She patted Suzanna's hand and whispered, "Don't worry. Things will be better in the morning."

"I'm not looking forward to facing my father."

"I know what you mean." Jessy glanced up at the imposing figure still standing in the doorway. George Webb, Esquire was law and order personified. "If I were you I'd have your mother face him for you. I think she's on your side."

"Good idea. See you tomorrow."

Jessy turned around and bumped into Adam. "What were you two whisperin' about?"

"Nothing."

He grabbed Jessy by the collar, his voice low and lethal. "And what was the idea of bargin' into that house like that?"

"I didn't barge in. I knocked on the door. Where are we going, anyway?"

"New elementary school down this block. I heard someone say they got a soup kitchen and cots set up for families that got nowhere to go."

They queued in line for soup and bread, their first meal in two days. They sat apart, trying to avoid the gossips that had hounded Adam ever since he first moved to Bethel. Jessy noticed a complete cross section of the township present, every age and occupation. Few had been spared hardship.

Even though the room was full of people, life didn't seem complete without Suzanna and Stephen. Jessy kept silent, not wishing to increase Adam's unhappiness. He looked exhausted, strained to the utmost. The food did little to revive his spirits. She finally asked, "What are you thinking?"

In his softest voice he said, "Maybe I'll try loggin'. There're these camps always needin' big guys like me. Tried it one winter, first year I knew Bo. We went to Canada. Beautiful country. Plenty of wild game, liquor, cards. No one asked any questions. Always figured that's what I'd do if I was ever really down on my luck."

"We're not down on our luck. God will help us. He always has and He always..."

Adam shut his eyes tight. He reared his head back, grimacing and straining to catch his breath.

She stood. "You need a doctor. I'll see if there's one here..."

"No." He grabbed her wrist so hard she sat down again. "Listen to me. Suzanna can stay here, have the baby. I'll go away a year, make some money, send it to her. I'll find us a new place to settle down, start all over again."

"Couldn't you do circus work again?"

"I'm through with that kid stuff." He glanced around. A family at the next table was staring. The father nodded hello, but Adam turned away. "I gotta get away from here. Might as well face facts. The Gaads woulda helped me rebuild, but they're gone."

Jessy sobbed at the memory of the family that had been so kind to them. Visions of their ruined home flashed through her head.

"I never should of stayed around here as long as I have. They pay good money for lumberjacks. Dangerous work, lonely, hard—but it pays good."

"But why not stay in Bethel? There must be three or four hundred people in this shelter, homeless like us. There'll be lots to do, putting everything right. They'll need carpenters, men like you—"

"I'm an outcast," he said flatly. "I'll never fit in."

Although Jessy had accepted her brother as he was, and hardly considered that an issue, the people of Bethel had long memories. Adam Flint's presence still caused a stir and Jessy had to respect his feelings.

That Webb, she thought angrily, pillar of the community, visits to the capitol, a son teaching at seminary, a daughter who learned to play every song in the hymnal as a girl. From what Suzanna had told her, Webb had attended Christian church services all his life, but tonight he didn't hesitate to toss needy people into the street. *What a hypocrite*, Jessy fumed. There he was, standing on his big veranda lording over her brother like judge, jury, and executioner. Her exhausted mind raced with images—the big Victorian house, his plush lawyer's office, the piano he had sent to Suzanna. The piano was gone now, along with everything else, lifted up into the air and disappearing as if it were nothing. Jessy shuddered, remembering how it felt to huddle in the cellar, helpless, while the house had been ripped away by the wind. She touched her cheek in a sort of dazed aftershock. She felt feverish. It was hard to think straight after all that had happened.

Adam was telling her about the logging business. She forced herself to focus on him. "Sounds primitive."

"You don't know the meanin' of the word."

"I've lived on a farm, haven't I?"

"Lap of luxury compared to loggin'! In them camps, men sleep with their favorite *ax*."

She smiled at the idea, but inwardly she was worried. The thought of Adam going off without Suzanna, doing dangerous work in the wilderness, forlorn, with nothing to console him but whiskey, terrified Jessy more than anything that had happened over the last two days. Someone had better look after him. "I could go with you."

He snorted in contempt.

"I'm perfectly capable. I could fell trees for a living, if I had to." In truth she had become adept at handling an ax. Jessy thought back to the long winters they had spent felling trees from the fringes of his property, snaking them out of the woods, cutting them down for fuel, hauling them to a saw mill to be planed into lumber. When he didn't respond, she affirmed, "Well, I could, you know. As long as the trees weren't too big . . ."

He shook his head helplessly at her. "My little sister . . ."

The sight of him filled her with such pity she said softly, "Maybe they could use a cook? You and Suzanna can have whatever money I earn, all of it."

Jessy wasn't prepared for the magical effect her words had on him. Tears welled in his eyes. "You're a good girl. If only everyone were good."

"People *are* good. I believe it."

"Shows how much *you* know. I seen people who'd kill you for a dime. Less."

Jessy didn't know why but she heard herself say, "Mr. Webb will help you."

"In a pig's eye." Adam pressed his hands against his temples and bowed his head over his bowl.

She knew it was pointless to argue but still she reached out to him, saying gently, "Tomorrow I'll go talk to him."

Adam's head came up with a snap. "You'll do no such thing. You're not crawlin' to him or to anyone else for anythin' in this stinkin' town! You hear me?"

"But it wouldn't hurt to . . ."

"Over my dead body."

"I only —"

"Try it and see what you get." Adam clenched his fist for emphasis.

"You folks doin' all right?" An emergency worker stood smiling down over them.

Adam didn't bother to respond. Instead he glared at Jessy who smiled sweetly at the man. "To tell you the truth, we could use a doctor."

"I'm a medic. What seems to be the matter?"

"My brother has a head injury."

Now Adam really scowled at her but he did allow the medic to look at the back of his head.

The medic whistled. "You need Doc Grady! You better take it easy." He patted Adam on the shoulder. "Wait here while I go get him."

While the medic went off, Adam shot a menacing glance at Jessy.

"I care what happens to you," she said in her softest voice.

Everyone paused when someone at the front of the hall began making an announcement: women and children were to sleep in the cots on the upper floor, while men, boys, and the emergency crews would occupy the lower floors of the building. Breakfast would be served at 7:00 A.M. and work details assigned at 7:45. A limited supply of hot water would be provided in the basement, near the latrines. Everyone was asked to keep the temporary dining rooms clean. Gas lights would be turned off in one hour.

Chairs pushed away from tables in all directions. The men were heading in one direction, the women and children in the other. Jessy stood to leave. First thing in the morning, she would go to the Webbs.

As if reading her mind, Adam turned to her, his deep voice rumbling. "Stay away from the Webbs."

She looked at him, her chin trembling.

"You hear me?"

With great reluctance, she nodded before following the women and children out of the hall.

Jessy sat on the hard iron cot and pulled off her boots. Old and worn, they were encrusted with grime. She had done hard work and hard walking in those boots, and this is where they had taken her. All her labors, all her prayers, had led her to this place. She tried to perceive the plan behind all that had happened, to accept this situation as God's will working through her and those around her, but nothing made sense. "What's the point, Lord? I don't understand. What are you teaching us?" Feeling numb as lead, she let the boots drop to the floor.

She heard the crisp sheets moving as she crawled under the covers. The big drafty study hall appeared blue in the night. She tried to imagine life in a logging camp but women and children near her rustled about on their cots. Many were either coughing or crying. Jessy pulled her mind upward to God in prayer, but she was so tired she slipped off to sleep. An instant later, or so it seemed, daylight was streaming in through the windows.

Jessy carried her breakfast tray to the table where Adam was sitting. "Good morning. How are you today? What did the doctor say?"

"Wants to see me again in a coupla days. I'll be long gone by then."

Jessy was just about to bite into a piece of toast. "When are we leaving?"

"You're not comin' with me! Loggin' camp's no place for a girl."

Jessy put down the bread. "I'm seventeen."

"All the more reason you shouldn't go. Men are crude. Cruel. They don't understand goodness. Purity."

Not go! Jessy felt crushed, not knowing what to do, where to look, what to think. "I never dreamed that the storm would b-break up everything, even our family." For Jessy this was the true catastrophe, the most dire consequence of the tornado, her greatest loss.

"Hey, don't cry," he said, awkwardly. "The government helps people left homeless after bad storms and such. See that couple over there? I talked with them just this mornin' 'bout you. They promised they'd find a place for you, most likely outta state, a work camp, collective, a farm or somethin'. Oh, stop cryin'. It won't be so bad, just for a year or two . . ."

"A year or two?"

They were interrupted by another announcement. Someone was being introduced to say the blessing. Jessy struggled to get hold of herself, lower her head, and pray.

"The Reverend Jeffrey Webb."

"Suzanna's brother!" she said to Adam in surprise. "From seminary."

Adam mumbled in disgust. "They're like bloody cockroaches. Everywhere."

Jessy tried to quiet him but now the invocation was over. She saw someone near the Reverend talking to him, pointing toward the crowd.

Jessy tried to eat, but the great lump in her throat made swallowing impossible. Adam was leaving without her. She might never see him again. While she stared down at the table, a shadow fell over her. She looked up to see the Reverend Webb.

"Mind if I join you?"

His hair was dark, unlike Suzanna's, and thinning at the temples, but he had the same warm blue eyes. His glasses made him appear serious, but Jessy liked his open, thoughtful expression. She pulled out a chair for him. Adam crossed and recrossed his legs under the table, as angry as she had ever seen him.

Jeffrey reached out his right hand toward Adam. "Don't believe we've ever met officially."

Adam shook his hand but said nothing.

"My brother, Matt, and I were always envious of your wrestling abilities. We never missed a match."

Adam nodded shortly. He looked as if he were getting ready to stand up and blow up. He couldn't go like this, she wouldn't let him. Jessy pressed both hands on the table, straining for words.

The Reverend went on talking effortlessly, blissfully unaware of any tension. "I came as soon as I heard about the twisters. Most of my students are here with me to help. Suzanna told me what happened to you, to your neighbors. I'm awfully sorry."

Jessy relaxed for the moment. "God will provide."

"Yes. And so will my father."

Adam laughed bitterly.

"I had a long talk with him last night. He's outside waiting for us. He would have come in but he thought I should mediate first. We all want you with us. Both of you. Mother's overjoyed with Stephen. To be perfectly frank, he's charmed the sox off Dad."

Jessy's nephew! So the little cherub hadn't let them down!

"What do you say, Mr. Flint? Can you forgive my father?" When Adam didn't—couldn't—speak, Jeff guided him to the window. "See for yourself." He rapped his knuckle on the glass and waved. "He's feeling like the goat this morning so go easy on him, will you?"

Still Adam said nothing. Jessy went over to the window. Sure enough, Mr. Webb was standing outside looking up at them.

Jeff patted Adam on the back. "George Webb seldom admits he's wrong, and believe me, I know. I've been knocking heads with him ever since I was two years old. If you ask me, you've won your greatest victory, Mr. Flint."

"Call me Adam," Jessy heard her brother say. He shook Jeff's hand in earnest now.

❧ 23 ❧

"Son," Mr. Webb said simply, extending his right hand and hugging Adam with his left. "Can you forgive an old man his folly?"

"Your daughter is the best wife a man could want. Who could blame you for bein' protective of her?"

"You've made her very happy. I couldn't be more pleased. No hard feelings?"

"None whatever."

"Come on, then, let's go home." Webb extended his hand to Jessy. "And you, young lady, Suzanna told us how you saved her life, and our grandson's. We could never repay the debt we owe you."

"It's my brother who deserves your thanks — always telling me to go to the cellar in bad weather."

"But the most amazing thing of all is how you managed to lift Suzanna up and carry her, and her seven months along."

"I've had lots of practice lifting, but after I made it to the cellar with Suzanna I was surprised myself, and weak all over. I believe God gave me strength only at the moment I needed it. Suzanna called it a miracle. I guess it was, as much a miracle as our coming together now as a family."

"Profound thought, Jessy," Webb said, "and as for your rescue operation, I've heard of similar feats. They're rare, but not unknown. A few years ago, in Kansas, a man was replacing a wagon wheel when somehow the jack slipped and the wagon fell on him. His wife, who weighed no more than eighty-five pounds, lifted the wagon off of him just enough so he could roll out of harm's way. No one could explain her sudden burst of strength except to say it was a miracle." Webb patted Jessy's hand. "Whatever the explanation, we're grateful to you. Eternally grateful. Isn't that right, Jeff?"

"Yes, Dad. Suzanna's my only sister."

"I couldn't love her more if we were blood sisters," Jessy said.

185

The group had reached the Webb home. Before they could go inside, Stephen, wearing a sailor suit, came running out to greet them. "Dad-dee! Look what Gamma gave me!"

"How's my boy?" Adam lifted up his son with gladness. "What you got there? Your grandmother give you a boat?"

The two-year old, clutching a toy sailboat, nodded happily.

Mrs. Webb stood at the doorway, smiling down on them. "We've been in the attic, getting out the children's clothes and toys for Stephen."

Adam climbed the stairs with Stephen in his arms. Suzanna hugged them both. "Oh, Darling, it's so wonderful to have you home."

To think that only a few moments ago, Adam, believing all was lost, was about to leave Bethel! Blessed indeed are the peacemakers, thought Jessy.

Suzanna was rattling on about all the news. "Mother's given us some lovely things for Stephen and the new baby."

"Shouldn't you be off your feet, Sue-Sue?" Adam asked, showing his concern.

"I've been sitting ever since I got here! Everyone's been waiting on me like a queen! Oh, but the news is dreadful: 142 dead so far, and none of the Gaads escaped. Mr. Gaad was in the barn with two of his sons. They found Mrs. Gaad, her daughter, and two of her grandchildren in the house, crushed."

Everyone looked shaken at this news, especially Jessy, who wept bitterly. Suzanna wrapped her arms around her.

"This town has become bedlam," Webb explained to Adam. "Rescue workers arriving in droves, Mrs. Webb and the Auxiliary sorting clothes, cooking, tending the injured. Five houses on this block have been set up as clinics. It'll take months to put the town right."

"Lots to be done, Darling. There's a sudden and desperate need for carpenters. Daddy says we can live here as long as we need to. We can stay in my old room. Your room is next to ours, Jessy. Come on!"

Upstairs, Jessy beheld the most elegant, spacious bathroom she had ever seen, with beveled mirrors in silver frames, crystal doorknobs, perfumed soaps, monogrammed towels, and a bathtub elevated on ball-and-claw feet.

"Would you like a bath, Jessy? It might help you feel better."

She nodded through her tears. After standing in line for an hour at the shelter last night, Jessy considered herself fortunate to be able to wash her face.

"Here's your room." Suzanna led her into a large garret with a full-length mirror, pastel walls, sparkling woodwork, and plush draperies. The big brass bed was covered with embroidered white linens. Broad windows overlooked the grounds — three acres of lawn, Jessy estimated, with flower beds and a whitewashed gazebo. Beyond were trees, thick masses of pines.

"I took all this for granted as a girl," Suzanna said. "After that storm I'll never take any blessing for granted again."

Jessy picked up the Bible on the reading table beside the bed.

"That's a gift for you from Daddy. When I told him you lost everything, even your Bible, he decided you should have that one."

"Oh, Suzanna, you're so thoughtful. I can hardly believe all this is really happening." Jessy lowered her voice so Adam wouldn't hear. "But how on earth did you talk your father into ..."

"I didn't. Jeff did. He gave Daddy a sermon! Of course, he gave me one, too. I agreed to ask Daddy to forgive me for eloping if Daddy would forgive Adam. When Daddy realized how happy I am and what a good husband and father Adam is, he was sorry not to have made amends sooner. The three of us talked for hours, just like old times. Once Daddy realized what we had gone through when the storm hit, he felt ashamed for refusing to take Adam in last night. He hadn't realized what terrible destruction we had survived, and how you saved my life. He wanted to make amends, but he didn't know how to go about it. So Jeff offered to act as a go-between."

Adam stepped into the doorway. "We're wanted downstairs for a town meetin'. All the bigwigs are here, even the mayor."

Downstairs, in a sunny parlor filled with fine furniture and snowy lace curtains, something caught Jessy's eye, a piece of hand-painted porcelain, a rococo scene of happy peasants haying and dancing, images that didn't square with reality. Fictitious peasants knew nothing of sweltering haymows, sudden rains, bugs and molds, hail, high wind, and disaster that took lives and ruined harvests.

A reporter from the capitol asked to interview Jessy, one of the stars of the storm. But for the present, she would have little time to bask in her sudden popularity. Community leaders, many of whom had sustained grievous losses, would use the Webb home to meet with emergency workers who would search the wreckage and rebuild Bethel. Everyone who was able, Jessy included, would help.

"If you help rebuild Bethel, I'll see that your barn is repaired and your home rebuilt," Webb promised Adam.

"The new house will have to be bigger than the old one. I was goin' to add on for the new baby, but now I'll have to start from scratch. Buildin' another house will take months," said Adam. "It'll have to be ready before winter. Suzanna's due in August."

"Don't you worry, Son. You just concentrate on rebuilding Bethel. I have an idea." For the moment, Webb refused to say more.

In the days to come, Adam helped search the rubble of shattered glass and sunken walls. He cherished one special victory, finding an infant crying, but otherwise unharmed, protected under its mother's body, a corpse in a gingham dress. Adam's carpentry, a source of pride and pleasure, had become a grim business of making coffins for adults and children alike.

Soon after the storm, Jessy spotted Adam with a team of construction workers repairing the roof of the church. Jessy thrilled to see him in the house of the Lord, even though the building was so badly damaged she could see blue sky through the rafters. Adam avoided the rededication service, however, shrugging and saying to her, "Nothin' mystical in repairin' a buildin'."

At the memorial service for all who were killed, Jessy prayed with the community, standing side-by-side with those who, having lost so much, stood confident, even at graveside, claiming ultimate triumph in Christ. Through their tears, the faithful could see the victory of life everlasting, of triumphant unity among believers of all ages, past, present, and future.

Suzanna admitted openly that her newfound peace was the precious gift of eternal life that had come to her with the winds that had so changed her being. Why worry about the terrors of earth when there was a heaven? In the light of God's promises, what did it matter that the tornado had come and gone and more might follow? The most desirable of earthly delights seemed shabby compared to the glories against which no evil would prevail.

Nature could be cruel, tearing down in an instant what had been built up over generations, but through all, and above all, God was with them. This Jessy knew for certain. The storm had torn all apart, but now all was being drawn together. After years of rebellion, Adam Flint had at last joined in the community, and for this Jessy rejoiced, but still her one great desire, that her brother would enter into a new life of faith, remained out of reach. Knowing the fervent prayers of the righteous avail much, she continued to pray that God would give Adam an unshakable, eternal faith and life everlasting but, as it had from the first day she met Adam, God's answer still seemed as remote as the stars.

❧ 24 ❧

Soon after her arrival at the Webbs', Jessy heard someone knocking insistently at the front door. When she, in a charming silk camisole, ran to answer, she found herself face to face with one of the handsomest young men she had ever seen. He was tall and lean, with a full droopy moustache, white teeth, olive skin, and bright blue eyes. They stared at one another in surprise. He looked Jessy up and down, drinking in her long silken hair, bare arms, and slender body. Jessy, angling the door into a shield, peeked around it. "Yes?"

"Is Matt here?"

"N-no, Suzanna's brother left just a little while ago, right after breakfast. I could give him a message, if you like, if I knew your name."

"Just tell him I'll catch up with him later. I'm Leo Kimball."

"Hi," she said lamely, her face partly hidden by thick brown shimmering waves that brushed her waist. "I'm Jessy Flint."

"Adam's sister? The one who saved Suzanna's life?"

Jessy blushed shyly. "Aren't you the great pitcher?"

"Do you like baseball?"

"I used to at school, back East." *Four years ago. Or was it four thousand years ago?* she mused.

"We have a three-county league. You ought to come out and see us play some time. But I don't know when we'll have time for a game. The storm's wrecked things for the moment. You don't get out much, do you?"

"N-No, I don't," she said softly.

"Your brother planning to rebuild? We heard you lost everything."

"Almost. A neighbor's tending what's left of Adam's livestock."

Leo nodded sympathetically, then paused, listening. "Chopin. Nice."

"Nattie Paulson, next door. She practices her piano every morning."

For one fleeting moment the pair enjoyed the romantic waltz filling the sunny morning air.

"That Nattie Paulson!" Mrs. Webb stormed in bearing fresh vegetables from her garden. "That woman has time for piano but no time for the clinic!"

From the upstairs landing, Adam boomed, "Jessy!! What are you doin' half naked talkin' to strange men?"

"Adam!" Jessy slammed the door shut in Leo Kimball's face.

"Where did you get that, that *thing* you got on?"

"Suzanna found it for me in the attic. It used to be hers."

"What happened to your own clothes?"

"They're soaking in the wash tub. They were filthy."

"Get up here!" Controlling his temper with obvious difficulty, Adam said in a deadly low rumble, "I'd rather see you dressed modestly in clothes soiled from honest work than like this. Half your body's uncovered. What would your mother think?" Before she could answer, he hauled her into the room where Suzanna was bathing Stephen. "This get-up your idea?"

"Why yes, Darling. Clothing is scarce, what with everyone being hit by the storm. This was the best I could do."

"But the girl's half naked!"

"She is not."

"Are you blind? Strangers will be wandering in and out of this house all day. Men are sure to notice her." He yanked Jessy's hair so hard she yelped in pain. "And why is your hair loose?"

Red with shame, she explained, "I washed it. It isn't dry yet." She didn't dare add that she had seen other girls in town with loose hair.

"I catch you like this ever again, I'll shave your head, I swear it."

Jessy stammered, "Oh, you wouldn't . . ."

"Oh, no? Pull a stunt like this again and see what happens. I don't want you attractin' attention. You're to be modest at all times, a pure, chaste young lady, which means you don't go paradin' around like one of the future whores of America. Is that clear?"

She nodded vigorously.

"Just because we're livin' in town for now doesn't mean you can act any way you please. Men'd see you like this and think you're ready to do whatever they feel like. I'm still your brother and you'll behave yourself. Don't go tryin' anythin' new without askin' me first."

"Dear," said Suzanna, pinning Stephen's diaper, "you're making a mountain..."

"Don't undermine my authority. I won't stand for it."

"You of all people lecturing Jessy about modesty! She's perfectly..."

"I know how men think. No one knows any better 'n me."

"Darling, you really ought to calm down. It isn't as if Jessy were going outside this way."

Adam snatched his son away from her, cupping the boy's damp curls in one big, protective hand. "I'll be glad when we get back to the farm. This is no place for raisin' children."

"May I remind you that I was born and raised here?"

With lips pursed and a devilish twinkle in his eyes, Adam studied her swollen breasts and protruding abdomen. "And look at how you turned out."

Suzanna hugged him close. "You just miss your normal routine. That's why you're feeling out of sorts. My darling. I love you with all my heart, do you know that?" He nodded sheepishly. "And I certainly don't mean to interfere between you and Jessy. I'm sorry I got her into trouble." Suzanna turned around. "I apologize, Jessy. Why don't you ask Mother if she might be able to help?" Suzanna turned back to her husband. "Now what can I do to make you feel better?"

He put Stephen down on his little feet and took Suzanna into his arms. "Oh, I can think of a few things—"

Jessy seized the opportunity to escape to her room. While she pinned her hair into a neat chignon, she could hear a work crew gathering shovels and pick axes from the back porch. Once they left, she sought Mrs. Webb and a change of clothes. It was then Jessy learned Mr. Webb was expecting her to visit his law office after she had finished her shift at the clinic.

Everywhere people were clearing debris and making repairs. At the Town Hall, a team of bricklayers was rebuilding a ruined wall. At Mr. Webb's office, two men were replacing a broken plate glass window. Through the empty frame, Jessy could see George Webb busy at his desk. "Sir, did you send for me?"

"Yes, I did. Come on in. I'll be right with you."

Jessy entered the place where Adam had signed his will more than three years earlier. Except for the broken glass, nothing seemed to have changed. The one important addition this afternoon was Stephen, bouncing on his grandfather's lap. "Read to me, Gra-da," she heard him ask.

Webb complied with good cheer. " 'This contract, made and entered into this [blank] day of [blank] between [blank] and [blank], both of said State and County, W-I-T-N-E-S-S-E-T-H that for and in consideration of [dollar sign] [blank] due and payable on the [blank] day of [blank] and in further consideration of ... " He paused to refer to his scribbled draft, made a few more notes, and went on reading in silence, absentmindedly pulling a heavy gold watch from his vest. The old gold gleamed in his hands. Stephen grabbed it before Webb had a chance to return it to his pocket. "All right, you can play with it." The attorney resumed his work on the contract.

How white his hands were, Jessy noticed, the nails scrupulously clean and trimmed. How unlike Adam's or even her own. In the golden light of day, Webb looked like an honored dignitary out of a history book. From her place on the settee she admired a clear crystal triangle on a side table. She wanted to pick it up but didn't dare touch it.

"Go ahead. It's all right," Webb said to her.

When she took up the prism she gasped at the effect. As she moved it around in the light, the room was filled with rainbows that danced in all directions over the stately interior of somber russett, green, and brown. Jessy let the light stream over her hands—red, orange, yellow, green, and blue as pure and bright as on their day of creation. When she turned the prism in Webb's direction, he too became drenched with color, his white shirt covered in rainbows. Stephen squealed with delight. Jessy shook her head in wonder. "Life's full of grand surprises, isn't it?"

"It is indeed," said Webb, patting his grandson's little arms.

"The rainbow, the sign of the covenant God made with Noah after the Flood."

"How does that verse go?" mused Webb. "And I saw another mighty angel come down from heaven, clothed with a cloud: and a rainbow was upon his head."

"Revelation," Jessy said, remembering. "Thank you again for the Bible."

"It was my pleasure to give it to you."

"Gosh, you certainly must love to read." With great care Jessy set down the prism and began looking at Webb's books. The largest section was devoted to law and reference works, but there were other kinds of books on subjects such as history, geography, philosophy, religion, classics, biographies, and commentaries. "You have a wonderful library," she said with awe.

"I've been thinking of giving away some of those. I'm out of shelf space." He pointed to a stack of new books piled on the floor behind an armchair. "I need to make space for these. Pick out what you'd like."

"Oh, Mr. Webb, that's very kind of you, but there's no need to . . ."

"You'd be doing me a favor, taking them off my hands."

Stephen squirmed off his grandfather's lap and ran to the prism.

"No, Stephen! It's delicate!" She held it from him. He began to wail.

"Look at what I've got, young man," said Webb, holding up a snow globe. Stephen went running back. "See the snow falling over the village? Your mother and your uncles used to play with this when they were about your size."

While the boy played happily with the paperweight, Webb said to Jessy, "Now you go ahead and take some of those books. They say it's more blessed to give than to receive."

"Acts Twenty?"

"You know your Bible, don't you?"

"It's my favorite book," she answered. "But of course it's more than a book."

"And what do you conceive it to be?"

Without hesitation she answered, "Love letters from God! And the best mysteries, most exciting adventures, the most moving dramas, the finest poetry, the greatest treasure — the Living Word of God."

"Amen!"

Jessy paused before saying what was uppermost in her heart. "Mr. Webb, when you made it possible for this family to stay together, it was the answer to my prayer, one that never could have happened without God's intervention and your help. God helps us in such marvelous ways, so much better than we can help ourselves without Him." Jessy smiled shyly. "Once I went to the circus and — I know this sounds silly — but I think God, high up on His throne, sees our world as clearly as we do looking down on a flea circus! He sees each one of us and every little piece of the puzzle."

A repairman interrupted. "All done, Mr. Webb. It'll be four dollars even."

As Webb paid the man, he said, "Now, Jessy, you'll take some of those books, won't you?"

"Oh, yes, if you really don't need them any more. Thank you very much."

"And that prism? Take it too, as a sign of our friendship."

"Thank you, Mr. Webb, for everything."

As she left, she noticed Mr. Webb hunting through a stack of files. What was he looking for? When he lifted his sights to survey the top of his littered desk, he nodded wisely to Jessy. Off she went with the prism making rainbows over the ravaged city streets.

❦ 25 ❦

Adam stepped into the Webb kitchen where Suzanna was trying, with little success, to feed Stephen his breakfast. He frowned at his boy for idly poking at his cereal. "Son, either eat it or I'll take it away from you and you'll go hungry."

Stephen seriously regarded his father and then the bowl of goo which would have so nicely adorned walls, floors, and furniture. When he tried reaching for a handful, his father took both mischievous little hands into one of his own. "No wastin' food, hear me? Takes too much work to grow it. Say, Mom, would you mind watchin' Stephen for a while? Suzanna 'n me're goin' for a ride."

"Mind? I thought you'd never ask."

"We won't be gone long."

"Take your time! Take all day. Goodness knows, you need to get away!" Mrs. Webb lost no time spoiling her grandson. "You don't like your cereal? Well, you don't have to eat it. Have a sugar cookie!"

"Mom!" said Suzanna peevishly. She squealed as Adam came up behind her, wrapped his arms around her, kissed the nape of her neck, and deftly untied her apron. "Darling! Where are we off to in such a hurry?"

"You'll see. Fetch Jessy while I hitch up the team."

While the three passed through Main Street, Adam told of the talk he'd had with George Webb the previous evening. After supper, Webb had called Adam into his private study to ask what he knew about Lucy Meredith. Adam managed to keep calm as he answered his father-in-law: "Folks figure I had somethin' to do with her disappearance but I never even met the woman. I don't know what happened to her."

"Lucy's husband, a railroad engineer, was a good friend of mine," explained Webb. "We grew up together and attended university at the same time. He passed away before you came to Bethel."

"I heard," said Adam, wondering, as he was to tell the story later, what Webb was leading up to.

Webb continued, "Meredith died, leaving a widow but no children and no will. After Lucy's disappearance, I was called on by the court to help settle the estate. In the meantime, the house stood vacant and fell into disrepair, as you've probably noticed. When the estate was settled, the house and its contents were put up at auction. I always felt sentimental about the place so I bought it for my older son, but Jeff plans to continue teaching at seminary. My younger son, Matt, yearns to go out West. That leaves you and Suzanna."

At this point in Adam's narrative, Suzanna interrupted. "Oh, sweetheart, you aren't trying to tell us that Daddy's giving us . . ."

"That's exactly what I'm about to tell you. The property's four times the size of my old place. Close to town, too, and school."

"Us live at that old horror house of Lucy Meredith's? You can't be serious," said Jessy.

"It ain't a horror house! It was bein' restored when the storm hit. There's 360 acres in all, a barn, and stables. Hasn't been farmed in thirty years or more." Adam turned to his wife. "Your father will help us get started. Give us furniture. Loan us money for equipment and livestock. Course, the house still needs repairs, but I can do them. If you ask me, your folks want to be near their grandchildren, pure and simple. What do you think?"

"I think it's wonderful. Oh, just look at it."

They had arrived at the Meredith place, just a half mile from town. Together the Flints beheld the spectacle in the early morning light, when the dew-soaked earth seemed to rise up and meet the first angling rays of morning. The two-story, freshly painted pale yellow with white gingerbread trim, seemed to glow amid the dense green of an overgrown yard. Light shining all around him, Adam stepped down and helped Suzanna out of the carriage. Despite the recent heavy rains, the land felt solid underfoot.

"Twelve rooms and a country kitchen," explained Adam, as they approached the porch. "Four bedrooms up, two down, two bathrooms, parlor, dining room, sun room, den, screened back porch, attic, basement, and ten fireplaces!"

Jessy paused at the front door. "And how many ghosts?"

"None!" Adam led the way to the front hall. His voice boomed in the big empty house. "Plenty of room for us, and the new baby."

"Oh, Darling," said Suzanna. "I used to come here visiting with Mother and Daddy. I never dreamed I could live here! Look at the size of this kitchen!" Suzanna clutched her husband's arm. "What pretty wallpaper. Mother must have picked it out. A pump at the sink! We won't have to haul in water any more."

"This place gives me the creeps!"

"Oh, Jessy, come on! It's beautiful. Look at the craftsmanship."

"Suzanna's right." Adam rapped the back of his hand against the woodwork. "Solid oak. Last several lifetimes."

"What if Lucy Meredith comes back one night?" Jessy glanced with apprehension at the parlor, gracious and vast but as yet unrestored. With its fourteen-foot ceiling, it looked like a ballroom. The crystal chandelier was dingy with cobwebs and dirt. Wallpaper sagged in sheets that had separated from the walls. The room was damp and cold. "Feels like a moldy old mausoleum."

"What we could do with this room!" Adam paced the inlaid floor. "Repaint it, clean that chandelier. A fire in the fireplace..."

Suzanna continued where Adam left off. "Custom drapes, Queen Anne furniture, or maybe Italian, and a new piano over there..."

"Whoa!" said Adam. "You're talkin' *money*! Don't forget, your poor husband lost everythin' in that storm."

"Oh, Darling, I'm sure Daddy would want us to furnish our home properly." She looked at her husband with cunning. "No?"

"No. We'll need to put the money into farm equipment, livestock, feed, major repairs. There's a lot to do."

"Still, I think it's wonderful, Darling," she said, holding his hands close to her lips.

"I think *you're* wonderful."

Jessy rolled her eyes toward the dingy ceiling. Paint had been flaking off by the handfuls, creating piles of debris on the floor. Big cobwebs hung like vapors high above her head. "I still say the place gives me the creeps."

"Come on, let's take a look outside."

"Mind if I sit through this next dance, Darling? My feet."

"Allow me," he answered, lifting and carrying Suzanna to the front porch.

While Suzanna rested on the porch, Adam forced a path from the house to the barn, with Jessy trailing behind him, hip deep in weeds. Nature had claimed back what man had once cultivated. The place was overgrown with saplings. Pine trees had sprouted up and now flourished in what was once open pasture and fields. Adam whistled. "What a job this is gonna be."

"Let me guess who's going to cut down all these trees and pull up all their roots before any plowing can be done," said Jessy, frowning.

"You guessed right."

"I feel tired just thinking about it."

"And you wanted to go *loggin'* with me?"

The raucous calls of red-winged blackbirds, thousands of them, interrupted Jessy. The thick brush felt alive with their grrk-grrrrrrking. "Lucky birds. You neither sow nor reap nor weed."

"You see the weeds. I see the potential."

"I see blueberries!" Jessy picked a handful. "Mmmm. They're delicious. Want some?"

Adam took a few. "Mmmm. So whatdya think 'bout our movin' here?"

"I'll miss the old place, the sugar maples, the bluebird nests..."

"I do believe you're sentimental, Jessy Flint!"

"I am. I liked the old place."

"We'll be more than five miles closer in to town here."

"True!" Jessy smiled. "Close to dances, parties, socials, parades, the opera house. Church. Just think of it."

"That's not what I had in mind." He pointed to the railroad line. "Station's just down the road."

"And the cemetery's even closer. Talk about convenience."

Ignoring her, he went on, "From here we could get hogs to market in a fraction of the time it used to take."

As if on cue, the thunderous sound of an approaching train drowned out Jessy's reply. "I don't think I could get used to that." Genuinely upset, she screamed, "Sounds like the tornado bearing down on us all over again!"

"I like the sound of trains. Reminds me of my travelin' days."

"The Man of Iron. Nerves of steel and all that."

"You bet. Dad says the barn's a beauty. Let's have a look." They pushed through the weeds to the rustic masterpiece pierced with windows in the shapes of snowflakes, no two alike. "Look at this workmanship," noted Adam, rapping a massive handhewn pillar. "Clean, too."

"Cleaner than the living room." Jessy looked up to the hay loft shrouded in darkness. "Wonder what's up there."

"Climb up and take a look."

"No, thanks," she said, thinking of Lucy Meredith with a shiver.

"Nobody's up there. The sheriff went through this place top to bottom. He never found a trace of Lucy Meredith. Come on, let's take a look out back. George says there's an icehouse, stables, two corncribs, pens . . . "

They wandered for nearly an hour without reaching the far property line. On their way, Adam would stop every now and then to examine the soil. "Looks good," he said, again and again. "Shame to let this place run to seed like it has but we can fix that."

Jessy stood on tiptoe, pointing. "What's over there?"

"Land."

"And there?"

"More land."

Jessy marveled at the scale of it, but she knew her work would be more demanding than ever. As they walked back toward the house, Adam spoke not of a few cows but thirty, not thirty hogs but 200. As Adam pressed for her reaction, she thought of all the work this place would require. For her there would be no escape from weeds and work and long days ahead, in cold and heat, rain and snow. She might as well have been bound up in chains. She glanced around again at the vast horizon and big sky above them, remembering how close the family had come to dissolving in one disastrous moment. At last, from her heart she said, "I want what you want, whatever you think is best for our family."

Adam smiled. "I want this place." He drank in the view. "In my life, till now, no one's ever given me anythin' 'cept trouble. This time I really hit the jackpot. Can't get used to the idea someone would give me somethin' this fine."

"Isn't it high time to thank God for all the wonderful things He's done for you?" When Adam didn't answer, she came to stand beside him. "People are good. Didn't I tell you?"

"*Some* people," he said. "Guess I been runnin' with the wrong crowd all these years." Adam snapped his fingers with his old dramatic flare, as if just remembering what he had been aware of all along. "By the way, it might interest you to know that George is givin' one-third of the property to you for savin' Suzanna's life. That's 120 acres of some of the richest farm land in the world. He'll put it in writin'. Do you realize that your share alone's bigger than my other farm?"

Jessy was too stunned to speak. On the way back to Bethel, squawking red-wings raised up their epaulets, saluting their passing carriage. For one brief moment, Jessy felt like royalty.

❧ 26 ❧

For a long time, Jessy had been wanting to ask. She waited all day before approaching Adam. Although it was only five o'clock, the sun was already slipping from view. Over her heaviest clothes she wore two frayed sweaters. Her double pair of wool stockings hardly kept her feet warm. In the chill air, she could see her breath, Adam's, and even the cow's. While she held Cressida's tail to protect Adam's face from being swished as he milked, Jessy asked quietly: "Adam?" She wet her chapped lips, then rubbed them with one equally raw hand. "We've been living here four years now, right?"

"Right." He continued to concentrate on his work.

"In the seven years since I came to live with you, I've never asked you for anything, not even one day off, now have I?"

"It ain't a picnic for me, either. To make this place pay, we gotta work near to death. You oughta know; you keep the books. Hand me that rag."

"Here." After she handed it to him, she took a deep breath. "What I mean is, well, tomorrow's Sunday." She looked down at her soiled rubber boots peaking from under the thick, hard-worn edges of her skirt. Her toes were so numb with cold she couldn't feel them. Aware that this was no time to dillydally, she spoke very fast. "In a few weeks it'll be Christmas and I want to go to church."

"Christ."

"That's what's wrong with you! You take the holiest name of all, the name that's above all other names, and turn it into a curse!"

Adam's jaw hardened and his shoulders flexed, but he didn't look up at her. "My answer's still no."

"Adam, please. It's been ages since I've been to church. I'll only be gone three hours at the most." She pulled a scrap of newsprint from her pocket. "Bible study is at ten, worship at eleven. It's a twenty minute walk, so I should be back here about ... "

"No!" He stood, took the lantern from its hook, and called out to Stephen. "Hey, son, it's time you stopped playin' with that calf. Go ahead of us with this."

Once he handed the lantern to Stephen, Adam picked up two of the four seven-gallon containers of fresh milk. Jessy picked up the remaining two and, with her heavy load, followed Adam and Stephen outside through the approaching darkness. They picked their way with care for a steady sleet, which had been falling since morning, had glazed the path to the cellar with ice. Once Stephen had opened the cellar doors, gone down the steps, and hung the lantern on a hook, Adam and Jessy followed.

As soon as Adam set down the milk, he began rummaging through shelves crammed with gear, muttering, "It oughta be here somewhere." When he noticed that Stephen was playing with something, he snapped, "Haven't I told you not to play with my tools! Put that down!" Adam continued hunting. "Now, where's that shell disc?"

"Last I saw, it was in the shed," said Jessy. "I'll get it for you." She stepped around the heavy milk cans she had just put down. "Why can't I go?"

"Go where?" asked Adam, distracted.

"To church!"

"Drop it, Jessy. Stephen, I said stay outa my gear! Go upstairs and help your mother!"

As the boy ran off, Jessy fumed with silent fury. From the start, she had sought out her brother to love and be loved, not to do battle, but now she was shaking with anger. "For seven years I've worked for you like a slave, with never a please nor thank you. I've never taken a day for myself for school or friends, and ever since we moved here I've been working seven days a week, year in and year out. I've shoveled manure and snow, scrubbed your dirty clothes, cut wood same as you. I've hauled water, gotten rained on, been half frozen. I've dug potatoes standing knee-deep in mud, and I've been up all night in freezing cold pens helping you deliver stuck piglets—and calves, half the time with a block and tackle. And after Mr. Gaad died, bless him, I've helped you butcher hogs every winter. Man's work, most of it, hard and dirty, and in all that time I've never asked you for a thing."

She rubbed her bare, aching hands together. "From the start, you haven't wanted me around, but I've worked hard for you." When she could no longer control her tears, she ran up the cellar stairs sputtering, "If only you loved me, even just a little, maybe you would treat me better. You have no respect for God or me or anyone!"

"Hey! Come back here! Jessy!"

She didn't stop running until she reached her bedroom on the second floor. After locking the door, she sat in the dark and cried. She could hear Suzanna and the children, rattling in the kitchen far below her in the big old Victorian house. For a long while Jessy stared at nothing. Sitting on the bed, she imagined herself packing her few belongings and going away. But to where? To do what? Every so often a gust of wind would drive the falling sleet into a swirling stream against her windows. Shivering, she began to pray: "Dear God, what should I do? This situation is impossible. Adam will never—"

"Jessy? You in there? Open up!" Adam's booming voice so close startled her. He had come up the stairs so quietly she hadn't heard. Now he was pounding on her door.

"Leave me alone!" she shouted.

"Open up, I said!"

"What for? So you can beat me?"

Adam chuckled. "Stop bein' a martyr and open up."

Jessy got up and stood near the door, saying, "No."

"Don't make me mad."

"Don't make you mad? What about me? What about my feelings? My emotions? My needs? I make one simple request and you're such a slave driver you can't even—"

"I got my reasons. Open the door and I'll explain myself."

"No need to bother," Jessy muttered. "I'm aware of your views on the subject of religion. In the past, you've made them all too plain."

He startled her by jiggling the door knob violently. "You know I could break down this door in no time."

"Brute force is your solution to every problem, isn't it?"

"I don't have time to waste fixin' busted doors, not with everythin' else needin' doin' 'round here. If you want me to explain, then do as you're told and open up."

"You tyrant!" She kicked at the door so hard it jumped. "All the years I've wasted praying for you! Well, never again! You're nothing but a hard-hearted heathen. Why should I bother worrying about you? You deserve your rotten fate!" At once she regretted her words. Abandon Adam? Would Christ?

"Oh, Adam, please forgive me. I'm sorry. I didn't mean—" Jessy threw open the door, but he was gone. She shut the door again, then crumbled against it. "Dear Heavenly Father, what horrible things I said to that poor lost soul. Please forgive me. I could never stop praying that You grace Adam's life with . . . Oh, what's the use? This is hopeless! Why waste time with that—that—barbarian?"

Fumbling in darkness for a match, she lit her lamp and sat at her desk. She wrote a goodbye note to Suzanna and the children. It didn't take her long to pack her things, but she couldn't find her gloves. She realized she had left them in the barn.

After a fitful night's sleep, she wakened and dressed. Though it was still dark, she could sense that yesterday's sleet had turned to snow, the thick pillowy kind that piled high, fast, and deep. The muffled roar of a train reached her. Its mournful wail suited her mood perfectly. To her empty, growling stomach she snapped, "We're fasting, remember? Fast and pray! Now be quiet!" She made her bed, put the note on her pillow, picked up her boots and bundle, and entered the hall in her stocking feet.

Passing the open door of the master bedroom, she noticed that the bed was already made. The room glowed in rosy lamplight, highlighting the mahogany four-poster from Suzanna's girlhood room, her handmade quilts, delicate curtains, marble washstand with pitcher and bowl. In the rooms nearby Jessy heard the gentle sounds of the children, all three still sleeping. "Your aunt will miss you," she whispered. "I hope you remember the prayers Suzanna and I taught you without your daddy knowing. Will you even remember me once I leave you? You're so small and sweet, and the world's so cruel. I love you!"

There was movement in the kitchen. The scent of cinnamon wafted on the air. Suzanna was baking sweet rolls, the family's favorite Sunday morning treat. The night before, after she'd made her decision to leave, Jessy had decided there would be no painful goodbyes. Quickly and quietly, she pulled on her boots and opened the front door. An arctic blast of air and snow gusted into her face, sucking her breath away. She had to push her way through the wind toward the barn. With relief she opened the side door and stepped into the warmth generated by twenty cows.

The air inside was redolent with mash, Adam's homegrown corn aged under pressure in the silo. Her gloves were near the stall of a newborn calf, the roan heifer she had found with its mother, beside a distant pond, just two days before, the one Stephen had taken such a liking to. To the calf she had carried here in her arms, she said, "I'll miss you."

On her way out, Jessy ran headlong into Adam. When he saw she was carrying a bundle, he grabbed it from her. "Where do you think you're goin'?" When she attempted to retrieve her belongings and step around him, he wouldn't let her. "What's your hurry? Meetin' somebody?"

"No, of course not."

"Why else would you sneak off in a blizzard in such a big hurry, if you weren't gonna meet up with Kem Curtis?"

"Who?"

"Don't act dumb."

"What are you talking about?"

"Curtis came by here a few weeks ago, remember? Soon after his wife died and left him with five kids."

Jessy strained to remember. "Oh, the man who raises Black Angus—"

"Used to, till his whole herd sickened and died. All the time I been livin' in this township that man's tried one thing and then another on that pitiful farm of his without any success whatever." Adam leaned back against a pillar. "Came by here to talk to me."

"While I was pulling onions," Jessy recalled. "I remember thinking how odd it was for him to visit us. He never did before."

"Or since."

"His visit seemed to put you into one of your moods."

"Know why? Course you do." Adam pursed his lips, savoring the rich irony of what he was about to say. "Kem Curtis asked me if he could take you to church." Adam's eyes glinted with sarcasm. "I know how men think, no matter how they try to cover up their real purpose."

Jessy blushed. "You mean he came to ask about me?"

"And him half bald and more 'n twice your age. Wears out his old lady till she dies, and figures he can get a nice young hardworkin' girl like you and start all over again."

"I had no idea."

"Sure." Adam's voice was thick with sarcasm.

"Honest."

"And you ask to go to church so you can meet guys."

"No! How could you even think such a thing?"

"I must say I woulda never come up with as underhanded an idea as Kem's, but when I was single I'd do just about anythin' to get girls to notice me. I'd show off, fight, talk big. Didn't care how I got their attention, long as they done what I wanted." He threw his impressive chest out to make his point. "By the time I was twenty, it took no effort at all to win them over." His successful marriage had only increased his appeal and heightened his charms. Adam Flint still had the looks, build, and voice women would risk all for.

"It's time you noticed the opposite sex and they noticed you but I just can't see you goin' for a guy like Kem. He's a sorry sort, if you ask me." Adam scratched his head and sniffed the cold. "Maybe I'm wrong, but that farm of his is an eyesore. Pigs with the mange, kids and chicks runnin' around in the rain, trash all over the place. House looks like it oughta be condemned."

Despite the grim picture Adam painted, Jessy looked a trifle enchanted. "Still, he did come to call for me. What did you say to him?"

"Whadya think I told him?"

She sighed dismally. "I can imagine. And what did he say?"

"He ain't been back, not to see me, anyway. I figured he might get to you somehow, and you'd go sneakin' off without tellin' me."

"Oh, Adam, how could you accuse me of such a thing?"

He tightened his grip on her bundle. "Who's the one tryin' to run off?"

"I'm not going to meet anyone. I've never spoken to that man in my life, and I certainly wouldn't go to church to meet men, Kem Curtis or anyone else."

While she sputtered on, he rummaged through her bundle: a change of clothes, a towel and hairbrush, the stub of a pencil, a small notebook, her toothbrush, a sliver of soap, and the Bible and prism George Webb had given her. Adam clicked his tongue. "Runnin' off without so much as a goodbye!"

Trying not to cry, Jessy looked away.

"What've you got in your pockets?"

"Nothing!" Turning to him, Jessy pulled them out for him to see. "As usual."

"You got a lot less now than when you first showed up at my place."

"Life is more than collecting things. What we are inside is what matters, and whether we honor God." She took the prism and admired the rainbow it made, the Old Testament symbol of one of God's great promises. "The whole world's out there, waiting to hear some good news."

Adam laughed at her. "You and your high-flyin' ideas. When I was your age, I woulda taken all the cash in the house."

"I'm not you."

"Come to think of it, that Leo Kimball showed interest but you didn't give him any encouragement whatsoever. Bright young man, too."

"Leo isn't a Christian. I couldn't be unevenly yoked."

"Plan on goin' into the haulin' business?" asked Adam, deliberately misunderstanding her.

"I wouldn't have Leo Kimball on a silver platter."

"Suzanna says half the girls in the county'd have him any way they could get him."

"Well, let them. He's so arrogant!" Jessy remembered Leo's boldness, how he had stared at her, openly, with mocking blue eyes. It had been a long time since they first met, that day he had knocked on the Webbs' back door, catching her in Suzanna's camisole.

Her second encounter with Leo Kimball had been one sweltering summer day when he arrived at the Flints' with a group of men to thresh. Every summer, threshing lasted six days a week for two weeks. The men visited one farm after another, starting around nine, when the grain had dried in the morning sun and could be separated by a co-op owned threshing machine. The men took the big steam-powered thresher from one dusty field to the next, while women and children worked in hot country kitchens along their route. The Flint crop had required a full day's work.

At midday, Jessy had just closed the gate around the flower beds when she heard Leo say, "I wish I had my camera. You make quite a picture, with all those flowers in your arms and that little girl tugging at your skirts."

She and her niece, Martha, had been picking flowers. Jessy was wearing her favorite dress, a soft, sweeping cloud of pastel cotton Suzanna had sewn for her. After that day, every time she wore it she had thought of Leo, and how she had hoped he wouldn't notice she was perspiring. But then, he too was drenched, his thin blue shirt sticking to him in such a way as to make her aware of his physique. He had gained muscle since she had seen him last.

"You haven't been to a baseball game since the tornado," Leo said. "I pitched a no-hitter a couple of weeks ago."

"I heard! Congratulations!"

"Beautiful flowers."

"They're for the table. I can't take the credit for growing them. Suzanna does. I'm just the field help around here." Awkwardly she had groped for her niece's small hand. "Excuse me," Jessy had said as she stepped out of Leo's way and onto the hem of her new dress. She felt a total fool long afterward.

Later that day, she had seen Leo again. Nearly everyone else was resting after lunch. Jessy was sitting on the back steps, shelling beans for supper.

"You sure keep busy. Don't you ever relax?" Leo asked.

"There's always something to do around here. How's the harvest?"

"So far, above average."

Although she did her best to remain cool and keep her attention on the beans, she couldn't help but notice and admire the way Leo moved. She especially liked the way he rested his back and one foot up against a column. When he caught her staring at him, his chest expanded in triumph. She had torn her eyes away and looked toward the barn where Adam was rattling around.

Leo pushed his hat back. "Don't worry. Your brother already knows that you'll be my wife."

"Your what?"

"I asked him this morning." Leo took off his hat. His hair tumbled toward his shoulders in loose, dark waves. He raked at it with one hand before putting his hat on again. "So how about it? Wanna get married?"

He's as arrogant as he is attractive, Jessy had thought, too stunned to speak. Everyone knew he had gone off to college but had returned before graduating. The gossip was that he was homesick. Homesick for what? Bugs and weeds and ailing cattle? The smell of manure? Or, riding bareback through sweet grasslands and swimming in crystal rivers? Who could blame him? These things had come to mean home to her, as they did to everyone in Bethel. Despite how excited Jessy became in Leo Kimball's presence, she had to face facts.

"I hardly know you," Jessy said simply. "And I don't even know that I want to get married."

"And just what do you think you were put on this earth for, anyway?"

"To give praise and glory to God."

"So you're one of them Christian types." Leo shook his head.

When she stood, offended, he approached her gently, with his hat in his hands. His spoke soft and low now. "If you could only go for a guy that had religion, then I'd get me some."

This made her laugh. "You don't just go out and get religion, like it was a wolf you catch in a trap or a sack of sugar you tote home from the store, or like it was something you could hold in your hands or lock away in a box. God can't be locked in a box."

"So how does a person find God?" He looked serious, but a smile played around the corners of his mouth.

"By saying yes when God calls us. And whenever that happens—" Jessy suddenly decided she didn't approve of that earthy look of his. "You're teasing me." She turned to go.

"Don't go. Please! What do I need to do to make you marry me? Tell me and I'll do it." When she didn't answer, he said softly, "I've seen every girl in this town—in the whole county. I've gone to all the dances, the picnics, every party. My mother and sisters introduce me to every female they know. I've been to college and back and I've never seen a girl like you, not one who interests me the way you do. I made up my mind. You're the one for me. There's something about you—"

"Leo? Leo!" Someone was shouting from the yard. "We're ready to start threshing again."

Leo turned from her, calling out, "Be right there, Dad."

Once Leo and the others had begun the afternoon's threshing, Jessy retreated to the kitchen. In just a few short moments her life had seemed to change. She gazed out to the sizzling field of oats being reduced to stubble by a dozen men. As she helped the women wiping dishes, she wondered what it would be like to have Leo hold her in his arms and kiss her, his black, wiry moustache brush-brushing against her lips. Blushing at the very idea, Jessy became so flustered she had chipped Suzanna's best serving dish.

Before twilight Leo and the rest of the threshing crew left the Flints, moving to other farms, other harvests, and to other girls in other country kitchens. She knew there would be other girls in their new, pretty dresses picking other flowers in other sun-drenched gardens.

"Leo told me he loved you." Adam's voice brought Jessy back to the freezing cold here-and-now.

Coming to herself, she shrugged and said, "I can't believe I'm the only girl he claims to love."

"Don't you like him?"

"I don't really know." And she didn't.

"Another time, he came to see you and you wouldn't even come downstairs and talk to him."

"I felt awful that day. I had a cold. My nose was all red and—"

And Leo hadn't been by to see her since.

"Suzanna says he's seein' a girl over in Carleton these days. Her father's got money."

So, that's the end of that. Jessy tried not to show her disappointment. She had missed her golden opportunity for romance, but more importantly, she hadn't been successful in her Christian witness. "I'm not at all convinced I should get married to Leo or to anyone else."

Adam juggled her bundle around. "So where you goin'?"

"Big city."

"Which one?"

"I haven't decided."

"Gettin' there on foot?"

"How else?"

"What're you plannin' on doin' for money?" He regarded her thoughtfully. "Will you be turnin' tricks in the streets? To be honest, I don't think you'd make a good hooker."

"You're disgusting! Your saying such a wicked thing proves you don't know me at all!"

Adam started laughing at her. "Hey, don't you think I don't know how tough it is to live the straight and narrow life out on the street, when you're hungry, broke, and friendless? Girls your age have to do most anythin' to survive."

"For your information, I'm planning to go into mission work. There are Christian organizations—"

"Goin' to Africa or China or wherever it is missionaries go these days?"

"Maybe. But there's no need to go that far to find sinners." She eyed him balefully.

"You'd fall in the wrong hands for sure."

"That seems to be my ongoing problem, doesn't it?"

"Now, wait a minute. Who's taken care of you all these years? Put a roof over your head? Taught you a business? Made you a useful, productive member of society? Huh?"

Jessy angrily grabbed her meager possessions. "If you'll excuse me, I'll be going."

He yanked back her bundle. "You ain't excused."

"I can go if I want. I'm of age and it's a free country. Besides, you ran away from home."

"That was different."

"What was so different about it? You had a tyrannical father; I've got a tyrannical brother."

Adam's eyes flashed at this unexpected reference to their father.

Seeing the hurt in his eyes, she asked with tenderness, "You've never forgiven him, have you?"

"What's the point forgivin' a dead man?" He wouldn't look at her.

"Better to forgive than let hate eat away at you." She patted his arm gently. "You ought to make peace with him somehow, for your own sake."

He shrugged off her remark, saying, "Anyhow, a guy runnin' off 's different from a girl. My little sister . . . " He regarded her with affection. "And while you're off savin' mankind, who's gonna look after your third of the property?"

"You can have it. Ask Mr. Webb to draw up a quitclaim deed. I think that's what they're called. When I get settled I'll write and sign my interest in the property over to you. Now, will you please give me back my things?"

"Nope." He clenched his arms around her little bundle. "You'll have to wrestle me for them."

"All right, then, I'll leave without them. God will provide." She attempted to leave but he blocked her way.

"Can't," he said. "You gotta help me write a letter. You know I ain't ever been a letter-writer."

"Can't Suzanna help you?"

"I'm askin' you cuz you know as much as I do 'bout raisin' hogs."

"What's all this about hogs?"

"Agricultural agents from the capitol." He pulled a telegram from his pocket. "This came last night. They seen our last shipment of hogs we sent to market. They want to have a look around here and write up a report."

Jessy took the telegram from him and read it through several times. "Gosh," she sighed, "what do you think of that??"

"I think we got a lot to do and them cinnamon rolls must be ready."

Morning had broken, bitter cold and blinding with snow. A rooster crowed from the coop behind the barn. Adam yawned noisily. "I need some coffee quick. So you'll stick around?"

She nodded reluctantly. "I shouldn't, but I guess I will, at least for a little while anyway." As she took back her bundle, she looked down to it meekly, saying, "Listen, Adam, I didn't mean what I said last night about not praying for you anymore. Of course I will."

He smiled devilishly. "Last night's the first I knew you was prayin' for me at all. Figures! Though why you waste your time —"

She looked deep into his eyes. "Prayer isn't a waste of time."

"What do you pray for, that I drop dead and go to heaven?"

His twisted irony made her laugh. "How can you turn everything around and make it come out sounding so wrong, so backwards?"

"Raw genius. Oh, and I guess you can go to church if it means all that much to you. But you better be back here by twelve twenty on the dot or I'll come after you."

"Thanks, but I'd better not go."

"After all this fuss you made?"

Jessy paused, listening to the storm rage on, unabated. "They'll probably cancel services on a day like this. And anyway, I didn't know about Kem Curtis. If he sees me in church, he's sure to think that I was there to—well, you know. What would I say to him?"

Happy shrieks of two little boys pierced the silence. Stephen and Taddy came running into the barn. They threw themselves against Adam's legs, pouncing and pummeling him without mercy. "Ooooooh," groaned Adam in mock agony, rolling with them in the straw. "Stop, you'll hurt me!" The boys laughed and shrieked all the louder. "Wanna play rough?" Adam scrambled around joyfully with his sons.

Watching them romp together gave Jessy an idea. "I know! If you were to go to church with me, you and Suzanna and the children ..."

"Not on your life." Adam clutched four little fists in his own.

"We could all go to church together. Wouldn't that be —"

"Suzanna's asked me 'bout church lotsa times since the tornado. Ever since we moved here, she started in on me." Adam wrestled with his two sons, then raised them high in the air as he growled at them. They laughed and squealed with delight.

Jessy wondered what would become of her brother and his three children. Kem Curtis had further soured Adam's opinion of church and churchgoers. Jessy knew her ongoing battle with Adam was not their fight, but the Lord's. Would Adam's response to God always be No? How long would God be patient? Jessy knew the spirit of the Lord would not always strive with men. There comes a day when He abandons them to their folly.

❧ 27 ❧

The following January, Jessy came downstairs early one morning to find Adam, in coveralls, at his rolltop desk frowning over the accounts she kept so carefully: every bushel they reaped, the money they earned, and the debts they owed. Adam's sharp green eyes traveled up one column of numbers and down another, his index finger tracking entries, dates, transactions. "Sit down and take a look at this," he said without glancing at her.

"Something wrong?"

"This total of yours."

She drew up a chair beside him and added long columns of numbers in her head. "I'm sorry. This ought to be a three not an eight," she said at last. "The rest of the totals are right."

The correction worked to Adam's favor. "That's better." He continued tallying dairy, poultry, and hog receipts. "Business looks good, 'specially since I started sharecroppin' the old farm. Nate Brambly's doin' a good job tendin' the place. Say, we better hurry. Visitors'll be here today."

"Those agents from the capitol? I forgot all about them!"

"Where's last month's receipts?"

"In your top lefthand drawer."

"You finish with them?"

"Yes, sir. I do my posting the last business day of every month."

The staircase shook under thundering footsteps. "Hi, Daddy!" blared little Taddy.

Adam paused in the middle of his accounting to put his youngest child on his lap. "Oooh, you're getting big! Just like Daddy. How's my boy?"

"F-i-i-i-i-i-i-i-i-ne!" he drooled, drawing out the word with glee, proud to use such a grown-up word.

"When are you gonna learn how to swallow? Huh, Goldilocks?" Adam flicked at his son's shoulder-length blonde curls.

215

Smiling, the boy shrugged and cuddled against his father's chest. Taddy still drooled so much he had to wear a tea towel wrapped around his neck at all times, even during formal occasions like Sunday dinner and visits to his grandparents. Suzanna had spent precious time trying to teach the boy, but finally gave up, deciding that swallowing was something Taddy would have to learn on his own. Adam coddled him before setting him down. He raised his eyebrows at the dampness of his lap. "The wettest child in this world," he said slyly to Jessy. "Wet at both ends."

Jessy lifted up Taddy at once, setting him on her lap and not minding at all his gooey little hands. As she pulled Taddy's fist out of his mouth, she returned Adam's sly look. Taddy was indeed wet at both ends.

"Those curls of his'll have to go. Today. No visitors will see any son of mine lookin' sissified. Tell Suzanna I said so."

"Me?" While Adam returned to the accounts, Jessy admired Taddy's beautiful ringlets. "Your first haircut. You'll look just like Stephen and Daddy when your mom is finished with you." Taddy nodded innocently. Jessy gave him a little kiss. "You're still young enough not to mind being kissed. Nothing like your brother Stephen these days. Now that he goes to school, he's a man of the world."

In a distracted fog, his eyes still on the record book before him, Adam said to Taddy, "Run along, son, go bother your mother."

Martha came next, respectfully greeting her father but filled with news for her aunt. Adam appeared more than a little miffed at her brief dispatch of him in favor of Jessy. When he protested, Martha kissed his cheek but winced.

Adam rubbed his unshaven face. "I was in such a hurry to get down here and work on these books I didn't bother shavin'."

"Yes, Daddy..." Martha gave him another chaste little peck.

He hugged her gently, then planted a big kiss on the top of her head.

"I dreamed of you, Aunt Jessy. We both went to the fair, and then we rode on the dobby horses and flew away!"

"How wonderful! Don't you wish we really could fly?"

Martha nodded, beaming with pleasure before going to the kitchen.

Adam and Jessy returned to their paperwork only to be interrupted again, by Stephen who had been outside examining a pen of rabbits. He had always considered his father's work of paramount importance and had, since age four, carried any tool he could manage, in imitation of him. "Good morning, Dad."

Adam set down his pen. "Son." The pride he felt for his firstborn was impossible to conceal. "You look a little damp around the edges."

"It's snowing outside."

"Lucky for us it's not snowing *inside*."

Stephen didn't catch his father's humor but Jessy did. She forced herself to look serious as they listened to Stephen's report on the rabbits. Then the boy rested his hand on his father's record books and asked, "When can I help you, Daddy?"

"Don't be impatient. You only just started school."

"I'd rather stay here and help you."

"You're not gonna end up like your father, havin' to fight for a livin'. You get yourself an education." Adam glanced at the grandfather clock across the parlor, one of many belated wedding presents the Webbs had showered on Adam and Suzanna. "Speakin' of school, you better hurry or you'll be late."

Jessy watched Stephen go, the boy she had once hidden from death in a carrot bin. Now he was tall for his age, vigorous and strong, carrying himself with the easy grace of his father.

"You love my kids, doncha?"

"With all my heart!"

"I can tell." Adam returned to his balance sheet. "Jessy, this past year, you cost me a total of $32.79."

"That much? What on earth for?" Jessy tried to pry the record book from under his elbow but he wouldn't let it go.

"Books, mostly, some personal items, and chocolates."

"I'm sorry, Adam, truly I am. I could do with less."

"You've missed my point entirely." Adam slurped on his coffee. "You're entitled to more."

"More what?"

"More of what you need. Like boots."

She smoothed her long wool skirt. "These are perfectly..."

"Let me see one."

"Adam." The look on his face was enough to set her meekly pulling off a boot and handing it to him.

"Just as I thought. Ruined inside and not dry from yesterday." He flung it down after a quick inspection. "Buy new ones, two pairs."

"Thank you, Adam."

"You should tell me when you need things."

"I don't like to complain."

"There's a difference between complainin' and askin' for somethin' you really need."

"Yes sir." She stood. "If you'll excuse me, I'll . . ."

"And another thing." He glanced over her and the chair in such a way that she resumed her seat. He handed her a wad of folding money. "Your share of last year's profits. You can check my figures." Adam pushed a tally toward her and leaned back to stretch. "We finally had a decent year. Suzanna says if you're to work like a man you might as well get paid like one. I think she's right."

Jessy tried handing it back. "You need this money for the children."

"That's for you."

"But what about the taxes?"

"Paid."

"Mr. Webb? The loans he —? Hail insurance? You didn't forget to renew the policy, did you?"

"We're current on all our bills and loans. This is your share of the profits. I figured your wage based on what a hired man would draw these days."

Jessy knew Adam was being more than fair. Hired women earned only a tiny fraction of a man's wages although both sexes put in the same long hours. Pointing to his figures, he explained: "Here's what you netted, which includes income from selling the hogs, eggs, dairy products, and poultry, and the jams you and Suzanna made and sold last fall. I deducted for the cost of supplies. I also figured in a profit from sellin' our surplus hay, barley, and oats." Leo Kimball's prediction had been correct: The harvest had been good. In lean years the Flints had been forced to buy feed, or worse, to sell or even slaughter animals they couldn't afford to feed. This had been a surprisingly good year. "Our hard work's finally payin' off. You know how to farm; now it's time you learned how to handle money." Adam closed his rolltop desk and yawned mightily, stretching his arms overhead. "I'm tired and today hasn't even started yet!"

Jessy rubbed her hands against her skirts before picking up the first monetary fruits of her labors. "Gosh, Adam, this is a lot of money."

"You earned it the hardest way there is, farmin'. How'll you spend it?"

"I don't know, but I want to tithe ten percent for God's work." Jessy delighted in the thought of all the good she could do, now that she had money of her own to share. "This is really very generous of you and Suzanna both."

"Can't tell you how upset she was to find that goodbye note you left her back before Christmas. She says if you left you'd take the heart out of this place."

"I didn't mean to upset her. But I may have to go someday, you know. Otherwise, I'll just end up the spinster everybody pities around here."

"Nope, not you. My guess is you'll be married in a year or two at most."

"It really doesn't seem likely, Adam."

Martha was shouting from the entryway, "Everybody, come and see!"

Oblivious to the cold gray midwestern day, three men wearing dusters over their coats and suits, along with rubber boots, heavy scarves, ivy league caps with visors, and touring goggles had come rolling up in a motor car open to the air. It was the first automobile ever driven to the Flint home. Adam admired the machine openly, the rich finish, black upholstery, folding cloth roof. The car lurched, tipping dangerously but not overturning. Jessy's heart nearly stopped at the danger but all the men, including Adam, only laughed.

"This the best pig farm in the state?"

"It is indeed," Adam roared over the sound of the engine, greeting his guests from the capitol.

The car backfired so loudly Suzanna rushed to the driveway, asking, "Has someone been shot?"

"No, my love," said Adam, tucking her under one great protecting arm. "Just the future come to pay us a visit, is all."

"If this is the future," she shuddered, "I'll take the past."

"Madam, miracles like this will save the American farmer!" shouted one of the men in goggles.

"This is a miracle?" Suzanna asked with dismay.

"Motorized farming, good lady! Think of it! Gasoline traction engines. One motor alone can already do the work of forty horses, with energy to spare. Can pull an eight-bottom gang plow with no effort whatsoever. I've seen it with my own eyes."

"Mind if I look her over?" asked Adam with boyish enthusiasm.

"No, not at all, help yourself."

Adam could hardly stop looking. The visitors raved about the virtues of cars while chickens and geese nestled on the sidelines.

"Climb in and we'll take you for a spin," offered the driver.

"Darling, you're not getting into that infernal machine, are you? Think of the children!"

It was no use. Adam had already squeezed into the front seat.

"Eight hundred fifty dollars from the plant in Dearborn," said the driver. "Look at this dashboard! Yes sir, a car for the people."

Later in the day, Jessy would take a dim view of the sooty stains the exhaust left in the pure white snow, but Adam, as it turned out, was as impressed with the automobile as his guests were with his farm.

Miracles like this will save the American farmer. Those words would echo in the still country air long after that day came to an end.

28

Two months later, in March, Jessy spotted Taddy coming up the drive, running as if he were being chased by demons. She ran out of the house to him. Suzanna followed. Taddy's nose was bleeding—broken from the look of it. Blubbering and taking in so much air his speech convulsed, he sobbed loudly, "Daddy's dead!"

"What?" Jessy scanned the stark horizon of late winter but could see no sign of Adam who had left for town with Taddy minutes before.

Crouching down, Suzanna wiped the child's face but still the blood ran. She tried to remain calm but her voice edged on panic. "Tell Mamma what happened, love. Where's Daddy?"

"I fell top-side down!"

Suzanna hugged him close, glancing over his shoulder down the drive before studying his face once more. "Tell Mamma what happened."

"Daddy's dead! He tried to grab me but he . . ."

An unfamiliar team approached them slowly.

"No, God, please . . ." said Suzanna, crying. She swooped up Taddy and turned him away from the sight.

Jessy ran to the end of the drive to meet Ed Mannon and his son. Adam lay in the back of the Mannon's wagon. "Easy, Princess, easy!" called the farmer to his horse. "Miss Flint! We found your brother by the side of the road. His legs were trapped under your rig. It toppled over on him somehow. My boys and me got him clear but your team . . . I'm afraid both horses will have to be shot."

"Dear God." Jessy murmured, touching her brother's ashen face. Minutes before he had been his usual, robust self, healthy and hale, full of plans, rifling detailed orders to everyone on his way off to the store with his youngest boy. "Taddy said he was dead."

"No, Miss, but he's hurt pretty bad."

"We've got to get the doctor."

221

"I already sent my youngest to fetch him." The farmer nudged his remaining son. "Let's get Flint inside."

Together Jessy and the Mannons rolled Adam onto a blanket they used as a stretcher. "I can't understand this at all. Adam is so good with horses, and it's only a half mile to town."

"From the tire tracks in that narrow part of the road, an automobile must have come up on Adam real fast, sideswiped him, and spooked his horses so that the wagon toppled over on him."

Once Adam had been carried upstairs, Suzanna ministered to him with absolute calm. One of his arms was twisted far out of line, and his leg was bleeding. Assuming it was broken, she turned to her daughter. "Go fetch my scissors, Martha, in the sewing basket." Gently she probed Adam's temples, searching for other signs of injury.

"Anything we can do, Mrs. Flint, just ask."

"You've been so very kind, Mr. Mannon, I can't thank you enough."

While waiting for the doctor, Suzanna listened for Adam's heartbeat. "My love," she whispered to his ashen face streaked with dirt. "To think someone would run you and our little boy off the road and leave you both for dead! What's this world coming to?"

Once the doctor made his first, quick examination, he went to Adam's carpentry shed with Jessy following. As the doctor examined and discarded boards of various lengths, he said, "Big tough fellow like Adam Flint should pull through, but he'll need time to mend. I expect he'll be black and blue all over by tomorrow morning. Broken leg, dislocated shoulder, fractured right arm, three broken ribs..." The doctor held his hands wide. "Help me find some boards about this size. I'll need two to set those bones. And see if you can tear up some strips of cloth. Old sheets will do."

Back upstairs, the doctor's steady stream of orders was interrupted by Adam's incoherent groaning. With each new wave of pain, he nearly rose up out of the bed.

"I'll give him something to calm him down. Suzanna, I'll be back this evening. In the meantime, keep him warm and quiet."

"Of course, Doctor."

"And here's something for you." The doctor handed her a small vial. "To calm your nerves."

She shook her head. "No, thank you, nothing for me. I've got too much work to do."

Jessy sighed. Three adults and three youngsters to feed, nearly four hundred acres to plant, a barn full of dairy cattle, a stable of horses, seventy piglets to raise, and Adam Flint out of his head with pain. "Doctor, how long will it be before my brother will be up and around again?"

"Hard to say. It's to his favor that he stopped drinking. From the look of him, he's been living a clean life since he got married."

Again Jessy pressed him for an answer. "Doctor, you well know we're about to begin the busiest time of the farming year. How long will my brother be laid up?"

"At least three months."

June! Feeling shaky, Jessy made her way to the bedroom window. From this second story vantage point she could see the earth moving away from her to the horizon, acre upon acre rolling out smooth and flat, a bare brown carpet waiting to be planted, seeded, cultivated, and tended, all by her and her alone. She clutched her arms around herself, wondering how.

"And you ladies should know that even after three months, I'd expect Adam to take it easy on that leg for a long while. It will take time for him to get back to anything like a normal routine. Eight months, a year . . ."

A year! Jessy continued staring at the bare acreage before her, silently praying for courage, strength, stamina, patience, wisdom. She recalled that in this life we shall have tribulation. The Lord had plainly said so, but He also promised strength for the trials, grace for the weary, peace for the troubled, and eternal life for the faithful. "I believe Your promises, dear Lord," she murmured. "Please show me the way through this."

Suzanna went to her side. "We'll get help."

Jessy turned to her sister-in-law. "I've been farming long enough to know what to do. It won't be easy, but I can see us through."

"Our neighbors won't let us down. They'll help us get through this, somehow."

"They have work of their own. And troubles of their own. I can handle an ax, a plow, a seed drill, a team. I've been at this business a long while. Adam has taught me every phase of farming." Jessy glanced toward her brother. "Sometimes I used to wonder why he expected so much of me, why he pushed me so hard, but now I see the blessing in all that's gone before." Jessy squeezed her sister-in-law's hands. "The Lord will see us through. We should be thankful no one was killed. How's Taddy?"

"Broken nose and bruises, but the doctor said he'll be fine."

"Thank God. Well, I'd better see about the horses. Mr. Mannon says they'll have to be destroyed." She pulled a shawl around her shoulders and searched the hall closet for Adam's rifle which she loaded with capable hands. "Two of Adam's best horses . . ."

Suzanna followed partway down the stairs, looking pale as the blonde curls that were swept up and away from her face. Stephen, Martha, and Taddy stood by their mother. She took their hands and told Jessy, "They've been crying because I've been crying!"

For the first time, Jessy felt this crisis as Suzanna might. She, a loving wife and wonderful mother, was too young and too vulnerable to be a widow. Jessy spoke to her sister-in-law with compassion. "When I get back, we'll make a plan — what needs to be done, our obligations, and our resources. I have some money saved, the money that Adam . . ."

"And there's always Daddy."

Jessy shook her head at the mention of imposing on George Webb. "No, not again! Adam wouldn't want to get into any more debt."

"We'll talk when you get back. I'd go with you but I'd better stay here with —" She glanced up to the top of the stairs.

"Yes, of course. Your place is here with your husband."

"But don't you go alone. Take Stephen with you."

"It's a sorrowful thing, what I have to do."

Suzanna clutched Stephen's shoulders with a sudden fierceness and turned him so she could look into his face. "Your father never shielded your aunt from the realities of life and I know he wouldn't want to shield his children, either, especially his oldest son."

Without hesitating, Stephen turned to Jessy. "I'll go with you, Aunty. I'll help you with the chores, too. I've already decided."

"Oh, you have, have you? Thank you very much."

Martha volunteered, "I'll help feed the new calves and all the baby piggies, too."

Not to be left out, Taddy chirped, "Me, too!"

"You little pumpkin." Taddy's angelic face was marred by a broken nose and dark angry bruises.

Stephen regarded his aunt through large, serious green eyes fringed with long lashes. "I'll give up school to help you."

"Oh no you don't, young man, you don't get out of school that easily!" Suzanna steered him out the door. "Only six years old and listen to you! For now, just be a good boy and help your Aunty. Now hurry!"

"I'm almost seven!"

"Not till May. Now get going!"

It was a short walk to the site of the accident. Their wagon was upended at the side of the road, but the horses were gone. Jessy found a note scrawled on wrapping paper and signed by Mr. Mannon: "Flints: We put your horses out of their misery and hauled to rendering man who will forward cash to you." So, Adam's two best horses were dead and would be sold for glue. Jessy had been spared the grim business but the loss was still significant. In the fading light, Jessy read the rest of the note: "Tomorrow we'll tow the rig back to your place. I should be able to fix it for you."

"Thank God for good neighbors. They've done the Flints a favor we won't ever forget," she said, tucking the note in her pocket. "Come on, Stephen, let's go home." As they walked, Jessy asked, "Do you want to know what the best thing is that you can do for your daddy?"

"What, Aunty? I'll do anything."

"Yes, I believe you would." She took his hand in hers. "If you really want to help him, you should pray for him, you and Martha and Taddy together. Every day. Can you do that?"

"Oh, yes, Aunty, Mother told us already to pray for Daddy and we have, very hard."

At this, Jessy felt an excited tingling deep inside of her. Something good would come of this dreaded event.

But the next day she nearly lost all hope.

"How are you feeling this morning, Adam?" Jessy said, approaching his bedside timidly.

He took an agonizingly long time to respond. "How do you think?"

It pained her to the core to see him so helpless, a superb athlete unable to move. The pillowcase under his head was stained with the sweat and tears of his suffering. She edged to his side. "I'm so sorry . . ."

"I don't want your pity, yours or nobody's."

"No, of course not." She paused, trying to gather sunlight into her voice. "I did the chores; everything's fine. Stephen helped me. The Mannons fixed our rig good as new. They've already been and left. They asked about you and send you their best. Do you want anything?"

"To die in peace."

"Oh, Adam, please don't even think such a thing. It must be terrible for you right now, but the doctor said you'll be fine, if you just give it time." She watched his prominent Adam's apple moving slowly as he swallowed. "Do you want some water? There's a pitcher right here . . ."

"If you really wanna do me a favor, get me some liquor."

Jessy caught her breath. All that he had built over these last several years would be wasted if he turned to drink again. His young family would be ruined.

"Adam, I know you're in horrible pain, but we can get through this without . . ."

His low, rich rumbling voice stung her like venom. "*You* got me into this. I was livin' alone, quietly drinkin' myself to death and *you* showed up. If it wasn't for you I would never have gotten myself saddled to a wife and a buncha kids and this monster of a house, and a mountain of debts, none of which I would a had without your interference."

"I'll take care of things till you're on your feet again."

He let out his breath sharply. "I might as well be dead."

"Oh, Adam, please. You have a right to be upset, but you have a beautiful family that loves you so much. This is a wonderful place to live, a home for all of us." She winced when he convulsed in pain. Getting as close as she dared, she said, "I'll pray for you, as I always have. We'll all pray for . . ."

With a burst of strength Adam raised his voice. "Get outa here and leave me be, you and your meddlin'! If I could throw somethin' at you I would. You and that, that nothin' you worship!"

"Adam!" In horror, she covered her mouth with the back of her hand.

"Get outa here! Leave me be! Leave me to the devil like you found me. I was better off that way."

"No! Never!"

"I said get out!"

Jessy ran into the doctor coming up the steps. She covered over her mouth, ashamed to let the man see her crying.

"What is it? Is he . . ."

"He's in terrible pain and it's all my fault! He's right to blame me!"

The doctor braced Jessy's shoulders. "Between the pain and the pain killers, Adam can hardly know what he's saying."

"That doesn't make it any easier to listen to him." Jessy ran down the stairs to face her burdens, now made even harder to bear under Adam's condemnation.

❧ 29 ❧

"Sam Ackworth's the name, ma'am. I do odd jobs and farming all over — down to Mexico last winter and up in California. I pass through this way from time to time. Heard you needed help."

Jessy, returning his friendly smile, noticed his backpack and bedroll near the porch steps. "My brother's laid up but we're managing all right. Thanks all the—"

"Must be hard for women to run farms when everyone's selling out and heading for Detroit."

Jessy's smile faded. He was right. Automobiles and assembly lines were changing everything, not only because of Adam's accident, faulted to a careless driver, but also because farmers were leaving the country for big city jobs. Why go up against an all-too-fickle nature, bedeviled by droughts, floods, tornados, fires, calamities of every description, when people could work indoors, claim steady paychecks, buy new cars, and enjoy time off with family and friends? When did she ever enjoy a holiday?

"I can handle a plow good as the next fella."

"I can plow, too, Mr. Ackworth."

"You independent females," he snorted. "I see you're not so good at repairs." He looked over his shoulder at the colter lying in the yard, the one she had broken that morning. Adam could have fixed that colter in no time, but equipment maintenance wasn't among Jessy's talents.

"I hear you won't accept free help. Maybe you'd pay for it?"

"What are you asking, Mr. Ackworth?"

"Four dollars a week and a place to camp out."

"Two-fifty and you can sleep in your pick of the outbuildings."

"A deal." He started to roll a cigarette in a pale blue paper flecked with red designs. "Get these end papers in Mexico."

228

"If you want to stay, you can't smoke. We have enough trouble without the place going up in flames." She hadn't failed to notice the flask in his back pocket. "No drinking either."

"Ain't natural for a man not to smoke 'n swig."

"Nature is what God commands us to subdue."

"I know the Good Book, too. Been saved three times."

"If you stay, I'll expect you to abide by the rules."

"Fair 'nuff." He sniffed the wondrous aromas of Suzanna's cooking. "I could use some lunch."

"Of course. We'll be eating soon."

"In the meantime, I'll take a look at that colter."

"Fine. Thank you. You'll find my brother's tools in that shed."

❦   ❦   ❦

"Sam Ackworth?" Adam struggled to sit up in bed on his own power. "Haven't seen him in years."

Jessy fully opened the drapes. "Look at this gorgeous day, perfect for field work. If this weather holds, I may even get on schedule by the end of the week." She turned back to see Adam struggling. "Let me help."

"I can manage."

"You know what the doctor said." She propped him up on extra pillows, taking care not to press against his taped ribcage or in any way disturb his fractured limbs. "I always thought you looked strong as a tree, but did you have to get yourself all twisted up like one?" As she straightened the collar of his pajamas and smoothed the quilt over him, she worked hard to sound casual, cheerful. "I hope you don't mind if Sam stays on for awhile. At the moment he's fixing the colter. He seems to know what he's doing."

"I'm glad you finally saw reason and got some help." Adam looked her over with his sharp green eyes. "You losin' weight? You look tired."

Avoiding his question, she busied herself with the tray she had brought up and uncovered a steaming bowl. "Suzanna's made one of your favorites—steak soup with corn, lima beans, onions, potatoes, and barley. Doesn't it smell grand?"

"Where'd the beef come from?"

"The Kimballs."

"Leo was here?"

"Mrs. Kimball brought it over this morning."

Adam's jaw was working devilishly. "Leo's wife?"

"Leo's grandmother." Jessy tucked a linen napkin under Adam's cleft chin. "Would you like a visit from the barber?"

"Good idea."

"Maybe he can shave Sam Ackworth while he's here. Poor fellow looks as if he hasn't had a bath since . . . Careful! Soup's hot." Jessy blew on the spoon as she maneuvered it into Adam's mouth.

"You sure can switch subjects double shuffle."

"Isn't this the best soup you ever tasted?"

Adam nodded like a child. The doctor had reset his shoulder, the one he had dislocated trying to save Taddy from their fall, but it would be a while before Adam could use his arm or hand.

"At least there's nothing wrong with your appetite. These corn muffins are straight out of the oven." When she slit one open, steam escaped. "Would you like me to butter it for you?"

He nodded again.

Now was the time, she thought, her first opportunity to ask. "You're not still mad at me, are you?"

"'Bout what?" His eyebrows lifted innocently.

"After the accident, you b-blamed me for e-everything."

"I don't remember sayin' any such thing." He looked genuinely concerned.

"The doctor said you were in shock." She broke off a bite-sized piece of muffin for him. "Anyway, I forgive you everything."

"What did I ever do to deserve you?" His old, buoyant cynicism was returning. He eyed her with boyish mockery. "What's in that glass, water?"

"What did you expect, gin?"

"A man can dream."

"Among other things, you cursed me for saving you from the evils of drink!"

"Well, in a way that's true. You are to blame! But even though now 'n then, I think it'd be good to have a bottle around, I'm glad there ain't. When I drank, I hurt people. I hurt myself. And now it looks like I hurt you. Again."

"I understand." She sniffled and smiled at him. "You'd better get some rest now. Eating lunch seems to have exhausted you."

He sighed. "Sleep! It's all I do, that and think. Never thought so much in my life."

"Thinking's good for you, once you get the hang of it."

His face flared with mock anger.

She removed the extra pillows and straightened the coverlet. "And what do you think about?"

"All sorts of things. The work needin' doin', Suzanna, our kids, you, the bills, the taxes, the hogs, the cows, the horses, the weather. The roof, the gutters, and downspouts—all of which'll need replacin'..."

"Easy! Easy!"

"You're wastin' away, workin' so hard. And I'll never forgive myself if you get hurt..."

"Fear not!" She rested her hand as tenderly as she could on his arm. "Promise me you won't worry about anything at all, not the taxes or the farm or me or anything. Just concentrate on getting better, okay?"

"If I ever got my hands on the driver of that car..."

"Getting revenge wouldn't make you feel any better."

"Wanna bet?"

"You know I'm right."

"Who could do such a thing?"

"I don't know, but God knows, and God will deal with that person in His own way, in His own time."

This answer appeared to satisfy Adam for he seemed to relax. With eyes closed, he said, dreamily, "Strange, but lately I've been rememberin' back to bein' a kid, about street fights and things I hadn't thought about in years. I think about everythin'. It's as if my whole life has been laid out like, like this quilt with little pieces stitched together. Only sometimes I come to a dead end, to a space, a hole where something's missin', where things don't fit. Then my thoughts go 'round in circles. I know my life had a beginnin', but where will it end?"

"We come from God and we go back to God. And what we do in between—what we're supposed to do—is give Him the glory." She pulled the quilt over his shoulders. "There! Just like little Taddy, all set for a nap."

Adam smiled happily. "At first, I hated bein' laid up even for two seconds but now I sorta like all this attention."

"In a way, it's like being a child again, and having the measles, and missing school, isn't it? Mother would fuss over us and, and . . . "

"And Pa would stay off our backs!"

Jessy laughed and nodded. "Now what else can I do for you before I go? Read you to sleep?" To her surprise, he nodded. "What would you like to hear about? The latest treatment for hog cholera?"

"You decide."

Without hesitation she reached for Suzanna's Bible on the side table by the bed. To her astonishment, Adam didn't object. She read aloud about the kingdom of heaven, hidden like treasure in a field, the pearl of great price which when a man finds, he hides and for joy goes and sells all he has, just to buy that field, so he can have that treasure.

Adam listened closely. When she finished he said, "I believe in *survival*."

"There's more to life than mere survival, Adam."

"Oh, yeah?"

"Yeah."

He smiled. "I'm too weak to argue."

"Rejoice, then, because God's strength is made perfect in weakness."

"A man's got to fight or people'll walk all over him." As a painful spasm washed over him, he stiffened in silent agony.

She took his hand and said gently, "When you're hurting, when you feel the world closing in on you, remember what Jesus said the night he was betrayed by a kiss, anticipating the awful pain He would face — the nails and thorns, the mocking, brutal crowds, the shameful death He was about to die — all He suffered to redeem us of our sins.

"You see, since the very earliest days, God has required a blood sacrifice for sin, and Jesus paid that price in full for all of us. We need His love and redemption. We can't earn it. We can only accept it from His nail-scarred hands. When we turn away from Him, we reject the greatest love there is to be had, and the greatest peace we can know. On the night He was betrayed, He left us with His peace. 'My peace I give unto you: not as the world giveth, give I unto you.' "

The words of loving kindness, hope, and eternal life with God that Jessy had read aloud came alive for they weren't mere stories that happened long ago and far away in different days to mythical people, or legends lost in time. They were nothing less than the greatest drama of the ages and it was unfolding here and now in a small upper room on the American prairie. Jessy believed herself to be part of God's intricate plan, and Adam, too.

Adam had nodded off to sleep while Jessy read to him. She wondered how much he had absorbed. Would the void inside him ever be filled with the spirit of the Living God? Would he ever be whole? And what would become of the great life force within him when he left this earth and stood before his Maker? After she closed the drapes, she paused at his side to say, "Dear brother, it is my heart's great desire that you be saved."

On that glorious spring day, little did she realize what grave danger he was in. He, Jessy, and the entire family were in the gravest danger of their lives.

❧ 30 ❧

"What are you doing, Martha?" Jessy referred to the way her little niece was bouncing around by the stables. "And what are you doing with your daddy's best screwdriver?"

"Come see, Aunty!" Martha waved frantically at Jessy.

Jessy looked askance at the four-year-old. "With your daddy laid up, you know there's no time for games!"

"I found something beautiful, Aunty, see?"

There was something undeniably intriguing in Martha's voice. Jessy allowed herself to be led inside, warning, "This had better be worth the time!"

"Look! It's under here!"

Martha worked the screwdriver under one of the floorboards. When the board popped up, the sight beneath it made Jessy catch her breath. "Gold!" She dropped to her knees for a better look. "A locket! It's inscribed!" She polished the face of the heavy locket on her skirt. *L.O.M. Lucy Orundel Meredith*!

"What does it mean, Aunt Jessy?"

"I d-don't know." Feeling uneasy, Jessy stood and looked around, then protected the child with her arms. "How did you know this was here?"

"I saw Mr. Ackworth through the window. He looked funny on his knees in here, so as soon as he left I dug up his treasure."

Jessy's mind reeled. She examined the hiding place but this was the only treasure it had held. Ten years ago, Sam must have murdered Mrs. Meredith and then hid her jewelry here, what he thought he couldn't pawn without rousing suspicion. Jessy reasoned that he left this locket behind because her initials might give him away, even now, so long after the woman's death. Jessy's quiet moment of truth was disrupted before she had time to react. Ackworth had heard their voices and came to see Jessy on her knees, examining his hiding place and holding the locket. "All

234

these years, everyone blamed my brother but it was you who killed Mrs. Meredith, wasn't it?"

He grabbed Martha who screamed in fright. Jessy lunged at him but he tore out of the stable, never loosening his grip on the little girl.

"If you follow me, I'll kill her! One more murder won't make no difference to me!"

❦   ❦   ❦

Night had come and the posse had yet to find Sam Ackworth or the child. The volunteers had just left the Flint home with a promise to resume their hunt at daybreak. The family sat together in the living room, forlorn, gathered around Adam in his wheelchair.

"How could anyone in Bethel have known Sam was dangerous? He's a hard worker and has such a friendly smile!" Suzanna shook her head helplessly for the thousandth time that day.

Adam reached out to her. "Come closer."

Jessy, red-eyed and hoarse from the strain of this dreadful day, said, "To think I hired a murderer! Poor little Martha, the angel!"

"Don't blame yourself, Jessy. I would have hired him too." Suzanna glanced at the clock and turned to Stephen and Taddy. "You two should have been in bed hours ago!"

"We're afraid."

Adam chided them. "My sons *afraid*?"

Stephen pleaded the case for both of them. "Mr. Ackworth will come and get us if we close our eyes."

"Nonsense." Suzanna grabbed their hands. "Sam Ackworth wouldn't dare come near here tonight. Now you two march straight upstairs and get ready for bed."

"We want to stay with Daddy."

"They can stay down here with me tonight," said Adam. "I'll stretch out on the day bed and the boys can pitch camp under the table."

"Oh, boy, Taddy, we can play fort!" cried Stephen, heading for the dining room table.

"Not so fast. Go brush your teeth and clean up first!" came Adam's voice again. "And after that, I'll tell you a story." When Suzanna started after them, Adam stopped her. "Let them go. I been wantin' to tell you somethin', you and Jessy both. Sit down, both of you."

Weary, strained, exhausted, neither of them complied readily. Adam, too, appeared exhausted and yet wistful as a child.

"For the last few weeks, I been listenin' to the two of you prayin', and the kids, too. I can hear you in my sleep sometimes."

"Oh, Darling, we've been disturbing you and we only meant to help!" Suzanna held him tight by way of apology.

"No, no. No need to apologize, not at all. I mean, why, it's ... I hardly know how to say this but, well, it's been a comfort!"

This delighted both women. Relieved, they stood to go, but Adam hadn't finished. It was clear from that look on his face. They both sat down again.

"Well, to hear my own little children prayin' for a sorry sort like me, well, it's ... And I been so hard on you, Jessy, all these years, and I'm sorry, I truly am. Can you forgive me?"

This sudden confession overwhelmed Jessy. "Well, of course! I never could stay mad at you for more than two seconds anyway, you big ox!"

He laughed good-naturedly, and sniffled, too, overcome with emotion. "I been thinkin' while I been laid up, you know, 'bout different things, and that maybe I ain't been as good as I coulda been, and so I ... Well, there's somethin' else. I don't remember my dreams as a rule, but I can't get this one outa my head. I dreamed it last night and it was so real it just felt like it was happenin' right now. I was layin' by the side of an old dusty road somewheres and Jesus came by and healed me so I could walk again. And the first thing I did was get up and follow Him! I walked with Him and a buncha other believers. We walked and talked ... He was sure kind to me, and after all the bad things I done, all the names I called Him. And I been thinkin' a whole search party can't find our little Martha, and here I sit, the Man of Iron, helpless! I can't save my daughter and I can't save myself. God's the only one who can save any of us. It's finally dawned on me there's one thing I can do, somethin' I thought I never needed to do, and that's to pray, if you two teach me how. God won't answer on my account, but maybe He'll listen to us together."

Jessy was in tears. Suzanna appeared thunderstruck. The boys ran downstairs pretending they were steam engines going full speed, straight into their father's arms. He hugged them a long while, too overcome with emotion to speak. When at last Adam was able to speak, he said, "It's time we all pray together."

On that night, Adam Flint learned to pray for himself, for his loved ones, and for his enemies, including Sam Ackworth. That night, Adam Flint stopped wrestling against God and instead began to trust Him.

❧   ❧   ❧

Events of the following day shook Bethel. As the search party resumed hunting for Sam Ackworth, a farmer eight miles from Bethel discovered a curly-haired little girl with a dimple in her chin who had taken refuge in one of his sheds during the night. When questioned, Martha, unharmed but sleepy, was unable to explain where her captor had gone, knowing only that he was angry with her for "slowing him down."

Now here she was, safe at home. The Flints gave immediate and profuse thanks to the Lord. While everyone greeted and hugged their Martha, the sheriff who brought her home went straight to the business at hand.

"Since yesterday we been watching the railroad line so Sam will have a hard time if he tries making a run for it. I wired an alert to all neighboring states, too, to be on the lookout for him, but we think he hasn't gone far. Today we're breaking the search party out in four directions. One's headed toward your old place." The sheriff looked at Adam. "I'd ask you to come along, Flint, but since you're laid up, I thought maybe your sister might want to come with us, seeing as she knows the area. We'll look out for her."

Without hesitation Jessy agreed, saying, "I'd be glad to help."

"Good! If you know how to use a gun, bring one along."

Full of sorrow, Jessy went to fetch and load Adam's gun. "I certainly hope I won't have to use it."

"This is a dangerous man. Time he was locked up, before he hurts anyone else. We want him alive, though. No doubt about that. Got lots to ask him!"

As Jessy bid her loved ones farewell, Adam squeezed her hand tight.

❧   ❧   ❧

It was late morning when the search party neared Adam Flint's old home place. They were about a mile from the little farm that had been Jessy's first home in Bethel Township. The road was familiar to her, each step of the way. Jessy felt strangely moved as they went along under the shade of giant elms. She remembered her first ride to her brother's house with her beloved friend Ollie Gaad. Jessy didn't dare tell the sheriff she had once considered walking her brother, at gunpoint, in the opposite direction, thinking he had done the murder Sam had committed. It shamed her to realize she had accused her brother falsely. The evening before, she had apologized but still felt ashamed that she hadn't believed him when he claimed he was innocent.

Jessy hadn't been on this road since the tornado, except for the one time, nearly four years ago, when she accompanied Adam to meet with the sharecropper. Nate Brambly had agreed to rebuild the house and work the farm for a share of the profits. Now something caught her eye. She gestured to the sheriff, who motioned for quiet. She dropped to her knees. There by the side of the road, she picked up a cigarette butt, a tiny bit of blue tissue flecked in red. "Sam's been here!" she whispered. "He buys these end papers in Mexico!"

The sheriff pocketed the evidence, then motioned to the others in their party.

With hearts pounding, they neared the old farm. Nate Brambly, the sharecropper, did not appear to be at home. Jessy knew the man often assisted his aging parents on their farm two miles away. She led the way over the creek and toward the house. The group had clustered around her, protecting her and watching the buildings ahead of them, especially the barn, big as a cathedral, topped by a weather vane, the still-flying horse Jessy remembered so well. She was glad the rusty old thing had survived the storm. Nate had repaired the hole so the roof was good as new. He'd also rebuilt the house very much as it was, conforming to the same size and proportions, but had painted the new structure white. He had planted numerous fruit trees and flowers, which pleased her greatly. The place looked well cared for, even loved. Adam would be pleased to hear all she would tell him, but for now she forced herself not to become sentimental. She had to keep her wits about her. Was Sam here or had he wandered to another farm?

"Nate? Nate Brambly!" The others called and looked about.

Not a sound could be heard, only the song sparrows so dear to Jessy Flint.

"Where would you hide, if you were Sam?" asked the sheriff in a whisper.

"In the hayloft," she whispered back. Again she had a recollection, one she dared not describe to the law. She had hidden from Adam in the barn the night he took up his gun and shot wildly, drunkenly, into the darkness, but there was no time to think about that now. "I'll lead the way," she volunteered.

Before she could do so, two of the men pushed the big double doors open before her, and others gathered around her to protect her. They called Sam's name but heard nothing. The sheriff spotted another cigarette stub.

Jessy's eyes widened in fear. They had come close to the murderer, very close. She looked about, knowing every inch of the place, the expansive loft above them, the stalls and bays that had remained unchanged even after the storm. The tension became unbearable as the party slowly moved about.

From somewhere above their heads, a cat hissed and dropped to their feet, nearly causing a shootout. The animal scuttled out the open doors before a shot was fired. Sighing with relief, everyone on the team eyed each other. They were depending on each other for their lives. One of the men nudged the sheriff. All eyes rose to the loft. Jessy couldn't see what the others had noticed, but she readied herself.

"Sam, you might as well give up," the sheriff called out.

"I'll give up, but don't shoot me."

Jessy, and everyone with her, sighed in relief.

Sam Ackworth climbed down quickly and quietly, empty-handed and laughing. "Had you guys fooled a long time!"

This enraged Jessy. "Laugh, will you? For years my poor brother has had to put up with everybody's suspicions, while you run around the country robbing and murdering and kidnapping little girls! I ought to . . ."

"Now, Miss, don't point that thing at me! You promised you wouldn't shoot!" He looked to the sheriff for protection.

"Too bad I gotta protect the likes of you, Sam Ackworth. Everyone hold your fire. Johnson, put the cuffs on him."

Everyone watched as Sam Ackworth was handcuffed. Several cars had been brought up as word spread of Sam's capture. The murderer would ride to jail in comfort, spared the walk back to town.

For two days after his arrest, speculation ran rampant in Bethel. Why hadn't the townspeople been given satisfactory answers — or any answers—to their questions? And what was a digging crew doing in the cemetery? The place had been roped off and was even now restricted by armed guards. The Flints, living so close by, had tried to resume their normal activities, but reporters and the general public wouldn't leave them alone. Curiosity peaked when word spread through Bethel that the sheriff would pay another visit to the Flints.

As he entered the house, he removed his hat, but his handcuffs jangled on his hip. The children would have enjoyed nothing more than to continue gaping at him and the pistol in his holster, but he asked them to leave the room while he spoke with Adam, Suzanna, and Jessy.

"You watch out for the others, Stephen!" shouted Adam as his children left the room. "Gotta look out for your sister," he said more to Jessy than to them.

The weary officer settled into an easy chair as Adam, Suzanna, and Jessy gathered in the living room around a fresh pot of coffee. "Sam's finally talked. Thought you folks should be told first. He killed Lucy Meredith, all right. Buried her in the cemetery across the way."

"The cemetery?" Everyone was incredulous.

"Strange as it sounds, that's what he did. Mighty clever if you ask me. When she disappeared, we looked for her everywhere but there. Sam had done odd jobs around here for years, and then off he'd go, riding the rails, jumping trains without paying his way. Well, after Mr. Meredith died, Sam still showed up here to do odd jobs for the widow, but he got it in his head to rob her. She had plenty of jewelry and such, and he knew the place well. He figured she was an easy mark. All he had to do one night was get off the train across the road here, grab what he wanted, and then jump another train without anyone knowing he'd been around. Except things didn't go like he planned. Seems the night he came by to do his thieving, Mrs. Meredith was having trouble sleeping."

"And so he killed the poor woman," said Suzanna, forlorn. "She was one of our family's dearest friends, too."

"Talks of it like he was proud of himself." The sheriff looked disgusted. "He's a clever one, but crazy." He paused. "Look, Adam, I owe you an apology. I always thought you killed Lucy."

"Can't say I'm sorry to disappoint you!"

"Thank you, ma'am." Taking another cup of coffee and a sweet roll Suzanna offered, the sheriff continued. "The strangest thing about this whole business is how Sam decided to hide the body. He figured the least likely place she'd be found was in a new grave, the one place none of us thought to search. Took us two days to figure out which grave, but it turns out Lucy's been buried with Charlene Trumble all these years."

Suzanna gasped. "Charlene died of typhoid!"

"Sure did, her and plenty of others that summer. Sam really used his head. You have to hand it to him. And there were two bodies buried with Charlene, not just one." The sheriff set down his cup. "Look, Adam, you been through a lot lately and I'm sorry to have to do this but there's something I need to show you. Excuse me a minute."

He went to the front porch and took something from an assistant of his, a brocaded valise encrusted with dirt. The floral pattern was distinctly feminine. He handed it to Adam.

"No, it can't be." Adam refused to take it, shaking his head in disbelief.

"What is it?" Suzanna asked in a hush.

The sheriff began removing its contents: a thin overcoat, black silk stockings, a sequined garter, a small pot of rouge, and a sepia photograph of Adam Flint in his prime — Samson with a lion cub curled across his bare shoulders.

"Laurann," Adam murmured at the sight of his long lost girlfriend's belongings. "No . . . " The Man of Iron shuddered in his wheelchair.

"Sam killed someone else that night. He told us that, while he was trying to figure out what to do with Lucy's body, a young woman knocked at the door."

Instinctively, everyone turned to look at the very place where Laurann stood ten years earlier seeking help, but instead finding death.

"Being a stranger to Bethel, she got lost looking for the railroad station in the night. When she saw the lamplight here, she asked for directions, not realizing Sam Ackworth had no business here."

"And not realizing she had stumbled across a fresh murder," said Jessy grimly.

"Exactly. Sam told us she was the best-looking girl he ever did see, a shapely little brunette with beautiful hazel eyes. As he puts it, 'It was a shame to kill her, and her so in love.' "

"In love?" Adam well knew he was the one she had loved and left that night ten years ago.

"She told Sam she would have gone back to her man in a minute if he would marry her. I knew Sam was talking about that girl you told us left your place on her own. I remember your description of her. Easy she was, friendly, Sam recalls. 'Shame to kill her,' he told me, but he couldn't run the risk of her being able to identify him. He figured any girl wandering around alone at night was asking for trouble and deserved what she got."

"Laurann," said Adam, overcome with emotion.

"I'll contact Laurann's family. I still got the files on the case. I figure she's got kin in St. Louis, like you told me back then."

Adam nodded. He took his wife's hand and said, "Her death's my fault. That's what drinkin' 'n fightin' got me. Nothin' but trouble."

Suzanna put her arms around him. "What's done can't be undone."

"Oh, and another thing before I go," said the sheriff. "Sam's wanted in at least four states we know of: Kentucky, Missouri, Kansas, and California. There's rewards for him everywhere, including one the citizens of Bethel offered for information about Lucy's disappearance. Seems to me you folks are entitled to the money."

Jessy shivered. "What a terrible, dangerous man..."

"He won't bother anybody else. I had him moved to the high security prison in Millbourne. To think I used to let Sam do repairs at my place, me with a wife and eight kids to think about! Shows you just can't tell about a person. Sure am sorry I suspected you, Adam." He reached out to shake hands.

"'Cept for murder, I broke about every commandment there is." Adam brightened a little. "From now on, I promise you I'm a new man."

The sheriff made an informal salute to him and his loved ones before leaving their home, Laurann's valise firmly in his grip.

ɤ   ɤ   ɤ

The sun was hardly up the next day when Jessy was startled by a strange new sound. The fresh dewy air was filled with the noise of cylinders and the odor of gasoline. She and Stephen, in the midst of chores, peeked out from the hog house to see Leo Kimball operating an eight-bottom engine oil-pull gang plow. With the exception of the co-op owned steam-powered thresher that was hauled around every summer, Jessy had never seen such a monster engine.

The Kimballs, father and son, tipped their hats to her. "Mornin'! With your hired hand in prison, we figured you needed help."

Jessy and Stephen ventured toward the noisy machine. The manufacturer's crest was emblazoned in red and gold across the body. The beast, made in Ohio, had rear wheels, molded in steel, that spanned eight feet across.

"Wave of the future," Mr. Kimball said proudly. He helped an excited Stephen Flint up into the cab for a ride.

"Wave of the future indeed," muttered Suzanna from the porch. "My husband was nearly killed by a 'wave of the future.' It's a miracle he's going to be able to walk again."

"Now, now, just take a look." Mr. Kimball guided her and Jessy around his newest acquisition. "Horses can be as dangerous as engines. I've been knocked out cold more than once by a horse. Lost a couple of friends to riding accidents. Ladies," he said, patting his machine, "this is for me. No panting horses to feed and water and curry, no galled shoulders and horse liniment. No days lost waiting for them to heal. We can rig up lights and plow all night if need be. Now, my son Leo here would rather ride this thing than eat or sleep. Says it's as much fun as a party." Mr. Kimball gave Jessy a wink. "Leo plowed our whole farm in less than six days."

Doing her best to ignore Leo, who was grinning at her from behind the wheel, Jessy said, "Just think of it, Suzanna. A month's work accomplished in less than a week. This could be the answer to our prayers."

❧   ❧   ❧

One bright, clear Sunday morning in the heart of summer, when the land was deeply green with thriving crops, the Kimballs' shiny new roadster pulled into the drive with Leo at the steering wheel. Jessy would always cherish the morning her entire family, dressed in their Sunday best, crowded into their neighbor's new car for a ride to worship service.

As the family helped Adam out of the car and toward the church steps, he admitted, "I'm sorta scared." For the first time, Adam stood at the doors to the little white church, his children bouncing around him. "I didn't expect to see such a crowd," he admitted softly to Suzanna.

"This is the church," Jessy said, indicating the people.

"Adam! Good to see you back on your feet!" A neighbor shook his hand.

"I'm glad to be up and around, thanks to God."

"Don't blame you, big active fellow like yourself. Be usin' that cane long?"

"Doctor thinks I'll be able to walk without a cane one day, if I take it slow."

"Track down any more murderers lately?" Leo asked Jessy.

"Pitch any no-hitters lately?"

"This coming Saturday."

"As arrogant as ever," Jessy said, laughing at him.

"Come see for yourself. I'll pick you up at noon."

"I don't know about you . . ."

"Wonder no more. I joined the church."

"No!"

Someone came out from the sanctuary and asked Leo if he would help usher. As he went inside, he turned to Jessy, asking, "See you Saturday?"

"Well, what do you know about that!" Jessy covered her dazzling smile with one daintily gloved hand.

"Nothing better for a man than a good woman," Adam whispered to her. His own wife strengthened her grasp on his hand.

"Mother! Daddy!" Suzanna kissed her parents.

"Remember, after church we're expecting all of you for Sunday dinner. There's a roast in the oven."

"Welcome, Adam Flint!" said the minister, taking Adam's arm and shaking his hand vigorously. "Welcome home."

Adam nodded warmly. His green eyes, no longer sharp or angry, were filled with hope and peace as they followed the minister's to the great bare cross at the altar.

At the sound of the organ, vast strains of ancient hymns in wordless medley resonating in the light of this glorious new day, Jessy's heart overflowed with joy. The faithful poured in all about them, bearded men in black, ladies in gray silk, girls in bright ruffles, noisy little boys in bow ties being hushed by their elders. While some leafed through hymnals, other worshippers flooded in — county officials, teachers, the mayor, the high school athletic coach, business owners, clerks, ruddy farmers with cheerful, weathered faces and loving eyes for their handsome wives. Once every seat was taken, latecomers crowded the vestibule.

As quietly as light, Jessy settled in the pew beside her brother, whose head was bowed in prayer. When the communion bread was passed, Adam hesitated.

Jessy encouraged him, whispering, "The body of Jesus was broken for you. He asked us to do this in remembrance of Him, until He comes again."

Jessy thrilled to hear Adam's rich singing voice mingled with Suzanna's delicate soprano amid all the congregation's. The King of the Universe had come to dwell in all their hearts. During the collection, the Flints donated a tithe of their income and reward money.

Adam, meanwhile, hadn't failed to notice the church jammed with people. "Looks like Bethel needs a bigger house of worship."

Suzanna patted his strong, capable hands, the hands of a carpenter.

❧   ❧   ❧

"What a day!" said Adam. He had survived a noisy Sunday dinner at the Webbs' where his children had raised the roof with their happy chatter. "I must be gettin' old."

"Nonsense, Darling," Suzanna assured him. "You're still convalescing!"

"Too tired to look at the crops?" ventured Jessy.

Adam responded with a newfound vigor. "Soon as I change clothes!"

❧   ❧   ❧

Jessy ached to see Adam bending slowly for a better look at the young corn. Had she done right? Using that check-row corn planter for the first time had been a nerve-jarring experience. Would he be pleased with the results? She offered her arm to him. "Can I help?"

"No, no, I can manage." With effort, he straightened up.

"Well, what do you think?"

"We could do with some rain."

"I think I smell rain coming."

Adam sniffed the air. "I believe you're right!"

Laughing, they walked along slowly, arm in arm. Adam still relied on his cane, but she could sense he was regaining his strength.

"The land looks good," he said after a while.

"I learned a lot being with you."

Adam stopped in his tracks. "I learned a lot bein' with you. Your spirit, your sense of values, your unshakable faith..."

"Your know-how, your quick wit, your common sense..."

"Now we're a combination of both." He looked around, scanning the horizon, seeing the crops coming up in neat rows around them. "If it wasn't for you, I don't know how we'd have managed these last few months. None of us, Suzanna, the kids, me. You've done a fine job. Remarkable, really!"

"I had a good teacher, and a lot of help!"

"I owe you a lot."

"You don't owe me a thing."

"I owe you my life, Jessy." He grew serious. "If it wasn't for you, I would've ended up in the gutter or at the gallows, no better than Sam Ackworth. No tellin' what trouble I mighta done if I hadn't quit drinkin'. And once that tornado hit, when I lost everythin', if it hadn't been for you and Suzanna and the Webbs, well, I woulda been wiped out. You made the difference."

"We need one another, and we all need God. We should live and work together in love, for His sake."

"Imagine what this world could be if everyone understood that!"

Together they resumed their walk, surveying the wondrous midwestern prairie and their home in the distance so filled with love, transformed from the gray, barren cottage Jessy had first seen upon her arrival in Bethel.

"What did you think of the service this morning, Adam?"

"It's right to worship God. Now I know you were sent to rescue me. Big, tough, thickheaded guy like me, I didn't even know I needed rescuin'!" Sheepishly, he added, "And I'll tell you somethin' else I never told you before. It's an honor to know you, Jessy Flint. You've always wanted what's best for me, even before I wanted it for myself. Thank you for never givin' up on me, no matter how rough things got. I love you very, very much!"

"Dear Adam! The very dearest Adam in the whole world!" As they hugged, she said through happy tears, "You're my very best friend and the best brother God could ever have given me. I thank Him for you every day."

And so Jessy's most fervent prayer, the great hope she shared with their mother, had been answered. Adam was a new man in Christ — forgiven, reborn, *whole*. Eternal life was his. The everlasting spirit that bound her to God now enfolded Adam and their loved ones, uniting them with the countless faithful of the present and of ages past, for all time to come.

"Do you remember that first day I arrived, when you found those checks? I had no idea of their true value until you explained it to me."

"How could I forget?" he laughed. "You had nearly seven thousand dollars in a schoolbag."

"Well, now that I think about it, coming to Christ is like that. We have riches beyond price within our grasp, but we don't understand until a believer explains, and until the Spirit of God becomes known to us. All we need to do is claim His gifts and they're ours, freely and forever."

"Amazin'," he said. "Adam Flint, a Christian."

"And this is only the beginning," Jessy answered, her heart brimming with joy that would never end.

For such is the undying power of divine love.

❦ About the Author ❦

Chris Drake, a freelance writer and historian, has worked in the fine arts and law firm administration.

She earned her B.A. with honors at Mount Holyoke College, an M.A. at Michigan State University, and worked on her Ph.D. at the University of Michigan. She has published articles on a wide variety of topics including modern art, humor, crime, business, and religion. Her byline has appeared in *The Wall Street Journal*, *The American Bar Association Journal*, *The Atlanta Journal-Constitution*, *Biblical Literacy Today*, *Atlanta Magazine*, and other publications. Her first screenplay placed 18th in the national Writer's Digest contest in 1988. That same year, the Dixie Council of Authors and Journalists gave her honors for her first novel, *The Price of Love*, then in manuscript form.

She lives and worships in Atlanta, Georgia, with her husband David, a tax attorney. Both deacons at their church and members of Phi Beta Kappa, they have traveled extensively together.